playing ROUGH

Perfection **SAGA**
BOOK THREE

BETH PELLINO-DUDZIC

My 3 Girls
PUBLISHING

My 3 Girls
PUBLISHING

To my brightest little light, Penelope June
Love always

PROLOGUE

PAUL RYAN'S OBSESSION with Gina McNaughton had reached a disturbing level. As he left the apartment he rented three doors down from Gina and Trevor, he looked around the room he had created as a shrine to her, Gina's pictures affixed to the walls. He lingered, wondering what could have been. Gina was never going to choose him. She loved her husband. His thoughts still swirled about her, and he was fixated on his next move to make Gina his. He wondered when he could create another wall dedicated to his soulmate. In his twisted mind, having her pictures surrounding him meant she was his. Before leaving the room, he took the opportunity to pleasure himself while he stared at her face. He wasn't done with her yet.

TREVOR'S UNCERTAINTY

TREVOR AND GINA MCNAUGHTON weathered the storm in their marriage. Their life was back on track. Gina understood Trevor's desire to get away, recognizing that he was still frail after months of intensive rehab. She would follow his lead. His stay at Turquoise Skye brought up deep emotions that Trevor buried after his mother died. Whatever lay ahead, Gina was determined to help Trevor with his demons.

Then there was Perfection, what to do?

The other band members, Tommy, Kevin, and Skip, were using the studio on a daily basis. Perfection had over twenty songs ready to work on. Rio was exceptionally focused on the music. He became preoccupied with the band's next steps.

Rio let himself into the McNaughtons' Montecito house. Gina and Trevor were on their outside deck taking in the view of the Pacific Ocean. Rio knew he was intruding on a quiet moment.

Rio said, "Hey, how are you, family? I have been trying to give you two space, I know you need your *alone time*. We miss you at the studio. We have been listening to the music we have in the vault. Trev, your guitar work is killer. I was wondering if you two would be interested in coming down and just listening to the music? No recording, no rewriting, getting reacquainted with music we already wrote. What do you think, Trevor, Gina? Any attention you could give to Perfection?"

Gina looked at Trevor, she wanted him to voice his opinion first. Trevor stared into space, then looked at Rio, "Rio, I got the message you want to get Perfection moving. I actually agree, music needs to be worked on. Gina and I could give you a few hours a day. I won't promise anything more. I still have some rough edges, bro. Adjusting being back home with my wife. Gina, what are you thinking, babe?"

Gina did want to get back to the band, she heard Rio. She felt uneasy about Trevor's return. He was having severe nightmares, waking up disoriented. She would remind him he was home with her. She had to appease her cousin and protect Trevor.

"Rio, have a seat. I appreciate you taking the lead with Perfection at this moment. Trevor and I will assume our roles as the faces of Perfection. We need to glide into the band slowly. Do you comprehend? Trevor has a great plan; we will give you a few hours every day. We want to be present in the band's activities. The key word here is 'slowly.'"

Gina gave Rio a faint smile and got up from her chair. "Rio, it would be cool if you and Jae would come over for dinner tomorrow night. We're family, let's hang out like we used to. Come on, Marisol will have a great dinner planned. Don't answer, I will take that as a yes. Let me walk you to the side door."

Trevor remained seated, relaxed, looking at the ocean. "Cool, dude, it will be great seeing you and Jae tomorrow night."

Rio nodded his head. "Yeah, cool, looking forward to it."

Rio walked with Gina. He knew she was likely to give him shit for trying to get Trevor into the studio. Gina's eyes teary, she held his arm. "Rio, please don't push this too hard. I'm not sure how Trevor will react to being in the studio. Please, I can't let him slip. I need you to be there for me. I'm giving the band about five weeks. Either Trevor becomes engaged or he will feel overwhelmed. If that happens, we are taking that RV trip.

There is so much going on in his head, those demons. I need them to fly."

Rio pleaded, "Gina, Perfection needs to start working with both of you. Have you written any songs? You need to start writing some lyrics, that's your job. Besides selling yourself as the *Sexy Bad Ass Bitch*."

Gina had tears down her face. "I don't feel like the *Bad Ass Bitch*. I don't feel Trevor's ready, I don't. Let's have dinner and I want you to feel his demeanor. Rio, please, if you want the band to reboot, I need to reboot my husband."

Rio hugged her. "I hear you, Gina. I thought when he came back you had reconnected and all was well."

Gina looked at him curiously. "Rio, just because things in our bedroom are excellent doesn't mean all is well with Trevor McNaughton. I will see you tomorrow night and talk about the time in the studio. You get the drift."

Rio kissed her on the cheek. "I'm trying to grasp it all. Jae will be happy to spend time with you. See you tomorrow."

Gina spotted that Trevor had gotten up from the deck. He was sitting at the kitchen island eating one of Marisol's Mexican delights. She walked over and kissed him on the head.

Marisol motioned for her to sit down. "Mrs. Gina, I made some empanadas, sit and eat. Mr. Trevor might eat everything."

"Thank you, Marisol. I will dive into this. I know this is last minute. I invited Rio and Jae over for dinner tomorrow, if it's too much, I can cook."

Marisol shook her head. "No problem. I would like to see them both. Any requests?"

"No, whatever you'd like to make."

Gina sat next to Trevor, wiped his hair from his forehead, and kissed him. "Babe, what are your feelings about going to the studio? Really."

Trevor told her truthfully, "I'm willing to give them a few weeks, to listen and suggest changes. No writing, rerecording. I don't have the head for it. I need to spend more time with you. Maybe see Roxanne."

Gina sat down next to him, took his hands into hers. "We give the band five weeks. We'll go from there. You make the decision. I'll be by your side no matter the decision."

Gina told Marisol to go home and she would clean up.

Trevor was hoping for a quiet evening of watching television and loving Gina.

The next afternoon, Trevor looked at Gina, "Let's take a walk to the studio and see those misfits. I'll sit for a bit. Come, G, I want to get an idea of where they are."

Gina was excited, cautiously so. Trevor entered the studio, with everyone cheering him. He explained it was only for a few hours a day. He would give input; he was not ready to do writing of any kind.

Tommy, Perfection's producer, said a few words. "Trevor, we need you, but we aren't rushing you. We all want and need you to feel comfortable with yourself. We all agree. As long as you and Gina are happy, we know Perfection will follow."

Tommy switched on the reel-to-reel of the music. The band listened. After that it was a chaotic situation of discussions, fighting, name-calling. It was how Perfection worked on music. Gina watched Trevor, sensing how uncomfortable he was. After ninety minutes, Gina and Trevor went back to the house.

Marisol cooked a lovely dinner. Rio and Jae were happy to spend time. Rio brought up the band, he was pushing. Jae gave him a *back-off* look.

Gina changed the subject to their family, the Riccis. Laughter about the family eased up the evening. Rio and Jae said their goodnights.

That night Trevor and Gina lay in bed, wrapped up in each other's arms. Trevor looked at his wife, "G, today was too much. I'm not concentrating on music. I promised five weeks; I'll commit to that. I do feel I need to take the trip. For one quick moment, I thought about having a drink. I refuse to regress."

Gina held him closer. "I won't let that happen."

The next several weeks in the studio were filled with listening to songs over and over, about five to ten times. Tommy wanted to get that hook, or classic guitar signature of a song. He asked for Trevor's opinion. He looked glazed and said he was unsure what direction the song should take.

Gina was watching intently, she believed Trevor was overloading. It also didn't help that Rio and Jeff, the bassist, were taking their smoke-a-joint breaks. Their manager, Skip, talked about potential tour dates with Gina and Trevor. "Perfection is not ready to think about tour dates."

Skip pushed back a bit on Gina. She categorically told Skip if Trevor was not ready, then Perfection was not. She thought to herself, *Why isn't Skip comprehending the concept?*

Arguments of how the song would be remixed continued. Jeff wanting a heavier bass track. Rio insisted that he and Trevor needed more guitar intros. Even Ian, the drummer, as mellow a guy as he was, would get involved in the vigorous arguments. The weeks were chaotic with the remastering of their music and a push for Gina to start writing lyrics.

At the end of the five weeks, after spending two to three hours a day in the studio, the McNaughtons felt that stepping back into Perfection was dicey. Trevor needed to spend time away from the studio.

He looked at his band and told them that, in rehab, the therapists suggested he connect with nature, that it would clear his head. Trevor also told them he needed to deal with some strong emotions.

Gina took that as her opportunity to let the band know they would be leaving in a few days. The RV trip was happening.

Trevor did, however, promise to work on music while they traveled. Away from the studio.

It was mid-May when the McNaughtons chose to leave.

Rio looked at Gina, almost pleading, "Gina, Perfection is on the top of the rock scene. We have been away for six months. Please get your husband ready to step back into the music."

Gina implored her cousin, "Rio, I am aware that the band is a significant presence in your thoughts. Please allow me to cope with Trevor's frailties. I will do my best to get us back home. I need your support, please, bro." Gina became teary.

Rio hugged her and whispered in her ear, "I will trust you with Trevor. However, Perfection is waiting for two of its vital members. Work your magic, Gina."

UNEXPECTED DISCLOSURE

GINA UNDERSTOOD TREVOR and she needed this RV trip. Trevor's rehab was an emotional journey down a very fragile place in time. She knew some of his demons, and she was sure she'd learn more on this trip. The McNaughtons wanted, and learned they needed, to stay away from the rock star lifestyle. They hoped getting into nature and simple living, a minimal lifestyle, would keep him sober.

Trevor's sobriety was most important to Gina and Trevor. And for Gina, the time away could help clear her head of the sadness, loneliness, and total despair she felt while her husband was absent. Now, knowing that Trevor was choosing to be clean for the love of her, their family, and the future of Perfection, she was eager to take the RV trip and explore the road Trevor was going on.

Gina contemplated items she would need for the trip. She would take some of her kitchen utensils, clothing would be easy. Simple casual clothing, one or two fancy outfits. Gina was gathering and packing when she heard the buzzer at the driveway gate. She looked at the camera and didn't recognize the person.

She answered, "Hello, may I help you?"

The woman answered, "Yes, my name is Jane Waters, I own the house three doors down."

Gina comprehended she owned the house that Paul Ryan was renting. It was odd, why would she need to talk to Gina?

Gina answered, "What can I help you with?"

Jane Waters said, "Mrs. McNaughton, I think I have some information you might want to know about my previous tenant, Paul Ryan."

Gina reluctantly buzzed her in. She didn't want to hear anything about Perfection's former publicist, she hated him.

The gate opened; Jane Waters came down the driveway.

Gina stood at the front door, "Hello, Jane, I don't need to hear anything about your earlier tenant. My husband and I believe Paul Ryan is an extremely disturbed individual. We choose not to discuss him."

Jane had a stoic look about her. "May I call you Gina?" Gina told her of course. "What you are not aware of is what I found in my house after Mr. Ryan vacated the home. He did a poor cleanup job. He hastily whitewashed the walls, slightly painted. However, with closer inspection I became aware that I could see through his paint job, uneven surfaces. What I found sent a shiver down my spine, truly chilling."

Gina was nervous. "Jane, it sounds like you want to tell me something that is uncomfortable. Please just tell me."

Jane could not make direct eye contact as she spoke. "Gina, he had a room solely devoted to pictures of you, plastered all over the walls. It was so bad I had to get the walls redone. Also, pictures of your husband marked out with a marker. Some even had his own face on it. I am shocked because I was of the belief he was a top professional PR man in Hollywood. This is not normal; I wanted you to know. There were other things now I can see clearer on. He found me through a real estate agency; I was transitioning between this home and another. I had no intention of renting this home, he begged me and offered a large rental fee. He was looking to get close to you. Gina, you didn't think it was odd?"

Gina felt slightly panicked. "Jane, I did think it was strange. Especially when it came right after I had an issue with Trevor. We are fine now. Any other psychotic moves?"

Jane Waters warned her, "Gina McNaughton, be careful. There are some files he left showing how far he was willing to go to separate you and your husband," she said while handing Gina the documents. "I found them in the closet of the room. Apparently, he was collaborating with a man named Brian Mayfield. The two worked together to cause havoc in your marriage. The plot was to get your husband back on substances. Ryan thought you would leave Trevor. Don't be surprised if he doesn't resurface somehow. Be vigilant." Jane was about to leave. "It's nice to meet you. It might be a good thing you're taking a little trip. I see the RV. Enjoy. Here's my number if you need anything."

Gina was frozen. "Thank you so much, Jane. I appreciate it. Here is my phone number. Seriously, thank you. Apparently, he was sicker than I already thought."

Wow! This is crazy. Should I tell Trevor? Will it cause him to regress? They were about to go on an RV trip to forget about the disastrous Los Angeles concert, Trevor's fall, and Paul Ryan.

The McNaughtons packed themselves into their brand-new large RV. After teary goodbyes to Marisol, they told her they would stay in touch during their travels.

As the McNaughtons were ready to enter the RV, Rio, Ian, and Jeff showed up. They were still unsure what this trip meant for their band, Perfection. They did know that Trevor tried for five weeks to step back into the band. He wasn't ready and neither was Gina.

Before leaving, Trevor assured them this trip was a necessity. He explained that together the McNaughtons would be in a clearer headspace when they came back, and the band was still of the utmost importance.

Rio had concerns. "Trevor, we will be waiting. Perfection needs both of you. We are getting the paperwork for our record company, remember that. You are my family, I love you. Work on whatever issues you have. Jae and I will miss you, so don't take too long."

Gina opened the door of the RV, kissed her cousin, and whispered, "Rio, please don't put this pressure on Trevor now. He is still very shaky. We will be in touch regularly, promise."

They pulled away from their Montecito home when Gina had a realization. "Trev, we know nothing about camping. The closest I can relate is the time my family had to stay at the Hyatt because the Ritz was full. We should stop at one of those huge camping and hunting stores and buy whatever we need."

Trevor agreed. They did some research and then drove to the nearest outdoor supply store.

A salesperson named Jonas recognized them. "What can I assist you with, McNaughtons?"

Gina stared at Jonas, then threw her hands up. "Everything ... We have no idea what is needed for an RV trip."

The knowledgeable employee gave them a checklist of necessities and camping equipment. Trevor and Gina trusted him to compile what was needed.

Jonas asked, "How long of a trip are you planning on taking?"

Trevor simply said, "Probably a month, maybe longer."

Jonas also asked if they had an itinerary and RV locations picked out and reserved. The two rockers looked at each other—who knew they needed to reserve a spot? He told them there was a book on RV parks that should help design their plan.

Trevor didn't vocalize what the exact plan was.

So, Gina suggested hers. "Trevor, I would enjoy driving up the coast, California, Oregon, Washington. We can take in beautiful sights on the way and continue to Vancouver. We can explore a bit of British Columbia and visit your father … and I would like to drive to Boise."

Trevor looked over at her. "G, I love the idea of driving up the coast. Even seeing some BC. Do we need to see my father? Why Boise, what is there?"

Gina explained, "I want to look for a house in Boise that we can go to in the winter. A place where there is snow, have family Christmas trips. Roxanne loves to ski. We can make some sweet memories. I thought it could be a chill place to get away from California. We are going to go through Vancouver. I would like to see your father, is that an issue for you?"

Trevor responded, "Babe, I'm open to looking at a house in Boise. It sounds important to you. I want to indulge your chill vibes. Visiting my father is something different. I'm dealing with intense memories brought up in rehab. Not sure how I'm feeling about that. Let's rain check that."

Gina did not want to interfere with anything that would keep her husband from working out any issues he had. She did, however, know that after buying a house in Boise, she wanted to slowly circle back to California so Perfection could start a hardcore reboot.

They pulled up to a Safeway market, donning baseball caps and sunglasses, hoping not to be recognized. Gina wanted to buy what they needed and get in and out. The travelers completed their purchase and loaded up the RV with enough food for at least a week.

They were underway, back on the road. Gina looked over at Trevor, he seemed to be enjoying driving the RV.

Gina reminded him, "Trev, didn't we promise Roxanne we would visit her after you came home? Shouldn't we go and see her first? I know our daughter, she needs to see we are working on our issues."

Trevor smiled. "Yes, I want her to know how much I love my two girls. First stop, Stanford."

PROMISES MADE

TREVOR LOOKED AT GINA and he touched her face. "It's about a five-hour drive to Stanford. Can you look at that book and find the nearest spot to Stanford?"

Gina scanned the book from Jonas, she found one.

"Trev, Sequoia Trailer Park is about five miles from the university. It has hookups—water, sewer, electricity. I will call Roxanne and tell her we are coming to see her and plan for the weekend. And I'll invite her to join us on our trip."

Trevor concurred. "Good idea, hopefully she doesn't have plans. I think it's important for the three of us to reconnect."

Gina was slightly nervous. "I will let her know we can't park; she should meet us outside. She will be shocked to see how big this thing is. I'm warning you now, please don't be blindsided, she may want Zach to come."

Trevor looked at Gina. "G, I'm not having my daughter sleep with her boyfriend when I'm about fifteen feet away. I won't have it."

Gina interjected, "Trev, does that go for us? We shouldn't have a play-date with Roxy being fifteen feet away. How does that sit with you? She doesn't want to know her parents are having sex, it's weird."

Trevor looked away from the road for a second. "G, are you kidding, we have our own room. If you weren't so loud, we would have no issue."

Gina laughed. "Trevor McNaughton, are you complaining or stating a fact? Because you aren't the most quiet person when we make love. But I love it."

Trevor got that look. "G, can I have an opportunity to enjoy you in the outdoors first? We have a few hours to get to Roxanne."

Gina shook her head. "Trev, you are a very horny guy. Is this the outdoorsy Trevor, being very sexy? I hope you don't mean really going outside, right?"

Gina knew he was a horny guy; he missed her, he was making up for lost time away.

Gina turned on the radio to one of their favorite rock stations and caught the end of Pink Floyd's "Comfortably Numb," followed by an earlier Perfection song, "Music Is a Circus."

"It's good to know that our songs are getting played," Gina said, looking over at Trevor.

Gina knew he was getting anxious about stopping so they could make love. The separation, being away from Gina made Trevor need her more.

Gina knew at some point she would have to tell Trevor about the visit from Jane Waters.

Paul Ryan definitely had some psychotic tendencies. But she was nervous about Trevor's reaction. He knew Paul Ryan was after Gina. That was his motivation for working so strongly on his sobriety. He needed to get back home to his wife.

Trevor pulled off to the side of the road.

"Babe, why are we stopping here?"

Trevor was already out of his seat. "G, I heard our song, it reminded me of when we recorded it. I want to have you now."

Gina was shocked. "Trev, seriously here, in a rest stop? We aren't kids, what if someone sees us and recognizes us? We will be in the news."

Trevor led her to the back of the luxury RV. "G, we have a bedroom with a door, come on. This trip is about us."

Gina stared at him, "So let me ask you. Do we need to have pit stops along the way solely for sex? Or are we going to legitimately drive to our destinations? Simply asking."

Trevor was waiting for Gina to join him.

She was moving slowly. "Did you lock the doors of this thing?"

Trevor smiled. "Of course I did, I'm waiting on you, that song reminded me of how beautiful it is to collaborate with my wife and create music together."

Gina smiled seductively. "I'm coming." She wiggled out of her jeans and stripped down. "Trev, I love you so much, promise me we are genuinely going on a trip." She brought her face up to his. "Let me truly look at you for a minute, I love your face, I love when you don't shave your whiskers, I love your eyes, I love your mouth. Don't ever forget that. I never stopped loving you, I could never."

Trevor held her body close to him. "G, we are never going to be apart again, I love touching you. I missed you so much in rehab, I wanted you, I cried for you. But I have you now."

Trevor laid her down and made sweet love to her. He was slow and deliberate in his movements. Gina melted with every thrust of his body. They kissed and touched each other passionately during their lovemaking.

As they lay in bed after, Gina stroked Trevor's hair, she glowed. "I feel like my old self now, Trev. I know we made up at home and we're good. I crave the feeling you give me; I feel regenerated. When we decide to go home, I have so many ideas for songs."

Trevor laughed, he was feeling high on love. "Babe, we can write music anytime, I brought guitars. I promise we will write. I think we should get dressed, unbelievable that I'm saying that to you. We still have a good three hours until we get to Stanford."

Gina smirked, "In that case, Mr. RV, let's roll. I'm going to call Roxanne and let her know our plans."

Gina looked out the window and enjoyed the scenery for a while. When they toured they barely got to see much except hotels and concert venues. This was a relaxing moment to drive and really take in their surroundings. Gina was enjoying the simple sights of the drive. The several types of trees, the beautiful wildflowers. Highway signs with interesting street names, all the small local stores, fruit stands, anything that was normal for other people was a treat for Gina.

She picked up her phone and dialed Roxanne, who answered at once, "Hi, Mom, is everything going well? I mean, you and Dad are okay?"

Gina laughed. "Yes, we are driving up to see you. There's one thing—your father bought a huge RV and we are driving in it now. We should be there in about three hours. We won't be able to park this thing for a long time at your apartment. Your dad thought you could pack an overnight bag and we could go camping for the weekend. You'll have your own space and bathroom. It'll be fun."

Roxanne was astounded by this. "What the fuck, Mom, you and Dad are traveling in an RV and you want to go camping? You two know nothing about camping or RVs. Wait, are you two high or anything, please say no. Whose idea was this?"

Gina shook her head. "Roxanne, your father came home with this 'house on wheels' and wanted to have some time away from all the distractions we have at home. We are still writing songs. Your dad thought we would drive to you. You are correct, we know nothing about this camping stuff. Please start getting ready, your father really wants to see you."

Roxanne was flustered, "Well, I could come for a couple of days but I'd want Zach to come too. You realize that he moved into the apartment with me. I would appreciate him spending time with my parents."

WELCOME TO THE ADVENTURE, ROXANNE

GINA KNEW TREVOR WOULD NOT BE happy about the additional guest. "Of course, Roxy, we would like to spend time with Zach also. We didn't realize that you were living together. Wow, that's a discussion most definitely."

At this point Gina looked at Trevor who was visibly upset. He got quiet, Gina knew he was seething with anger. She needed to finish her call with Roxanne before she dealt with Trevor's rage.

Roxanne told her mother, "Mom, I have actually camped lots of times, I probably need to show you and Dad how to camp."

Gina begged, "Roxanne, can you start getting ready please? Wait, when did you go camping, I don't remember that. Was it with one of the Montecito Moms? You will have to tell me about your camping experience. At any rate, you have no idea how big this RV is. See you soon."

Trevor was pissed, he looked at Gina. "Did I hear all this correctly, our daughter wants to bring this guy who is now living with her? He's sleeping with our daughter, doesn't that bother you?"

Gina was adamant, "No, Trevor, it doesn't, because as our daughter recently reminded me, I had to take you to my parents after we lived together for six months, in their house technically. You were nervous and also wanted to let my parents know that I was safe with you. That you loved me very much, do you remember? Because I do, I was scared of my father's reaction. If Mario Ricci accepted you, I think you can hold it together with Zach. He is a football player with a Stanford scholarship. How bad can he be, Trevor? They have been sleeping together for a while, you know that. We aren't those parents, Trev."

"You're her mother, it's different. As her father it bothers me spending time with a guy who is having all kinds of sex with our daughter. For me it's my little girl."

Gina snapped her fingers, "Hey, baby, don't think about it. What she does is her business, she's almost twenty-one, we have no control. When we were their age, we made love all the time. It's not any different. I choose not to think about what goes on in their bedroom, come on."

Gina leaned in closer to Trevor and gave him a kiss on the cheek. "Here, baby, try not to think about their living situation. Roxanne has lived in a house knowing that her parents were that hypersexual couple. It's all good."

Trevor shrugged. "I still don't have to love the idea. You're right, I'll try to be that guy, accepting."

Gina smiled. "Apparently our daughter has been camping, so we may need their expertise." Trevor pleaded, "G, please, no more revelations until we get Roxanne … Tell me about what you're writing."

Gina was excited. "I want Perfection to come back with solid hard rock songs, maybe some kind of a love song. But I want to come back roaring, rocking people off their asses. I'm sure Rio, and you of course, can't wait to play some hardcore guitar. I don't want to go down the road of making a name by becoming soft and sappy."

Trevor moved his head in agreement. "G, I like it. You're on to something, come back harder, this is our newest music. We did listen to some of our music they want to rearrange. I like it. You always think of the business side, G. I could give a shit, simply hand me a guitar."

Gina smiled. "You be that quintessential rock star, babe, that's who you and Rio are."

They were about thirty minutes from picking up Roxanne. Gina was snacking on some cheese crackers and stuck a bunch in Trevor's mouth.

He talked with his mouth full, "G, it's good. We are almost there; would you call your daughter?"

Gina laughed. "Seriously, my daughter, a few moments ago you were referring to her as your *little girl*. Trev, play nice for me, I promise you will be rewarded."

They were getting closer to Roxanne's apartment. They drove past some of the Stanford buildings. They felt proud their daughter attended one of the finest universities in the country.

Gina called, "Roxy, we are ten, fifteen minutes away … Oh, you and Zach are already waiting, good. Why do you need a tent and sleeping bags? This thing is huge; you have your own space. Oh, I see, you're embarrassed around us, so you two want to sleep outside. That's silly, you have your own bathroom and space."

At that moment Gina heard her mother's voice come out of her. *Oh, shit, I sound like Franny.* "Nevertheless, Roxanne, you do what you want. If that makes you feel more comfortable, I won't interfere. We just want to spend time with you."

They drove on for another ten minutes. Roxanne and Zach were waiting with a tent, rolled sleeping bags, and overnight bags.

Trevor pulled the RV into the large parking lot, thankfully it was a wide space. He got out and hugged his daughter. "Roxy, I'm glad you are going to spend some time on our journey. Hello, Zach, good to see you again."

Roxanne hugged her father. "Dad, it's good to see you, but why the RV? I'm not sure you and Mom understand how this thing works."

Zach chimed in, "I know a bit about RVs. My parents had one when I was growing up."

Gina smiled, it was a happy reunion. "Fantastic, we have a pro with us. Sorry for the short notice, you two, but it's going to be fun. Trev, baby, let me give you directions to the campground."

The campers checked into the facility and got their spot. Trevor carefully backed up the RV. Gina was impressed. Gina looked at the water and sewer hookups, could they do this? They found the equipment that Jonas suggested. Gina could tell that Trevor was frustrated and didn't want Zach to think he was a total moron. Trevor looked for the proper equipment and took it out, but he had no idea how to hook anything up.

Zach looked at all the hookups and told Trevor, "I think we could do this, no problem."

Gina threw Trevor a look and shook her head as if to say, 'See, you can be his friend and learn something.'

Gina went into the kitchen, pulled out food for dinner. "Roxanne, you want to help me put something together for dinner? I would love the help."

Roxanne sat at the dining alcove. She was hoping for the real answer for their trip. "Mom, why this whole camping thing, why does Dad want to do this, really? What are your thoughts? I definitely think it's strange."

Gina was truthful with her daughter. "Look, Roxanne, he came out of rehab, he had a week by himself. He was nervous when he came home. We spent five weeks working with the band; it was too much. Your father thought of having a drink. Even though he says he is strong, he knows that's where he can fall down. We gently have to reintroduce him to working. I want him to feel in control. If this trip is what he needs to get back to Trevor McNaughton, the rock star, we must and need to support him.

"As I said, your father is still a bit fragile. Please respect that we need to make him feel like his old self. I promise you I want to get back to business also. I remember those of you who kept your father from me for a good while, a brief time ago. I'm over being angry about that. Now I need to manage him, so he's strong. When we get back to Perfection, I want to make sure his demons are gone. I know that's what you want for your father also. I love you, trust me."

Roxanne still wanted more. "I am aware of all that, but you do need to go back and pick up your lives. I realize the two of you are back together and love each other. Mom, you need to give him a gentle push back into your lives. I know your intentions are in the right place."

Gina knew she was right. "Roxy, I have a plan, no worries. We will go up the coast to Vancouver for a few weeks, see your grandfather. My plan is to go to Boise and find a house where we can go for winter. Afterward I'll gently push to come home. Trust me. Speaking of trust, you chose not to tell us about you and Zach living together. Roxanne, you know your father, he is the one with the issue, not me."

Roxanne was pissed. "Why is he being so Dad-like, you two are not conventional parents. I don't get it."

Gina smiled. "Because, Roxy, you're his daughter. Fathers have a thing about the man who is intimate with their daughter. What can I say, your grandfather gave your father a little bit of grief. Roxanne, if Mario Ricci could accept that long-haired musician who took his daughter away, your father will come around to Zach."

SHARING THOUGHTS

GINA WATCHED TREVOR AND ZACH hook up the RV at their spot in the park. All necessities were managed. Trevor and Zach joined Gina and Roxanne inside.

"I'm hungry now, let's get that grill going. Zach showed me how to hook everything up, so we have water and our toilets should flush."

Gina put her arm around him. "Thank you, that's a relief." Gina laughed.

Gina and Roxanne set the table in the motorhome's kitchen. Gina whipped up a nice salad. Roxanne placed the salad on the table and helped Gina with the steaks on the grill outside. Trevor and Zach sat outside watching the grill. Trevor was enjoying the peacefulness of sitting in nature.

Gina looked at Trevor and Zach. "Steaks are done, let's go inside and eat." The four of them moved to the kitchen table.

It was quiet at first and Gina led into a conversation. "So, we survived the worst part, parking and getting water and other lines hooked up. We appreciate your help, Zach … What is your major, or have you come to a decision?"

Zach was a bit unnerved sitting with Gina McNaughton, a rock celebrity. He muttered, "I'm thinking of doing sports physical therapy and training. I like the strength coaches and trainers we have. I think I would enjoy it."

Gina smiled. "Well, half the battle of finding a career is doing something you love. I didn't think singing and being in a band was my life's calling until I sang onstage the first time. I became hooked, I knew it's what I wanted to do. I was lucky to find a man who shared the same dream."

Roxanne looked up. "In the past I feel that you two together put too much of yourselves out there. To be honest, it was embarrassing. Listening to my friends or strangers talk about my parents being superstars. They forgot I was your daughter. It's tough having the world see your parents being rock stars, being that sexy couple onstage. Honestly, as I get older it is burdensome."

Trevor looked up. "Roxanne, I'm sorry we are celebrities, rock stars if you will, but we love what we do. You used to love coming to our shows. You were the princess backstage. Your mother and I thought it was sweet how you would give us hugs and kisses when we were done. I remember in high school, you hated it. I thought you were over that. We know it's a challenging lifestyle; you always came first and still do. Please remember that. We are excited that Perfection is coming back harder, and under our own label. We will be in control."

Roxanne wanted to hear her father's reasoning for the trip. "Dad, finally, sounds great, I can't wait. So, you aren't going to be driving around for a super long time. You will want to get back in a few weeks. This camping thing is a little diversion, something different."

Trevor passed the salad. "Roxanne, your mom and I need a little time away, for ourselves. We thought we would have fun in this thing, see sights we don't get to see on the road."

Gina didn't want the conversation to go further. "How is dinner, is my family happy? I bought something corny; I got stuff to make s'mores for dessert. Roxy, would you help me?"

Gina pulled Roxanne aside, far enough away to have a private conversation with her daughter. She used the pretense of getting everything to make s'mores. Gina needed to emphasize why this trip was necessary. She spoke softly to her daughter. "Roxanne, please don't allude to anything we discussed. I don't want your father to think we can't trust his vision."

Zach and Trevor went back outside to enjoy the evening air; the stars seemed brighter.

Trevor commented to Zach, "The night looks so beautiful, the soft light from the moon. The smells of campfires. The lighting bugs, nature, it's beautiful."

Zach nodded his head in agreement.

Meanwhile, inside, Gina and Roxanne were clearing the plates off the table. Gina was thrilled to have water to wash the dishes.

Trevor and Zach came into the RV.

Trevor smiled at Gina. "Where are those s'mores stuff you want to make, let's do it. In my whole life I never had one."

Gina brought out a plate with all the makings for s'mores. They gathered outside and enjoyed their dessert. Trevor had three, he thought it was heaven.

Gina had plans for the next day, "I thought we could go to Sequoia National Park and see those beautiful trees and nature. We can rent bikes or even go to Hume Lake and rent a boat, does that sound good to the three of you?"

Zach was the first to agree. "We should go on a hike; I also like the idea of going out on the lake. You want to enjoy the outdoors; this will kick off your first nature journey."

Trevor loved the idea. "It's a plan. We will wake up early, have breakfast, and blissfully wander through the park. Good call, Zach. I think we should all get ready for bed. Roxanne, you really aren't going to sleep in that tent, we have room for you and Zach, even your own bathroom."

Roxanne stopped her father. "Dad, you always say you and Mom need privacy. Well, we would like our privacy, so we will sleep in our tent next to the RV. We will use that bathroom for sure. We're good, we have done this before. So, goodnight, hope you sleep well. Because we will have a full day of hiking and boating. Something you have never done. It should be entertaining. Love you."

Zach chirped in. "I want to thank you for inviting me to spend time with you. Getting to know Roxanne's parents, not members of Perfection. I'm sure this will be a fun experience for us all."

Gina got up and took Zach's hand. "That's settled, you two do what you feel is right. Goodnight, sleep well."

Trevor and Gina went to their room.

Gina laughed. "I see you are trying with Zach; I appreciate it and you will make your daughter awfully happy."

Trevor's facial expression changed as he looked at Gina. "That outdoor air is refreshing for the soul, I could only take this path with you along my side. You know I love you. The worst feeling I had in rehab was going through withdrawals and calling for you, then I imagined you were there telling me how much you loved me." Trevor was tearing up. "That was so hard, knowing you weren't with me."

Gina got close to him in the bed and touched his face. "Trevor, if I knew, I would have been there. When you went through withdrawals, I hadn't been able to come. If you imagined me telling you how much I loved you, then you weren't wrong. I would have told you how much you are my entire life; this life is completely perfect with you."

Gina raised her eyebrows. "Tomorrow you will be getting a big dose of nature. I hope I can deal with it. Let's put some of those good rehab vibes to work."

THE MAGIC OF NATURE

GINA WOKE UP EARLY THE NEXT MORNING and prepared food. She opened the door and called Roxanne. No answer. She turned around and saw by their matching terrycloth bathrobes and Roxanne's towel-wrapped head that she and Zach had already showered. They smelled fresh, similar to coconuts. They had their toothbrushes in hand, and she held a cute carryall with the rest of their bath supplies.

Gina smiled, assuming they showered together. She would keep that secret from Trevor.

Gina pleasantly asked, "Good morning, you two, did you sleep well in that tent? Breakfast is almost ready. I was hoping to get an early start for our adventure. I will say, camping gets you up early."

Roxanne reached for plates. "It's refreshing, we slept well; we like the outdoors. Mom, you really cooked for a lot of people. It's just us four. Where's Dad, is he up?"

Trevor walked out in hiking shorts and an aloha shirt. "Good morning, my two girls, Zach. We'll have breakfast and then I'm ready to go hiking."

Gina laughed. "Who is this guy, not Trevor McNaughton for sure. But I like it. You three eat, I'm going to take a quick shower."

Shortly after, Gina walked into the kitchen in a nice sundress and sandals.

"Mom, not sure if you're dressed for hiking. I know you are Gina McNaughton and you always look great, but nobody is here to see you hiking."

Gina strutted by. "Roxanne, thank you for the compliment. Coming from you it means a lot. So, I'm ready, let's go to the office, get some hiking guides and bikes."

The walk to the office wasn't far. They hiked down a rocky path, bordered with wildflowers. Gina bent down and smelled them. She loved the earthy but sweet smell. Other campers were starting their mornings, some cooking their breakfast on a campfire or grill. People were friendly, waving *Hello, neighbor.* Gina and Trevor felt a sense of freedom that the outdoors gave them. The smells of bacon and coffee filled the campground. They heard the mockingbirds singing and flying overhead. For Gina it was jarring to hear the birds squawking. She looked at Trevor's face, he seemed relaxed, blissful. Gina loved the smells, the tall trees, nature. She and Trevor walked into the RV office and asked for brochures for hiking trails and rowboat rentals.

The girl working the desk was young, around mid-twenties. She looked up from her book. She then had to look again. Standing in front of her were Trevor and Gina McNaughton. Still stunned and amazed, she gathered herself together. "Can I help you? What are the world-famous rock star McNaughtons doing at our little RV park? What do you need?"

Trevor gave a bit of a smile, he just wanted the bikes. "Yes, it is us, we are here to have a retreat of sorts, we are interested in a brochure that shows us all the hiking and bike paths. Do you have bikes available?"

The young girl, whose name was Yvonne, said, "The bikes are around by the storage area. We should have a few there. Can I have each of you sign this for me? I saw you in San Francisco, you were unbelievable."

Yvonne gave them a baseball cap and asked them for their autographs.

Gina tried to get what they wanted and leave. "Sure, if you promise not to mention that we are here. We are really trying to unwind and relax. You get me. We aren't touring yet, but write down your information, and when we go to San Francisco again, I'll make sure you get tickets."

Yvonne promised not to say anything, she was so excited to meet them.

Trevor and Gina got four bikes. Roxanne and Zach had taken their time walking down to the office. They stood outside waiting. Gina waved over Roxanne and Zach. Each inspected the bicycle they liked. Trevor looked at the map. He then shared it with Zach and asked what path he thought was best. Zach chose a path he felt that Gina and Trevor would be able to tolerate.

The quartet went off down the bike path that Zach chose. It led them to the giant sequoia trees. They were fascinated by their size. The air smelled clean, woody, the sky seemed brighter and more alive. Roxanne watched as her parents walked around like it was a fairyland. She enjoyed seeing her parents walk hand in hand around the trees. She understood the amount of love they had for each other.

Trevor had his arms around Gina's neck as they were whispering to each other, laughing. They were touching the huge trunks of the sequoias. One tree had a path through the trunk. The McNaughtons walked back and forth a few times, awestruck by the fact that these trees were centuries old. They spotted huge ferns around the trees and the wildflowers. And huge mushrooms. After ninety minutes of enjoying the serenity, Gina became aware that she hadn't packed any food or water. She stopped. "Oh, shit, I didn't pack lunch. Now we have to go back, and I wanted to go to the lake."

"Mom, I packed snacks and water. I was sure you wouldn't realize that you needed to pack food."

Trevor grinned. "Roxanne, I am thankful that you are as smart as you are. We are such novices. Let's enjoy lunch amid this beautiful location. It's fucking peaceful, I'm in awe of these trees."

Trevor kissed his daughter's head, like when she was a small girl. They all sat in a clearing, Roxanne made peanut butter sandwiches and handed out fruit and bottles of water.

Gina took a deep breath. "It seems magical, these towering trees. They smell like sandalwood incense. The grass smells like fresh-cut grass, but it's tall, uncut. I can hear birds flying through the branches. I even saw a bird's nest. I'd never seen one in my entire life. Roxanne, have you smelled all the wildflowers? Each one has a distinctive smell. The dirt has an earthy smell. Nature cleansing the air, heavenly. I never did anything like this when I was younger. I lived on that big estate and went around the world but never sat and enjoyed the peacefulness of nature. It's fucking impressive, right, baby?"

Trevor seemed as inspired as Gina. "You know, this is what I envisioned, the quiet, stillness of nature. It renews my soul. Gina, we should write a song of the magic of nature as a cover for a love song. We'll work it out."

After they ate, they biked to the lake and found where they could rent a rowboat. Zach and Trevor took the lead in rowing. About an hour later they rowed back. The crew rode and returned the bicycles back to the RV office.

Gina was tired, she hadn't had that much exercise in a while. Trevor seemed invigorated by the entire day; he didn't look like a rock star, merely a man in tune with nature and loving it.

Once back at the RV, Gina needed a nap. Trevor took out his guitar, went outside, and played wherever his heart led him.

SERIOUS TALKS ABOUT NEXT MOVES

ROXANNE AND ZACH OPTED TO take a walk along one of the other hiking trails. It was over an hour's walk according to the brochure.

Meanwhile, back at the RV, Gina and Trevor were about to have some serious talks.

Trevor came into their room and crawled onto the bed next to Gina. "G, today was exactly what I wanted out of this trip. Be around nature, not amps and recording, writing songs. Us, together enjoying life around us, no one cares who we are out here."

Gina smiled at him and motioned for him to come next to her. "Trev, we aren't nobodies out here. The girl at the office recognized us, we are who we are. You may want to run away from it for a bit. That's not happening, not for us. This trip is for you to let some demons fly. I'm here to follow what you need. You and Roxanne have always been my priority. I would do whatever is necessary to protect my family. It's truly the deepest love a person could have, my husband and my child. Never forget that. However, we can't run away from Perfection forever. You know that. I do believe we need this time for you to sort out your feelings from rehab, for your sobriety, and for us."

Trevor looked out the window, "G, thank you for your loving support."

Gina didn't want to take away Trevor's idea of a break. "I didn't want to ask you this earlier. Trevor, what does getting back to our real life look like to you? I'm not going to fail you, I promise. Our love is strong enough to carry us through."

"G, you aren't wrong, I can't lie to you and tell you I'm strong enough to deal with the pressures of the band. I can tell you I won't fall down. Having you next to me like this, I can't fail."

Gina rolled over to her side and touched his face, rubbed her nose against his and kissed him. "Trev, it doesn't matter if we are here or with Perfection recording. We're good, baby, nothing can or will ever come between us."

Paul Ryan is going to be a problem. Is now the time to tell Trevor what I learned about him? No, not yet. He's not ready.

Trevor faced her and ran his fingers through her hair. "My intent is to lay down next to you and hold you."

They were falling asleep when Trevor's cell phone rang. He groggily answered, "Yeah, who's this?"

It was Rio, his voice loud and enthusiastic, booming through the phone, "Hey, man, how are you two doing in the woods and nature, all that shit? Bro, we have some good music going on. I want to play it for you and give you some inspo on adding some guitar or lyrics. You have time now."

Trevor answered, "We had a wonderful day out in the woods and on a lake. It has inspired me to write, but we're totally exhausted. Gina and I passed out. Can we call you later?"

Rio sounded a bit annoyed. "Definitely not tonight, Jae and I are going to a gallery opening. I do have other things in my life that are not Perfection. But we need to connect tomorrow, give me a time."

Gina yawned. "Babe, is that Rio? What's going on?"

Trevor held the phone out so Gina could hear. "Listen, Rio, we have half a day here at Sequoia and then we take Roxanne and Zach back to

Stanford. I promise you that when we find a place to stay, we will call. It may be around five-ish. Are you good? Another day is not going to have influence on any music."

Rio made one last loud statement. "Listen, I know you need to have this time, but seriously, you two can't be gone for months. A few weeks I get. Perfection needs to start thinking about our new stuff soon, you got me?"

Gina grabbed the phone. "Rio, don't worry, we hear you and agree. When you see us, we will be stronger, you get me? Gina and Trevor McNaughton will be better. Can't wait to hear the music tomorrow, bye for now."

Gina laid her head on Trevor's chest. "You okay, baby? It will be good to listen to some music again, new and what we have in the vault. Maybe once we drive Roxy and Zach back, we could listen to it. Can we do some writing at our next stop?"

Trevor looked resigned to the fact that Perfection needed to be part of this trip. "G, yes, we will listen to the music, which should get you inspired to write some lyrics. I'll focus on the guitar and bass lines. It's better to hear the music out here than in the studio. I keep convincing myself that I can do this with a clear head, yet a tiny part of me still is unsure, you can appreciate that, my beautiful wife, correct?"

Gina held him close. "Trev, we will never walk down the road that almost destroyed us, I got you."

They held each other, they were each other's lifeline in life, nothing would break that connection. They were still sleepy when they heard Roxanne and Zach come into the RV.

Roxanne was reluctant walking in. "Mom, Dad, is it all right to be in here?"

Gina came out. "Oh my God, Roxanne, you must think all your father and I do is have sex every minute. Stop, we were taking a nap. Silly girl. Did you enjoy your hike? Tell us about it. Roxanne, we love you, we want to know everything you do."

Roxanne took in what her mother said. "That was a lot to say in one sentence, Mom. Glad you two rested. Yes, the hike was beautiful, we enjoyed it. Now we're getting hungry, what did you plan on cooking? You do have an oven …"

Gina looked at Roxanne, amused. "You want me to make chicken parmesan, don't you? It was always your favorite. Okay, let's see if I have all the ingredients. Does that office sell food if we need something?"

Gina checked their provisions, "You are in luck, Roxy, I have all I need, even linguine. But I need your help. Zach, you okay with that? If I take her away for a bit? I know it's your last night with us."

Trevor walked out of the bedroom. "Zach, come outside with me, I'm going to play some guitar, you cool?"

Zach couldn't believe he was actually going to hear not Roxanne's father, but Trevor McNaughton the rock star, playing the guitar. He was happy to sit and listen.

Trevor began playing an exceptionally melodic tune—soft, beautiful, almost peaceful. Gina was trying to listen to the music while cooking.

She called them in to eat and the four campers exchanged their favorite parts of their bike ride and being on the lake. It was pleasant. Trevor seemed to bond with Zach, which was meaningful in itself. After their meal, they sat outside wrapped in blankets listening to Trevor play his guitar once again, first some old Perfection songs, then new music.

Gina was happy; she felt a red glow move through her body, the warmth radiating outward. Her face felt flushed, her body tingling with the sensation of the complete love she had in this moment. A few hours passed and Roxanne and Zach said their goodnights and sauntered into their tent. Gina and Trevor climbed into the RV. She disrobed, washed her face, and began putting on something to sleep in.

Trevor stopped her. "G, stop, I want to look at your body. I love looking at you naked, having the vision of you this way. It got me through so much in rehab. I would close my eyes and see you."

Gina walked up to him. "Trev, you never have to close your eyes, I'm here. Look, I'm touching you; I feel like you are afraid of losing me. That will never happen, we made it through the worst time of our lives. Nothing can break us, come hold me and give me a kiss."

Trevor simply said, "Can I take my clothes off first?"

Gina smiled. "You are a silly man, of course."

They fell on the bed and made love "quietly."

The next morning Zach and Roxanne packed up their tent and belongings. They were ready incredibly early. Gina and Trevor thought about having to cook breakfast. They knew they had a two-plus-hour drive to their next destination, Bodega Bay. They also had a phone call with Rio at five.

Roxanne and Zach were getting breakfast ready for her parents. "I love you two and wanted to say thank you for letting Zach and me join you on your trip. We made breakfast for you two."

Gina smiled. "That's so sweet, my girl, your dad and I appreciate it. We looked at our next stop, it's a bit over two hours away. This is wonderful, although I am going to miss you desperately, Roxanne. I'm feeling sad about bringing you back, can we kidnap you? Shouldn't you be coming home soon? Classes are almost over."

Roxanne hugged her mom. "I'll miss you guys, I do have a lot of studying for finals and so does Zach. And I might be taking a quickie summer class. I'll be at Stanford longer."

"Roxanne, I'm guessing this class is important for your psychology major, your father and I support that. We do want you to come to Montecito for a few weeks. We are hoping to spend time with you."

Trevor spoke up. "Roxy, take your class and do what's necessary, I'm happy we got to see our girl. You know I wouldn't have been able to finish all my time in rehab without your support and love."

Trevor reached over and kissed her on the head.

GINA MAKES A MISTAKE

AFTER BREAKFAST THEY DROVE BACK to the university and dropped off the Stanford duo.

Hugs and kisses all around, and Trevor and Gina got back into the RV and prepared for their two-hour drive to Bodega Bay.

Gina remembered, "Trev, babe, we should stop by a store and restock our supplies. Hopefully, we can get in and out."

They found and entered the store and began shopping, walking arm in arm and giggling as they perused the aisles.

As they reached the checkout line, a woman recognized them and shouted, "Oh my God, it's Gina and Trevor McNaughton right here!"

The McNaughtons were stunned; they weren't sure if they should make a quick exit or stupidly wait and check out. A crowd surrounded them; it was like a "meet and greet" but a bit frenzied. Trevor smiled and said they would sign autographs but wanted to pay for their food. The crowd agreed and allowed them to check out. Gina and Trevor spent about thirty minutes signing autographs and then politely told the crowd they had an appearance they needed to get to. Fans wanted to know about their latest music. They assured them it was coming.

They walked across the parking lot and entered the RV. Gina took her cap off and looked at Trevor. "Babe, I want to continue this trip, but you realize that as much as we want to pretend, we can't be people who blend in. We aren't those people. You are too handsome," Gina laughed.

Trevor leaned over and kissed her. "Let's move on, we have a bit of a drive."

Gina questioned Trevor, "The music you played last night was beautiful. Are we going to use it for Perfection? I don't know how we fit it into our hard rock style. A love song?"

Trevor answered, "G, I was in the moment feeling it, the music flowed, I am trying to get back in the writing mode. I think we may have an issue with Rio; he is pressing hard for the reboot of the band to happen immediately. He is too laser-focused on the band. I wonder how Jae feels about it. He is all about the band, what about his marriage? At any rate, we need to think of us. We have a good three, four weeks, possibly longer, on the road. I want to commit that time to us and to build on my sobriety. You grasp what I'm saying?"

Gina fell between two sides; she wanted to get back to the business of Perfection sooner like Rio. However, her love and promise that she would never put Trevor in a compromising situation again would always win.

Gina said, "Trev, let's drive on to Bodega Bay and we can relax and have the phone call with Rio. Are you good with that? Wasn't Bodega Bay where they filmed *The Birds*?"

Trevor was confused. "Gina, what are you talking about? I'm sorry, my mind wandered a bit, what about birds?"

Gina looked at Trevor, astonished. "Trevor, the Alfred Hitchcock movie *The Birds*, where the birds attack the people. You have no idea what I'm talking about, do you? It's a classic. See, this is interesting, we never talk about this stuff. I find it fascinating that you have no idea."

Trevor was agitated. "Gina, you know what my childhood was like, I didn't enjoy watching classic movies or even certain television shows. I lost my mother, I didn't go to school, I was drunk at thirteen and got in trouble, plus my father couldn't care less."

Gina recognized she had touched a nerve, she knew she needed to back off. "My love, I'm sorry I seemed insensitive. I didn't mean it that way. I realize you had a rough childhood and teen years. I forget that because you and I have built such an unbelievable life, one that people envy. I'm sorry, please forgive me."

Gina did not want to be the cause of anything that could push Trevor to slide in his health.

Trevor smiled. "Why don't you turn on the radio?"

Gina fumbled to turn on the radio, hitting all the buttons until she found something they could listen to. There was silence between them for the thirty minutes of driving.

Gina was rerunning the dialogue in her head and realizing how awful she seemed. As she looked out the window, she teared up. How could she hit the one nerve that she never really uncovered with Trevor all these years, feelings about his mother's death? They drove with no words spoken for another twenty minutes. Gina felt his pain. She needed to make him grasp how special he was. She unbuckled her seat belt and got on the floor. She set out to rub him gently in the crotch and placed her head in his lap. Touching, caressing him softly. She could feel him getting hard.

Trevor was still driving. "Gina, what are you doing? You are making it difficult to drive."

She could tell by the tone of his voice he was either aggravated or stimulated, the first time in over twenty-three years she couldn't read him. She continued but became bolder. She unzipped his shorts, grabbed him in her hand, and then surrounded him with her mouth. Trevor was certainly excited, as most men would be. Gina wanted to show her husband love. He needed to know the unconditional love she had for him, all that he missed early on.

Trevor was getting extremely aroused but managed to pant out, "G, I know what you're doing, I'm not angry, but you forget that we grew up on different ends of the spectrum. Damn you, woman, you're driving me nuts. I have to pull off the highway, I can't drive with you doing that."

Gina looked up at him, a bit teary-eyed. "You want me to stop?"

Trevor exhaled, "No, baby, I don't, you go ahead and do what you want. I just need to pull off the road."

By the time Trevor made his way to the side, he was just about ready to climax. Gina slid off her panties and moved on top of him, making Trevor her driver's seat.

She moved slowly, wanting to give him incredible pleasure. She cradled his face and told him tenderly, "Trevor, please forgive me, I love you so much. I never want to bring up those old memories. Let yourself go."

Trevor did let himself go. He stroked her hair. "Gina, I focused my pain from my father onto you. That was wrong. They taught us how to recognize when we're transferring anger to someone else. I was doing that to you. I should never do that to the one person who has loved me without question. My sweet Gina, baby, you are so damn hot."

BODEGA BAY

TREVOR SOFTLY SAID, "Can I start to drive again, so we can get to this place, Bodega Bay, and call your cousin?"

Gina knew she dodged a bullet. "Yes, my love, let's get going."

They had about another twenty minutes before they'd reach the Bodega Bay park. She felt they would get there in plenty of time to talk to Rio. Gina suddenly felt inspired to write a song about their emotions before reconciliation. She found her writing pad and wrote a song, "Almost Done." She would show it to Trevor when they reached the site.

ALMOST DONE

I wanted you; no one was there, I swear I saw you. You said
you loved me. I cried out to you, you weren't there. Every time
I saw you, I cried out to you I felt lost, you seemed to be there.

Was I pretending to see the part of you that we both loved and needed?
These walls remind me of you, wher did you go? Are we almost done?

*Where did you go, we can't be almost done, I reach out for you, a
vision of you, you come to me, you say you love me but when I reach
for you, you're still not there. What did we do? To see the ghosts of our
love, are we almost done? Please don't let it be done. Just be with me,*

*I need your touch, your love, don't let this be almost done.
We can't be done, there has been so much we have done in
this life, full of happiness and joy, are we almost done?*

*Where did you go, our love was the sweetest of all loves. I see you
in a dream and tell you I love you. Come home to me, I forgive
you. Don't make us almost done. I can't have us almost done.*

*Did you hear me? I can't lose you. Don't make us almost
done. I wonder where you are, can you see me like I
see you in a dream or maybe something real?*

*Our memories haunt me, then I see you, do you
need me, I need you, are we almost done? Just come
home, so I can tell you how much I need you.*

*Did you call me? We can't be almost done, please don't let this be
almost done, I call out to you, I love you, is this almost done?*

*Then a messenger, an angel came to me and told
me you loved me, I sank down and cried and said,
I thank God, for what we'd almost done.*

Gina felt this song was truly the way she and Trevor felt separately.
Trevor, during his detox, calling and reaching for her. He needed her, she
had no idea. Gina cried every day living in their house, seeing him all around

her, she thought he was gone. She was in a black hole she dug for herself, she hoped he would come home. The song was rightfully how they felt. This would be easy for them to sing together. More of a soft song turning into a hard rock ending. She hoped he liked it. As she was writing, she cried.

Trevor looked over. "Baby, why are you crying? I'm not mad at you."

Gina loved his face. "I finished a song that we can mutually relate to, it has sadness in it. I turned it into something positive; that's all, babe. I can't wait for you to see it. It should shut up Rio since I wrote it within three days into our trip. I love him but he drives me crazy, he's a dick sometimes."

Trevor smiled. "I can't wait to see it. You said it was sad."

Gina got up to kiss him. "Baby, it's all good, we're together and that's all that matters."

They saw a huge gas station; they needed to fill up and go to the bathroom.

Gina hoped she could pee without being recognized and avoid someone sticking a piece of paper under the stall. It happened—the pitfall of being a celebrity.

Trevor filled up the RV while Gina walked into this huge truck stop and found the bathroom. Nobody seemed to notice. She walked into the bathroom and found two people washing their hands; she slipped in unnoticed, or so she thought. Certainly, they were in the middle of nowhere.

Gina washed her hands and the two women came over. "You're Gina McNaughton, how cool. What are you doing here? A concert?"

Gina smiled. "You got me, no, I'm actually on vacation. You are seeing a plain, regular Gina. Can you please not tell this entire place that you saw me? I would appreciate it."

The fans were looking for a pen or something to get her autograph.

Gina hated this.

The women asked, "Could you sign our shirts?"

Gina caved. "Sure, but remember, you don't say anything when we leave this bathroom. I want to buy some snacks, I don't want people coming at me, okay?"

These women must have been in their thirties, something like that. They knew Perfection. *We are still relevant.*

She walked out and examined all the junk food, pulling her favorites. Trevor walked into the store; they simply exchanged glances. If they were together, it would be a dead giveaway who they were. If they were alone, they had a chance to get in and out. Gina began laying down all the junk food, water, fruit, she even asked for a lottery ticket. Once she took out her credit card, the cashier gave her a look; a Black Amex card was a dead give-away. The cashier smiled and bagged all her food. Gina signed the receipt and on the back wrote, *"Thanks for not giving me away, Gina McNaughton."*

Trevor walked straight to the RV.

Gina carried four stuffed bags. "Well, I guess even out here, people recognize us. I had to sign three autographs, two were in the bathroom. Should we be happy? Perfection is still a hot commodity."

Trevor laughed. "I was trying to pee, and some dude came up to me, midstream mind you, and asked if I was me. I said, 'Hey, guy, can I finish going to the bathroom?' I signed his cap. Hopefully, when we get out of California, we will have less of that."

Gina took out a bag of caramel popcorn and handed it to Trevor. Junk food, they loved it, they also knew to be careful of weight gain. However, they each had lost weight while they were apart, and Gina felt it was a celebration, *so why not indulge?* When they were about an hour away from Bodega Bay, Gina looked at the directions for their next stop. She checked the book they got from Jonas. There was a beach on one side and on the other was the bay. It looked like a great rest stop. She hoped they would stay two nights. Suddenly, she remembered she didn't reserve a spot. She called the office and was able to get them a spot. Gina didn't want any hiccups since they had to talk to Rio.

NOT ALMOST
DONE

TREVOR WAS TIRED AFTER DRIVING over two hours, but they had to hook up the RV. She hoped he remembered what Zach showed him. Trevor walked to the back of the RV to the bed.

He fell down hard. "G, baby, this is exhausting, I would rather go on tour. Driving for hours, I'm not used to it. This was my plan so I guess I shouldn't complain. Come next to me."

Gina got up and looked up at the ceiling. She had a thought, "Trev, this is supposed to be relaxing. If this is too much, we can change plans, I won't be upset. I don't want you to stress." He needed Gina to know the importance of this trip. He reached over to touch her face. "Gina, this is part of my therapy. I need to do this to go back to Perfection clearheaded. You get why. Let me kiss you, so I know this is real."

Gina brought him closer. "Trevor, it's real, I had those same emotions. The song I wrote is about that exact feeling."

She touched his face. "Here's a kiss. We have to hook up this beast and take a shower. I'll figure out what we are eating, good?"

They lay there for about fifteen minutes and went outside to hook up the water and sewer line. These two rockers had the right idea but couldn't execute. There was an older couple watching them. Finally, they came over and asked if they needed help. They were quick to accept. Myra and Lionel Ludden introduced themselves; the older couple had no idea who they were. Merely two novice RV-ers. Lionel took the time to show Trevor in detail how to hook up all they needed.

Gina felt she needed to thank them for their help. "Would you like to have supper with us? We appreciate all your help. We have a call at five o'clock but are free after."

Myra jumped in, "It's always nice to meet folks who pop into the park. We would love to join you."

It was getting close to five o'clock. They were determined to call Rio so he knew they had their heads in the game.

Gina took out her cell phone and called Rio, one ring and he picked up at once. "Well, well, you actually called when you said you would. How's camping? You two are actually hilarious, you have no idea what you're doing. But you're still alive, so that's something. I hope you have something to give me."

Gina knew he was correct about their camping experience, but she was offended by his comment that they were hilarious. "Rio, are you done being a fucking dick right now?"

Rio laughed. "Now that sounds like the Gina I know. Seriously, you're still doing this all the way to Vancouver, then to Boise, Idaho? We took bets to see how long it takes you to come home."

Trevor was listening to this; he never gave a full explanation to the band. It was time to let them all know why this was so important to him.

Trevor paused for a moment. "Hey, Rio, there is a reason I chose to do this trip. First, I wanted to spend time with my wife, with no intrusions. Entirely us, to reconnect after we went through hell away from each other. We need to work through that as a couple. Most importantly, I need to know that I'm absolutely back in the right headspace to reboot Perfection. I'm better, I simply need to know I don't have fragile edges. I need to commit totally to Perfection. I need to be clear of all those demons; they can never come back. It's for my sobriety and my love of music that I need this time."

Rio acknowledged, "Trevor, I hear you. You and Gina remember Perfection will have its own label now. We own all our music. Skip is finishing the paperwork with the attorneys."

Trevor held the phone out so Gina could hear Rio's comments.

Gina let out a long sigh. "Rio, I vaguely remember this discussion, I certainly don't remember details."

Rio said, "The two of you were distracted. I am also reminding you that Tommy is no longer with Brown Fence, he is solely working for the Perfection label. He is now a partner."

Trevor responded, "I remember bits and pieces of these conversations. Gina and I support Tommy being a partner. Perfection is successful as a result of his outstanding production work. He should have a piece of the label. That's cool."

Gina had Rio's ear, "How's Jae? I miss her. Jae was the catalyst to shed all my anger and focus on the love I had. I wrote a song, it's sad but it captures the feelings Trevor and I had separately though were the same. I named it 'Almost Done.'"

Gina read the words to Rio, and it was the first time Trevor heard them. He now understood why she was crying.

Gina was inquisitive. "Rio, what do you think? I think a soft rock edge in the beginning to let you see the pain and end it in something harder, thoughts?"

She looked at Trevor, who had tears running down his face.

Gina asked again, "Rio, your thoughts?"

Rio was quiet and said, "Gina, it sounds like an especially personal song, but I think it's killer. Write about the pain but don't forget all you regained in the process, write about both. Trev, let all the stuff fly, really get it all out there."

Trevor held it together. "I had nothing to do with it. My wife wrote from pain. Yes, it's personal but the truth. I'm good, I want to produce a sad melodic tune to go with it. I'll work on it with G. We will talk in two days, good? We have our own label, that's major. Call us with anything, I told you we are reachable."

Gina wasn't sure what Trevor meant by *personal. Was it too much to share?* Trevor was trying to handle the many emotions he was feeling. This time his tears didn't stop, she held him so close.

Oh, no! Did I inadvertently open that fragile edge? "Trev, my love. I'm holding you so tight, I'm here, no ghosts, it's all real. We love each other, we are addicted to each other and that's beautiful."

Trevor sniffled back tears. "I wish we didn't make plans with our new friends; my preference would be to be alone with you, touching you, loving you. After hearing those words, the pain that we went through separately but was the same."

Gina devotedly and with love stroked his cheek. "Trev, baby, we made mistakes. I should have saved you and you should have let me know where you were for five months. It's over, baby. It's not *almost done.* I need to get my head around the Luddens, so let's get food ready."

DUNES OF BODEGA BAY

TREVOR GATHERED HIMSELF. "I love you, Gina, always. I'll get things going."

They used their folding picnic table and set four places. Gina was able to put together a pasta dish with chicken, peas, and mushrooms. Myra came over with a casserole. Gina was not accustomed to eating casseroles, but it looked good. They also brought a bottle of wine, no need to say anything. Myra and Lionel were middle-class retired teachers who chose to travel to four spots throughout the year. Their suggestion was to walk the beach in the evening, bring a flashlight, and enjoy the sound of the surf. The dunes were beautiful and the Luddens said sometimes tourists used them to *do it*. The McNaughtons shook their heads in disapproval, but it was noted, and in a positive way. The Luddens were early risers, so they excused themselves for the evening and invited the new adventurers to join them on a walk on their favorite trail around lunchtime. Gina and Trevor accepted the invitation; they elected to stay a couple of extra days.

Gina was clearing and washing the dishes when Trevor came up behind her and whispered, "I think the dunes are calling us."

A smile came over her face. "I was wondering how long it would take you to bring that up. It took exactly thirty-eight minutes. Of course, I'm in. Bring two comforters, I don't want sand all up me."

Gina wore one of her gauzy sundresses, without anything underneath, and Trevor wore a pair of surf shorts. The two lovers walked the beach at night with a flashlight, the surf appeared gentle and peaceful. The flashlight caught the foam of the ocean, which appeared multicolored. They walked together holding hands. Next they found a set of secluded dunes. Trevor placed the comforters down.

Gina lay down first. "Trevor, I'm waiting for you."

Trevor placed the comforter on top of them. Gina kissed his neck all over and continued to plant tiny kisses on his face. She marveled at how handsome he was, how many women fantasized about her husband. He was hers, always.

She looked into his eyes. "Mr. McNaughton, I have loved you my entire life, our lovemaking is always extraordinary, so show me again how special we are."

Trevor responded, "I really want to kiss you, like we are kids having a make-out session, and see if I get lucky."

Gina laughed, "Oh, I think you will get lucky."

He kissed her neck, who was he kidding, that was the place she would melt. She placed her hands on his face, like so many times before. Gina was totally turned on, kissing him hard and deep. He responded by lying on top of her. She placed her arms around his neck and drew him into her, slowly they moved together.

Trevor whispered, "Baby, we were never almost done. I would never let you get away. Even when it seemed hopeless. I was never going away. I needed to get to you, Paul Ryan was in my head knowing how much he wanted you. I knew you would never be his. Gina, I hate that man."

Gina simply answered, "Thank you, baby, for having faith. Oh, shit, Trev, a family is coming this way. We are one of those couples who *do it in the dunes.*"

Trevor had a plan. "You take one comforter, wrap it around you, and I'll take the other; it'll look like we're cold, honestly it is a bit chilly. Come on."

Gina heard Trevor's words; he hated Paul Ryan. When would she share how psychotic he really was? It frightened her. How would Trevor react to the news she received right before their trip?

Gina raked her hands through her hair and felt sand throughout. "Trev, I'm going to take a lukewarm shower."

After she showered and dressed, she went through her suitcase and found her pastel cigarettes. "Trev, look what I found, want one?"

Trevor laughed. "Those things that made Gina Poole so different. I actually haven't had a cigarette in a long time. We could have cigarette breaks during therapy; it reminded me of you. I stopped, but sure, I'll see if I can deal with one of those."

Gina lit two cigarettes and handed one to him. "While I was home, crying my eyes out, I saw our lives like a time capsule. It went by fast and later it slowed down when it was the worst. I remembered the pastel cigarettes. It made me laugh and also cry. You don't have to smoke that, babe, if you're not interested."

Trevor was nonchalant. "G, it actually tastes good. The song you wrote, if there are more feelings to put out there, do it. Our music will make it relatable to people who have gone through the same experiences. It can still be hard-edge, only with a soft hook. Perhaps this is your therapy, to express your feelings in our songs."

Gina looked concerned. "Trevor, you think I need therapy? I thought of it but never acted on it."

Trevor held her. "I learned most people can use therapy, but it doesn't look the same for every person. It could be good for you. I take you the way you are. I guess we should get some sleep. God knows what the fuck we got ourselves into with this hike."

Gina dried her wet hair a little and got into bed. "Hold me, I want to go to sleep, knowing I have your arms securely around me; I'll do the same, never almost done, babe, goodnight."

The next morning, once the sun rose, they were up.

Trevor was looking at his phone. "G, does that say six thirty?"

Gina groaned, "Oh, shit, it does, why are we up this early? It's the camping, up at sunrise. I'll get up and make coffee."

Gina fumbled her way out of the bed to the kitchen for mugs. She stood in front of the machine waiting for it to brew. Gina needed the caffeine. Once the brew was made, she took some long sips and felt she was stable enough to hand Trevor his mug. They sat in silence until the caffeine from the coffee woke them up.

Gina had an idea. "I would love to walk Bodega Bay this morning before we meet with the Luddens, do you mind? I want to see if there are any signs where they filmed the movie."

Trevor smiled. "If that's what my wife wants, let's go."

The walk from their campground to the bay was about fifteen minutes. The sun was out; it was a mild May day. Trevor and Gina walked hand in hand. She was excited to see the bay that was in the movie. There was a coffee shop called The Birds Café; she thought they should check it out on the way back. The duo walked along the bay and enjoyed the scenery.

Trevor remarked, "Exactly what I wanted to experience, the peacefulness of nature, scenery, the two of us, baby. Enjoying the simple things. I learned that the simple things are the most cherished."

Gina was surprised. "Trev, what a beautiful sentiment, that facility really gave you a different outlook. I wish you would tell me more so I could enjoy some of this wisdom. I really would love to be at the same place as you. Seeing things through your beautiful eyes."

Trevor was honest. "G, I would love to share those eye-opening talks. At times it also reminds me of the worst time in that place. I know I needed to do it. I'll share some with you, promise." Gina loved the smell of the salt air, she felt somehow invigorated. "Trevor, please remember you can share those troubled times too. I want to know the feelings you had in rehab. You know that's behind us. All those feelings are a part of that journey."

They looked at the water, it was calming, they walked the beachfront for a bit and came to a decision to walk back. They promised the Luddens a hike at noon. They had a couple of hours to choose what to do. They chose to go back to their RV.

Gina made a late breakfast. Trevor sat on the couch and played his guitar. Gina enjoyed listening to him play while she cooked, like old times.

Gina called out, "Babe, food, are you hungry?"

Trevor looked up. "Sure, I can eat."

They sat and ate a late breakfast. Gina asked about the music he was playing.

Trevor was proud of the music he just created and smiled. "I thought we could use it for part of 'Almost Done.' I know you wanted a big rock ending. I have to work that out. I love the song, your words capturing all that we were each feeling. Gina, I know how mad you were, the whole incident backstage. I don't even remember, Rio reminded me. I was embarrassed because Roxanne knew what I did. I felt like an addicted loser. How could you love me? I was at my lowest. I kept remembering our wedding in Vegas, you said 'I do' a million times. I assumed we had a few more 'I do's' in our life."

Gina teared up. "I forgot I said that, I meant every word. You remembered that when you were at your lowest? You needed me. Had I known I would have come whether they wanted me there or not. I would have demanded to be there. I pulled you out before, I should have ..."

Trevor halted the conversation, "G, you wouldn't have been allowed. I needed to do it."

Gina sat on his lap, "These are the things I want you to share. This trip is letting all this emotion seep out of each of us. Changing the subject, Roxanne thinks all we do is make love every hour. Did we really expose her to that much? I feel she resents us. Did we not show her how much we love her? Roxanne came first, or did the band become more important? I can't figure it out."

Trevor laughed. "You said it, it's weird for her to think of her parents having sex. I appreciate what you are saying, she might resent us for everything we do onstage. Roxanne is uncomfortable with it. I remember her telling me when she was in high school, she was embarrassed. She felt awkward that her friends thought her parents were *very cool and good-looking*. G, maybe it was immensely emotional for her."

Gina touched his face. "I don't remember you ever telling me that she felt awkward. It makes sense why she is unhappy with us at times. I believed we always tried to make her comprehend that what we did onstage was a show. When we were home, we were normal. Obviously, not to our daughter."

GINA'S BRUSH WITH DEATH

THE LUDDENS KNOCKED on their door. "Hi, folks, ready for a two-mile nature walk?"

Gina opened the door, "Sure, let me pack some snacks."

The two rock stars and the experienced hikers took off on their walk. They hiked from the water into a wooded area with a path, having conversations about raising children and whether the Luddens enjoyed teaching. Never once did they ask what they did for a living. They walked for about thirty minutes, sat down in a clearing, and enjoyed snacks. They continued to walk for a while and turned back to the park. The couples said their goodbyes and hoped they would see them before they left.

They enjoyed an evening playing music. Gina was trying to think of lyrics that weren't so personal.

When Gina woke up the next morning, she had a huge rash on her legs and arms, it was burning and itching.

She screamed for Trevor. "Trev, something's wrong with me, I have this rash on my legs and arms. It looks like yellow bumps. It's itching me like crazy."

Trevor took a look. "G, I think you may have poison oak or something like that. Have you ever had it before?"

Gina was confused. "Trev, I have never hiked in the woods like that. Is it bad? I feel like it's all over my body."

Trevor looked her up and down. "Gina, we need to take you to the ED, I never saw someone have a bad case like this. I'm going to go to the office and find the nearest hospital."

The office employee directed them to Santa Rosa Memorial Hospital. Lionel Ludden offered to drive them there.

When they got to the ED, a doctor examined Gina and had a simple explanation. "She was in contact with poison oak. Unfortunately, she is having an allergic reaction, she needs to be treated immediately so she doesn't go into anaphylaxis."

The doctor said they would give her shots of cortisone that would help, but she had to stay overnight.

Gina got nervous. "Trevor, please don't leave me, I'm scared."

He sat next to her. "I'm not leaving, I will ask for a cot or something. If I have to sleep in the waiting room, I will."

Gina was frantic, panic set in. "No, please, baby, I'm scared. This shit is all over me, I hope it doesn't get to my ass and vag. What's the cortisone shot supposed to do?"

Trevor wasn't too sure but tried to calm Gina. "It should help reduce spreading. Also the itching. G, my love, you look miserable. I guess hiking in the woods is out. We'll stick to the beaches for the rest of the trip. Does that make you happy?"

Gina, shaking in fear, asked, "How long did the doctor say I have to be here? Anaphylaxis, can't you die from that?"

Trevor spoke in a calming manner, "Yes, baby, that's why you're here, we got you in here before you went into shock. You might be here for a couple of days. You need to relax, I'm here."

The nurse came in to do a vitals check on Gina.

She hesitantly asked the nurse, "What's the deal with these cortisone shots? Will I be able to leave tomorrow?"

All the nurse told her was that they were giving her a few cortisone shots. The nurse added she didn't think Gina would be able to leave as fast as she wanted.

Trevor asked the nurse for a cot. He wanted to be beside his wife. The nurse told him she would find a cot for him. It was a frequent request from most husbands when their wives were in a hospital room. Bonus, the nurse knew who they were. A few hours later the doctor came in to give Gina another injection. "Your eyes may swell and close up, but it will only be temporary."

Gina flipped out, "Oh, hell no, am I going to be scarred? Baby, this isn't good."

Trevor explained, "Listen, my wife is extremely upset now. Her looks are important to our work, that's why she is concerned."

The doctor told them, "I know who the two of you are—the McNaughtons. The swelling will be temporary, a day or two. But Mrs. McNaughton is extremely allergic to any poison oak, ivy, or sumac. She didn't even need to touch it; the plants secrete oils, and if you're allergic, you can get the rash from that. You two shouldn't hike in the woods." He turned toward Gina. "I promise you will not be damaged, however, you will definitely be uncomfortable."

Gina was crying, "Trev, I'm sorry, I'm going to look like a freak. I don't want you to stay. I don't want you seeing me look horrible."

Trevor sat next to her. "G, I'm not leaving you. I told you never again will we be disconnected. I love you no matter what you look like, it's temporary."

Gina continued getting panic attacks, so the doctor ordered a sedative to calm her down. It took about twenty minutes for her to fall asleep. Gina had been sleeping for about an hour when she heard Trevor's cell phone ring. She was still out of it but managed to say to Trevor, "I bet it's Rio, baby, I can't deal with him. You manage him. I want to hear what that pest wants now." Trevor picked up the phone, he let Gina listen. "Dude, what songs do you have for me? The one Gina wrote is killer. Not trying to stress you out, are you two working on music?"

Trevor spoke bluntly. "Rio, I'm at the hospital in Santa Rosa. Gina has poison oak. She has a massive rash all over her body. She's allergic so she has been hospitalized. They are giving her cortisone shots. She has been given something to calm her down. I will have to stay in the hospital for a few days. No music until we are out of here, sorry, man. I can't leave her to go write songs."

Rio was speechless. "Wait, you said all over her body, it's that bad? She must be freaking out, is that why they drugged her?"

Gina heard Rio and barely said, "Rio, this sucks. I'm going to look like a freak."

"Try to rest."

Rio was careful in his words, knowing Gina was listening. "Trevor, I don't know what to say. You do know who you are dealing with, a rich girl from Long Island. She's not used to nature and shit. Gina always hated walking in the woods. When we were younger and smoking weed, we would sometimes go into a wooded area by Saint Mary's, she hated being there. She was afraid of animals and bugs … Can I ask you a personal question, were the two of you fucking in the woods?"

Trevor was annoyed. "No, Rio, we went on a hike with some nice people. The doctor said we were lucky to get her here fast. Rio, this is no joke. Gina is covered with this shit. Her eyes are going to swell closed from the cortisone shots. She's not happy."

"Rio, screw you, this sucks." Gina wasn't having it.

Rio felt bad for his last comment. He did love Gina like a sister. "Trevor, man, I know Gina, she's definitely freaking out. I do have band business I need to mention. Tommy came today. He loves what we have, he wants to rearrange some of our music. I'm good with his changes, I need you to agree to them too. I need lyrics from you and Gina, obviously we will have to wait on that. I'm not trying to be insensitive but you two should head up to Vancouver and finish this trip. You two are essential to Perfection. I know you need this time away, but this whole nature shit is not your thing."

Trevor couldn't believe the urgency of the situation escaped Rio, especially when he knew how close the two of them were.

Trevor raised his voice, "Rio, she could have died if we didn't get her to the hospital. This isn't a bullshit thing. We will work double the time after we leave, I promise. But my wife is sick, she's my priority. Gina is the biggest part of Perfection. If she is in trouble, we all are, you get it?"

Rio was resigned. "Trevor, she's my blood, my sister, of course I'm concerned. Get her well, I'll call you tomorrow to check up on her condition."

"Rio, we are on it, please, we will bring it all together. We do want to get back to business. Let me emphasize slowly—Gina and I still need a moment in our therapy."

Rio reeled it in. "That's all I need to hear, Trev, take care of Princess. Did you call Franny?" Trevor didn't want this situation to escalate. "No, you know Gina's mother, she'd be on the next flight out here."

Rio just said, "Trevor, take care of her, I'll call tomorrow."

The hospital staff brought in a cot. The aide recognized him at once. "Wow, man, you're Trevor McNaughton. Your wife, is she going to be okay?"

Trevor thought he most definitely wanted an autograph. "Hey, man, thanks for the cot, if you have paper or something, I'll give you an autograph."

He was excited. "Here, could you sign my sleeve? I won't say anything, promise."

Gina slept through the night; Trevor slept next to her on the cot.

When she woke up, she screamed. "Trevor, I can barely see, the bridge of my nose is swollen and my eyes must be too. How bad is it, baby, please tell me."

Trevor shot up and saw Gina with her eyes almost closed.

He sat on her bed. "Gina, your eyes are swollen, but the doctor told us this would happen. Try not to get upset. How is the itching and soreness?"

Gina couldn't get over not seeing properly. "I look like a freak, people in the hospital must know who we are. This sucks."

Trevor kissed her head. "G, you had to have this treatment. By tomorrow, I'm sure the swelling will go down. Please hang in there, this was serious. I'm sure the doctor will check on you soon. I love you, it's cool. When I detoxed, baby, I looked terrible. I am sure I pissed and shit in my pants, so it could be worse."

An aide came in with breakfast, it looked like hospital food. Gina was starving so she ate the crappy oatmeal and fruit. Trevor told her he would go to the cafeteria and see what they had. He would be as fast as he could. He came back with weak coffee and a bagel for her.

The doctor came in and took off the bandages that covered Gina's arms and legs. "Well, here's the good news, your arms and legs look like they are drying up. I feel confident that it won't spread anymore. I understand, Gina, that you're upset about your face. The swelling should go down late today and tomorrow. I don't want to release you until that happens. You okay with the plan?"

Gina tried to look at him. "Honestly, I don't want to go out looking like this. I have no choice, do I?"

Trevor thanked the doctor. "I want her completely or as close to 100 percent as possible. Another day won't matter."

Gina threw him a look. "Trevor, I want out of the hospital. It brings back some bad memories, my miscarriages, being sedated. Helpless—"

Trevor stopped her. "G, the last time you were in the hospital you gave birth to our daughter, try to think of that. Not the bad memories, I'm here with you, it's fine."

Gina was exasperated. "Maybe, I should write a song, 'Don't Go Fucking Hiking,' which would be interesting."

As promised, Rio called to check in and was thrilled that they would be leaving in about two days. He was still pressing to get some lyrics from these missing rock stars. Trevor told him to hold on, don't push.

Trevor tried to calm Gina's insecurities. "G, when you get out, we will be having a big playdate. How does that sound?"

Gina pouted. "The way I look, you must really love me."

RIO PUTS ON THE PRESSURE

AFTER TWO DAYS THE DOCTOR FELT Gina could leave the hospital. The swelling dissipated. She had scabs on her body. They grabbed a cab to the park and would stay the night and drive up the coast the next morning, hoping to make it to Redwood National Park.

When Gina came home, she immediately looked in the mirror. She was horrified to see what had happened to her face.

She sat on the bed and cried, "Trev, I'm ugly and all scarred up."

He sat down next to her. "G, it was an unfortunate experience but you are still beautiful." He put his arm around her. "Come here, wife, I missed you."

Gina whined, "Trev, can you hold me even with the way I look?"

Trevor held her up close. "I told you on the day we got married I would love you forever, no matter what. Stop, you're still Gina McNaughton."

She leaned in and kissed him. He immediately went in for a *deep I'm hungry for you kiss.*

Gina begged, "Trevor, please let me take a shower, I feel disgusting. I want to at least feel clean."

They spent a lazy afternoon enjoying each other. They agreed to go for a short walk to the coast to enjoy the sea air. Gina felt normal, no smelling like the hospital. The stroll helped with Gina's mood. It felt great after being in a hospital bed for days. On their way back, they stopped to say thank you to the Luddens for all their help and to let them know they were leaving tomorrow in the morning.

They woke at seven to start their five-and-a-half-hour drive to Redlands National Park.

Gina remembered how exhausted Trevor was getting to Bodega Bay. "Babe, sure you're not going to be exhausted? It's a long drive, over five hours. I don't want you stressed."

Trevor surprised her. "G, we are stopping halfway and we will find a lovely place to go and eat."

Trevor's phone rang. He kept the phone on the console of the RV so Gina could listen. "Hey, Rio, are you calling me about songs, because yesterday evening Gina and I left the hospital. We obviously have nothing for you yet."

Rio had the band on his mind once again. "Hey, man, that's good news, so Gina is all cleared up, no more poison oak. Princess, stay in the RV, don't take any chances on getting any other ailment. Just kidding. Tommy wants you to hear some of the songs we rearranged. We need your input on what we've done. Tommy will be back tomorrow, can you two be available?"

Gina yelled into the phone, "Rio, seriously, it seems like you have forgotten why Trevor and I need this trip. We can be available; it sounds like a long phone call. How many songs have you rearranged?"

Rio laughed. "Gina, I know you're pissed off; I'm telling you, write bitch."

Gina sneered, "Rio, I love you, but like I've said before, you're a dick. I don't know why Jae loves you so much. So how many songs are we talking about?"

Rio got serious. "Right now, five songs, we have fifteen more that we have to go through. It's difficult to do this on the phone. We will work on the five songs, we have an immense amount of work, we can wait on the other songs till whenever you get back. No stress, man, really."

Trevor took command of the conversation, "Rio, let's do the five songs Tommy wants to rearrange. Gina wrote a great song. I'm putting some music to it. Once I have something solid, I'll play it for you. What time tomorrow with Tommy?"

Rio pondered. "Probably around noon, where are you two planning to be tomorrow?"

Gina chirped in, "Redwood National Park, afterward we will be going up the Oregon Coast. We are working our way up to Vancouver. About four or five days to get there. I think Perfection will be fine. How are Ian and Jeff? They have their heads in the game?"

Rio was positive. "Yeah, man, they want to get this going also."

Trevor nodded his head. "That sounds great, we need the guys' commitment. Rio, we are trying to be a part of the process, we ask you to be cool. Gina and I got this."

Rio reminded them, "Gina and Trevor McNauaghton are what helps sell the band. I'm glad you are all in. Really try to condense this trip the best you can."

Trevor was resigned, "We will all talk tomorrow."

Gina was infuriated. Rio was putting some hard demands on them. She knew Rio would always have Perfection's interests before anything else. She wondered if Jae should be his first priority. She also remembered that he lied to her about where Trevor was. Gina thought he put the band before his own cousin's sanity. She did forgive him but wouldn't forget.

Gina finished in the kitchen. "My dear captain, are we ready to ride off?"

Trevor smiled. "I'm ready, let's vámonos. We have about a three-hour drive until we get to Westport for lunch. Babe, if you have any ideas of making the trip more interesting, I'm not opposed to it."

Gina winked, "I'll keep that in mind."

Gina wished she had recordings of all their songs. She knew one existed but the trip happened so fast, she didn't think clearly.

Gina called Marisol to make sure that she and the house were alive and well. She was thankful that Marisol, their live-in housekeeper, kept the McNaughtons' home running smoothly. She didn't know what she would've done without this godsend, who took care of Roxanne when she was young and her parents weren't available. She was a member of the McNaughton family. They loved her.

Marisol said all was quiet, nothing to report, and that Gina's friends had stopped by to check on her. Those Montecito Moms, the best of friends. Nice that they thought of checking on Marisol. With that out of the way, Gina looked out the window as they drove through Mendocino County. The scenery was amazing—spectacular cliffs and ocean views. They also went past some beautifully landscaped wineries. Gina's biggest excitement came from seeing lavender fields. Lavender was her favorite fragrance. She asked Trevor to stop so she could surround herself in a lavender field. She felt like she was in heaven. As they drove further, the huge trees dotted the sides of the road with ferns and extremely large wild mushrooms.

Trevor was inhaling all the beauty of the coastline, trees, and the flowers that his wife was enthralled with. Gina noticed a place called Earth Spoke Farms, which had many varieties of dahlias. She was surprised by the variety and colors. She was mesmerized by the vibrant fields of color. She bought several tubers of dahlias to plant at their home.

Trevor accommodated her, knowing it would slow down the drive. He didn't care; his wife immersed herself in the natural beauty of their surroundings. The roads were winding, and through the tall trees they could see the Pacific Ocean. With all the beauty around her she stared at her husband, to her he was perfect.

Trevor grabbed her hands at the table. "G, I am so happy you got to run through the lavender fields and see all the gorgeous flowers. You had a look on your face I don't think I have ever seen. Peaceful and childlike. Something new I learned about my wife."

Gina smiled back. "Trev, I have never just sat back and enjoyed all the beauty of nature. Most importantly, my love for flowers. I can thank Franny for that." Gina laughed.

They arrived in Westport and stopped to eat at one of Westport's must-visit pubs. It was time to enjoy food and relax. The lovers sat admiring the view, in the distance they could see the ocean and cliffs. They found a place to park the RV and set off walking until they found the pub they were looking for. It offered live music. They felt listening to someone else sing was a treat.

Gina looked at Trevor with all the liquor that was being served.

Trevor told her, "No worries, G, this might be a pub, but I have no desire to drink."

Gina wasn't worried, she knew her husband went through a miserable time getting clean, she believed he finally exorcised those demons. She knew Trevor had other fears waiting to creep out.

MCNAUGHTONS

GINA'S HEART OVERFLOWED with happiness, she asked the server for a nice red cabernet, something that came from one of the local wineries. She asked Trevor if that would bother him.

Trevor insisted, "Gina, you don't have an issue. I do, have a glass."

He asked for sparkling water. They surveyed the menu.

Gina said, "Oh, look, shepherd's pie. Did you remember when we went to London, Roxy loved shepherd's pie. Sweet memory, wasn't it?"

Trevor grabbed her hand. "G, yes, that was a great memory. I don't remember the last time we simply ate out together like this, it's been a while. I was a horrendous drunk."

Gina shook it off. "Trev, we are so past that, I know you are such a better man. All you went through, no worries, baby. I trust you with our lives."

The server came over. "I can't believe Gina and Trevor McNaughton are sitting at my station. What would make you two be in a place like Westport? I mean, it's incredible."

Gina asked her politely, "Listen, we want to order our food, enjoy the ambiance of your pub. Can we please not let the entire restaurant know we are here? We're on a vacation, so …"

The server promised she wouldn't say anything.

Trevor looked at Gina. "She's going to tell the whole damn place; I fucking know it. I'm so hungry, I want to eat."

Gina agreed with him. "I feel you, so I want to show you the song I wrote. Here, take a look." Trevor read Gina's lyrics. "G, this is beautiful, I love how you tied together nature and what our love means to us. You are the beauty in my life."

They began to notice the stares from around the restaurant. *Did their server say something or were they completely out of place?* The house band kicked off playing some 1980 covers. Gina and Trevor sat back and enjoyed the show. The two chatted about the cities they were going to hit on the Oregon Coast.

From out of nowhere, the band announced they had a special surprise in the restaurant. The next thing they knew, the band announced that Gina and Trevor McNaughton from Perfection were in the house. They looked at each other, unsure what they should do. At that point, the entire pub stood up clapping and asking for a song. They were speechless. What would they sing? The pub wanted a Perfection song. Gina and Trevor were a bit shocked. Trevor asked a band member if he could use a guitar. One of them happily handed him one. Gina asked the band if they knew the Perfection song "Life Flies By." She was surprised when they said they could play the background music. Gina threw Trevor a look, she hadn't sung since she did the anniversary gig on the strip, and for Trevor it had been longer.

They were going to fake it; this was unexpected so the crowd shouldn't expect much. They stood up on the makeshift stage. They told the audience that they were vacationing and hadn't sung for a bit. Trevor played the intro to "Life Flies By." Gina searched to get her voice going. She and Trevor sang and harmonized and got through the song. The restaurant patrons stood and applauded the couple.

All Gina and Trevor wanted to do was pay their check and go. They asked their server for the check and said the owner told her no charge. He was excited to have such huge celebrities eat at his pub. They exited quickly and stared at each other.

They got back in their RV.

Trevor broke the silence. "G, has that ever happened to us before? In a public place? I know we have done it professionally with other bands, but in a restaurant. Strange, but we gave those folks a story to talk about."

Gina laughed. "It actually did happen to us on the ski trip with the Montecito Moms. Remember, Roxanne got mad at us for being those 'different' parents. You told her we sing for a living and she wasn't happy about it. We really didn't have a choice, but it would be great for Perfection. The story will get some play."

Gina looked at some brochures she had taken from the restaurant and suggested instead of taking the highway they should take the scenic route to Redwood National Park.

Trevor smiled. "Let's do it. It may take longer, who gives a shit? We are here to enjoy everything we never get to see. Baby, I love you for taking my idea of nature seriously."

Gina shook her head. "Trev, so many beautiful sites. We have had many special trips, but this one is personal, our journey together." She leaned over and gave him a kiss.

Trevor sat back and geared up for the two-plus-hour drive to the campgrounds at Redwood National Park.

As they were driving, a song came on from Brent Nolan and Orange Wave, their touring partner. They laughed; Brent was a character. Gina grabbed her pad from the console; she had some thoughts for a song.

Trevor looked over. "G, are you inspired by something?"

Gina, mindful, said, "Yes, Trev, how amazing to be in the beauty of nature. I need to think of incorporating them together."

Trevor smiled, "Baby, you write your heart out."

Gina was deep in thought, once again she used the McNaughtons' life as inspiration. She wrote about how their love endured even when each of them thought all they held precious was almost lost. She wrote a song, "Lost Our Way." She would show Trevor when they stopped for a break.

LOST OUR WAY

*There was a time when we both lost our way, too
much drink and jealousy. We knew our love was
stronger than that, we just lost our way.*

*Almost lost everything, we just lost our purpose. Had
to make it better, just you and I riding together.*

*You and I enjoying life the way it should always be. Our love
stronger than most to enjoy the world outside four walls.*

*Enjoying the sites and a simple life. We just lost our way
Almost lost everything, but will love save the day?*

*Now the love we have beautiful and brilliant among the waves,
hills, and trees. I love you more, so simple to see that you're beautiful.*

*And mine forever. So lucky to see that we didn't nor ever will lose
our way. We are forever and will never again lose our way.*

Gina knew it was a rough draft of her emotions, certainly Trevor would
add his perspective.

Rio need not worry about their songwriting, Gina and Trevor had so
much in their hearts waiting to come out.

They embarked for Redwood National Park, taking the scenic route
that Gina had mentioned. On the drive the couple bounced ideas for songs
and the next steps for Perfection.

They knew having a brainstorming session with Tommy tomorrow meant they needed to be totally engaged. They got to Redwood National Park. Trevor hooked up the water and sewer lines.

Gina couldn't wait to wash her face and get into her comfortable T-shirt and lace panties. The campground had cable so they could watch TV in their bedroom. Gina was all comfortable and Trevor stripped down to his boxers.

She eyed him up and down. "My God, you are so handsome, how do you get more handsome?"

"I'm with a woman who makes me feel special and loves all the parts of me, good and bad. I have a good woman; I am lucky to say it."

Gina was sultry, "You have a good woman, who does love every part of you. I was hoping you could bring one part over here, your mouth, so I can kiss you."

Trevor crawled up on the bed, grabbed her face, and kissed her hard. She kissed and sucked his neck and gently bit his lip.

Gina felt Trevor's heart. "Show me how much you love me. Any and every way you want."

Trevor smiled, he came behind her. "Turn over, I want you this way."

Gina smiled. "You are playing a little dirty, I see. I like it. Take me then. I want you to know how much I love this part of our life. Baby, I love taking this trip with you. I feel free. Now do what you want, I'm waiting."

Trevor knew her hot spots, taking her face down from behind was one. After their lovemaking, they watched TV, wrapped around each other. This was their bliss.

Gina still had to have a talk about the Paul Ryan situation. But when was the time?

She hoped that Jane Waters had given her all she had on Paul Ryan, no more delusional disclosures. Gina was intuitive, she knew deep down Paul Ryan would reemerge.

OLD EVIL RISES AGAIN

GINA HAD JAVA AND BREAKFAST READY. They wanted to be fully prepared for the call at noon with the band and Tommy. It would be the first time speaking with all of them since leaving Perfection behind. They would need to talk about band business and next steps.

Gina was a bit nervous that this might overwhelm Trevor, but she knew he needed to get a little taste of business. Even in some capacity.

Gina took a sip of caffeine and then placed a piece of bacon in her mouth. "Trevor, are you in the right headspace for this phone call? I want you to be ready mentally for all this. We have our own label now. Everything musically is on us. You need to quiet Rio down a bit. You and I have always been the main voice of Perfection, with Rio playing a role. You know what I'm asking you."

Trevor stopped eating. "G, I get it. Rio feels like he's in control. He kind of is in charge for now, but the McNaughtons will come back as the face of Perfection. Hell, G, you already wrote two songs. I was thinking we need to write a hard rock song, something that isn't about what we have gone through. I'm expecting Rio to bring that up. You and I have to work hard. I do wonder what Tommy is thinking, we'll find out. I'm prepared, baby."

Gina cleared the kitchen up. "Trev, I need to get all ready, get dressed. So mentally I feel as if we are sitting in the room with them. And not miles away. I need to feel the room."

Trevor came into the small RV shower; he still wanted the consistency of their relationship.

Gina wanted space. "Trev, I love you but I have to shave my legs, it's quite small in here."

Trevor smiled. "I'll leave after our playdate, I'll be clean."

Gina queried, "Trevor, are you taking those pills? You are exceedingly horny again."

Trevor laughed. "That's what a stay in rehab does to you. I want our lives back the same way they had always been. The way I dreamed about you."

Gina took his face and kissed him, water cascading over them. "Fine, then a brief playdate, baby."

Trevor left the shower while Gina finished primping. She got out wearing her ratty bathrobe and a towel wrapped around her hair. Gina dressed and styled her hair. She noted Trevor was already dressed and cleaning his guitar. He wanted to be ready.

She felt the call with the band would be lengthy and tried to mentally prepare. She had been away from the business side of Perfection for a while. Gina knew she would need to jump in and deal with business issues, Perfection, Inc., their label.

Gina sighed. "Trev, I'm not sure what to expect, I'm a bit nervous."

Trevor smiled. "G, don't be, we are Perfection, let them all throw whatever at us."

At noon precisely, Rio called and put them on speaker so all of Perfection was united, including Kevin—the sound engineer, Skip, and Tommy.

Rio was a bit cocky, no empathy. "How are you two wanderers doing? No problems with poison oak?" He laughed as he said that. "But seriously, Gina and Trevor, your presence here is missed. Have you two done any writing?"

Gina answered, "Well, hello, my asshole cousin, we're doing great.

You should try getting in tune with nature, it might help you not be such a douchebag."

She heard Jeff, Kevin, and Ian laughing in the background.

Trevor spoke to the guys, "Hey, Ian, man, you doing good? Jeff, no crazy ladies, all cool with you? I appreciate you are all aware that I needed some space after rehab. Reuniting with my wife. I still need some time. I still have ghosts and demons in my head that need to escape so my head can get fully back into business. Before you say anything, Rio, we are still continuing with our trip. Skip, what band business do we need to discuss?"

Skip spoke, "Trevor, good to hear your voice. There are a few things—the label is established and ready for production. We are good there."

Trevor said, "About the label, we are now in charge of all we do from now on. Perfection is well set with music we haven't released yet. I'm assuming everybody is immensely proud of what we have created."

Skip continued, "Yes, Trevor and Gina, good to know we are in charge. I have a few requests for Perfection to play stand-alone concerts in various locations. We can discuss those requests."

Gina stepped in, "Skip, scheduling concert dates is something that you and I are in charge of. It will wait until we get back to Montecito."

Skip hesitated; this was an uncomfortable issue to bring up. "One particularly critical issue is our public relations situation. Paul Ryan was told he and his PR firm no longer have a contract with Perfection. He is being an asshole, actually. He is claiming he still has a contract, which is not true. He was fired. However, he won't break what he says is a legitimate contract. I have a lawyer working on it. Perfection needs to separate from him entirely."

Gina threw a shoe at the phone. "Skip, I want that lawyer to keep him out of our business entirely. I can't have him around. He is actually enormously scary; he's gone over the edge. Trust me, if necessary, I can prove it."

Skip winced at the last comment. "Listen, it's no secret he couldn't come to grips with you and Trevor reconciling very well. He is putting out some not-so-nice reasons explaining why you got back together. He is a bit of a stalker. I don't want to upset you, but we need to investigate all legal issues."

Gina spoke up, incredibly pissed off. "Wait, Skip, one of the last things I told you was to get rid of him in every way possible. There is no more contract, this man has an unhealthy obsession. He crossed the line many times, I even told him to his face. He is sick, demented, insane. Letting you all know, no more PR agencies. What could he say about my marriage? He always knew I was in love with Trevor, sorry if he didn't get the memo. What not-pleasant thing is he saying? Please don't hold back."

Skip was still afraid of Gina. He knew never to get on her bad side or give her information that would set her off. "Gina, he is saying Perfection may no longer be a band, since you and Trevor took off. That no one knows where you are and the two of you are in a codependent relationship. Also, both of you now are abusing drugs and alcohol. Oh, and that Trevor has you in some sort of controlling relationship, that's why you can't leave him."

Gina's body shook in anger, her face reddening. "Are you fucking kidding me? This is slander! I want a lawyer to send him a cease-and-desist letter. I will personally sue the fucker. Skip, you hear me? I won't have it. He's pissed because I didn't choose him. If Paul Ryan wants to lie, I have a huge story about him that would destroy him. I am saving it. Then I will exploit it."

Gina was incensed at all this information. This was still an issue she hadn't told Trevor. She would have to tell him sooner than later.

Trevor was angry but cool. "Skip, arrange for a friendly interviewer to talk to Gina and me, we can counter his assertions. If people hear us speak and tell our truth, it should help. I personally hate the guy, he gave my wife an engagement ring, for Christ's sake. I agree with Gina that we should do our own PR. What a scumbag and a sicko."

Skip spoke, "Listen, I have about ten requests for you two to do interviews. Can I get two good ones? Would that be acceptable to you?"

Gina grabbed her cigarettes from the drawer and began to chain-smoke. "Look, I can't have this person spreading these lies, so whatever I have to do is acceptable. Can I ask a question? Do we know where Brian Mayfield is? Has he popped up on anyone's radar? I heard before we went on our trip, he was causing problems. Is he still in Los Angeles working for that band? I know if given a chance he would try to get to Trevor. He hates me, hates my marriage. I want him neutralized. If I need to talk to the band that he's working for, I will. You all hear me? I can't have him and Ryan around, I won't."

Trevor pleaded, "G, Mayfield can't hurt us anymore. But I know you, this won't be done until he gets sent back to Canada."

Skip injected, "Yes, Gina, you are correct, he's around doing what he does, creating havoc with the band he's working for. I can find out who their manager is. Gina, please no punches if Mayfield pops up."

Tommy spoke up, "Now you know what's going on here. Let's talk about the music. I heard five songs so far, no lyrics yet. I would like to punch up the guitars to make them harder, hard rock type of thing. It means reworking guitars, drums, and vocals. Let's start with those. Have you two written anything?"

Trevor answered, "Gina has written two beautiful songs. One can turn into a harder edge, the other is a more softer tune. I will tell you, both songs speak to our relationship."

Rio must have been going crazy to get a word in. "Trevor, we can set a time for you to hear the songs that Tommy wants to pump up. I want you to listen, then you and I can rework the guitars. It's going to be meaner and harder. You get me? When does it work for you? Don't tell me two days from now. We need to get rolling."

Trevor was anxious and furious. "Rio, we have to leave here tomorrow, give us a day to get to Oregon. If you want us to move our trip along, we need to drive about five hours a day. Give us a break, man. Now we have to deal with a shitstorm, an out-of-control public relations douche speaking about our band and my wife."

Rio interjected, "Hey, together we can manage this. Please don't get worked up about that opportunist asshole. We got your backs. Let's look at all legal paths to kick his ass."

Gina was fuming and holding a valuable piece of information. It was time to expose it. "He crossed the line with Perfection and with me personally. I might as well get this out now. Trevor, baby, I found out some disturbing news right before we left for our trip. The woman who owns the house that Ryan rented, Jane Waters, visited me the day we left. She didn't want to rent it, but Paul Ryan was relentless, which was weird. Jane told me that Paul had a room in the house with my pictures all over the walls. She called it *a shrine*. He blacked out Trevor's face in some pictures. He is crazy, I'm telling you legit crazy. There is more, we will talk more about this. Trev, I'm sorry, I have been waiting to tell you. I was afraid."

Rio stepped up. "Gina, this guy took us on because of you. He flaunted his desires in front of Trevor. Who knows what he's up to? Now this latest information. He's a douchebag for sure. Perfection as a band will put out our response to him. He is sounding scary, mentally out there. What about a restraining order? Skip, we have to look into that."

He told the McNaughtons, "Look, this is a problem for all of us now. I know a judge who I can talk to about the restraining order. It needs to cover the band and Gina personally. I will move on this."

Trevor was quiet after finding out about the house. "I want him crushed and ruined. I spent hours of every day in Turquoise Skye worrying about this asshole. Now I know I was correct, but this is worse than I expected."

Gina continued chain smoking, "Look, I want to do those interviews at once. Will they come to where Trevor and I end up for that day?"

Skip answered Gina, "If they want the interview, I'll make it a condition."

Trevor got his fire back. He was pissed. "You get them to us. Gina and I will take it on. Tommy, anything else you need from me?"

Tommy was caring. He said, "Trevor, truthfully, getting you back and thinking of some great guitar riffs is good enough for me. I want to express to you and Gina, I want you to have your personal life in order first."

Ian, Jeff, and Kevin said their goodbyes, they couldn't wait to record and write music. Then schedule some concert dates. They purely wanted to play.

Gina ended the call, "Get ready, Gina McNaughton is back on the attack, don't fuck with me, my husband, or my marriage. Paul Ryan has opened a hornet's nest of garbage."

SET UP THOSE INTERVIEWS

THE CALL ENDED. TREVOR LOOKED AT GINA. "We have some work to do, don't we? I don't want to talk about the Paul Ryan issue, let me distinctly say that. Any man who wants my wife and does it in front of me doesn't deserve shit from me. I hoped you would have shared that information with me. I am your husband; I am here to protect you. I get you felt I wasn't strong enough to hear that insane fucking bullshit. Gina, Ryan is sick. I want to put him away."

Gina teared up. "Trevor, I'm so sorry, this guy is insane, scary insane. I mean, I never gave him encouragement. I always loved you; you know that."

Trevor was calm, too calm, Gina thought. "We will do interviews and I will start playing in the evening. We can sing together. Baby, I'm not back all the way. There are some memories I need to work out. Your love keeps me going. We will neutralize all the negativity. We need to stop talking about Paul Ryan and stick to our plan."

Trevor came over, grabbed her, and kissed her. He knew Gina was always going to be his. Gina adoringly looked at his face. "We should get rollin', hopefully we will get a day ahead."

Their goal was to get to at least Yachats Beach in Oregon, which was about five hours away. They would be happy with anything close to that.

They knew that there would be many cities on the Oregon Coast. If something looked interesting, they would stop.

The McNaughtons were trying to digest what they heard about Perfection. Trevor was thinking about music while Gina was thinking about the Paul Ryan situation. She knew there was one secret she never wanted exposed. One weak moment, when she drank too much. She almost forgot about it. If Paul ever exposed the tryst, she would say he was a liar. Gina would never risk her marriage over something she could barely remember. She became quiet.

Trevor looked over at her. "Baby, you're worried, tell me it's not Paul Ryan. Why would you give that prick a second of your thoughts? He can't hurt us with his lies. We will do the interviews. We hate these types of interviews, but we need to do them. I know you don't like exposing our life, this time we need to show how strong we are."

Gina smiled. "I know you're right. I'm mortified and hate that these lies are out there. We have picked up our lives from misery and came back stronger. I won't have one disgruntled, pyscho man make us look like we are codependent or that you are a controlling prick. We have always been known as that loving couple; I won't let anyone destroy that."

Trevor touched her face lovingly. "G, it can't happen. I want you to set your mind for some kick-ass lyrics."

Gina replied, "I can think of kicking someone's ass lyrics. Oh, shit, that might be something. I'll need to think on that. In fact, I want to cover the song 'Break Stuff.' It's my way of saying it's all bullshit. Yes, I will break someone's face in."

A few hours later they were in Oregon, the coastal cities were beautiful. The views and drive made them forget about the Ryan situation. They drove awhile and found a coastal city, Bandon. It had the beautiful quaint Coquille River Lighthouse. They also stopped at the Face Rock State Scenic Viewpoint. The coast was rocky and serene. The couple got out and held hands as they walked to the lighthouse. Gina and Trevor took their shoes off and walked the rocky coastline.

The McNaughtons felt peaceful, considering they were about to enter a PR blitz. They picked a place to eat, The Loft Restaurant and Bar. They sat outside and enjoyed the view of the ocean and the delicious seafood. Gina told Trevor she needed a drink after the conversation with Perfection. She ordered a large red sangria.

Gina grabbed Trevor's hands. "Trev, I think after we leave Yachats we should drive to Portland, stay a few days, get those interviews done, and you can spend time listening to the music. Portland has a weird vibe, I like it. No one will care if it's us. What do you think? We certainly can get interviewers to fly in easier. What're your thoughts?"

Trevor did not hesitate. "G, I like how you think. I want to get those interviews done as soon as possible. I hate the idea that people think I'm a controlling asshole husband. The lies that we are all over the place abusing shit. I spent a long time doing the honest work of cleaning up. I take my sobriety seriously. Ryan is a sick motherfucker. We will crush him together, he won't see it coming."

Gina took his hands in hers and kissed them. "I know you do and you should. All the work you did, the horrible moments. We need to highlight what we did because we love each other. We won't have someone tear us down. I won't have it. Let's enjoy our lunch."

During their relaxing meal, Gina thought that somewhere in the chaos they needed to call Roxanne and check in with her. They would call after the interviews. Roxanne would need an explanation.

As they walked back to the RV, Gina looked at Trevor and asked, "Ready for another long drive? The views are amazing. I am hoping to get inspired to write another song."

They had over two hours to drive. Gina turned on the radio and fiddled with the dial, trying to find something to listen to. She landed on Perfection's, "Punch the Night." She sat back and listened.

The DJ came on and said, "That was Perfection. No one knows where the McNaughtons are, probably laid up somewhere doing something they shouldn't."

Gina glanced at Trevor. She knew that look, it was rare that his anger came to the surface.

"Gina, please call Skip right now and read us the list of who wants to interview us."

Gina immediately called. "Skip, read us the top candidates for the interviews. We were listening to "Punch the Night" on the radio, and the DJ made some nasty remarks. We are going to a small coastal town in Oregon. We will continue to drive on to Portland. That's where we will sit for the interviews. It will also give Trevor time to listen to the music. What do we have for interviewers?"

Skip had his list ready. "Gina, these are the interviews I think would be the most prudent for you—the Entertainment Station wants an interview, in-depth. Of course, that weekly magazine *US*, which is all about celebrities. That should reach many demographics. When should I book them? The TV station may want a good deal of your time and bring in cameras. The other one can be the next day. Does that sound like something you and Trevor can live with?"

Trevor raised his voice. "Skip, we will be in Portland in two days, book them three days from today. I want this shit to stop. Did we send Paul Ryan a cease and desist and a restraining order? That has to happen at once, no bullshit on this."

Skip heard him, he also never heard Trevor be so strong-willed.

Skip said, "I'm in the office. I will use the landline to organize all the interviews. Can you hold on while I arrange everything?"

Gina said, "Skip, you received Mr. McNaughton's orders, let's execute. We will hold."

Skip came back on the line about twenty minutes later. "Gina, you are good with those interviews, I have them all arranged. I got a room at a hotel for you to do them. I didn't think you and Trevor would want the world to see what you're driving around in."

Gina laughed. "I didn't think of that, good for you. Yes, we don't need to publicize this beast."

Skip was on his shit. "You know the TV interview will in all probability be long, but you know they edit the shit out of those interviews. I will make sure that I get to look at it before it's aired. This way they can't edit it and make you two look bad."

Gina sighed, "Oh, Skip, I can't believe we have to do this. What time and what day?"

Skip had all the info. "Gina, in three days you will have the TV interview at 11:00 a.m. Next day, I have the celebrity magazine at two thirty. You ready? Trevor sounds extremely irritated by this whole thing. I have never heard him this pissed off. I know this is intrusive for you equally. I believe sincerely that doing these interviews will calm the waters. I will call you tomorrow and get you more information about the interviews. Try to enjoy your drive to Portland."

Skip hung up. Gina felt he was indeed on point.

Gina knew Trevor was aggravated, she was trying to divert his attention.

Gina turned off the radio. "Baby, why don't we sing with each other? You know, get our singing voices together."

Trevor grabbed her hand. "G, I'm agitated, I'm sorry, not mad at you. I want to get to the next stop and relax, look at the water. Your controlling husband wants to spend a romantic evening with his favorite victim."

Gina touched his face. "Trev, I know it's hard not to take this personally. The McNaughtons will see to this together, get our story out there. Should we tell them how many times we have playdates? That should shut them up."

Trevor smiled. "They would love that."

After two hours they pulled into the park where they would stay. It was in a beautiful location with a water view. They sat looking at the ocean for a while, while Gina chain-smoked.

Gina got up and placed her head on her husband's lap. "Trevor, can we go inside now? Sitting by the water reminds me of our Turks and Caicos vacation. Very sexy, remember?" Gina moved to sit on Trevor's lap, wiggling her body against him, making him hard. "Trevor, I can keep doing this until you get the hint. I would like that playdate."

Trevor turned her face to him; he picked her up and brought her inside. "G, have I ever made you feel like I was controlling? I did work on myself; I never thought I was that guy."

Gina was shocked. "Trevor McNaughton, you are exactly the opposite. If anything, I would be the controlling one. Please look at me, you're perfect. Kiss me."

Trevor seemed to relax once they got into the bedroom. Gina started throwing off her clothes. She put on a sexy voice, "Baby, come here, I want that romantic evening you promised."

Trevor was excited, "Get ready for a very romantic evening. I want to give you sweet love, baby."

After a few hours of that sweet romantic love, Gina got up wearing only her lace panties. "Trev, I'm hungry, you want something to eat?" She opened cabinets to see what was there. "Oooh, Trev, I can't decide between linguine and clam sauce or potato chips."

Trevor came up behind her, buried his head in her hair. "Whatever you want I'll eat, I had my snack."

Gina turned around. "Well, it's potato chips and TV in bed. That's what I want."

They fell asleep and forgot about Perfection's PR issues.

In the morning Gina made lattes and some toast and called Trevor to the kitchen.

He came out, and the first thing he said was, "All last night I kept thinking that people believe I'm using and I control my wife, I can't have it. I'm trying hard to work out issues, this doesn't make it easier."

Gina put her arms around his waist. "Trev, we will be a united front, we will have to talk about our separation. The public has no idea you were becoming a sober man. We're good. Please come and have some toast and coffee."

Trevor was eager to hear how Gina laid out their schedule. "We need to be in Portland by tomorrow. We will find a place to park this thing. Skip also arranged for a car for us to get to the hotel. We should dress as rock and roll as we can. I don't think we brought those types of clothes."

Trevor looked up. "We will dress in black, both of us. I'm sure we can find something. I want to try and have a relaxing day. Walk on the beach, enjoy the peacefulness of our surroundings. Come here, G, I don't want you to think I'm upset with you. It's the whole situation that aggravates me."

Gina tried to smooth it over. "Let's enjoy the beach and the beauty here. Prepare yourself, as we will soon be entering the lion's den. We are good, we know our truth. I'm sorry I was talked into hiring Paul Ryan; it is what it is now. Let's go shower and walk on the beach."

The McNaughtons got dressed and enjoyed Yachats Beach. They loved watching the water hit the coastal rocks and rise up. They walked down the main street to check out some local shops. Most were touristy. They loved looking at the local art and beachy vibe trinkets. They chose to have a quiet lunch at their RV, sitting outside to enjoy the fresh air. Gina made a crab salad.

Trevor was sedate. He told her he was thinking about music. Gina didn't want to push him. She let him play his guitar as she thought of lyrics. They selected the Luna Sea Fish House for their evening meal. They walked to the RV office to find a taxi or car service to drive them to the restaurant. The person behind the desk recognized them at once and offered to drop them off and pick them up when they were ready. All it took was an autographed T-shirt. The clerk dropped them off at the restaurant, where they enjoyed a seafood feast. When they got back that evening, Trevor was extremely tense. He wouldn't do anything to ruin his sobriety.

Gina offered a suggestion. "Trev, let me give you a back massage and work out some of that tension. I see it in your face, please, honey. I hate seeing you like this. Come on, lay down on the bed."

Trevor winked at her. "Okay, G, a back massage, that's what you're calling it now."

Gina said, "Get on the bed and take your shirt off. I have massage oil, please, baby, do it."

Trevor gave in. Gina found classical music on the radio and rubbed the oil on his back. Slowly, her hands worked over his back and neck.

She finally said, "Trevor McNaughton, please relax. I can feel you're tense, let my hands work their magic."

Trevor finally relaxed a bit. While she was massaging his back, she told him how much she loved him and their life, reinforcing all the positive; they had a beautiful, intelligent daughter. It seemed to start working. Gina thought he was falling asleep. In a minute, he had Gina on her back.

He enjoyed the massage but had better ideas. "What a crafty way to get me to make love to you."

Gina laughed. "I was seriously giving you a massage. If I wanted something else, I would have let you know. However, it seems like you are determined to get your way. So, I concede."

The two expressed their love for each other for a good part of the evening. They fell asleep, trying not to think about those interviews.

The next morning the McNaughtons got up early and were gearing to get on the road. Before they took off, Gina wanted to check out what type of clothes they packed for these interviews. She was able to piece together outfits that screamed The McNaughtons, rock and roll's favorite couple.

They had a few hours to get to Portland. Gina found a place close to downtown to park their RV. Skip had arranged for a car to get them to the hotel for their interviews.

Gina called Roxanne to give her a heads-up about the upcoming interviews.

Roxy picked up, "Hello, Mom, is everything all right? Where are you and Dad now? You still traveling in that RV?"

Gina knew Roxanne would be concerned about the interviews, so she had to play it down. "Hello, sweet girl. Yes, your father and I are heading to Portland. How is your summer class? When do you think you'll heading home?"

Roxanne was vague. "The class will be over in about ten days. It is a quickie summer course. I'll be home, don't know when exactly. I'm waiting to see what Zach's plans are. I will be able to give you a better idea once I know that."

Gina just blurted out the news. "Roxanne, I want to tell you that your father and I are heading to Portland to do some interviews. Paul Ryan is putting out despicable lies about your father and me. We need to put our story out there. Rehab, me falling apart, the whole chain of events. You may hear things you will hate. I need to tell you we love you. I'm sorry you will be upset. Please just know we need to defend ourselves. It's quite a bit for you to take in, I'm sure. We are doing this to protect our family, understood?"

Roxanne was silent, then responded, "I knew Paul Ryan was a problem, I hate him. He's spreading lies about my parents. Who is doing the interviews so I'm prepared?"

Gina told her, "One will be on the Entertainment Channel, I predict this will be long and difficult. The other is with *US Weekly*, I expect that one to be intrusive also. Heads up, my sweet girl. I don't want you to be blindsided."

Roxanne seemed distressed, she began sniffling. "Mom, you and Dad have to relive all the shit that happened. I hate it, hearing my parents baring the souls for an asshole. I am aware why. I just need to be prepared for my friends and others to ask me questions. This sucks."

Gina felt the angst her daughter was experiencing. "Roxanne, just trust your father and I will tell the truth. It's up to other people to decide if they believe us. After all, we are the McNaughtons, it does have some cache."

Roxanne was still upset. "I'm going to go now. I have an appointment. Let me know the details. I love you and Dad but hate the drama."

Gina agreed and hung up, then recapped the conversation for Trevor. It added another layer to Trevor's distress. They would individually be on their *A game* for the next days' interviews.

MCNAUGHTONS SPEAK THEIR TRUTH

THE MCNAUGHTONS HAD DRIVEN to Portland the day before. They were tired but knew their commitment to the interviews was paramount.

It was the day of the TV interview; Trevor wore a pair of black jeans and a black skull T-shirt. Gina had no idea why she packed a black tight-fitting dress, but there it was. She became the *Bad Ass Bitch* instantly with the proper makeup and clothes.

Her phone rang, she glanced over and saw it was Jane Waters. What holy hell was this?

Gina took the call. "Hello, Jane, are you about to give me more bad news regarding your former tenant?"

Jane came right to the point. "I heard you are doing an interview with a TV station. I told you everything I knew at that time. There is one more item I discovered. Paul Ryan had a private detective find Trevor's rehabilitation hospital. Gina, from the beginning he knew where your husband was."

Gina felt like she would lose control of her body at that moment. That piece of shit Ryan knew where her husband was. Gina needed to sit. "Jane, anything else? Not sure I can handle it, but please tell me."

Jane drew a huge sigh. "I found a music tape he listened to. Are you familiar with the song 'Wicked Game'? The song that describes the allure and danger of attraction, when it is someone who doesn't care about you. He played that on a loop. Paul Ryan had a playbook of the whole scheme with Mayfield. Including the destruction of the backstage. Clever man, he knew you would react to the setup of a certain lady. I apologize. I do have the files just in case you need them. You should be aware that he is a sociopath when it comes to you. I don't know if you can use this relevant information in destroying him."

Gina sat stupefied, tears running down her face. This was horrific information, she had to tell Trevor. Would they use this in an interview?

Gina gathered herself. "Jane, that was mindboggling. Wicked, yes. Sociopath, most definitely. Trevor and I went through the descent into hell. For what? Two wretched men. I'm sorry, I appreciate having this informa-tion. I regret you had to get involved. I am digesting this. Any other *files* you find, please alert me."

Jane said her goodbyes.

Gina sat there, unable to move. Her legs felt like Jell-O. She sat frozen, her body still weak. She felt numb, her arms and legs tingled. What to do? They were getting ready to do a taped interview. Trevor needed to know. The fear of Trevor regressing was on her mind. She screamed out for him in a loud, frightening tone.

Trevor ran to her. "G, what the hell, are you afraid of the interview? I'll be there to protect you."

"Trevor, I'm about to tell you a story you need to know before the interview. It could change our tactics."

Gina, still immobile, told Trevor what Jane Waters had dropped in her lap. Trevor collapsed into a chair, placed his hand over his face.

He tried hard to keep it together. "Gina, are you telling me you and I were pawns of two psychopaths—a stalker and a person who wanted a rock star lifestyle? Our lives hit the bottom, to their pleasure. What the fuck,

Gina? Ryan was listening to 'Wicked Game,' delusional. At Mayfield, you should have killed him. Now we have to sit and answer questions about Paul Ryan. I want to destroy him."

Gina gathered herself. "Babe, let's stick with the plan. I want to hold this information. We shouldn't play our hand yet. This isn't the end but the beginning of a war. The McNaughtons are more savvy. Breathe deep. Trevor, baby, they put us down. We come back stronger, no division between us."

They stayed in a state of shock. The car was waiting to shuttle them to the hotel. They each sat quietly, in their own heads.

Gina broke the silence, she grabbed Trevor's hand. "Trev, my father could make them disappear."

Trevor had love in his eyes but a bit of hatred on his mind. "Remember, we hold the cards. No more talk about your father."

Gina and Trevor were performers; this was like another show. Time to get their game faces on. They headed to the car and showed up at the hotel like rock stars.

They found the room; the cameras were already situated and one of the station's popular interviewers, Tracy Easton, was waiting there. They introduced themselves. Tracy said she was happy to meet them and offered them water and food from a table nearby.

Trevor made it clear that he was ready to answer all questions relating to the lies in the public about Gina, himself, and the band.

Tracy warned them that some of the questions might be difficult, but she wanted to hear their story. The interview commenced.

"There are many stories of how you landed on the name Perfection. Was that an argument among the band?"

Trevor and Gina laughed. She answered, "It was a discussion for sure. Everyone had different ideas for the band name, some were crazy, stupid. First, you need to know, Rio, Jeff, and I were in our own band, Vision Skye. Trevor, Ian, and our sound man, Kevin, were in a band, Stanley Park. We broke up our bands when Trevor and the guys had to go back to Canada for visa reasons. Once they came back, we formed our band. I suggested, after many discussions, that our name should be Perfection. It was the perfect mix of our two bands. Trevor agreed with me, everyone else fell in line. Hence the name, Perfection. That is the true story, any other story is false."

"Why are you two separated from the rest of the band back in California? Has there been a falling out? That's what people think is going on."

Trevor shook his head. "Really, that's the first time I heard this theory. Sorry, no falling out, we are collaborating with our producer, Tommy Whelan, and remixing some of our music. I'm in touch with them every other day, nothing nefarious, Tracy."

"So, where have you two been for the last six months? You've both been off the radar when you have a band that has become one of the top rock bands in the country and the world."

Trevor began, "I was in rehab for five months. I had an addiction issue with alcohol, cocaine, and pills. I went into rehab without telling my wife. The only people who knew where I was were my daughter, Rio Poole, and Skip Glazer. I wanted Gina to know I could do it myself. She had helped me three or four times when I slipped, she always pulled me out. She did it all for love. I was wrong in not letting Gina know where I was. I accept that now. She went through her own hell, not knowing where I was."

"Gina, what went through your mind, not knowing where your husband was?"

Gina teared up when answering the question. "I went into a black hole, I was extremely depressed. I thought my husband went off with another woman. I was a wreck. Our home was a storybook of our life. The awards, the pictures, our daughter's achievements. It was horrible to sit in our home filled with our family memories, not knowing if I would ever see my husband again. I sat and listened to all the sad songs I knew. I was a basket case. The worst part was that my daughter and Rio didn't visit me. I would see Rio but he was evasive. I called my sister-in-law Jae, Rio's wife, she visited every day. I don't know how she put up with me. It was extremely hard, especially after I learned the truth. I blamed myself. I saw Trevor struggling and I should have listened when he said he would go for help at the end of the tour. I didn't believe him. I was angry that the information was not given to me, but I recognized that my love for Trevor was stronger. I had to let my pride and jealousy vanish. My life with Trevor is powerful, immensely so. When he came home, I was the happiest person."

"There are rumors suggesting that you both might be in a codependent relationship and that Trevor may be a controlling husband. How do you both answer that?"

Gina spoke first. "When people say codependent, it makes me think of two people who are doing drugs or are alcoholics. I am neither. Trevor has had issues. However, in a marriage two people work through their problems. If being codependent means we rely on each other out of love, then yes, we are codependent in love. I'm incredibly happy to admit that our love is wonderful, real, and has been from the first time I saw this beautiful man. As far as controlling, Trevor has never been that man. I am the controlling one."

Trevor spoke, "My wife and I are sincerely in love. If that's codependent, well, I'm fine with it. People have different definitions for types of relationships that they don't comprehend. Our type of business has pitfalls; we have avoided many of them. I was an addict, which was our biggest pitfall. But not our commitment to our marriage. Anyone who thinks I am controlling does not know me at all. Gina wears the pants in our family, she always has. As far as Perfection, she is a savvy businessperson. I wouldn't make her angry."

"Why do you think these accusations are coming out, and who would start such rumors?"

Trevor wanted to answer. "I imagine they are coming from the person whose agency we hired for public relations. Paul Ryan made it noticeably clear from the beginning that he was interested in my wife. He actually flaunted it in front of me. When I was a falling-down addict, losing who I was, he thought that it was an opening to get to Gina. But I know my wife, she believes in our love. If someone is determined to undermine your relationship, they use any means to do so. I suppose there is a man who believed he could have my wife. He was constantly trying to get Gina to file divorce papers. To make matters worse, he also gave her an engagement ring for when the divorce would be final. That takes a lot of balls, if I'm being honest. When we reconciled after my rehab, he became upset, brokenhearted. This person is unbalanced, delusional, and psychotic. We now need to protect ourselves, not knowing what lengths he will go to."

Gina answered, "Trevor is correct, it is coming from Paul Ryan, who we hired. Our manager thought it was a wise choice, we all agreed. In Perfection we are a collaborative. The entire band decides the path we take. Ryan was intrusive from the beginning. Concurrently, Trev began his descent into addiction, he was slipping. I warned him that Paul Ryan was watching his every move. When you are in the throes of addiction, you don't think straight. After Trevor went to rehab, Ryan rented a house three doors away. He would come over with wine or food every few nights. I did all a person could do to discourage this. I told him I wanted to be alone and I was mourning my marriage. I preferred to do it in private; it became difficult to keep repeating the same words. I know there are pictures of a trip to Hawaii. It did happen, separate rooms and no romance. I needed to get away from all my memories for a bit."

"Let me ask you both, are you truly in love or is this a publicity stunt?"

Trevor fired up. "Excuse me? A stunt? You don't stay married to the same woman for over twenty-three years and call that a publicity stunt. Gina and I genuinely love each other. As my wife told you, we fell in love the first night we met. It was electric, and through the years it has gotten more so. Our love is very deep, intimate, loving."

Gina spoke. "I hate this bullshit, needing to tell your viewers, anyone else that we have a great marriage. Roxanne, our daughter, my family, and our friends know the truth. We sometimes embarrass our daughter because she says we are too hypersexual, and that's true. What you see onstage is the way we really are. We have had some tough emotional issues we needed to deal with. I had two miscarriages and we became stronger through what was an unbelievably tough time. How many people can say that? So, I say bullshit to those people out there who think our relationship is anything other than what it appears."

"Why have you been hiding out, and why Portland?"

Trevor answered, "I saw an RV for sale, I bought it. I wanted to reconnect with Gina alone, without the pressure of the band. To take in nature and enjoy things that most people take for granted. I needed a bit of time to make sure my sobriety was strong. We have taken off for several weeks, however, we are writing music and in touch with the band. Gina and I told the band we would get back to Perfection. We have a lot to be excited about. We've launched our own record label. Any claims that Perfection has broken up is most definitely wrong, it's the exact opposite. A few more weeks and we will be back with the band."

Gina smiled and added, "Trevor is correct, I take the business of Perfection extremely seriously. Let's put all our fans on notice, we are coming back harder and stronger. Do you want to know anything else? You're not going to ask how often we have sex? I know people are interested. Let me proudly say a lot so that's clear. The fact that Trevor and I had to debunk this crap out there is painful. How many of your viewers would like their lives examined like ours? This stuff hurts our daughter and our parents; lies, it's all lies. Now we have to think about Paul Ryan out there, creeping us out. He is insane. Now it has us fearful."

"In your own words, what would you like to say to your fans and people in the audience that hear this negativity?"

Trevor responded, "I am a lead guitarist and lead singer with my wife. We feel privileged that we are in a small group of people who get to do this for a living. We enjoy being rock stars, it's been our life. It isn't always glamorous. The public gets to see a show and we blow them away. It's a hard life touring in different cities, not being in our home for months. The interviews, the meet and greets that radio stations assemble. We do it because it was the life we chose to follow. Let's be clear, our family is the most important part of our lives. The McNaughtons are totally like your audience; we enjoy a normal lifestyle, that's the truth. We have been trying to do it now for a few weeks. I want to end this bullshit about who we are. We are what we let you see onstage and have a normal life at home."

"Gina, you come from a vastly wealthy well-known Italian family. Some people say with connections. It's rumored that you threatened someone and actually gave him a beatdown. Is this true?"

Gina was stunned. "I know who you are talking about. What people don't know is that my family was able to get Trevor, Ian, and Kevin back in the US legitimately. This freeloader was suddenly added to the group. I hated him immediately; he was using Trevor. He wanted the rock star lifestyle. He did nothing except give the band drugs, women, alcohol. These are traits we don't embrace. He was personally responsible for giving my husband drugs to get him re-addicted. He did not respect my marriage, my position in the band. The incident that you are referring to, Trevor and Rio were doing an interview for a guitar magazine.

When I saw the photos with my husband and my cousin surrounded by half-naked women, I exploded. No one puts my family in a compromising position. I made it clear he was prohibited in our studio. I used a lot of vulgar words; he made an aggressive move toward me. I reacted. I punched and kicked him. I told him to leave my home. That's how I dealt with that situation. The tough Italian girl in me can come out, but he provoked me. Let's get something clear. Nobody should make any accusations about my family. I grew up tremendously privileged. I would never know those things you are asking about my family. I appreciate people leaving my parents, siblings, and aunt and uncle out of any discussions on Perfection. Do you feel you have enough information about us for your interview? Please try to keep the continuity intact. Otherwise, it would be a waste of our time."

Interviewer Tracy Easton was confused by Gina's comments.

Gina stared at her, "Don't ask us to clear the air to then mess with us. You asked for honesty; we gave it to you. We sat down with you explaining our lives, we gave that to you. Please respect that."

Trevor leaned over and gave her a kiss. "That's why I love my wife."

They got up, said thank you, and walked out. The interview took about ninety minutes. They felt drained by the process.

Trevor sarcastically said, "I think that went well, you?"

They laughed hysterically. Partly because they were still astonished by the revelations they had ingested before their interview. They knew they needed to call Skip and update him on the interview. But first they strolled around Portland to clear their heads. They loved the *Keep Portland Weird* sign. The McNaughtons walked around, no one paid attention. They strode in a daze, their lives manipulated by people who were unbalanced. The comeback of the McNaughtons was in motion.

Trevor took Gina's hand. "Gina, it doesn't matter what they tried, it failed. We still need to deal with the aftermath. We are doing it together. I did fall; you exploded. It's over. I love you and you love me."

They found a hotel lounge to sit in to decompress. Gina stopped at the bar for a pineapple martini, and Trevor stuck with ginger ale.

Trevor looked at Gina. "I like how you changed the Mayfield story up a bit. You decked him before he could react. Baby, you went hard core with that scumbag."

Gina half-smiled. "That's the story that Ryan gave to the public. I'm merely following that lead. We need to be consistent with the script. I should have really hurt Mayfield. Now knowing what he and Ryan had planned out. Makes me ill. But you were quite the fiery one."

Trevor looked down. "I wasn't thrilled talking about my addiction issues, it makes me look weak. Knowing I was set up makes it worse."

Gina held his hands. "No, it makes you look strong, but more importantly, human. We all have faults. Let's call Skip, hopefully he got feedback from the interview."

Gina dialed and placed the phone on the table so Trevor could listen. "Hi, Skip, did you get feedback yet?"

Skip dove in, "Yes, I did. She felt you were a bit defensive."

Gina laughed. "We couldn't have been more honest. I know they edit interviews; I don't want us looking like shit, Skip. I would think you would agree."

Skip relented. "Gina, all right. Was it vastly evasive? Paul Ryan crap came up, you two debunked it?"

Trevor spoke up. "Skip, we were honest and talked about shortcomings. We're done."

Skip said, "I will let you two get some rest. Tomorrow is another interview. Let's talk again after that."

Trevor sighed. "I have to call Rio and listen to Tommy's changes. I have some work to do," Trevor told Gina. He called for the car to pick them up.

REHAB MEMORIES

THE RV WAS BEGINNING TO FEEL a bit like home. They both felt out of harm's way inside.

Trevor called Rio. "Okay, bro, you got me, is Tommy there? Let's listen to these tracks."

Rio and Tommy played the music they had recorded, and the three of them were playing with different chords and progressions for the guitar work. Doing it over the phone was not the best but they were getting somewhere. Rio expressed he was pleased with the progress of their work. They were at it for about three hours. Rio, Trevor, and Tommy called it quits; they went over three out of the five songs. Tommy asked both of them to work some of the guitar riffs and leads. Trevor said he wouldn't be available until about four because of the interview they needed to do the next day. It was going to be another trying day.

Gina had made herself busy by making a lobster and crab bisque soup with some homemade biscuits. Cooking took her away from the mind-numbing revelations that Jane Waters revealed.

Trevor walked up behind her. "G, this looks delicious. Let's try to savor the simple joy of your cooking." He reached over her and grabbed a biscuit.

Gina turned around, facing him. "Is it good? It's supposed to be a cheesy biscuit. Do you like it?"

Trevor's mouth was full, "Babe, it's delicious and amazing."

Gina tried to be cheerful. "It seemed like you and Rio got some excellent work done. I hope someone had a reel-to-reel tape to catch it all."

Trevor thought for a second. "I'm sure Tommy did. He is always on his shit, you know Tommy. G, I have to tell you, that soup looks amazing, When can we eat that? I'm starving."

Gina looked smug, she knew she had cooked him a treat. "As Marisol always tells you, your stomach is calling. Come sit down and I shall serve you a feast. After that interview I thought you deserved an exceptional meal."

She sat back and watched her husband indulge himself in the soup and biscuits. "Trev, you enjoying?"

He was fixated on the soup. Eating it feverishly, Trevor closed his eyes with each spoonful. "G, have you tried it? This is unbelievable … I know what you're thinking of those pieces of human waste. Baby, things were set in motion against us. We both fell into their rabbit hole. When the time is right, we will attack."

Gina smiled. "It was a rough day, we deserved this. I thought it would be good to relax and watch some TV. We have the *US Weekly* interview tomorrow. I wish I knew what we were walking into. We got it, right?"

Trevor assured Gina he was in agreement.

Gina cleaned up, led Trevor into the bedroom, and turned on the TV. He undressed and got under the comforter, saying he was trying to relax.

Gina found an old movie she liked when she was a teenager. She didn't ask Trevor if he had seen it, she was afraid of another *The Birds* issue.

Gina was watching the movie. She felt Trevor staring sadly at her. "Trev, the last time you did that, we got married in Vegas. What's up with you? You're looking all naked and beautiful, what's on your mind?" She lowered the volume on the TV.

Tears escaped from his sorrowful eyes. "G, you want me to tell you the feelings I had while in rehab. I felt so lost without you around. You had been my savior for years. I would think to myself, why isn't my wife here, when other patients had their spouses? I had to remember that I was the reason. The worst is when I would see you in my room, telling me you loved me and forgave me. I now am aware they were delusions or effects from withdrawal; it made me sadder. Did you ever think of giving up on me?"

Gina knew honesty was what he wanted. "Baby, there were very dark times when I thought you were with someone else; I told you that. It shattered my heart. Into pieces. I wondered if you gave up on me. I asked, 'What did I do that would make you want you to leave me?' The spiral down the dark hole was endless. I thought, am I not sexy anymore? Am I not exciting anymore? What could I have done better? Was I not a good wife? The hurt that I couldn't give you more children. Trevor, I thought that would make you want to be with someone else. Every day a different scenario led me to black. I hated thinking that way. I had no hope."

Trevor reached for her face, tears streaming down his own. "I know I was wrong not allowing you in. I've said it so many times, now it's out in the public. All the people who lied to you because of me. Detox may have been more manageable if you knew. I was an asshole, I'm so sorry. Even though Mayfield and Ryan had a plan, I needed to be in rehab."

Gina turned off the TV. "Trevor, we don't need to talk about this, we both made mistakes, and the public now knows. Many will have sympathy; some will think we are rich assholes. Who cares, I want to hear about your feelings. You keep saying Ryan, which never was happening. We discussed this, my love. Never, never was he any thought in my mind."

"I was obsessed with him trying to get to you. I thought he was definitely going to put you in bed. I asked Rio, Roxanne, and Skip every time they visited. I did this; I turned my wife against me because I was weak. Now I know you were Ryan's plan from the beginning. I was correct, he wanted you."

Gina wiped his tears. "No man could make love to me like you, that's first. I wasn't the best at making you feel supported; I turned my back.

Why would you have that kind of faith in me? Trevor, it's good to get this out now. We have that interview tomorrow. I want us on the same path. Knowing that Ryan and Mayfield orchestrated this whole event makes me sick. The magazine will zone in on our life. I want us to be truthful; we don't need to give interviewers discussions that we haven't even had with each other."

Trevor rolled on top of her. "I had faith in you, Gina. That faith is what made me get better, quicker to come home to you. I never wavered that I wanted to be home with you. Roxanne thought I needed to wait until she spoke to you. What would you have done if I did show up?"

"I don't know, honestly." She held onto him like someone was going to take him away, squeezing harder every time she thought about losing him. She kissed him and held him in her arms. "It's all good, we are going to slay that interview tomorrow. Let's go to sleep. I love you always."

They kissed goodnight and held tightly to each other, as if no one could ever separate them.

INTERVIEWS AND EXPLANATIONS

THEY WOKE UP AROUND SEVEN to prepare for their twelve-thirty interview. They wanted to look put-together, like rock stars. Gina brewed some beans and called Trevor for breakfast.

Trevor got up and looked at Gina. "I'm not sure if I'm ready for the interview. Yesterday was bad enough. How much sharing do we really have to give them? It's fucking ridiculous. Why don't they put cameras in the RV?"

Gina touched his face. "I'm sure they'd love to! Babe, I know this is difficult. Talking about your rehab is invasive for sure."

Trevor sat down and sipped on his coffee. They finished getting ready and hopped in the car to go to the interview.

Trevor was exhausted and the interview hadn't even gotten underway. "I'm wondering how long we have to relive this bullshit."

Gina looked at Trevor lovingly. "It will be the last interview we have to do on this shit. You know what, babe, we don't talk about it after this. With all we know now, I believe seriously we will have to sue Paul Ryan for slander. Skip should have that restraining order in place for him and Mayfield. We shouldn't talk about it after this."

Trevor agreed. He was hoping to put the hurt on Paul Ryan, even if it was financially. Gina was thinking of ways to get to Brian Mayfield. She hated both of them.

They ate, made small talk, and saw that they both missed a call from Roxanne.

Gina scrunched her face. "Trevor, why don't you call her? She doesn't give you the third degree like she does me. Please."

Trevor looked down at his phone. "G, can we get this last interview done? This one is going to be the worst, *US Weekly*, a gossip rag."

Gina knew he was right. They found their way to the hotel for the next interview. *US Weekly* offered coffee drinks and a spread of Danish, croissants, and donuts. There was a photographer and the magazine interviewer, Linda Cross. She was the magazine's top Hollywood reporter. She introduced herself, offered them a seat, and asked if they needed anything. They both took a bottle of water. She started off by telling them she had a recorder. Linda would be using it for the interview. She wanted them to know it was for their protection as much as hers. Linda didn't want to misquote anything in their interview. The McNaughtons agreed but added they wanted to see the interview before it went to publication. She agreed, she always did that out of courtesy. Linda asked them to get comfortable, explained her questions would cover a wide range of areas, and dug right in.

"*Looking at you both, it's clear to see how much you love each other. What is your secret?*"

Gina felt this was a good start. "It's easy to be in love with the man you fell madly for so many years ago, love at first sight. We get better together as the years go by, a happy marriage. In our business, many couples don't make it. We enjoy working together, creating music together, having our personal life together."

"Since you mentioned your marriage, Gina, the lyrics you write do seem personal. Are many of your songs about your marriage? Or is it an impartial statement that's a universal sentiment? Because the song 'What Do You Want to Know?' sounds personal. Elaborate for me."

"That song was personal. Our home in Hollywood Hills was overrun by paparazzi, fans, and news outlets. I felt like we were living in a cage. We give people a great show but they want more. Women want my hairstyle, want to know where I get my clothes. Dudes want to know what guitar my husband loves the best, it goes on. It's never enough, we like our private life. Not everything in our life is a song, nor do we want it to be. Our choice to move to Montecito; it was far enough away from prying eyes. Our lives became normalized. In Montecito no one cares that the McNaughtons are rock stars. I haven't written a song about our life there."

Trevor spoke. "Gina writes lyrics, but we all put our perspective in the song. It's not solely her feelings; we all feel the songs. So, we can embrace the music. Yes, we have loud discussions and swear at each other about how a song should go. We always get to a place where we all agree. We like each other; we all have been friends for over twenty-five years. People don't hang out that long if there isn't respect. Our families celebrate holidays together; we are a family. If we all had inflated egos, do you think that would happen? If Gina feels she needs to get her voice out there, we make it work. It's simple. Every member of the band is elite."

"Are either of you jealous? There are so many distractions, women wanting your husband, men wanting your wife, how do you cope with it?"

Trevor did not want to bring up Paul Ryan, so his answer was easy. "I have always trusted my wife, I know we were always meant to be together. I am lucky that she loves me as much as she does. I don't worry about that at all."

"And you, Gina, women have to deal with all types of people who want to meet rock stars. Do the groupies and the women bother you?"

Gina answered honestly. "Yes, it bothers me, women can be horribly manipulative. Either they don't care or they try to be your friend to get close to your husband. I have seen it happen with other people. Trevor and I don't allow groupies or that kind of element at the backstage of our shows. I am jealous, it's nothing I'm proud of, but I'm truthful."

Linda added, *"Trevor, does that bother you?"*

Gina intercepted. "I have caught women trying to get close to Trevor back in the days when we were a bar band. The more famous, the harder women come in. I already admitted I am a jealous person, but my husband has never given me a reason to be jealous. Everyone in the band is happily married. Except Jeff, he does have a special lady. If ladies are looking for Perfection men, they are out of luck." Gina laughed.

"You have a daughter, Roxanne. She's at Stanford, congratulations. How did she feel growing up with parents who were rock stars? Did it bother her?"

Gina and Trevor looked at each other, debating who was going to speak first. Trevor did. "We are immensely proud of our daughter; from an early age she was exposed to touring and her parents being recognized. When she was young nothing bothered her. She was the princess backstage. I remember one time she ran onstage while we were singing. She used to look at us as simply as Mom and Dad. When she got older, it changed."

Gina added, "Roxanne, in her teenage years, was embarrassed by what we did at times. She didn't like how suggestive we were onstage. Friends would make comments. It's hard to see your parents being sexual for the entire world to see. It did bother her, I believe it still does. We had to tell her that it is who we are, who we have always been. But it's still hard for your daughter to see that. I'm sure there were times she wished we weren't her parents. It makes me sad."

"Gina, you had two miscarriages before you had Roxanne. Did that ever play into you raising Roxanne?"

Gina teared up. "Wow, I was not expecting that question. We were happy that with the help of a great OB/GYN, we were able to have a healthy baby. It was something we both wanted and we were devastated losing two babies. My mother was a significant help during those times. Roxanne was never a child who was shielded. She knew about things a child shouldn't have seen. But honestly, she grew up to be an honor student, loves cheerleading. She chose a different path than her parents. Even when she is embarrassed of what we do, she is still our little girl. She is a daddy's girl."

Trevor opened up. "Roxanne is my joy. She has many qualities of her mother for sure. She has always shown how much she loves both of us."

"Let's talk about the five months that you two were estranged. There are many stories out in the public about your separation. One is that, Trevor, you did actually leave your wife for someone. Another theory is that you were admitted to rehab. The last one is that you, Gina, had an affair with your PR person, Paul Ryan. Which one is true, or is it all of the above?"

They knew it was coming. Trevor answered, "I did not nor would I ever leave my wife for another woman. Most definitely false. Rehab was the reason, I felt Gina needed to see me clean. Gina never had an affair either. When we reconnected, we knew nothing could break us. That's the truth."

"What exactly does Paul Ryan have to do with your story? There are some rumors out there about how he is involved, or is he?"

Trevor was tired of the question. "Look, Linda, this is another long interview we agreed to. This keeps coming up. It's lies, all of it. Our management hired Paul Ryan's agency to work for Perfection. He did clean up some issues we had. He made it clear that he took on Perfection to meet my wife. Once we reconciled, at that point the stories came out. He is telling people that we are codependent. Your readers should know that Paul

Ryan, the Wiz of PR, actually has a psychotic obsession with my wife. We found this out before we headed out on our trip, it is now a scary situation, that's all I will say."

Gina was angry. "I'm tired of this false story. You should tell your readers we are happy and that our band is moving forward. We are working on our latest music. But wouldn't your readers be interested in our home decor, anything to do with our real life? Did you ask about what a great cook I am? No, just these horrendous rumors. Maybe ask us about our adventures in our RV? We really want to have a normal vacation. Can you appreciate that?"

"Gina, I was actually going to ask you where you get your clothes. I've heard certain designers would love you to wear their clothes, but you have rejected that. Why? Do you have your own idea about fashion?"

Gina answered, "Certain designers have asked me to wear their designs. Most seem slightly fussy. I like simple and classic. I lean to that. I also want to own anything I wear. I don't rent or wear and return. That cuts out many designers. Even though I'm rock and roll, when Trevor and I go out for a public event I like it simple and classy."

"I will say I was nervous doing this interview with you both. So many stories out in the public. I have to choose what I think might have a bit of truth. I didn't believe most of them. I have followed your careers, I know how much you are committed to each other. Thank you for being the people I thought you were, so many are so phony, it is hard to interview them. I think we're done, thank you."

Gina and Trevor exchanged pleasantries with Linda, and she asked for a couple of pictures. She was hoping it would be the cover of the magazine. Gina sat in a chair and Trevor wrapped his arms around Gina's neck. For the next one, Trevor placed his head on Gina's head and placed a kiss on her cheek.

Gina was determined to have fun. She sat on Trevor's lap and put her arms around his neck, similar to the picture they took all those years ago. Gina requested to view the pictures prior to printing.

They were done with *US Weekly and* all the interviews.

The car drove them back to their home on wheels. The McNaughtons were so exhausted they dropped onto their bed.

Gina looked at Trevor. "Thank God it's over. Let's go back to why we are doing this trip. Can we leave here tomorrow?"

"Of course, I want to do the same. Let's watch the scenery from the road and go to Seattle. Can I ask for one more thing?"

"I assume I know what you are thinking. Do you want a playdate?"

Trevor stared into her eyes. "You know I do. We have been wiped out with these interviews. The whole Ryan and Mayfield, the duo from hell. We have had no energy or time for us."

Trevor rolled over on his side and kissed his wife, then eagerly took her clothes off. She lay on the bed.

Gina spoke in a husky voice, lying on the bed. Her gestures gave him every sign she wanted him. Gina was taking the lead in this sexual scenario. "Can I help you take your clothes off? I might have a trick up my sleeve."

Trevor's eyebrows shot up. "Let me see what you have planned for me."

Gina, with only her sheer nightgown on, sat on top of Trevor, took his shirt off. She moved deliberately, kissing his chest and running her hands over his arms, neck, stomach. She unzipped his pants and slowly kissed him from the belly button downward. She yanked off his pants and boxers. Gina wanted to show him how much she loved him. She ran her tongue around him and took him in her mouth. Trevor made fun of Gina being loud. He was highly aroused, he played with her hair, told her between his excitement how much he loved her. He didn't want to let go yet; he pulled her up and she straddled him. She slowly worked her magic and leaned down to kiss him. He drew her closer and they kissed and loved each other until they fell over in exhaustion.

Trevor held her close. "Gina, it was difficult to relive those painful times, twice. You never blamed me; you stood by me. To say I love you sounds so minimal, not a word could describe how I feel about you."

Gina felt so loved. Trevor's words were heartfelt.

Next stop, Seattle.

UNEXPECTED PHONE CALLS

TREVOR'S CELL PHONE RANG. "I don't know if I want to answer it." He picked up anyway, "Yeah, who's this?"

"Trevor, it's Skip, I want you to know that they are going to air your first interview on TV tonight. I caught a preview of some of it. It's good, you and Gina came off uniquely authentic. It will go a long way with all the BS out there. How did Linda Cross go?"

Trevor was sick of talking about interviews. "She was a fan but she had to ask some of the same questions, you know all those rumors. I imagine it went well."

Skip said, "We will see when the reviews come out. I'll let you two go. Watch the interview. Bye for now."

Gina chimed in, "I don't want to ruin a nice evening. However, we really need to watch the interview on TV. You agree, my love?"

After sweet lovemaking, Trevor was hungry. The duo landed in the kitchen, drunk on love. Gina gave Trevor the rest of the soup.

They sat at the table looking at each other, happy. They would watch the interview and hope it would answer people's questions. Their loyal fans should get excited that new Perfection music was coming.

Trevor took out his guitar and started playing the music he and Rio worked on for Gina, hoping it would inspire her to write lyrics to go with the music. Gina was plotting out song titles in her head. After she found an idea for the title, she wrote the song based on that.

Trevor looked at the clock. "G, the interview is going to be on soon. You ready to see us expose ourselves?"

Gina shook her head. "Well, it will be what it is. I hope Skip is able to gauge the reaction tomorrow. That's what I care about. We were authentic. Let's hope the public views it that way. Come on, let's get comfortable and watch this."

The McNaughtons got comfortable in their bed and flipped through the stations to find the Entertainment Channel. There it was, now they sat back and waited.

The show always dove in with some hot Hollywood gossip. Then Tracy Easton came on, the McNaughtons were the next hot news.

Tracy began, "Everyone has been wondering what is going on with the band, Perfection. Why have two of the main members been off the radar for months? Well, I sat down with Gina and Trevor McNaughton and got their very truthful answers."

Then the interview commenced. At moments watching the interview, both Gina and Trevor winced at their answers. They felt vulnerable as they witnessed themselves completely exposing their lives over the last months. It was powerful and painful at the same time. Gina paid close attention to see if any of their answers were edited out. They seemed cohesive with the questions asked. Then the interview abruptly stopped. Tracy went on to tell the audience that the second half of the interview would air tomorrow. Her last words were "The McNaughtons are truly who they say they are."

It was over, for tonight.

Trevor looked at his wife. "Seeing that shit, it was hard as fuck, baby. To admit to the public how flawed I was."

Gina grabbed him in her arms. "We are both flawed. Who cares, we were truthful. We live in the world of rock and roll. How many people in our world are flawed? Most. It's fine, our fans know we haven't gone away. That's the takeaway. We're good."

They sat holding each other. They knew there would be calls from Roxanne, Rio, maybe Skip. They waited for the phone to ring.

Gina's phone rang first. She thought it must be Roxanne. "Hello …?" There was silence, and then she heard the voice on the other end of the line.

"Gina, it's Paul, what are you doing? Why are you saying things about something that I thought was private?"

Gina was incensed. "Why the fuck are you calling me, Paul, didn't you get our cease-and-desist letter? And you will be getting a restraining order. I know what you did in that house, Jane Waters told me. You are sick, you are obsessed with something that was never real. I know that you and Mayfield plotted against us. Why are you telling the world that Trevor and I are codependent, that he is controlling? You know that it isn't true!"

Paul answered her, "Do I, Gina? I saw you fall apart for a junkie, that's not healthy. I told you I wanted to marry you and you dismissed me for a loser …"

Gina went berserk. "Hey, Paul, go fuck yourself. I told you always that I loved my husband. I never wavered. You are seriously disturbed, psychotic, there is a mental defect within you and that fucker Mayfield. I hate you and Mayfield; I'm coming for you both."

Trevor grabbed the phone. "Hey, asshole, leave my wife alone. I heard about your room filled with my wife's pictures, my face blacked out. You are a deranged sociopath, all for a woman who was never going to be yours. You had the balls to give my wife an engagement ring, hoping she would get a divorce. I should really fuck you up, but I'm not that guy. I got what I want, and obviously what you want. It's going to come out who you are. I know what you did. I will leave it there; we know about you. I hope your agency can come to grips with the bad press, plus possibly going under. Don't ever call my wife again."

Trevor slammed the phone.

Gina was enraged, with tears flowing. "Trevor, I don't trust him. He could say anything, he wants to divide us."

Trevor was seething, he needed to calm Gina first. "G, he can't. We need to change your phone number. I don't want these calls anymore."

Gina didn't want to change her life like that. "Babe, why should I change my number, the people who need it have it. Why should I change things for that mental asshole?"

Trevor was adamant. "I'll make sure those people get your new phone number. I won't have him harassing you. Get ready, Gina, the shitshow is about to happen. Whatever we said, he will counter, that's what he does for a living. He creates a false narrative to make stories disappear; however, he is in the middle of this bad story. He created this, he should have walked away. He chose to get in the middle of our marriage again. Please let me be your husband and take care of this. Gina, please, this is part of my sobriety."

Gina was teary. "Trev, did I not prove to you how much I love you? I couldn't share the intimacy that we have with anyone else in this world. Babe, you fought those demons. You are part of my soul. If you are uncomfortable, I'll let you manage it."

"We need to keep track of what we said. I smell a lawsuit coming, we told the truth. As you said, we still have that card to play. Although, if I saw Mayfield, I might bury him also."

Gina agreed. "Trevor, you take the lead on this, we should call Rio and let him know we have serious band business that isn't music. If we don't, he'll dick around with us."

Trevor picked up his phone and called Rio, he answered on the second ring. "Hey, bro, you calling to go over music? Or are we talking about the interview Jae and I just watched?"

Trevor stopped him. "Rio, Gina and I spent two days doing those interviews because of all the Paul Ryan rumors. Couldn't you tell it was difficult to get over the same shit over again? My rehab. Gina falling apart, it was brutal, bro. There's another problem, Paul Ryan called Gina about fifteen minutes ago. I have to change her number; I won't have that prick harassing my wife."

Rio was silent for a minute. "Okay, I watched the interview. It covers the bad publicity Ryan set in motion. Will the second part cover the band still working, shit like that? Why did he call Gina, to what end?"

Trevor simply told Rio, "Ryan is delusional. I don't know, he must have seen the interview and had one of his delusions and chose to call Gina. He called me a loser and a junkie. I would kick his ass, hand his balls to him on a plate, but that's not me."

Rio laughed. "But we can arrange to have that done. It's merely a phone call away. When are you leaving Portland?"

"Tomorrow, hopefully we can get to Seattle in about three hours. I'll call you and be available for the music. This Paul Ryan bullshit has me aggravated. I guess my concerns in rehab were real."

Rio was worried, "Hey, don't let that shit get into your head. You know your wife chose you, Gina was always going to choose you. However, Perfection needs to deal with some of his accusations. We can't have that fucking shit floating around."

Gina grabbed the phone. "Rio, I need you to speak out if it's necessary, don't forget it."

Rio could hear the hurt in her voice, "Gina, I always got you, know that."

After the phone call ended, Gina's phone rang again. *Please don't let it be Ryan.* She picked up.

It was Roxanne. "Mom, what's going on? I saw the interview. You both put everything out into the public. It was authentic, simply hard to see you both living through all that shit again. Mom, you and Dad looked so much in love. Not one person on this planet would ever think you both were anything but in love. That codependent BS is awful; I'm sure few people believe it. The Paul Ryan information is terrifying. Mom, aren't you afraid? Are you taking legal action? Please tell me something."

Gina let out a long, hard sigh. "Roxanne, it's entirely Ryan trying to be a prick. No matter what you hear, it's not true. Your father and I did two interviews to set the record straight, we put it all out there. The truth, all the truth. It was difficult but we did what we needed to. You watched our first interview tonight; the second half is tomorrow. We also did an interview and photo shoot with *US Weekly*. We'll most likely be on the cover. Please don't worry, we're fine. We love you, and the three of us will be better for it. Would you like to speak to your father?"

Roxanne grabbed the opportunity. "Mom, yes, please let me speak to him."

Gina handed the phone to Trevor. "Dad, think of all the work you did to get better. Don't let that man take that away from you. You are a fighter; you fought for us."

"Roxanne, no person in this world will ever take my fucking family away from me, ever. You good now?"

Her voice was choked up. "Yes, yes, I know that. I'll let you go."

Trevor and Gina stared at each other across the table.

Trevor touched Gina's hand. "Let's take a walk outside. Get some fresh air, hopefully we can clear our heads. Roxanne is worried about Ryan. I heard you tell her we are strong as a family. Don't worry."

Gina had a faint smile. "She's afraid of Ryan. Roxanne's not wrong. Let's see how it all plays out."

The two walked around their new location for about twenty minutes trying to shake off the distressing feelings they shared.

Gina looked at Trevor. "Babe, I have a headache, can we go lay down?"

The two lovers went to their bed, enveloped in each other's arms. The McNaughtons put a difficult part of their lives in the public. Now it was up to the public to figure out if it was real.

SUCCESSFUL INTERVIEWS OR FAIL

IN THE MORNING, THEY WERE ON THE ROAD. They both tried to put the interviews behind them and enjoy some sights in Seattle. Gina was hoping to get Trevor to the Space Needle and some of the beautiful gardens, something Zen. They enjoyed the drive to Seattle, even though it was on the interstate. Purely driving was relaxing, seeing the sights on the road.

They reserved space at a park in Bellevue, their stay for three days. They checked in and had time to wander, so they grabbed a cab and headed downtown. Gina was pleased that they got to walk around the gardens and have espresso at Seattle's Best Coffee. They had an eye on the TV to see if any stations had reactions to their interview. They hadn't seen anything negative, yet.

Trevor took a cab back to their little home. He and Rio could immerse themselves in the music over the phone. Gina kissed his head and told him she wouldn't be long. She went to Pike Place Market and was awed by the farm-fresh produce, fragrant bouquets, restaurants, dessert shops, and so much seafood. Gina was like a kid in a toy store. She bought several choice seafood items to make a spectacular dish. Trevor deserved it. He and Rio were working hard on the music. Tommy wanted several songs reworked; it was their future.

Gina was happy with her purchases at the market. She grabbed a mocha at Starbucks, then a cab back to the campground. She poked her head into the bedroom to let Trevor know she was back. Gina thought a great seafood buffet would lighten the mood. She was watching a small TV in the living area of the RV when a clip of her and Trevor caught her attention. They were talking about their five-month separation and how it was hell for both of them, but how their love was the most important motivation to get well. It seemed to play well. Even though Gina wanted to let Trevor know they got positive reviews; she would wait until after they ate.

Trevor stepped out about every hour to stretch his legs, give Gina a kiss, and tell her how much work they had ahead of them.

She smiled each time. "It will be happy work."

Rio and Trevor felt good about what they'd accomplished. Tommy was more than pleased. Break for the day. Trevor told Rio he was looking forward to a sightseeing day with Gina. When he came out of the bedroom, where he was playing, Gina surprised him with a wonderful seafood feast and placed it on the table.

He sat down, pulled Gina onto his lap, and told her he was so lucky to have her.

After some talk about the music, Gina asked if she needed to start thinking about writing lyrics for the music.

Trevor told her, "Anytime you want to write it will be helpful. Putting your words to the music."

Gina couldn't contain herself, "While I was out, I saw a short recap of our interview, it seemed to be positive. Good news, right, babe?"

"That's because we told the truth. Tomorrow, we have a date to spend the afternoon together. We are also changing your phone number. Make a list of people who need to have your new number."

Gina tried to smile. "Whatever you need me to do."

They relaxed with Trevor playing some of the music that had been reworked. Gina loved the sound, it was harder and grittier, it was what the band was hoping to achieve. They were exhausted after the full day and fell asleep.

The next morning Gina woke up and had coffee and a quick bite to eat. Trevor was excited to tour Seattle. He wanted to go to the Space Needle and view the Emerald City from the sky. Some people did look at them knowingly but never approached them. Trevor found a store that was Gina's phone carrier. He told the salesperson he wanted the phone number changed, but for it to still be a California number. The salesperson was able to change it fairly fast. Trevor felt the most important errand of the day wouldn't be an issue anymore.

Trevor and Gina held hands walking down the street. Crowds passing them by didn't recognize the two. How good that felt, after they opened their personal lives to the entire world. Gina eyed a trendy shop and stepped in. A unisex shop where she knew she would find things she would love and Trevor would tolerate. Gina knew once they went to pay, the salesperson would know who they were, but she didn't care. She grabbed numerous dresses and piled them on the counter, then had Trevor pick out six or seven vintage concert T-shirts that would be great for their shows. The bill was a bit over five thousand dollars. Gina looked over her sunglasses and handed her the Black Card. She asked her to please allow her to pay and leave. The salesperson saw Trevor walk up to Gina; she screamed, "It's *Trevor McNaughton!*" Thankfully, it wasn't crowded.

He whispered, "Yes, it's me, can my wife please pay the bill?" He shook her hand and said thank you. They walked arm in arm and found a place to eat. A bistro with a rock vibe, posters from past concerts, pictures of popular grunge bands that played in Seattle. Gina loved looking at all the memorabilia. The food was mediocre but the atmosphere was amazing. They hailed a cab back to the park. Once back in the RV, Gina flung her hands around Trevor's neck. She told him that today was one of the best days she'd had in over a year.

He wrapped his arms around and kissed her. "I'm glad I could make it special, baby."

Gina was hopeful. "Trev, we were normal people today, enjoying the simple things, I love it. I'm also going to love spending time with your dad in a few days. I want to buy him something special."

"G, my darling wife, I appreciate your love for my father. I have an utterly strained relationship with him and always will. It runs deep."

Gina held him. "Can't I try to make it better, isn't there something I can try?"

Trevor was honest. "G, I love you, can we let things stay where they are? He loves you and he loves Roxy, which makes me happy."

As Gina unloaded her shopping bags, Trevor stared at her, it seemed deep. "While you were shopping, I slipped away. There was a store two doors down and I bought you something."

Gina was excited, Trevor had given her gifts but they usually were things they found together. It was a beautiful box tied with a pink ribbon. Gina had no idea what he could have bought her and couldn't contain herself. "Trevor, can I open this now?"

Trevor smiled. "I definitely want you to open it now."

Gina could tell by the box wrapping that this was an expensive gift. She opened it slowly, and inside was a luxurious white satin robe with a gorgeous matching long, white satin nightgown trimmed with lace.

"Trevor, this is beautiful, what made you choose this for me? I can figure out the robe, but, baby, this is a beautiful nightgown. Do I need to be more sexy for you?"

Trevor shook his head. "No, G, I thought you would look amazing in this. I hoped it would be similar in meaning to your white dress."

Gina raced to the bathroom. "I'm putting it on."

While Trevor was gone, she had worked out a bit, hoping to take her mind off her loneliness, and she lost about fifteen pounds. Gina slid on the nightgown and it hit every curve of her body. She went out to model it for

Trevor. The way the evening light hit her, she looked alluring. He dropped to his knees and held her.

Gina leaned down to face him. "Trevor, thank you, this is divine. I loved that you picked this out for me."

Trevor ran his hands over the exquisitely expensive satin, he went up her body and stopped at her face. "This is the way I saw you, when you came to me all those weeks at the facility, a white satin nightgown, telling me you loved me, you forgave me, you wanted me home."

Gina teared up. "Trev, I'm here with you now, I love you, I forgave you, we are home together. Let me kiss you, it's real. Did you want to show me how much you love me?"

Trevor seemed entranced, like he was seeing her for the first time. "I want to love you, is it okay if I do?"

Gina sat on the bed, affectionately telling him, "Trev, I'm your wife, you can do anything you want."

Gina was nervous, was this something that made him regress? Or was it precisely that he saw that nightgown and it brought him back to rehab for a moment?

By the morning, Trevor was himself. The McNaughtons remained one more day in Seattle. Another day Trevor would collaborate with Tommy and Rio. The reel-to-reel would catch all the good stuff.

Gina called Shawn to let him know they would be in Vancouver tomorrow. "Dad, it's Gina, I can't wait to see you tomorrow. Are you ready for us? Do you need anything before we get there?"

Shawn was happy to hear from her. "Gina, you said both of you are coming tomorrow, right? I saw the interview with you and Trevor. I didn't know you had any problems. Those demons caught Trevor again, they always resurface. You love him that much; I can see that."

Gina's response, for the most part, was all she could give him. "Dad, I do, it was awful without him. Roxanne made me see a lot of my own faults that didn't help Trevor. I promise you he is profoundly serious about his sobriety. I would love to see you both have a better relationship. I'm not sure why things are the way they are, I believe you love him and he does love you. I suppose it is wrapped up with losing his mother."

Shawn told her, "That's why he loves you, he transferred the love of his mother onto you. Gina, you are his protector; he missed having that. You are the one woman who has been there for him through all these years. He has been lucky to have you and Roxanne. You all created a life that people envy. Your parents also have accepted him, some long-haired, half-shaved musician from Vancouver. I know he wasn't what they thought you would end up marrying."

Gina stopped him, "Dad, I could never have married anyone but Trevor. My parents knew that fairly quickly. My mother even went to see Trevor while he was in rehab. I didn't know until my mother told me. That's Franny, she has always had a soft spot for him. Like I have one for you."

Shawn was a bit dismissive. "Okay, Gina, I look forward to seeing you both. I hope I can get another Italian meal cooked by you."

"Consider it done, see you tomorrow."

Gina knew she owed her parents a phone call. What would Franny and Mario think about the interviews?

Gina made the next phone call. She would soon find out. "Hello, Mom, it's me. How are you?"

Franny answered, "I should be asking, how are you? I'm hearing all this terrible gossip about you and Trevor. I know it's not true."

Gina interjected, "Mom, thank you for your faith. It has been awful having to go through our separation again with the public. We needed to counteract Paul Ryan's bullshit. Mom, he is psychotic, he had a room filled with pictures of me. It goes unbelievably deep. Ryan and Mayfield, twins of the devil, worked together. It's insane. Did you think the interviews seemed genuine?"

"Gina, most definitely. You looked like a couple who are in love, you just had a hiccup. Your daughter and cousin had your back, knowing how much you love your husband. Let me add your mother also."

Gina chuckled. "Franny, we know you have a special spot for my husband. I love you for that. Listen, I had to change my phone number because Paul Ryan called me. Trevor was frantic. Here is my new number … Trevor is taking a break from working with Rio. Tomorrow we are going to be in Vancouver visiting Shawn. I'll keep you updated. I'm hoping to go to Boise, Idaho, and buy a family winter house. Then Perfection needs to get back together. Let's hope my plan works. My love to you, I'll talk soon."

The conversation with her mother perfectly solidified the love that she had for both of them. Franny really took Trevor in as one of her own children, it amazed Gina.

She needed to call Roxanne and give her the new number. "Roxy, I had to change my phone number so you need to take it down."

Roxanne was slightly concerned. "Why did you change your number, Mom?"

Gina told her, "Roxy, Paul Ryan called me, he said we were saying terrible things. That your father was a loser and a junkie. Your father went apeshit. He insisted I change my number, write this down. I love you, my sweet girl. Bye for now."

Trevor came out of the bedroom looking exhausted. "Your cousin drives me fucking nuts sometimes. He always needs the guitar sounds punched up to the maximum. We need to give the drums and bass some love, of course vocals. Tommy will take him to a good place. That's why we have him. Skip was there, he said he is getting good feedback about the interviews. I asked about the cease and desist against Ryan. He has no information yet. I never disliked anyone as much as him. I guess it's the way you felt about Brian Mayfield. Now we know that the two people we despise were working together. An unholy alliance, if you ask me."

Gina made a face. "Trevor, don't ever bring up that dude's name again. I thought of actually beating him and almost killed him. I wouldn't go to prison for an asshole like him. That's the way you need to look at Ryan. Did

Skip get the judge to get the restraining orders for Ryan and Mayfield? That's got to happen at once."

Trevor looked a bit off. "Don't worry, baby, not sure what's going on with that."

"Trevor, you didn't take anything, did you?"

He sat down and looked up at her. "We have so much work to do. I'm feeling overwhelmed by it all. I had a huge break. I need to wrap my head around working intensively hard again. Perfection is our baby, that I neglected for a while. I'll be fine. No, I didn't take anything. Remember, this trip is about my sobriety, G. I won't be alone this time. I'll be fine with you next to me."

Gina was uncertain, she needed to be reassuring. "I trust you. I need to have a sanity check, that's all. I spoke to your dad, he is looking forward to seeing us. He asked for Italian food again, he's cute."

Trevor shook his head. "He is looking forward to seeing you, Gina. He would like to see me, sure. We don't have that relationship; I know you want to make it better. I told you, let it be what it is. I'm happy he cares for you; it's probably the one thing I did right by him."

Gina tried to change the subject. "Trevor, this is our last night here in Seattle. Want to do anything special?"

Trevor surprised her. "Let's get our chairs, sit outside, and look at the stars. You can smoke your pastel cigarettes."

Gina hugged him. "I love that idea, maybe some soft music while we sit."

They sat outside so close to each other, holding hands and looking up at the sky. Gina swore she saw a shooting star; Trevor laughed at her. They sat for about thirty minutes when a song came over the radio, an old, slow eighties song, "Waiting for a Girl Like You." Trevor pulled Gina up slowly, sexy, very touchy with her as they danced, like they used to in the beginning of their relationship at Carriage House. It felt like so many years ago.

Gina got teary. "I wish we danced like this more often, it's wonderfully romantic."

Trevor questioned, "Aren't I romantic all the time with you?"

Gina was careful here. "Of course you are, but this makes me feel special. Oh, shit, I remember another time when we slow danced, in Turks and Caicos, when you were taking ecstasy. That was some vacation."

Trevor laughed. "I'm not going to lie; I was planning on dancing you back into the RV and having my way with you."

Gina giggled. "Trevor McNaughton, you have always had your way with me, that's why I love you."

Trevor didn't exactly dance into the RV; he swept her off her feet, carried her, and playfully threw her on the bed.

He pretended to pin her down. "The song was correct. I was hoping I would meet a woman like you. I knew I was never going to find her in Vancouver."

Gina gave him a sultry look with her eyes. "I was waiting for you also. I didn't know where I would find you but I did. Let's show each other that love we have for each other."

Trevor was gentle and romantic. He chose to love her in the standard missionary position. Gina placed her hands on his face and looked into his eyes, kissed his ears, lips, and whispered, "*I love you.*" They moved together sweetly. Gina could always tell by Trevor's face when he would reach climax. He laid his head on her chest. She kissed his forehead and told him they needed to sleep. They called it a night.

UNSETTLING VANCOUVER VIBES

GINA AND TREVOR PREPARED for their three-hour drive to Vancouver.

Gina asked, "Trev, you seemed overloaded yesterday. Are you able to cope with all the work with Perfection? It sounds like Tommy wants a lot to be remastered. What are you thinking?"

Trevor was eating, he looked up at Gina. "I'm not going to lie, I haven't worked that hard on music for a long time. I'm getting back into the work, it's good for me. I'll put my energy into the music. I won't think of those other things. Keep me busy. I know I have to dedicate the time; you are going to get involved soon enough. You will need to start playing around with the lyrics and singing. Tommy will want you to add them sooner rather than later. We are going to be fine."

Gina kissed his forehead. "That's right, you have me, I'm not going anywhere. Although, we do need to drive to Vancouver. Trevor, do you have your papers? I remembered my passport. I forgot to ask you."

He nodded his head in agreement. "I have all my paperwork. I want to be able to cross back over the border."

Gina cleared the dishes and headed for the shower; she was almost done when Trevor walked in.

They were ready to hit the road. Taking I-5 N, it would be less than three hours. They did have to go through the Peace Arch Border Crossing, which could take some time. This was one time they hoped they would be recognized. The drive was quiet for a bit.

Trevor became obsessed with the Paul Ryan situation. "G, we need to make sure that Ryan's PR agency is gone. When will we sue him for slander, get those restraining orders? Skip appears to be dragging his feet. Do you think he actually likes that guy, and that's why things aren't moving faster? I don't want to see Ryan's face. I might let loose on him. Maybe I should call your father and see if we can dig up some dirt on him. Calling me a loser and a junkie. We have three Grammys, what does he have? Nothing. The one thing he wants is you, my wife."

Gina wasn't used to Trevor being so outspoken. She was alarmed that he actually had this hidden temper.

Gina begged, "Trevor, please don't call my father, he might want to do more than what you're thinking about. Leave Mario out. I agree, Skip should be on top of those restraining orders and any other legal actions. When we get to your dad's, I'll make a few phone calls. The Montecito Moms have husbands who are lawyers. I'll get their advice; they can help speed up the process. Baby, I want him buried. I'm on your team, don't forget that."

Trevor leaned over and kissed her hand. Gina turned on the radio for background noise. She didn't want to get Trevor worked up again. Gina turned on classical music, she knew Trevor liked listening to it. The music and the road made the trip magical. As they drove toward the border crossing, Gina remembered the first time she went to Vancouver. Her time away from Trevor due to visa issues. She had been excited to get on a plane to visit him. Gina remembered Trevor had a beautiful hotel suite overlooking the waterfront, flowers, champagne. It was a charming gesture, time alone. They had missed each other completely.

They got to the border crossing. Surprisingly, it was actually moving pretty fast. The agent asked to see their passports, he looked at the passports and back at them a couple of times.

A smile came to his face. "I have two members of Perfection sitting here waiting to cross into Canada, sweet. You folks don't have any weed or anything?"

Gina's head was spinning, they did have about an ounce of weed. She was not offering that up. She laughed. "Hell no, have you seen the interviews we did? My husband was in rehab, no, we don't have that shit, Officer."

He smiled. "I was having a little fun, giving you shit. But could you sign something for me?"

The answer was *Yes, most definitely.* They crossed into Canada. The ride was about forty-five minutes to Shawn's house.

"G, remember, don't try to force my father and I to have a breakthrough moment. I know you care about him, but you didn't grow up with him. I love that you care enough about my relationship with him. That's all I need."

Gina was disheartened. "Trev, whatever you need from me is what I'll do. I don't want you being uncomfortable. It's fine, I won't rock your boat. Let's stop at the store so I can cook. Your father requested Italian."

Trevor reluctantly agreed. Gina loaded up the cart with all the makings for chicken parm, spaghetti carbonara, antipasto salad. Once Gina pulled out her Black Card, the cashier knew who she was but didn't say anything. They made one more stop at the Canadian Liquor Store for some wine. Gina knew Trevor would be fine not drinking. This time Brian Mayfield wouldn't be popping in to share a meal. Gina did include her favorite potato chips and caramel popcorn when she got high.

They pulled the huge RV into the driveway. Shawn must have heard it; he came out to greet them. He looked quizzically at the huge RV. "Well, you two weren't kidding, this motorhome is huge! I have to take a look inside."

Gina said, "Before you do, a hug and kiss." He complied.

Shawn was awestruck when he opened the door. "This is like a small house on wheels. Trevor, you have been driving this monster?"

Trevor got up and gave his father a small hug. "This has been our home for the last few weeks. Gina and I might be on the road for a few more weeks."

Gina scowled; she had to get him back to Montecito earlier than he expected.

Shawn marveled at the bedrooms and baths, "They packed a lot of rooms in this thing. Must have cost some big money."

Gina laughed. "Dad, boasting a bit, but Perfection is one of the top hard rock bands in the world … I have a ton of food we need to put away. Can you please help me bring them in?"

Gina and Shawn brought the shopping into the house. Trevor collected a few things from the bathroom, packed up some clothes, and brought them into the house. Gina unpacked a bit and was ready to make some carbonara. Trevor came over and gave her a sweet kiss. He told her he would be in his room, their room. He took out his guitar, playing it relaxed him.

While she was cooking, Shawn approached her. "How is Trevor, really? He seems a bit withdrawn. He gets this way when he's struggling."

Gina looked concerned. "Dad, he had a tough time while he was in rehab. Apparently, when he was going through withdrawals, he kept calling for me, he was hallucinating that I was there. It took him three weeks to detox, you know withdrawals. I had no idea where he was. I would have gone to him."

Shawn looked at Gina. "You both had a challenging time, didn't you?"

Gina choked up. "I had no idea where he was for months. He went to rehab. I thought he left me for someone else. He came home and that was it. I love him, he loves me, Dad. This trip is helping him support his sobriety before we go back to the band."

Shawn took in the information. "He does need you, Gina, as I told you. Stability, that's what you are. He loves you, but you stand for all that he missed growing up."

Gina's tears were rolling down. Shawn said, "Gina, I didn't want to make you upset."

Gina shook her head. "I hated the feeling of not having him with me. I never want that again … Anyway, I'm cooking up a great spaghetti carbonara and an antipasto salad. I'm sorry, making these brownies from a mix."

Shawn put a hand on her shoulder. "It all smells wonderful. You should check on him."

Gina left the kitchen and let the food simmer. Salad was already made and brownies were in the oven. It would be another twenty minutes before the food was ready. She took Shawn's advice and went to check on Trevor.

Gina walked into the bedroom, sat next to him, and pushed his hair away from his face. "Hey there, how's my sexy man? Are you creating something new, or a redo?"

Trevor stopped playing. "A bit of both. Are you enjoying catching up with my father?"

Gina looked at Trevor. "Trevor, tell me you're not jealous of your father, please. I'm trying to be a good daughter-in-law. I'm not pushing you either. Something is going on."

Trevor leaned in. "I'm getting some visions; it's you all over again. I'm trying to rationalize this and sort out why. I'm not jealous. I want you to watch over me."

Gina tried to mask her emotions. "Trevor, I've been managing you in an incredibly delicate way. I know you have some low spots; you need to tell me. Is coming to this house bringing some suppressed feelings out, maybe? This is where all your demons originated. Baby, if being at the house is a problem, we need to think about leaving. I know your father is an issue. I won't interfere with that. This trip is about your sobriety, facing your demons. What do we need to do to make these visions and feelings disappear? I will always watch over you. Trevor, you need to talk to me."

Trevor was fearful, tears filling his eyes. "I am being flooded with emotions, G. I feel my mother around, it's haunting me. Then these visions of you bring me back to Turquoise Skye. I am trying to keep it together, but I feel like I'm slipping a bit. My father has locked away everything in my life after thirteen. I resent the fact that he never spoke of my mother after she died. Nothing, like she didn't exist, she did."

Gina pulled him close, holding him. "Trev, whatever is going on in your head, we will deal with it together. Are you able to sit down and eat with your father? You have been living with this resentment for years. I don't think your father will change. I need to check on the food, come with me."

Trevor sighed. "I'll come. Being with you here in this house makes me feel protected. Thank you for making something to eat, I'm starving."

Gina got the brownies out of the oven and left them to cool. She placed the salad on the table. The pasta was cooked; Gina made the carbonara sauce. Placed the pasta in a large bowl. She set the table and Trevor sat in one of the chairs. Gina called Shawn to say that supper was ready.

The three McNaughtons sat, had casual small talk, and enjoyed the food Gina had made. She and Shawn enjoyed a couple of glasses of wine. No talk about interviews, nothing deep. Shawn talked about stores that closed down. Nothing meaningful. Gina cleared the table and cleaned up.

Shawn retired to his chair after dinner. Watched his favorite television programs, had a few beers, and retired to bed shortly after.

Trevor led Gina into their room; he held the white satin nightgown. "Can you put this on?"

Gina was worried he was regressing. "Baby, I'm happy to wear this beautiful nightgown. It reminds you, though, of when you were in that place."

Trevor rationalized, "No, I want to know you're here. I know we had a playdate with this, can you please?"

Gina stripped down and slid into the nightgown. "What now, Trevor?"

He had a strange expression on his face. "Trevor, you're scaring me, what's going on in your head? Baby, tell me so I can help you."

He reached for her and pulled her close, he started to cry into her chest. "Let it out, whatever you're feeling."

She stroked his head and let him cry. He sobbed for fifteen minutes or so.

Gina quietly and lovingly asked, "Trevor, what you're feeling is totally normal. You're thinking of some of the bad moments you had here. I wish I could take them away, I can't. You and I have built many happy memories. Can you think of those, our wedding, our daughter, our music, our beautiful home that we built a life in? Try hard to get to that place, look at me."

He lifted his tear-streaked face. "I know I have a beautiful life with you and Roxanne. I come here and a wave of the lowest parts of my life flows through me. I needed to see you like this, you gave me hope, a drive to be better. I thought seeing you this way would help me with those feelings, like it did in the facility."

Gina still held him. "Has it helped, crying it out and having me here? I love you so much. Can we make it better?"

Trevor needed and wanted to be held, Gina lay down on the bed. "Come here, I'll hold you."

All he needed was to feel cocooned in love, Gina made him feel secure. At this point Gina knew Trevor was being flooded with so many bad memories, she had to manage him. She knew that all the time in rehab taught him to talk about his feelings. Connect with the feelings leading him to his addictions. She wondered if she needed to play a bit of a therapist role. She didn't want to see signs of regression. She never thought that coming back to his childhood home would bring up all those emotions. Rehab made him connect with locked memories. She knew Trevor was feeling strained. They were in Vancouver now. Gina would help him get through this.

Trevor's emotions about the loss of his mother were remarkably deep. The aftermath had to be devasting to a thirteen-year-old boy and a husband. They both were hurting and suffering in their own way. Gina knew Trevor was too fragile for him to talk about those feelings with his father. And Shawn wasn't incredibly open about his feelings about the loss of his wife. She felt it was sad that it would never be resolved. Gina couldn't fathom why father and son never grieved together. She really wanted to protect Trevor at any cost.

Gina was still holding him, wrapped in love, and whispered, "Baby, I got you. Let's go to sleep."

Trevor kissed her goodnight and whispered, "I love you, wife."

When Gina woke up, Trevor was still sleeping, overly attached to her. She kissed his head, slipped out, and started to make breakfast.

Shawn joined her. "Gina, you put on coffee, and you're making breakfast, this is a treat. I usually go down to the local 7-Eleven and get bad coffee. It's nice to have a woman around."

Gina smiled. "I'm happy to do it, sit."

Shawn was eating when Trevor stumbled out to the kitchen.

"Good morning, my love, did you sleep well?" She was afraid of his answer.

Trevor seemed agitated. "Not really, I had bad dreams. You were with me last night, right?"

Gina got nervous, was he hallucinating again? "Trevor, yes, I was with you all night, we held each other, remember?"

Too much information for Shawn, but he could see a crack.

Trevor sat down. "G, can I have coffee and I guess whatever you made for breakfast?"

"Yes, love, here you go."

She sat next to him and sipped from her hot mug.

Finally, she broke the silence. "What are our plans today? Anyone want to do something special?"

Trevor looked at Gina. "I have a fucking session with the band today, what's wrong with you, Gina? I told you that last night."

He hadn't but his agitation with her was troubling. Knowing she couldn't be herself and tell him to fuck off, she put on kid gloves.

Gina tried not to show her disappointment. "Yes, you're right, I forgot. So, you will have a lot to do, I get it. When do they want me to start joining in these sessions?"

Trevor looked up at her. "G, how the fuck do I know when Tommy wants you in? When they tell me I'll tell you, how's that? I'm getting in the shower."

Gina sat at the table, tears pouring down her face.

Shawn took it all in. "Gina, Trevor was rude to you. Why did you let him speak to you like that?"

"Dad, I sense he is dealing with some memories from when he was younger, when his mother died. His drinking began in this place. He is having an overload of emotions, he doesn't know where to put them. This morning I'm the target. Truthfully, Dad, this is something that should have been managed all those years ago. Did he ever get therapy after the accident?"

Shawn said, "We attended grief counseling, but he was disconnected and wouldn't take part. He was drinking as a kid profusely a few months after. He was in and out of all the different programs, nothing stuck. Then his stays in juvenile detention. That's why he is a mess today. I tried and then I stopped trying."

Gina was crestfallen, Trevor had no shot. It was up to her to deal with the damage of Trevor's early years. She needed to clear her head.

"You know, Dad, would you like to drive to Stanley Park and walk around? I need to distract myself. Stanley Park was how I first met Trevor.

I need to remember those early days when I fell madly in love with him. Would you mind?"

Shawn looked at Gina. "I see you're struggling. It would be nice to go out. I haven't been there in years."

Gina went to take a shower; she knew she had to go into that room. She didn't know what to expect.

She walked in to get some of her bath items. "Trevor, I'm taking a shower. I'll be out of your way; your father and I are going to Stanley Park. I need to remember when I first met you. I don't know what's in your head. You have never spoken to me like that. I don't like it."

She couldn't help the tears.

Trevor was angry and seemed confused. "Why did you leave me last night? I was looking for you. You left me, why?"

Gina was scared, this must have been some kind of transferred emotion he had from some other place, like his mother leaving.

Gina, restrained in her response, said, "Babe, I never left you. I held you in my arms, you were crying. You are really scaring me. I love you; I'm not leaving you. You don't remember, you made me wear the nightgown. You fell on your knees and cried. I held you the whole night, I never let you go. I'm upset that something else is going on, I don't know what to do for you. Please never speak to me like that."

At this point Gina was visibly sobbing.

Trevor had a moment where he thought clearly. "Gina, I hate when you cry. I remember you in the nightgown, I thought I was back in that place. You were here with me; you never left me. I remember you holding me, it wasn't a dream. I'm sorry, baby. I don't want you to cry. I'm having some issues with being here, all my anger from living in this house. It's flooding back, I'm trying to hold on. Please forgive me, this house, the band, the work. Am I strong enough? You were right, maybe we shouldn't have come here."

Gina tried to smile through her tears. "Tell me you're having a tough time. Don't misplace your anger at me. I'm the one who will always love you. It makes me sad you're having these visions of me leaving you. That was months ago, you are better. You are having a slight setback, but you don't feel like drinking or anything else, right? Please say no."

Trevor slouched on the bed, afraid of what was going on in his head. "Gina, I'm so sorry, I'm so screwed up right now. I keep going back and forth, I promise I'll get it straight. Maybe working with Rio will keep my mind on the music. I swear I didn't mean to hurt you, I would never …"

Gina placed her hands on his forehead. "Do you need to talk to the head of the facility to check in? If I need to, I will arrange it."

Trevor felt misplaced, "G, I'd much rather talk to my wife, you know me better than anyone."

"I do, Trev, however, professional help could be good for you."

Trevor begged, "Please, I'll get my shit together. When do we leave here?"

"Whenever you want to leave. It's up to you."

Trevor asked, "Do you still want to go to Boise and look for that winter home? You know we will never go skiing, we're terrible."

Gina laughed. "We do suck at skiing."

Trevor was thinking deeply about Boise. "Roxanne would enjoy it. Are we good? Can I give you a kiss to tell you I'm sorry?"

Gina tried to put on a calm face. "Of course you can, my sweetest love."

He gave her a long, loving kiss, Gina let that be enough for now.

UNHAPPY TRIP DOWN MEMORY LANE

GINA KNEW SHE'D HAVE TO CALL RIO and ask him to mellow out a bit. Being back in Vancouver was bringing out some heavy emotions for Trevor. She was worried it was overloading him. Gina wanted the work with the band to be cathartic. To keep his mind off being in Vancouver.

She knew Rio would be a dick, but he was her cousin. She knew how to deal with him.

Gina called him. Rio picked up, "Well, how is my wandering cousin? Aren't you tired yet of driving around in that thing? We could use some killer Gina lyrics here in the studio."

"Rio, I am calling to let you know Trevor is having issues. We are in Vancouver, at his father's house. He has some heavy memories bubbling up. This is the place his issues were set in motion. I need you to use kid gloves with him."

Rio was now concerned, "Princess, is he regressing? I watched him all through his rehab working hard. I don't want to see you both fall down. All the Paul Ryan shit out there makes it worse. I'm saying this because I care about you both. You should leave Vancouver as soon as possible. Come home. Working on music might help him."

Gina heard him. "I don't disagree with what you're saying. We are going to Boise to hopefully buy a winter home. My plan is to get him home after that."

Rio drew a deep breath, "Okay, Princess, I promise you I will be gentle. I will call him soon. Gina, we are family, we grew up learning that family is the most important thing."

Gina thanked Rio, knowing he heard her. Gina felt a bit defeated, she got ready.

Gina took a shower and got dressed for her outing with Shawn. She reminded Trevor that she and his father were going to walk around Stanley Park. He hugged his wife and told her to have a good time.

Gina kissed him. "Good luck with the guys today."

Shawn didn't wait a minute out of the driveway. "Is he having issues, Gina? Or did he realize he made a mistake?"

Gina tried to smooth it over with Shawn. "Dad, it's okay, he's working things out. He's having trouble deciphering emotions he had in rehab and reality. It will be fine. You know I will make it fine."

Shawn flatly said, "Gina, I trust you."

She tried to gather a smile. "I'm looking forward to having a nice walk in the park."

They drove downtown and walked to Stanley Park. Gina loved remembering having Trevor take her on that walk when she came to Vancouver that first time. They strolled around in the fresh air. She felt she could clear her head from the morning's events.

Gina walked up to Shawn. "Can I interest you in some ice cream? I haven't had any in so long." Shawn agreed. Gina told Shawn how she ate a pint of ice cream almost every evening when Trevor had to go back to Vancouver. They enjoyed the ice cream while walking back to the car. They passed by a pastry shop. Gina looked in the window and spotted a strawberry shortcake she knew Trevor would love. She walked in and bought the cake. She hoped it would give him joy.

On their ride home, Gina and Shawn talked about the gardens in the park, the lake. Small talk, no huge issues. As they were getting close to the house, Gina mentioned they had lots of leftovers to eat. Shawn was his usual self, indifferent but friendly. He pulled into the driveway, then walked into the house and plopped himself on the couch in the living room to watch television. Gina followed and heard Trevor playing and talking. She wouldn't disturb him. She puttered in the kitchen, getting the leftovers ready for mealtime.

Trevor came out and grabbed her around the waist and kissed her neck.

He whispered in her ear, "I'm so sorry, I was an absolute asshole. I had no idea what was going on in my head. I was a mess. I'm trying to sort things out. I think you were correct that we shouldn't stay here as long as we had planned. Gina, your husband needs more time alone with you. You make me feel incredibly loved, Gina. This house is bringing out too many difficult emotions."

Gina held him. "You make me feel so loved, the best gift you have given me. We both give each other something back. I'm going to heat up leftovers. I bought you something special for dessert."

She opened the box, showed him the strawberry shortcake with whipped cream, and watched the corners of his lips rise into a full smile.

Gina touched his face. "You have to wait until after you eat. It's almost ready."

In a childlike voice, Trevor said, "I guess I will have to finish dinner to have my dessert."

Gina snapped a dish towel at his ass. "If you're good, you can even have two pieces."

Trevor sat down at the table. "It was the usual, Rio, Tommy, and Jeff getting work done. How was my father and the park?"

Gina set the table and finished getting the food ready. "Nothing major. No big, amazing insights."

Gina motioned to Trevor and Shawn it was time for dinner. She placed the food on the table.

Trevor laughed. "G, I love how you always make so much food."

Gina retorted motherly, "Eat your dinner and you can have dessert."

The evening had a lighter feel to it. After the meal, Trevor devoured two pieces of the cake. He also helped Gina clean up the dishes. Trevor wanted the two to relax in their room.

Shawn sat in his chair, had a few beers, and went to bed. It was his routine, nothing upset that.

Gina said goodnight and Shawn returned it with a wave.

Gina and Trevor walked into his old bedroom. She sat on the bed and asked Trevor how the music was going.

Trevor laughed. "Rio can be such an asshole, but every now and then he will produce some guitar riffs that are killer. Later we work it out together. I'm getting back to where music is the place I can go to let my head go into a creative space. That's huge for me, G."

Gina smiled, touched his face. "Trev, I'm relieved to hear your positivity."

Trevor felt ashamed, he sat on the bed wringing his hands. "Gina, I know you're worried, I don't blame you. I hope you aren't frightened."

Gina looked up at him. "Honestly, Trevor, I was extremely frightened, but if you acknowledge that, I'll be fine."

Trevor sat down next to her and kissed her the way that made her melt. "G, no nightgown tonight, okay?"

"Trevor, lock the door." They got into bed. Trevor was ready to go.

Gina was coy, "Babe, are you trying to have your way with me right now?"

Trevor looked into her eyes. "Gina, I love you, I know my problems are coming through. It's this house. I was fine when it was us. I will work really hard not to let whatever is going on in my head ruin the next few days here. My father won't care if we leave early, trust me. I know you like spending time with him. I'll hang on. I know you are here with me. I need to keep reminding myself I'm not back at rehab. It's unsettling. I have you, my most treasured, if I can say, possession."

Gina exhaled, "Trev, I don't mind you calling me your possession. Many women might hate that. We have been to hell and back. Remember we're codependent, in love. I want you to want me anytime."

She kissed him and he made sweet gentle love to her and ended their night. Gina knew she would have to watch over Trevor gently and with all the love she had for him.

The next morning Gina woke up, kissed Trevor, and told him she would make her famous waffles and bacon. Trevor seemed more like himself. He even had a short conversation with his father about driving the RV. While eating, Gina had asked Shawn if she could see his garden. She thought that when they got back to Montecito, she would plant an herb garden.

She missed her house; she knew once she got Trevor home, having all those memories would help him ease back into their normal life. Right now, he needed this distraction. Shawn was excited to show Gina that he had added tomatoes. She marveled at how well he tended to his plants, she felt she could do this.

Trevor had a day off from the music. "G, would you like to drive around my old neighborhood and go down memory lane with me?"

Gina was hesitant, torn between whether this would send him to a bad place or if this was a way for him to deal with his issues.

Shawn whispered to Gina, "You sure this is a clever idea? He may relive some unhealthy memories."

Gina told him, "Dad, this may be therapeutic for him to get this out. I have to let him try. Trust me, I'll deal with it."

Trevor asked for the keys to Shawn's car. "Let's go, G, we'll drive around."

Gina hugged Shawn, an unspoken word that she would take care of him.

Gina feigned excitement, "Babe, I'm surprised you wanted to do this, but I'm looking forward to sharing this experience with you. Are you sure about this?"

Trevor touched her face. "I need you to know where it all began and experience it with me. I trust you to protect me. You ready for it?"

Gina kissed him. "Let's do this together, I always wanted that deeper part of your soul. Now you are willing to share it, I'm privileged to embrace this with you."

"Let's do this, baby." They drove to the downtown area. Trevor stopped by the liquor store. "This is where Ian, Kevin, Brian Mayfield, and I used to steal bottles of anything we could get away with. We were detained several times, and the police were called once. My father had to come and get me."

Gina's words were incredibly careful. "Trevor, how does that make you feel, being here? Are you looking at this as therapy to revisit where your addictions took over you?"

Trevor looked a bit confused. "I'm not sure, it doesn't depress me. I feel that I can make peace with it. I have you with me, I'm protected with you here in this place to share these bad recollections."

Gina put her arm around him, "Yes, Trevor, you will always be safe with me, I'll protect you." Trevor drove around the corner to where the school was. "Funny, I didn't feel like I was a part of being at this school. I really didn't go after a while. Too drunk, too high, and honestly not interested. Does it seem like I'm uneducated?"

Gina looked stunned. "Oh, God, no, Trevor, not ever did I think that of you. You are highly intelligent; school doesn't make you smart. I coasted through high school, I never applied myself. Do you think I'm uneducated?"

Trevor touched Gina's face, admiring his wife. "My lovely wife, you are the most intelligent woman I have ever known. You have a great business head. Perfection is better because of you."

Gina kissed him. "Thank you, my love, that means so much. I'll always have Perfection's best interest."

Trevor drove by Ian's parents' house and Kevin's house, he did not take her by the Mayfields.

He drove by a field with an old shack that must have been there for decades.

Trevor pointed out, "This is where we would skip school, drink, and get high on whatever we could afford. I was wasted for so many years. I don't remember a day when I wasn't doing something."

They continued driving. He showed her the juvenile detention center, where his father would sometimes make him stay for weeks before taking him home.

Gina felt numb hearing Trevor's sad life. Her eyes teared up. "My sweet man, I'm sorry you had to experience that kind of abandonment. It must have been awful. I wish I could go back and hug you and tell you that I was coming for you, and I would love you always."

Trevor told her there was one more place he wanted to take her; he hadn't been there ever. He said he needed to go. He drove on a winding street and pulled over on the side of the road.

He looked at Gina. "This is where it happened, this is where my mother died. I never could come here. I was so inebriated, I couldn't. It's wretchedly sobering to see it. The last place where she was alive."

Gina took a deep breath, she had a feeling he would finally let out all that emotion, trapped for all these years.

She got as close to him as possible. "Trevor, it's okay to let it go. You can now cry, it's time to let out those emotions now. You're loved. I have you, I'll always have you, we have our own family. We can't replace your mom. But Roxanne and I could not have the life we have without you."

Trevor looked up, tears streaming down his face, and he cried like that young boy who lost his mother. He rested his head in Gina's lap. He was clearly in pain. She wanted Trevor to cry for however long he needed.

Time passed, he looked up at her. "Gina, thank you for allowing me to come here and feel sheltered and loved, to let all my backed-up emotions come through. I couldn't identify with this feeling in therapy. Now, although it will always be a bad memory, I'll know I visited where she left this world."

Gina was now tearing up, this was a major breakthrough for her husband, "Baby, I am so proud of you facing this, it was tremendously brave of you. I'm at a loss for what to say. I feel the pain, baby, because I love you so much, our connection is profound. Although I empathize, I don't know if I can ever completely identify with your deep pain."

Trevor held her. "Gina McNaughton, I will forever feel protected by you. I love all the affection you show to me."

"Baby, always and forever."

They finally drove from the spot.

Gina tried to take the edge off this painful moment. "Trevor, let's get something gooey and sweet. Decadent."

They found a bakery and ice cream shop where they split chocolate cake and mint ice cream with hot fudge, something they would never eat while on tour. The McNaughtons drove back to Shawn's. Gina went to work cooking chicken parmesan and sauce. Trevor went into the bedroom and played his guitar.

Shawn came over to Gina. "Did he take you to some of his places where he got into trouble? The liquor store, the abandoned house where he and his mates would get piss-ass drunk, stoned?"

Gina gathered herself and tried not to show Shawn her emotions. "He took me around town; he wanted me to see where he grew up. Just places, one of significance."

"Well, the man finally met those ghosts, he should have done it years ago."

That wasn't the answer she was hoping for. She continued cooking. She saw what Trevor must have seen his whole life, his father being removed from the traumatic event that changed their lives. Gina wouldn't delve into it any further. As long as she felt Trevor had some relief from his pain, that was all she wanted. She continued cooking and added a surprise, she made her Nonna's pignoli cookies. She knew Shawn would never have experienced them before. Trevor came out of the bedroom and put his hands on her waist.

It surprised her. "Trev, how are you? You had an emotional day. I want you to be well."

Trevor drew her into him. "G, I feel some weight lifted off my soul. It was difficult going to the spot where my mother took her last breath. I immediately exploded."

Gina was overwhelmed with sadness and extreme love for him. "Trevor, I told you, what you did this afternoon was brave and difficult. I'm thankful we did it together, remember, Trevor, always together. I'll never be apart from you. Except if I go clothes shopping," she added with a wink.

Gina leaned in and gave him a big kiss. "I made an unbelievable feast. Are you able to sit down at the table with your father, no issues?"

"G, we barely have another day, half a day. I can deal with it."

Gina set the table and placed the food down. She hoped if Shawn mentioned anything about their ride, he wouldn't negate Trevor's feelings. Simply acknowledge and move on. Gina didn't want any type of conflict. They sat down, and Shawn remarked on all the food Gina made. She told him there were special cookies for dessert. The conversation thankfully was about who was still around in the neighborhood, agreeable, nothing impactful. And that was the problem, neither one of them discussing their feelings. Gina thought to herself that it was not the Ricci household, where all of them expressed their feelings, often too much.

Trevor promised his father a ride in the RV, it was small but it was something. After dinner Gina brought out her cookies.

Gina told Shawn it was her Nonna's recipe, a very Italian cookie.

Shawn ate about five cookies in a row, savoring each bite, closing his eyes with each mouthful.

A TROUBLING PHONE CALL

GINA HEARD HER PHONE RING as she was cleaning the kitchen. It had to be family or someone in Perfection.

She picked it up, "Yes, who's this?"

Rio was feisty. "Well, stranger, it's your dick of a cousin, isn't that what you said to Jae? But I called because there's some shit happening here. Paul Ryan is popping up again. He isn't saying brilliantly flattering things about you."

Gina exploded, "Wait, Rio, what the fuck? What is Ryan saying about me?"

That got Trevor's attention. *Would this be too much for him today?*

Rio did not waste time. "Gina, he is saying that you arranged the trip to Hawaii for you both to have a getaway. You called paparazzi for them to take pictures of you two secretly. But here's the best, and you will go apeshit when I tell you. He said he slept with you the entire trip, your decision."

Gina went atomic. "What are you fucking telling me right the fuck now? That prick arranged the whole trip. I didn't want to go; he is fucking flipping this sideways. Rio, how did you hear this? You know none of it is true. Right from the beginning it smells, that isn't me, I would never. Tell me, tell me how. This guy is psychotic, he had a creepy, chilling shrine in that house of me. He is insane, we need to move faster on that restraining order."

Rio went further, "Listen, he found someone at the Entertainment Channel willing to interview him. Can Trevor hear me?"

Gina could tell Trevor was digesting all his feelings and news about Ryan after the day he had.

He took the phone. "Rio, we have a lawyer for the band, I forget his name. I want to sue for slandering my wife, and get Skip to get that judge to issue a restraining order for Gina and me, plus the entire band, that cocksucker. He isn't a normal man; he creates a room for a woman who never was in love with him."

Gina was freaking. "You both don't believe that any of this is true because it isn't, I'm getting a panic attack. These are lies. Rio, Jae came over the next day, when he dropped off those tickets. I had a conversation with her."

Gina panicked. Rio tried to reassure her. "Gina, Jae told me the whole story, we all know they are lies. Why come out now? If he had a story, why not come out with it when it happened? I think it's another one of his lunatic, obsessed delusions. Ryan could try and sue us for nonpayment of his unfilled contract. We have our own laundry list of reasons for firing him. There is a chain of letters from Perfection, firing him. Hey, my dude, you haven't said much, what is going through your head, man?"

Trevor took in the information. "I am going to cut this guy's balls off, how's that? I'm not a violent man. I may be an addict but not violent. Paul Ryan needs to have his legs broken or his mouth sewn shut. Which way do I go, Rio?"

Rio came back, "Skip is not responding, of course, he doesn't want to give it any credibility either ... As far as our next music session, Tommy is taking a few days off. You two have a few days off also, you're welcome."

Gina downed three Valium. "Rio, lies, I am in disbelief again. Trevor and I had an unbelievably emotional day. This news about Ryan has compounded that. Trevor and I need to absorb this disturbing information. You need to be our conduit to what is going on. I trust you, please."

Rio assured her, "Gina, I always have your back and Trevor's. Jae and I will stay connected."

Gina glanced at Trevor and fell apart. "Baby, this isn't true, please trust me. You know, I was in hell without you. I did go to Hawaii, but it wasn't the way he wanted it to go."

Trevor held her. "Gina, it looks like we've both had an emotional day. Let's go lay down and watch my old-ass TV."

They walked together to the bedroom, both emotionally strung out.

They cuddled up to each other and Trevor touched her face. "Baby, it's okay. We're good. Come closer, let me feel your body close to me."

Gina wiggled closer. "Trevor, I want to head out to Boise soon, very soon. We can look for our winter getaway, we can hide out the whole season. What do you think about seeing if Roxanne would like to join us in the house hunt?"

Trevor lifted her face to his. "G, I think it's an outstanding idea. For a moment you took my mind off Paul Ryan. I'm sorry, do you feel worn out at this moment?"

"Baby, I freaked out, I took three Valium to keep me from caring about that asshole. I care more about your emotional well-being. Ryan is pure evil, along with Mayfield, they are the devil incarnate. You are my priority. Can we cuddle up naked under this comforter?"

Gina wasn't sure if Trevor was still thinking about the Ryan issue. However, he loved her idea for the evening. They both fell asleep watching TV.

THE MORNING AFTER

GINA WOKE UP THE NEXT MORNING feeling like she had a hangover. She told Trevor she was going to make coffee; she needed it badly.

Trevor yawned and pulled her back into bed. "Not so fast."

She leaned over him. "Are you wanting a playdate?"

Trevor had a dirty, hungry look on his face. He grinned, pouted his lips, a sexy smile. "You know, I have missed you for a couple of nights. With everything that has gone on, I wasn't sure you were up to it."

He yanked her naked body hard back into bed.

Gina shook her head. "Trevor, you make it difficult to say no to you. Not that I want to."

Trevor was a thirsty lover; he did miss his wife. He took her hard and fast. Gina liked it that way. However, his face looked different to her. She felt like he wanted to possess her.

Gina looked into his eyes, swept away the hair from his face, then rubbed his half-shaven face. "Baby, I love you wanting me this way. I know your face well when we make love." She grabbed him for a kiss. "Trevor, you have a distinct look on your face I have never seen. Baby, what's in your head?"

Trevor continued going harder, making Gina even hotter. Trevor finally reached his moment of climax.

He rolled over on his side, touched Gina's face softly. "Don't get angry, I needed to feel in charge. I can't explain it. Something came over me. We had a day of emotional shit. I needed to feel you were mine, taking you over. G, it's just some weird shit I'm dealing with."

Gina sat up, holding the comforter up to cover her naked body. "Trevor, it's fine that you felt like you needed to own me in some way. I have only been yours. Let me throw some clothes on and brew some beans. I'm dying for it and breakfast. I'm sure your father is up."

Trevor grabbed her arm. "Gina, we talked about this. I believe we should leave, like today. I'm having issues being here."

Gina got out of bed and reached for her clothes. "Yes, as we discussed, we will leave today. Hey, we are going to look for a house. I'm excited."

Gina finished getting dressed and threw Trevor his sweats and a shirt. They walked out of Trevor's room giggling. Gina got the machine going. She couldn't wait for it to be ready. She replayed all that happened yesterday. Even with Trevor's excellent lovemaking, she felt run over. The machine finished brewing. The smell of the coffee, like a bit of chocolate and toasted nuts, wafted through the kitchen. Gina grabbed some large mugs and poured herself and Trevor a cup. They sat at the dining room table, savoring each sip, just looking at each other and enjoying their mugs of hot brewed beans.

Shawn didn't seem to be in the house. Gina looked outside, he was in his garden, trimming and harvesting tomatoes.

He came in a few minutes later and she threw some onion bagels in the toaster. "That smells good, Gina. Are you making Canadian bacon too? No mistaking the slight smoky smell. It will be a nice taste with those onion bagels."

Gina nodded in the affirmative, "Yes, you can make a breakfast sandwich."

Shawn sat down at the table. "You starting your journey back on the road today?"

Trevor answered, "We are planning on it. I don't know if I'm up for five hours of driving, but if we leave here around one, we can make it to Yakima, Washington, at a decent time."

Shawn asked, "What is your next destination?"

Gina buttered her bagel in between big gulps of coffee. "We're going to drive to Boise, Idaho. We are thinking of buying a winter home. For skiing and for Christmas, a place where the whole family can spend time together. We, of course, would want you to join us if we find a house we like. Something where we can have some privacy."

Shawn took four tomatoes and placed them in a bag. "You must take these with you."

Gina placed her hands together, feeling sad about leaving. "Dad, did you want us to stay longer?"

Shawn looked at them. "It's fine for you to continue your trip. I'll be fine, it was great having you here for the last few days. You will need to get back to California sometime, I guess."

Trevor got up from the table. "Maybe sooner than we originally thought."

Gina was somewhat shocked but pleasantly so. She knew Trevor had the fight back in his personality, even if it was because of Paul Ryan. He left to take a shower and Gina cleaned up the kitchen.

Shawn remained at the table. "Gina, whatever happened yesterday seems to have cleared Trevor's head a bit. I couldn't help but overhear some person is starting trouble for you. Trevor will have the ability to manage this, he loves you. Anything that could hurt you, he will fight for you."

Gina smiled. "Thank you, Dad, are you sure you're okay with us leaving today? I feel maybe there are conversations that could happen."

Shawn looked at Gina. "I know you want my son and I to have that moment where we tell each other how much we love each other and forgive everything. That, regrettably, won't happen. Neither of us would be able to take that step. It's okay, he comes to visit, and I know in his own way he loves me. I'm good with that."

Gina looked disappointed. "I won't force anything. But if you're okay with us leaving, that's all I need to know for now. You know I always enjoy my time with you and love cooking for you." Gina gave Shawn a big hug and kiss and then went into the bathroom to find Trevor had already finished his shower.

He had hunger in his eyes. "Were you hoping for a playdate?"

Gina winced. "Trev, you know I'm uncomfortable doing that in your father's house. If we leave today, I promise when we get back into that beast we can struggle for a playdate. Once again, you are a horny man. I love it actually, but seriously, Trevor."

He laughed and let her take her shower solo while he was packing up.

Shawn knocked on their bedroom door and Trevor answered. "Trevor, whatever is going on with this guy, promise me you won't let it interfere with your marriage."

Trevor looked at his father. "No man will get in between my wife and me. I know you care about Gina. I will manage it."

That was good enough for Shawn. It wasn't going to get deeper, so he left the room.

"So, another five-hour drive, you up for it?" Gina asked as she stepped out of the bathroom.

Trevor pulled her towel off. "Yes, I am. I get to have you all alone."

Gina protested. "Trev, come on, let me get dressed. Let's call Roxy so she can book a flight. Hold on, Trevor, you know she will want Zach to come. You need to come to terms with it."

Trevor sat on the bed resigned that Zach was part of his world. "I knew you would say that. I now realize she really cares for this guy. I hear you, babe; I got to get over myself when it concerns Roxanne."

They piled all their luggage in the RV. Gina was reluctant to leave Shawn, she felt he was a lonely man. But it was time to say their goodbyes. It was nice to feel normal while in Vancouver. They headed into the RV for their long drive.

For about an hour they drove silently, enjoying the scenery. They went from the beauty of Vancouver's coast, driving south into the forests of the Cascade Range with the tall lodgepole pine trees.

Trevor blew up, "Ryan had to see our interview and the one in the magazine. Why still interject himself into our marriage? He is some crazy sicko, Gina."

Gina half-smiled. "He is a jilted man. It's hard for me to rationalize why he won't give it up. When I have the best lover in the world, why would I care?"

Trevor cracked a smile; however, he was still agitated. "I was thinking, with this new interruption, I need to consider going back home to Montecito. We can work on our music, even do some of those stand-alone concerts. We do owe Los Angeles a concert after that horrible incident, you agree? We will be able to respond to any allegations Ryan is throwing out there. When do you think Mayfield will resurface?"

The thought of Mayfield made Gina's stomach turn. How would she come to grips with coming face-to-face with him?

Gina was excited but cautious about Trevor saying *back home to Montecito*. "Trev, you sound like you aren't so worried about your sobriety. I'm happy. Are you ready to take on all the work we will have to do? It seems like it can be overwhelming. Also, concerts would be a single night anywhere in the country. That could be tiring and more work for us. I'm up for it. I would love to go home to Montecito. We haven't been able to spend time in our home together for a long while. That house has all our memories, good ones. I would love to get back to singing. I miss singing and playing music with you."

Trevor smiled. "G, you are correct on all those things. As far as me being strong enough, I'm not sure. I do know that Paul Ryan is giving me strength like I had in rehab. I'm determined to get back to our lives. I miss working with those bunch of assholes that are our band. Yes, G, I believe I'm ready to step back into Trevor McNaughton. Seeing where my mother died helped shake some of those demons off my back. Thank you for allowing me to feel that emotion."

Gina planted little kisses on his face. "Baby, seeing you so positive is so uplifting. I'll call Roxanne and see if she can meet us in three days. Does that give you some *alone time* with me?"

Trevor smiled. "I'm sure I can fit a lot of *alone time* in those days."

Gina called Roxanne; the phone rang several times and she finally picked up.

"Hi, Mom, is this you? What the hell is going on with that prick Paul Ryan? I saw his interview on TV. Mom, he said you slept with him the whole time in Hawaii. Did you really arrange it? Tell me you didn't."

Gina put the phone where both she and Trevor could hear Roxanne.

Gina was a little hurt that Roxanne would have any doubt that the rumors were true. "Roxanne, don't even question that, I can't believe you. You knew how much I missed your father. Why would you think I would ever let another man in my bed? I'm being real with you; you're a grown woman now. It's false. That is not why I called you. I admit, I'm a bit annoyed at your reaction. I'm not sure I want to ask my real reason for calling you."

Trevor heard Roxanne on the phone, he looked at it disapprovingly. "Roxanne, you shouldn't question your mother like that. I don't believe a word of it, you shouldn't either. What your mother was going to ask you was her idea. We are going to Yakima, Washington, then onto Boise, Idaho. Mom wants to look for a winter house where you can go skiing. She thought it would be special if you came and helped us find a house. Roxanne, you owe your mother an apology."

Roxanne hated to be admonished by her father. "Mom, I'm sorry, I know you love Dad, it's amazing how much. But I hate hearing this BS. Yes, I would love to help look for a ski house or winter house since you two don't ski. If I come—"

Gina interjected, "You want to bring Zach, yes? You would be going home to Montecito soon anyway. Think of it as a side trip. Let's meet in three days. Your father and I need to preview houses before you arrive. It's up to you, Roxanne. We thought since it's a family home you would like to be a part of the process. Speak to Zach and call us back, let us know. We're going no matter what."

Roxanne apologized to Gina again and said she'd call back later in the day. Trevor drove for about two hours, and they elected to stop at a rest area with a few fast-food restaurants and little stores.

"My God, Trevor, let's hope we can buy some junk food and get in and out."

Gina thought for a moment. "We have a record label now, we should get business credit cards, don't you think?"

Trevor laughed. "You think of everything."

They got all their junk food they loved to snack on while driving. Once back in the RV, Gina was thinking of what kind of house they would want. Was it big, or small, specifically for their family? Gina also wanted a home that was turnkey. Furniture included. A home that they could move right into. She wanted land nestled in the foothills, privacy.

Gina thought aloud, "Trevor, we need to have privacy at this house, and some land around it. No prying eyes while we are vacationing."

Trevor conceded, "Gina, this is your idea. I'll love whatever you want."

They drove on, talking about their music, including the two songs Gina wrote. It had been a while since the two of them had talked about the next steps for Perfection. Gina was encouraged because it seemed that they would get home sooner than originally planned. They were about an hour out of Yakima; Gina saw a big-name supermarket. They needed to replenish their pantry.

They could go out every night if they wanted, but they liked being in their own environment. They loaded up their cart with meat, fresh vegetables, coffee beans, milk, all the essentials. Despite their disguises, the McNaughtons were unmistakably still rock stars. They realized they were made when they saw a girl wearing a Perfection T-shirt.

She came up to them quietly, "I know who you are, I can't believe you're here in the middle of nowhere. Do you think I can have my shirt signed? I won't say anything, I promise."

Trevor smirked. "As long as we can get out of here without any commotion, sure."

She handed him a pen, she was ecstatic. One happy fan. They bought their rations without any other issues and drove to the next location. Trevor hooked up water, sewer, and electricity. As Gina was putting away the remaining groceries, Trevor pressed up against her and she turned around.

"Trevor, I know what you're doing, I feel you against my body, you are hard as a rock. I've been married to you absolutely too long not to notice your moves. Seriously, that's the first thing you want to do?"

Trevor grabbed her face and gave her an extremely hard kiss. "You know this is what I wanted; you and me totally enjoying each other. I have had a backlog of Gina time."

She laughed. "Trev, don't you think you're caught up yet?"

Trevor pushed himself harder against her. "Is my wife telling me that she's not interested?"

Gina shook her head. "Have I ever denied you?"

Trevor dug up an old memory. "Yes, you did. I was drunk or high, you locked the door on me. I came in. I told you I wanted you and you said no. You told me sex isn't going to make this better. I remember that because you were right. Not realizing that I was wanting you in spite of the fact that I was fucked up. Having you love me took away the ugliness of what I did. I'm sorry. But now I am wanting to love you, to give you my soul by making love to you."

Gina stroked his hair. "Love those words. Trevor, you always give me the affection I need and more. Come on, let's hit that bed."

After the two lovers were drunk on their lovemaking, Gina walked into the kitchen to put something together for a snack. She prepped the food and placed it in the oven. The two enjoyed a peaceful meal, a simple life made. After they ate, they sat outside on the lawn by the RV and stared at the stars.

HEADS UP, BOISE, THE MCNAUGHTONS ARE HERE!

THEY GOT TO BOISE AROUND 3:00 P.M. and set up all the connections at the RV park. Trevor played his guitar and wrote down some music. Gina believed he was getting to a place where his emotions were in check. No thinking about Paul Ryan. It was late in the afternoon but Gina tried calling a local real estate agent to line up some homes.

Dennis Tate picked up. "Hello, Great Boise Real Estate, can I help you?"

Gina asked him if he would be discreet with her phone call first. "Dennis, my name is Gina McNaughton, my husband and I are in the band Perfection. Not sure if you've heard of us?"

Dennis said, "Of course I have, saw you when you played Boise a few years ago."

Gina continued, "Dennis, my husband and I are looking for a home here in Boise. We would like to have land around us for privacy. We would like five bedrooms; it could be more. I think six bathrooms; we like that open-floor plan concept. We would like to have several living areas. We would be entertaining our family and friends. I spotted a home in the foothills that might work for us. I'm sure you have some homes that fit that narrative. We would like to have it furnished or have the ability to buy the house as is. We don't want to start decorating another home. Can you help us?"

Dennis Tate had to be floored by this phone call. "I believe I have at least four homes that would fit what you're looking for. We may have to negotiate on the furniture, but people usually have a price if that translates to a sale. Houses you are interested in are over the million-dollar mark with furniture, doable?"

Gina laughed. "Dennis, don't worry about the cost, we would pay cash. That should really entice owners and you to sell us a home. But remember, discretion is key, you with me? Get that list together and we would love to look in about two days. Does that work for you?"

An excited Dennis Tate said, "Mrs. McNaughton, or can I call you Gina? I'm on it. I promise you will be happy with what I show you."

Gina said, "Yes, Gina is fine. Okay, it's a date, two days. By the way, we are in an RV. Is it possible for you to pick us up?"

Of course, the answer was yes. Then Gina remembered she hadn't heard from Roxanne. She worried that if Zach couldn't come, Roxanne would stay back at Stanford. Gina saw Trevor playing his guitar, she didn't recognize the music. She sat down next to him on the bed, and closed her eyes and listened.

Gina interrupted him. "I'm sorry to stop you, but we haven't heard from Roxanne and we have a date with a realtor in two days. Do you want to call her? She responds better when it's you."

Trevor sighed. "She needs to be more attentive to you; I don't like it when she gives you shit. It's not what I expect from our daughter. Especially when I love you so much."

Gina pleaded, "Trev, can you call her? I may have to change our realtor appointment."

He laughed. "I thought you sat down next to me for an encore."

Gina chuckled. "After we eat you can have your encore, deal? Call your daughter."

Trevor put the call on speaker and called Roxanne. She picked up at once. "Hi, Dad, what's up?"

"Hi, Roxy. Have you looked at flights to come here to Boise? I thought your mother and I asked you if you wanted to be a part of buying a home here. We have an appointment two days from now, so what's up?"

Roxanne was frustrated. "Dad, I'm looking at tickets. I would have to go through Seattle, then to Boise. I can make it there tomorrow, along with Zach. The tickets are expensive."

Gina added to the conversation, "Roxanne, when was price ever an issue? Don't use that as an excuse. That's why we gave you a credit card, for this type of situation. What time would you get here?"

"Probably around noon, how would I get to you?"

Gina shook her head. "My darling girl, we will send a car to get you. You will have to stay in the RV, you realize that."

Roxanne moaned. "Oh, okay, but can you and Dad behave yourselves while we are there?"

Trevor chimed in, "Roxanne, please don't worry about what we do. Your mother and I need to worry about you and Zach. So, you remember that. Details arranged, you will be here."

"Yes, Dad, I'll be there. I want to see this house the two of you are going to buy."

Trevor ended the call, "We will see you in a few days."

Trevor groaned. "She is getting harder to deal with, G. I think it's Zach."

Gina laughed. "No, sweetheart, it's her. She feels she has her own little life with Zach. We are annoying. I remember I felt that way about my parents when we were first together. Funny how life comes back and hits you in the face."

Gina prepared a small snack and summoned Trevor, "Come on, food is ready. Then we will see if you can carry out an encore."

Trevor smiled. "I might be an older dude, but I'm still able to give you an encore."

"Okay, older dude, let's eat."

Trevor helped Gina clean up. "Mr. McNaughton, to what do I owe this special treatment?" Trevor kissed and sucked on her neck to show how much he wanted her. "The faster you clean up the faster I can try to woo you. Actually, I thought we could sit outside, look at the stars, sing a few songs. We haven't sung in quite a while."

Gina smiled. "I love that idea. I need to get my voice back in shape."

They sat outside in the moonlight, not too many people around. Trevor took his acoustic guitar out and started playing one of Gina's favorite songs, "Can't Find My Way Home." She used to sing it with Vision Skye and at the beginning of Perfection. It was a song where she could use her low range voice to sound incredible. Then Trevor played, "I Can't Get Enough of Your Love." They sang it together but it was Gina's song to sex up. She made a mental note; it should become a song to sing together. They took a moment to have fun singing whatever came to their heads. Gina took out her pastel cigarettes and had a glass of wine. They sat outside for a few hours. Gina told Trevor she had a surprise for dessert. She prepared a banana split for them to share. Hot fudge, wet walnuts, and whipped cream all over their faces. They laughed while they ate this decadent dessert. Gina took a paper towel, wiped Trevor's face, and he cleaned hers. Then she had a brilliant idea, one they needed to do before Roxanne came.

She asked Trevor, "You still want that encore, baby?"

Trevor looked wide-eyed. He folded the chairs outside and placed them against the RV. Gina took the dessert dish and cleaned it. Trevor walked in with his guitar. He had a smile on his face.

He propped himself up against the bedroom doorway, "Did you mention an encore? I am interested."

Trevor went into the bedroom, stripped bare, and waited.

Gina used her sultry voice, "Baby, get ready for me, I have a surprise for you."

Gina added, "I enjoyed sharing dessert with you, but I'm still hungry, so I thought maybe I could have you for dessert, and maybe you could do the same."

Trevor got extremely aroused. "G, I love that idea. Who goes first?"

Gina smiled, "Oh, I will go first, you ready to get a bit dirty?"

She drizzled some hot fudge along his penis, Gina licked the hot fudge and added some whipped cream. She was driving Trevor wild; she made sure that her tasting finished him off.

"Baby, you better get ready, because I'm ready for my second dessert and it's you."

Gina smiled. "Let's see how hungry you are."

Trevor didn't need much prompting to place his face between Gina's legs, but this was a total turn-on for him. Trevor loaded her up with sweets and devoured her. Gina was in total ecstasy. This was always Trevor's secret weapon. He would excite her. When she couldn't take it anymore, Gina could see he was ready again. He smeared hot fudge and whipped cream on her face and they licked them off each other. He moved her slowly; he was totally in charge. Once they finished, they felt how sticky they made themselves. Gina lay back, exhausted from passion.

Trevor leaned over. "Gina, loving you is never boring, you always surprise me."

Gina kissed him. "I always want to give you something you don't expect. Trev, I need to take a shower, I'm all sticky."

Gina got up and went into the shower. This time, Trevor came in to get clean. Gina then put on her satin robe and wrapped a towel around her head. Trevor dried off and put those ratty sweatpants on.

Gina was very satisfied, she pulled the comforter up to her knees. "You outdid yourself, I loved it. Can we cuddle, find a movie, and watch TV? Are you okay with that?"

They got comfortable in their bed. Gina scrolled through the few stations that the camp had. She couldn't believe what she landed on, *The Birds* on a movie channel.

She was so excited to share this with him. "Trevor, remember when we went to Bodega Bay and I told you about the movie they made there? This is it. *The Birds*. Please let me share this with you."

They cuddled up. "G, baby, you blew my mind, anything you want."

Trevor enjoyed the movie and they fell asleep. They knew that tomorrow Roxanne would be visiting and there would be no special desserts on the menu.

THE HOUSE HUNT BEGINS

THE NEXT MORNING GINA LET TREVOR SLEEP IN and made lattes and a quick bite to eat.

Trevor staggered out. "Good morning, baby, it was some night last night."

Gina teased him. "I know, you finally got to see *The Birds*. Oh, yes, dessert was fantastic too."

He gave her a good morning kiss. Roxanne was due around 1:00 p.m. and their appointment was in a couple of days.

Gina called out to Trevor, "Trev, baby, Roxanne is delayed a few hours. What would you like to do, and please don't say the obvious. Would you like to go for a walk around our new area and get some chill Boise vibes? We deserve it. I was thinking of maybe even smoking a joint if you are okay with it."

Trevor walked out, guitar in hand, "I could use a walk in the fresh air. Remember, getting back to nature clears your mind. I was thinking about all the work we have to do. Perfection needs our attention. Going back to our home in Montecito. Then we have some ugly business we need to deal with. Let's take that walk before Roxy gets here. I'm still going to try to get a playdate."

Gina grabbed his hand, "Come on, sexy man, let's get a dose of fresh air. Then maybe a quickie playdate."

The air smelled fresher, they could see the foothills in the distance. Gina thought she made the right choice by picking Boise for a wintery escape. She didn't know why, it felt right. Maybe because she did smoke that joint. An hour later they circled back to the RV.

Trevor smiled at Gina, "That was relaxing. It cleared my head for a while. Then my mind went back to Vancouver, Ryan. Baby, I just want you to know I'm processing everything. I give you my promise I won't fall down."

Gina touched his unshaven face lightly. "Trevor, you have my trust always. So, it's one thirty, we have time to get those sexy Boise vibes."

They enjoyed a lazy romantic afternoon.

Roxanne and Zach would be en route to her parents. Trevor sat outside the RV waiting for Roxanne and Zach. Gina was making chicken and dumplings for dinner; it was one of Roxanne's favorites. Gina wanted Roxy to know how valued her opinion on the house was.

The Stanford duo arrived, kisses and hugs were exchanged.

Roxanne tried to temper her emotions, "We are really buying a house to go skiing. I'm excited."

Everybody chatted about school, family, nothing controversial. Roxanne asked where they would be sleeping since it was an early day of traveling, they wanted to rest. They went to their tiny bedroom, watched television, and fell asleep. Gina and Trevor did the same.

Gina jumped on the bed, "I'm so excited to buy a house tomorrow. Our escape. Thank you, babe, for making this happen for us."

Trevor smiled, "I want you to be a happy wife. Let's get some sleep, tomorrow will be a hectic day."

The next morning was busy, with everyone getting ready to buy a house.

Dennis Tate would be picking them up, hopefully his car was big enough. Trevor and Gina dressed casually, black jeans, white T-shirts, and leather jackets. They hoped he would think of them as those rock stars he saw many years ago. Roxanne would hate it.

"Quick thought, family," Gina said. "I can whip up some omelets before the realtor comes."

They all enjoyed a quick bite.

Gina smiled at her daughter, marveling over how she was the perfect mix of her and Trevor.

Roxanne looked at her mother strangely. "Mom, why are you staring at me like that? You and Dad don't have something weird you want to tell me …"

Gina laughed. "No, silly girl, I look at you amazed, I see your father and myself in you. Roxanne, you got the best parts of each of us. That's all. Zach, don't you think so?"

Zach was a bit nervous. "I always tell her some days she looks like you and some days she looks like her dad."

They finished eating. Then a knock came on the RV; it was Dennis Tate.

Gina opened the door. "Hello, Dennis, it's nice meeting you. Obviously, you know me and my husband, Trevor. This is our daughter, Roxanne, and her boyfriend, Zach. We are ready to buy our winter home here in Boise. I hope you have enough room in your car."

Dennis was a bit starstruck, he fumbled over his words. "I have a Range Rover, I'm sure we will all fit."

Trevor said, "Let's go find us a house."

They drove about twenty minutes to the foothills. All the houses they were going to see were five bedrooms and had office areas and large open-floor plans. Gina and Trevor didn't mind some exposed wood features but didn't want the house to look like a log cabin. Two of the four houses fit the bill, large lots, the house set way back from the road. Both had gourmet kitchens and two large living areas, the primary baths looked like spas. Trevor winked at Gina, their playdates in the shower. Gina fixated on the furniture. She loved one house that had a great room that had three areas established as separate sitting areas in the one expansive room. The outdoor area was beautiful with a view of the hills.

Gina looked at Trevor. "I like both. It is the furniture that will be the deciding factor." Roxanne favored one house because it had a separate guest house.

Gina eyeballed her daughter. "Roxanne, both of these houses are huge. There is plenty of distance between the rooms."

Trevor told Dennis, "Let's make offers on both, with the stipulation that we want the furniture, and here are our offers. Let them know we are paying cash. That should be an incentive to someone."

Poor Zach's head was spinning at the ease with which the McNaughtons made a deal.

Gina looked at Roxanne. "Seriously, which one do you like better? Forget the guest house. I would put Nonna and Poppi there."

Roxanne didn't care, although one did have a ski locker next to the garage. It happened to be the one Gina was hoping for.

Dennis dropped them back at the RV a few hours later. He told the McNaughtons he would talk to the realtor about the houses they were interested in. Dennis told them it could be a waiting game. He would try to encourage the owners, as this was a bona fide offer.

They thanked Dennis for his help and believed he could broker a deal.

Dennis said he would get back to them when he heard back from the sellers' realtor.

Trevor was excited; this was Gina's dream. He seemed open to spending Christmas here with snow and lit fireplaces. Gina was watching her husband come back to that easygoing Trevor McNaughton. Not the man who came back to her slightly fragile and had memories he needed to work out. She knew taking him back was obviously the right choice for her. Gina and Trevor sat outside and took in the enjoyable, easy RV life. They both knew it would be ending. They knew Perfection needed their attention. They would enjoy every minute of the trip. A few hours passed, and nerves were starting to show. Gina headed into the RV to prepare the steak pizzaiola and antipasto salad for supper.

Trevor's phone rang, "Babe, your phone. Answer it, Trev, please."

Trevor picked up the phone. "Dennis … yes, we can have the furniture, how much … another 200K, go back and tell them 150K, the house is five years old. The furniture has some wear. I will wait to hear back."

Gina was relieved that Trevor was taking charge. She asked, "Which house are we talking about? The one *I REALLY* like or the other one I like?"

Trevor flashed a Cheshire cat grin. "The *really*-like one. I want you to have it, this is your vision for our family. I want you to love it. Do you realize this is the first house we'll have bought ourselves? Your parents bought us the Hollywood Hills house and our home in Montecito. This house is special because we'll have bought it."

Gina threw her arms around him. "Trev, so true, I never thought about that. Mario and Franny always taking care of us. Thank you, my love, this home is our escape. I guess we will see if our offer is accepted."

Dennis called twenty minutes later and said a deal was made for $1,750,000. Trevor told him to get the paperwork ready and he would have the money wired to the escrow account. He asked how fast they could close on the house. Dennis felt thirty to forty-five days. Trevor asked for a quicker closing, it was a cash deal. The owners wanted it sold quickly. Dennis said he would get it done. The McNaughtons were excited.

Gina made banana splits for her family and winked at her husband.

Roxanne hung her head in agreement. "Yes, I was hoping to spend some time at home, in Montecito. Relax. Zach and I need to be back at school in July. Football and cheerleading practices start then. Don't forget, college games start in August. We need to practice earlier."

Gina smiled. "I am aware, Roxy. After we buy this house, I am going to try to get your father back home. We can all spend time together. Family time. I look forward to it."

Once Gina sorted out Roxanne's schedule, she told the two, "Your father and I are going into our room to hang out. Think of all the details of the new house. Feel free to do whatever you want."

Roxanne had to add, "Can you two definitely not, please?"

Trevor quizzically shook his head. "Are you asking us not to have sex, Roxanne?"

Their daughter was in shock. "Oh, my God, Dad, seriously. You said that aloud."

Trevor laughed. "I know, hope it pissed you off, good night, Zach."

Gina was giggling in the bedroom. "That was great, babe. She totally didn't expect that from you. I love it. I really want to curl up with you tonight. I want you to know that I see you coming back stronger, Trevor. I'm so proud of all the progress you've made. For us, for our family, for Perfection, but mostly for you, babe. Whatever your motivation was, I was waiting. My husband, 'I do' a million times, 'I do.'"

Trevor kissed her, remembering that he had mentioned that vow to her when he first came home from rehab.

Their plan for tomorrow was to explore Boise and the surrounding areas, including skiing locations. They were incredibly content after buying their new house. The McNaughtons found a place of Zen. Away from their wild lifestyle. Gina looked forward to spending the holidays in their winter getaway.

WORRISOME TRIP TO NEW YORK

GINA WOKE UP EARLY THE NEXT MORNING. She was excited to have a day filled with learning about her new city—restaurants, kitschy clothing stores, markets. She relished the idea of a farmers' market in town.

The aromatic smell of citrus and cinnamon filled the air as her coffee percolated. She observed that the door where Roxanne and Zach slept was slightly open. Surely, they were up. Roxanne came out of the bathroom, solo, in a bathrobe and hair tucked under a towel.

She pleasantly said, "Good morning, Mom. Is the coffee ready? I'm dying for a cup."

"As am I. Today we find out what is in Boise. All the shops and interesting places. Are you as excited as I am?"

Roxanne's request was, "Can you make pancakes before we go exploring? You make the best."

Gina grimaced. "I was hoping not to make breakfast, but since you asked, I will. Get dressed so you can help me. Where is Zach?"

Roxanne said he was going to take a shower now that she was out.

Trevor came out showered and dressed for their excursion today. Gina handed him a mug.

Trevor looked over. "G, you making breakfast? I thought we would get an early start."

Roxanne came back dressed in her designer jeans and a crisp blue-and-white striped button-down shirt. Her hair was braided in a long ponytail.

Roxanne said, "Dad, I asked Mom to make pancakes. They're my favorite."

Trevor relented, "They are my favorite too. Where is Zach?"

Gina said, "He is showering and I need to do the same. Here, you all eat while I get ready."

The McNaughton family plus Zach engaged in some small talk around the kitchen table. Roxanne was excited that this year she would make co-captain of the cheer squad.

Gina came out dressed in a Boho midi dress. It was somewhat sheer but it had embroidered flowers and vines. The waist had some smocking, showing off her waist.

Gina clapped her hands. "We all ready to see Boise? I know I am."

Trevor called a cab to take them into town.

As the four of them were stepping into a cab, Trevor's phone rang. He was hoping it wasn't music-related. He wanted a day of carefree exploring.

"Trevor, I need to speak to you," Rio announced. "This is some heavy shit I am going to tell you. Prepare Princess, she is going to flip out."

Trevor waited, "Hey, man, what's going on? I don't want to hear about Ryan, we are heading into Boise. The McNaughtons will soon own a beautiful winter hideaway. What? … When?"

Gina looked at Trevor's face, something was wrong.

Rio simply told him, "Uncle Mario had a massive heart attack. The doctors are waiting to operate. They want him to be stabilized. My father is a mess. You need to park that fucking RV and get on a plane at once. Pack whatever you have. You'll need to call Roxanne and get her here."

Trevor said, "That's not an issue, she's here. How bad?"

Rio said, "He was having a heart attack. Aunt Franny called the ambulance, they took him to the hospital. They revived his heart twice. They are planning a quadruple bypass. My poppi died slumped over in his chair from the same thing, Uncle Mario at least has a chance. By the time we land, I'm sure the operation will be performed. Trevor, take your wife and get her on a plane. Jae and I are leaving for the airport now. You need to tell Gina. She will take it better from you, love you, man. I'll see you soon."

Gina looked at Trevor's shocked face. "What's going on, something is wrong. What is it?"

Trevor had tears in his eyes. "Gina, we need to leave for New York now, you too, Roxanne. Gina, please try to be calm. Mario had a massive heart attack."

Gina screamed. "Trevor, is he ..."

Trevor was firm. "Baby, we need to pack and go. The doctors are waiting to stabilize him, then will perform a quadruple bypass. Right now he is sedated, waiting for the operation. Franny needs you. We need to go, now."

Gina crumpled, Trevor picked her up. "Baby, we need to get ready, okay? Zach, I'm guessing you want to fly back to Stanford."

Roxanne was tearful. "I want him with me."

Trevor looked at Zach. "This is going to be a highly emotional situation, Zach. Can you manage it? Lots of New York Italians, it's a lot to take in, are you ready for it?"

Roxanne spoke, "We need to go see Poppi. Dad, it's really bad then ..."

Zach finally spoke. "If Roxy needs me, of course I'll go."

Trevor viewed Zach differently. "You're a good guy, Zach, this will not be easy. I need to check on your mother, Roxy."

Trevor walked into their bedroom. Gina was on the floor crying and throwing clothes into a suitcase. "Trevor, tell me, do you think he's going to leave me? My father and I don't always agree, he has a huge personality, but I can't have him leave me yet. I'm not ready, and my mother. Franny is probably at his side with rosary beads, praying."

Gina was still sobbing hard.

Trevor knelt down next to her. "Baby, pack the reasonable essentials, we can buy whatever we need. We will stay at your parents' house."

Gina shook her head. "We will stay at the Carriage House if it is still livable. Trevor, I can't imagine. My father is the strongest person I know. To have this happen. Baby, I guess we should get to the airport and figure it out from there."

Trevor lay on the floor with her. "Gina, I know how upset you are, Mario has helped us so many times. Hurry, baby, so we can get to the airport. Did you pack for me?"

Gina, through her tears, said, "Of course I did, I don't think you've ever packed for yourself."

Trevor checked on Roxanne and Zach. "Pack up whatever you have. We can always buy what we need in New York."

Since the original one left, Trevor called a cab and they headed to the airport. The mood was undeniably anxious, uneasy. The flight would go through Denver and on to JFK in New York. Their flight would get in around 8:00 p.m.

Trevor called Rio. "Hey, Rio, we are at the airport, we have to fly through Denver into JFK. We don't get in until 8:00 p.m. What's your arrival time?"

Rio exploded, "Our flight is delayed; we most likely will get in around seven fifteen. I have a limo coming to pick us up. I will wait for all of you. We can ride together. I think we should go straight to the hospital. I will have the limo driver drop off our luggage at Gina's house and my parents'. How is Gina taking the news?"

Trevor expressed, "How do you think? She hasn't stopped crying. I might tell her to take a Valium so she's a bit calmer. Rio, how bad is this actually?"

Rio explained, "My father is a basket case; he hasn't left the hospital. He's been crying for his big brother; it's an Italian thing. My mother is there calming him and Franny as much as possible. Of course, Frankie is there, all four of his kids. It's a fucking scene, man, get ready. The doctors still have him sedated to stabilize him. I'm sure we'll all be in the air when they take Uncle Mario in for the operation. I don't know, Trevor, if this goes sideways, it's not good. We'll see when we get there. Try to calm down Princess, she takes this shit extremely hard. You should know that by what you two went through. I'll see you soon, safe flight. Remember, we are family, we will get through this."

The McNaughtons hadn't flown commercial in a long time. With nothing else to do, the four of them sat in first class. Trevor asked if they could be seated at once to avoid being recognized. This was not a trip where Gina or Trevor were giving out autographs or pictures.

Trevor looked at his wife. "Listen, G, I hate when you take your Valium. But I think it's okay in this instance to calm you down a bit. Do you have them with you?"

Gina gazed into space, still teary. "I always have them on me, you're right. I need to relax until I get there."

She took three pills out of her bottle. She asked the flight attendant for a glass of red wine, and Trevor asked for ginger ale.

"Roxanne has never dealt with a family emergency like this one," she said to Trevor. "I'm going to see how she is coping."

Gina got up from her seat. She knelt down by Roxanne, who seemed in a daze. Gina grabbed her hand. "Roxy, try not to occupy your mind with the worst-case scenario. Poppi is a tough guy. With that said, we have no idea what to expect when we get there. Nonna will be a mess, we need to be strong for both of them."

Roxanne tried to scan her mother's face. "I can't help but think the worst. Mom, I know you are trying your best not to show how fearful you are. We went from going to a happy outing to this unbelievable circumstance. It's a lot to take in."

Gina offered up a Valium to calm her down. She refused and said she would have a few glasses of wine to try and mellow out. Gina kissed her hand, then went back to her seat and looked over at Trevor. "This sucks, we have to change planes in Denver. Walk through the airport. I don't want to deal with fans right now."

Trevor held her hand. "Baby, we will do the best we can, I got you."

It was the first time she had smiled since the news of her father. She settled into her seat for the hour-and-a-half flight to Denver.

An issue suddenly dawned on Gina. "Trevor, we abandoned the RV. We have no idea how long we are going to be gone. What's going to happen?"

Trevor told her he spoke to the management of the park; they would charge them while they were away. After buying the Boise house, Dennis Tate mentioned knowing someone who could drive it to their new home.

Gina noted that all changes happened so fast; she usually considered those details. Trevor took care of his wife. He took care of the minor details before they boarded the plane.

They got to Denver and had to go across the airport to another terminal. The airline said they would drive them in a cart so fans wouldn't run up to them. Of course, Roxanne looked disapproving. Why did her parents have to be rock stars? People always wanted a picture and an autograph. She hated it.

The first class from Denver to New York was much nicer. A meal was served, which Gina ate. Trevor did the same. They figured the minute everybody got to the hospital, who knew when they'd eat again?

Trevor lifted the armrest so Gina could lean into his arms. Both tired, they fell asleep for about an hour. Gina felt the pressure in her ears and knew the plane had started to descend. She reached into her bag and popped a stick of chewing gum in her mouth. It was her ritual while flying. She opened the shade on the window, and there it was. Gina always thought the New York skyline was the most beautiful sight, she missed New York.

She never pretended that she was a California girl. Her life was now there but her love would always be New York.

She offered a faint smile, then said to Trevor, "Trev, we're back in the greatest city, where we fell in love."

Trevor smiled. "It is an impressive sight, isn't it?"

STONY BROOK, LONG ISLAND

TREVOR CALLED RIO, "What terminal are you at?"

"Dude, I'm at United, where are you?"

Trevor sighed, "We're in United, where the fuck are you?"

Then Trevor looked at the arrivals for Rio's flight, they were about ten gates apart. Rio had been waiting by the gate he and Jae exited. They all met up.

Gina leaned on Rio and burst into tears. "What if he doesn't wake up after the surgery? Are they doing all the procedures possible? What did Uncle Tony tell you? Please, Rio, you always keep things from me. We are blood, this is our family in crisis. Don't hold back on me."

Rio knew his cousin was hurting. "Gina, we won't know anything until we get to the hospital. Try and stay as calm as you can. Aunt Franny is worn out and tired but won't leave. You need to take care of her. Can you do that?"

Gina stiffened up a bit. "Of course I can, it's my mother. If she doesn't listen to me, she will listen to Trevor, she loves him."

They waited for the luggage. The limo driver walked over to the group and told them not to worry about the luggage; he had someone to help load it up. They all sat in the limo while the driver and an agent from the airline packed the trunk. Gina stepped out of the car for a quick cigarette break. Her family in the car was looking at her to come in. She didn't care; a smoke was what she needed before the shitstorm that was about to start.

The limo driver said he was ready. Gina got in the car. Roxanne and Zach fell asleep the minute they climbed into the car.

Gina sat next to Jae. "Jae, I've missed you so much. I miss our talks, lunches, all our girlie stuff. I was roughing it with this guy. There were some emotional moments. We can talk about that later."

Jae smiled. "Are you two having fun? You both look so happy to be together, like old times." "Jae, it's better than old times. We discovered so much more in our lives and in our love. Thank you for telling me that day to find it in my heart to let go of the hurt, anger, and jealousy. To allow the man I love back into my life. Jae, I will love you always for that."

Rio looked on. "I don't really want to bring this up now, but are you both ready to reboot Perfection? Start recording and writing again?"

Gina wanted to blast him, but it wasn't the time. "Yes, Rio, Trevor and I are dedicating ourselves to the band with more energy. I don't want to talk business now. Once we deal with this situation, we will talk about Perfection's reboot."

The weary passengers sat back as they waited to get to Stony Brook Medical Center, which was further out on the island than where they lived. It was quiet, and it was getting late. By the time they reached the hospital it would be close to twelve thirty. The six travelers were exhausted and would soon have the reality of the situation smack them in the face.

Gina knew they were getting closer. She knew the neighborhood; twenty minutes and they would pull up to the hospital.

Gina cried again. "What if we're too late, it's taken us almost an entire day to get here. I wouldn't be able to say goodbye."

Trevor wrapped her up in his arms and allowed her to cry it out. "G, let it out now, you need to be strong for your mother. You can do this; we haven't gotten a call, right? Someone would have called me or Rio. Get that out of your head."

Rio began tearing up himself. "Gina, Trevor is right, Uncle Mario is fighting in there. Don't let those thoughts enter your head."

The limo stopped at the hospital entrance, and they all filed out. Rio tipped the limo driver and reminded him about the luggage. The driver told him not to worry, that Uncle Tony had taken care of the limo charge and tip.

First stop was the information desk. Gina asked, "My father, Mario Ricci, where is he? Please tell me his room."

The nurse said he was in the cardiac unit, but there were so many people there she didn't think six more people would be allowed.

The nurse next to her waved them on. "Mario Ricci, yes, he is in Room 505 of the cardiac unit, go right up."

Gina raced to the elevator and waited for everyone to pile in. There was silence as the floors passed by. As soon as they exited the elevator, they saw a nurse's station ahead. Trevor asked for Room 505, they directed them to the room. A small waiting area was arranged near his room, with the rest of the Ricci family all in attendance. She hugged her Uncle Tony and Aunt Deidre. Her uncle looked worn out. She knew Rio would comfort his father. Gina gave an obligatory hug to Frankie and said hello to MaryAnn.

Gina ran down the hallway, Trevor tried to keep up with her. She opened the door, afraid of what she would see. There was Franny looking extremely tired, not her put-together self.

Franny saw Gina and let out a cry. "Princess, you're here. I'm waiting for your father to wake up. They performed the surgery already. The surgeons said it was successful. What does that look like exactly? He hasn't woken up yet."

Franny sat in a chair next to Mario with her Bible and rosary beads. Gina went to hug her mother.

Franny let herself cry. "Princess, it's not your father's time, I know he will come back to us. There is still so much to do. Why him, he took care of himself, Princess."

Her mother let all her emotions out to her daughter. Gina held back tears. She knew Franny never let that veil down.

Here she was, on her daughter's shoulder, crying nonstop. "Mom, it's okay, look at the monitor, his heart is working. He's been through a major operation; his body is trying to recover. I'm sorry it took us so long to get here. We hoped we would arrive before or during the surgery. We did the best we could."

Franny whispered, "Gina Annamarie, look at all those tubes and IVs in his arm, I can barely see his face. Your father is under all that. He is not going to be happy when he wakes up, that's for sure. Trevor, Trevor, where are you?"

Trevor peeked in. "I'm here, Franny, I'm here."

Franny flung herself into his arms. "Trevor, why did this happen to my husband? He clutched his chest and fell. I was so scared. They brought him back twice. It was horrible."

Trevor was out of his element. Dealing with Gina was one thing, she was his wife. Franny was different. But he remembered that day when she came to visit him in rehab, he was so raw. He felt so defeated and Franny made him fight.

Trevor hugged her. "Franny, Mario is here and he is alive, that SOB is a fighter, you know that. He has all of you who love him. He can hear us talking about him right now."

Rio came in, he didn't see his mother or father. "Aunt Franny, it's me, Jae and I came to be here with you."

Franny hugged them both through her tears with love that all the people she needed were there.

Gina asked, "Where is Frankie and his gang? And where is Ant?"

Franny said, "I sent Frankie and his four hoodlum kids home. I know I shouldn't say that. I feel Frankie is waiting to take over the business. If your father doesn't make it, Frankie thinks he would run Ricci Inc. with his sons. I won't have it. I couldn't take it. Ant is still trying to get here; he's been stuck on a case in Dallas. Is my Roxanne here?"

Roxanne heard her name. She didn't want to go into the room, but she heard her Nonna ask for her.

She popped her head in. "Nonna, I'm here," she said, fighting back tears of fear and sleep deprivation. "I'm so sorry for Poppi. He is going to get better."

Franny pulled her in. "My sweet Roxanne, Poppi knows you're here. Heavenly Father is telling him. I'll get more chairs, let me buzz the nurse."

Rio asked if Franny knew where his parents were. She told him they were sitting in a waiting room that was for their family. She warned him that his father was extremely upset and his mother was keeping him from a meltdown. Rio and Jae went to find Tony and Deidre. Poor Zach was left alone in the hallway. Roxanne pulled him in.

"Nonna, this is my boyfriend, Zach, he came to be with me."

Franny Ricci was a mess but in perfect Franny Ricci form when she saw Zach. "What a pleasure to meet you. How nice of you to come all this way to be with our sweet Roxanne."

Even on ridiculously hard hospital chairs, Roxanne's and Zach's bodies gave up and they crashed.

Trevor looked at Gina. "There's a hotel ten minutes from here, I'm going to get about four rooms, these kids need to get sleep. I'll step out for a minute and make the call to get rooms. This way people can shower and sleep if necessary."

Gina looked scared. "Don't leave me!"

Trevor promised, "Baby, it will take five minutes, it's for all of us. We will all be close; you know it's the right thing to do."

Gina looked afraid. "Come right back, I need you."

He kissed her on the forehead and told her not to worry. As Trevor walked out, two nurses came in to check her father's vitals.

Gina asked, "What are you checking for? Is he doing better?"

The nurses offered calming smiles and said they would check on him about every twenty to thirty minutes; they had a monitor for her father at the nurses' station.

Franny looked up from her rosary beads. "Gina, you and Trevor are happy again? He loves you immensely, Princess, you realize that."

Gina told her mother, "Yes, Mom, we are happy and dealt with some of Trevor's very emotional issues. No worries."

Franny gazed at her daughter with red eyes. "I heard some lies. I knew that Rio, and of course, Roxanne, would know exactly where Trevor was. Never once did I think he took another woman. I'm sorry I never told you I visited him."

Gina was honest with her mother. "I'm not mad. I'm actually thankful."

Franny, tired and distraught, told her daughter, "Gina, he's a good man. He was so afraid of losing you. Those stories I hear about you aren't true, you can tell me. That Paul Ryan person, saying horrible things about you, Princess."

Gina was emotionally burned out. "Those stories are lies from that asshole Paul Ryan. Mom, not one of those are true. Now isn't the time to discuss that."

Franny acquiesced. "Gina, you are correct. Your father is our focus. I just needed to know you are happy."

Gina tried to smile. "If I haven't said this to you, I love that you have so much affection for my husband."

Trevor walked back into the room. "I got five rooms for a few days. People can rest, take showers, whatever. It's really late. I will talk to Rio. Gina and I will stay here with you, Franny. I called for a few cabs to take Roxy, Zach, Rio, Jae, Tony, and Deidre to the hotel. Let them rest so they'll be fresh for tomorrow. You good with that, Franny?"

Franny Ricci looked wrung out. "Trevor, thank you for taking control. I trust you. Please oversee all this, they are all here for Mario."

Trevor told the family he was having them shuttled to the hotel close to the hospital. Rio was appreciative, his father looked exhausted. As they all were. It was close to 2 a.m.

Trevor added to Rio, "Please keep your phone close, in case something dramatic happens."

Rio looked down, "Hey, man, Trev, let's hope he wakes up. I can't imagine the ramifications. My father is on the edge. Princess will be inconsolable.

Similar to when she was missing you. But worse. Can I ask, where the hell is Ant? It's like he has disappeared from this family."

Trevor told him that Franny said he was working on a case in Dallas, that he was trying to get there.

Rio looked through his tired eyes, "Trev, man, something isn't adding up with him. I'm not buying it; there is a bigger picture here."

Trevor shrugged his shoulders. "That's what Franny said, don't know. I need to go back to Gina. Are you good? Rooms are reserved and confirmed? Please make sure Roxanne is taken care of."

"I got you, bro, no worries. You two staying here?"

Trevor eyed Rio incredulously. "Do you think I'll get my wife to leave? We will stay here with Franny."

CRISIS AVERTED

BACK AT STONY BROOK HOSPITAL, Mario Ricci's machines were beeping and showing his heart rate, pulse, and other vitals. Gina would look over every few minutes, she had an idea of what were acceptable numbers. The nurses, knowing who was in Cardiac Room 505, brought another cot for Gina and Trevor. It wasn't for sleeping as much as a softer place for them to sit. Trevor leaned back and closed his eyes. Gina wiped the hair from over his eyelids.

Gina whispered to her mother, "Mom, why don't you take one of those hotel rooms and rest? You have been here for almost two days. I'll be here if anything happens."

Franny Ricci stared into her daughter's eyes. "Princess, let me ask you, would you leave Trevor in a situation like this? I think not. I have been married to your father for almost fifty years. I haven't left his side; I won't do it now."

Gina knew there would be no separating them.

Trevor opened his eyes and whispered to Gina, "I need to walk around, maybe find some caramel macchiatos that you love. I'm spent, baby, this has been a week."

Gina whispered back to him, "Franny needs to walk around. It's not good for her to sit in that chair all this time. Why don't you invite her to go with you?"

Trevor kissed her softly on her cheek. "I'll try my best. Anything for you."

Trevor stood up and looked at the clock, it was slightly after 6:30 a.m.

"Franny, you look like you need to stretch your legs. Let me take you to the cafeteria, you can't sit here without food. When Mario wakes up, he'll need you. Please take a walk with me, like I once did with you."

Franny was afraid. "If he wakes up, I won't be here. He'll wonder if I left him here."

"Mom, I'll be here," Gina reassured her. "If he wakes up, I'll call Trevor. You need to eat and walk around. Please, don't you trust me with my father? Please go."

Trevor held out his hand. "Come on, Franny, you have no choice."

Franny went with Trevor, she trusted him. She also wanted to have an important discussion with him.

Gina sat next to her father for about an hour, staring out the window and trying to tame the thoughts running wildly in her head. Then she heard some beeping and looked over to see Mario slowly opening his eyes. He glanced down at the tubes, wires, IVs all over him. And then over to Gina.

He said in a raspy voice, "Princess, why are you here, what's going on, where am I?"

Gina cried happy tears this time. "Daddy, you had a bad heart attack. The ambulance rushed you here to Stony Brook. They had to do an operation; they performed a quadruple bypass surgery. You have been out, sedated, in surgery and now in recovery. Please, you need to remain calm. We are all here, me, Trevor, Roxy, Rio, Jae, Aunt Deidre. Uncle Tony is bad, he's so worried. Let me call Mom, she's been sitting here for the whole time with her rosary beads and Bible."

Mario Ricci was a man who had to have complete control, but he was most definitely not in control of his current situation. He croaked, "Princess, not yet. Let me sit here with you. What the fuck is all this shit on me?"

Gina laughed through her tears. "That shit is keeping you alive, so don't even think of pulling anything out. Daddy, it's okay to be vulnerable. I know you think you're Superman, but you need to reel it in a bit. Actually, a lot."

Mario was becoming a bit more talkative, using a soft whisper. "Princess, how are you? Did you and Trevor make things better? You should never throw away a marriage that God put together. That's why the church is so important, you both made that commitment. That fucking guy. I wish I hated him, but I know he makes you happy. Princess, you made him a better guy. Your mother cares deeply for him. She says if he could love our princess, he's got to be a good guy. I also know he didn't come from a Ricci-family type of life. It was rough for him."

The monitors alerted the nurses that Mr. Ricci in Room 505 was up.

Mario started coughing and the nurses came in. "Mr. Ricci, nice to see you up. What is your pain level on a scale of one to ten?"

He looked at Gina, whispering, "Are they fucking kidding me, it's a frickin' ten, give me better drugs."

Gina looked disapproving. "Dad, they are here to help, you need to stop … I promised Mom I would call her when you woke up. I don't want her pissed off at me. Anything else you want to say before they come back?"

Mario moved his head slowly. "Yes, Princess, I love you. I know you are stronger than your brothers. You always have been the one, my strongest child. You made a beautiful life for yourself. Don't be mad at your husband for fucking up one time."

Gina tried to hold back the tears. "Daddy, Trevor and I are good, we love each other, we are all good. We each went through our own hell. But we are better for it. Can I call them now?"

Mario coughed, whispered, "Princess, I need you strong. Can you be that? Your mother won't leave me. Watch over her. Because I can't do a frickin' thing. I can barely see you." Then he softly added, "Yes, do it, Princess, call your mother. Franny has her beads and Bible?"

Gina laughed. "You know she does. I'm calling …. Trev, babe, bring Franny back. My father is awake."

Gina walked to the hospital door and peeked out. Rio, Jae, Uncle Tony, and Aunt Deidre were gathered in the waiting area. They still looked exhausted and were wearing the same clothes from the night before. It was about seven thirty when the family arrived.

Gina watched as Franny grabbed them. "Mario is up, he's awake, come. Tony, you need to see him. See, our Lord wouldn't take my husband yet. It's not his time."

Gina saw Franny touch Trevor's face and kiss his cheek. "Let's go see Mario. Franny, he probably wants to go home now," said Trevor.

Rio put his arm around Trevor. "Bro, you have always been a part of this family from the beginning. Are we getting a new, improved Trevor for Perfection?"

Trevor smiled. "A better man for many reasons. Come on, let's see Mario."

Gina was back sitting next to her father when Franny and Uncle Tony rushed into the room. Franny had given in to tears. She couldn't figure out how to kiss him with all the tubes and IVs. Gina got up to allow her mother to be next to her father.

She found his cheek. "Mario, you scared me, I thought I was going to lose you."

Uncle Tony's tears were flowing. "Jesus, thank God, my brother is alive. I can't wait to punch you for scaring the shit out of me."

In Mario's inevitable fashion he said, "I don't like all this fucking shit all over me. I'm not going anywhere anytime soon. Franny, my love, we have much more life to live. Capiche? Tony, do you think I would leave my little brother? Hey, we're a team, bro, I'm not going anywhere. Who else is here? Rio and Jae, you flew out here to see your sick uncle? Rio, you're a good boy."

Gina piped up. "Daddy, Rio is not a boy, he's a fucking grown man with a wife. You kill me. Sorry, shouldn't have said that. We are all here, you are the king of this family, Daddy. You are a handful, but you're our lynchpin."

Mario looked around. "Where's Roxanne?"

Trevor told Mario, "She was exhausted. I got hotel rooms ten minutes away."

Mario spoke in a scratchy voice, his throat still irritated from all those tubes. "Trevor, thank you, I think some of you should get some rest. You and Gina have been here without sleep. Franny, my love, you should get some rest at the hotel."

Franny was adamant. "Mario, no way I'm leaving, don't think about it. I want to talk to the doctors."

Gina accepted that her mother wouldn't leave. "Mom, at least rest on the cot to get some sleep here."

Gina asked the nurse for some pillows and blankets.

Franny looked at Gina and Trevor. "Gina, I want you to know it was upsetting to see my son-in-law so raw. I prayed for you and Trevor every night. I always knew Trevor was talented and loving. Don't let those demons come back. Both of you remember your vows of faithfulness. Trevor, I love you, I wanted you to know that."

The couple was a bit choked up by Franny's admission. Both knew how impactful Franny's feelings were.

Trevor was surprised. "I don't know what to say. I mean, I love this family. You and Mario have been so generous to us. Knowing you care for me like a mother. I'm at a loss for words."

Doctor Alex Wong, the cardiac surgeon who performed Mario's procedure, entered the room. "Mr. Ricci, you're awake, fantastic. I see you have your entire family here. You gave every person here a scare. But the surgery went well, we should have you out of here in about a week. Now I need to examine this patient. I need to ask you all to leave and give the patient some privacy."

Franny looked at the doctor, disbelieving. "Doctor Wong, correct? I am not leaving my husband. Whatever you say can be said to me with my husband."

"There she is," Gina whispered to Trevor. "Franny Ricci."

NEXT MOVES

GINA WAS DRAGGING AND ASKED TREVOR if they could go to the cafeteria for caffeine, the hot kind. She grabbed Jae's arm. "You guys should come with us. I haven't seen you in forever. I missed you. Let's go gab."

"Uncle Tony and Aunt Deidre, we're going to the cafeteria. You both go visit with Dad. We will see you all later."

It was a little after 9:00 a.m. as Trevor, Gina, Rio, and Jae walked to the cafeteria.

The four exhausted rock stars navigated the hallways to the cafeteria. Trevor and Gina didn't get any sleep. Rio and Jae rested at the hotel but looked tired and ordinarily unfamous. *Would anyone recognize us?* They were in their old territory, Long Island, where they launched their careers. Not one of them cared. It had been over a month since they were all together, so they bought some hot drinks and sat around a table to catch up. Gina knew Rio would bring up Perfection. She wouldn't be angry; a nudge from Rio might help. Trevor seemed stronger.

Rio laughed. "It fucking took Uncle Mario almost dying to get us together. What's going on in your heads? We have a band that is waiting to work, we can't do that without you two. What's your solution?"

Gina smirked. "Rio, you are so fucking predictable, I knew that would be the first thing you would talk to us about. It's not my decision. Trevor has to feel that he can take the pressures of the band on and not want to use. I'm sorry, baby, I don't know the right words. Trevor is my world, that's what I care about. I can sing, I can write, I can take care of the business. I'm ready to take it all on, but it's Trevor's decision."

Jae smiled. "Gina, you have your fire back. I remember the last time I saw you was to say goodbye for your RV trip. You looked scared. But this is the Gina we all love, that bitch who won't take any shit."

Gina grinned. "Thank you, Jae, I appreciate the compliment. Seriously, I have written two songs already. I'm sure I have a few more in me."

Rio looked at Gina. "We need you writing some killer lyrics. We owe Los Angeles a show, we have to honor our commitment."

Trevor asked, "How many venues are asking us to do a show? They would need to be spread out over the year. I'm not ready to go back on tour yet. We should have some of our latest music."

"Trevor, man, I need you. Ian, Jeff, and Kevin have been great but they aren't you. The guy who plays the best guitar, plus a killer voice. Don't forget you're composing the music; you are the strongest. Even stronger than me, that's saying something."

Jae asked, "Don't you miss your home in Montecito? I go and check on Marisol when I can. She is holding down the house."

Rio added, "I need to know what you're thinking, Trevor."

"I feel like I want to play, Rio. I do miss performing. My mind sometimes goes back to the last concert, the state of confusion that happened. I never want to be that guy again."

Gina interjected, "I would like to spend a couple of weeks in the new house we bought in Boise. It's chill. Not Los Angeles. Would you and Jae would like to come to Boise and we can map out songs?"

Trevor cut in to voice his concerns. "We have a huge problem, and this is paramount in my mind. Paul fucking Ryan. I want to destroy him. He is one delusional man."

Rio knew this would be Trevor's hot button. "I talked to our lawyer; he doesn't have a lawsuit. Are you still going to pursue the lawsuit for slander? Skip said the judge is about to issue a restraining order. I know you sent a cease-and-desist letter. Honestly, Ryan is talking to whoever will listen about Gina. What the fuck did you do to that dude?"

Gina, furious, stood up, stomped her feet, and felt her blood rise. "What did I fucking do, nothing! What the hell, Rio, we need to stop this bullshit, especially if Perfection is coming back full-blown. I won't have people talking about this shit. I emphatically won't, it hurts me and it hurts Trevor. We can't take the stage with this out there. Skip never got rid of Mayfield, as I had asked. I told him we didn't need a public relations firm, then we got Ryan. Skip ignored my feelings. What should we do?"

"I was the one who saw Gina every day," Jae broke in. "I saw her broken, depressed, crying. I was heartbroken for her."

Gina teared up. "Jae thought it was a healthy idea for me to get away from the house, all the memories. Ryan brought those tickets over. I didn't want to go, but I finally caved in."

Jae added, "Gina was hurt by not knowing everything. I remember my words to her, letting her know that Rio told me that when you two first met it was electric. It was immediate, that you were meant to be together. I asked her to find it in her heart to forgive and let all the pain go. I can tell that story to anyone who will listen to me."

Rio held Jae. "Baby, I'm sorry I lied to you and to Gina. When I hear you tell the story, it makes us look horrible. We did what we thought was the best, obviously it was wrong. This guy wanted to come home to be with his wife. That was motivation for him to get the hell out—"

"I want to tell the real story of who Gina McNaughton was when neither of you were there. Gina, I want to go on TV with you and tell the story. Do you think that could help? Are you strong enough for it?"

"Jae, yes, I am, even if I lose it, it gives credibility. It's the truth, I can relive it, knowing that Trevor and I are happy. Our marriage, well, is stronger. I'm good to get it out there. It's the typical he said, she said, but two women talking about it makes it more believable. That will win every time." She asked Trevor, "Baby, are you strong enough to let me talk about this?"

Trevor was firm, "If it means destroying Paul Ryan. This should be the last time we discuss a man who is truly mentally unhinged. Although, Gina, we did tell Skip we did not want to do any more interviews. Remember, we agreed it gives legitimacy by being dragged into a *he said, she said situation.*"

Rio agreed. "Don't you remember Skip didn't want to add credibility to Ryan's accusations? Why are we changing things?"

Jae had made up her mind. "Rio, I love you no matter what, you know that. But I really think I can help with the Paul Ryan situation. Perfection can be that band without any bullshit attached to it, please let me do this."

Trevor looked at Gina. "I know we said no. Let's do this only one more time from your and Jae's perspective. Then we legally deal with him. Just one more talk about this."

Rio, outnumbered, gave in. "So, that's the play. But do it as soon as you get back to Montecito."

Gina boldly said, "I'll call some people I know and arrange it. You didn't answer my earlier question. Will you come to Boise after my father is cleared to go home? We can do the interview there, away from the mess that's happening in California. We can play music there. Rio, you need to get out of the studio and free your mind and write. Trust me, it is liberating."

MARIO DODGES A BULLET

GINA STOOD UP QUICKLY. "Oh, shit, we should get back to Dad."

They walked quickly to Mario's hospital room.

Franny looked hopeful. "Doctor Wong said your dad is doing well after the surgery. His vitals are good. But all the tubes and IVs have to stay for now. The blood flow to his heart is great. My prayers were answered."

Gina looked at Mario. "Daddy, you need to be a good patient if you want to go home. No pulling out anything. They opened up your chest, which has to heal. Are you listening to me?"

Mario was exasperated. "Princess, I can't stand being this fucking guy in a hospital bed. I have a business to run. I can't trust Frankie to think things through."

Rio stepped up, "Uncle Mario, that's why you and Dad run the businesses. He'll take care of things."

Mario sighed. "You're right, Rio. My brother has always been my partner. I need to trust him."

Gina and Trevor were dragging, shuffling along the hallways, yawning. Their clothes were getting uncomfortable. Gina needed to wash her face, she felt filthy. It was about 11:30 a.m. No sleep.

Gina said, "That's settled, do you mind if we go to the hotel and get sleep? I haven't slept for over twenty-four hours."

Franny ushered them out. "Yes, go, I have a cot, blanket, and pillow. They gave your father a sedative for sleep. I'm going to lower the lights and try to sleep a bit myself. I know it's still morning; we are all exhausted. So go, all of you. I'll see you later this evening, or better yet, tomorrow morning, not too early, please."

Kisses were exchanged. Rio called a cab, they got to the hotel, got their key cards, and said their goodbyes.

The McNaughtons fell on the bed, exhausted mentally and physically. Their bodies ached from sitting on the cots in Mario's room. Gina fluttered her eyes at Trevor and touched his face. "I love you, so many emotions going on at the same time, my head hurts. I wish I had a joint."

"Seriously, G, that's what you want to do now?"

"Babe, I don't have the energy for a playdate now."

Trevor got closer. "No, like you said, way too many emotions today."

She rolled on top of him. "Trevor, I want to discuss the ways we demolish Paul Ryan. And I would love to make Mayfield disappear; I hate him. Can you help me take my clothes off? I have buttons on the back of my dress."

Trevor was tired also. "No playdate, sleep, yes."

After a refreshing nap, Gina had the hotel call a cab for her, Roxanne, and Zach, Jae, and Rio. Trevor stayed back in the hotel to relax. It was midafternoon as they climbed into the cab and headed to Target. Gina had never been to a Target, which Roxanne found hysterical. It was an experience. She picked out some clothes and toiletries and found some new treasures, along with an item that would alter her appearance.

Roxanne pleaded, "Mom, I'm starving, can we go and eat?"

Gina said, "Of course, I think we are all starving. Isn't there a TGI Fridays next door?"

Roxanne said, "Let's get cleaned up first."

They headed back to the hotel and Gina knocked on her door; she had no idea where she had put the key card.

"Gina, is that you?"

"Trev, who else would be knocking on the door?"

He opened the door, still wrapped in a sheet.

Gina laughed. "I wish I had the energy to take advantage of this look. Our daughter is really embarrassed by us. She didn't want to see what I was buying because we sell sex for a living. I told her we weren't porn stars. Are we sure she's our child? We didn't raise her that way."

Trevor looked through the bags. "This stuff is decent. I'll wear it, wait, junk food, Gina you're bad."

Gina smiled. "Even though my dad escaped a life-and-death situation, I'm still looking at you in a sheet and I find it hot. I need to find my shampoos and stuff; I have to take a shower badly. I feel my skin crawling. I don't think the shower is large enough for a playdate."

"I think maybe we could try if you're up for it. After dealing with our daughter, who might turn you off."

Gina laughed. "Well, I'm going to take a shower, what you do is up to you."

Gina jumped in and made it nice and hot, it felt good to get clean.

Trevor sauntered in as Gina was leaving.

"Trev, hope you still have hot water."

He didn't care; he felt filthy from the whole trip. He wanted to wash off the plane, the trip. They toweled off and scoured through the treasure trove of clothes from Target. They still looked like the stars that they were.

Gina surprised Trevor. She clipped in the hair extensions she had bought and faced him with her new long blonde hair.

Trevor looked up, astonished. "What did you do?"

Gina was disappointed. "I thought you would like me with longer hair. I can't stand that everywhere I look, women have my haircut. I wanted to be different, maybe people won't recognize me. You don't like it?"

Trevor came up to her and put his arms around her. "I have a really sexy wife, I do like it. Is this something you are going to wear daily?"

"I don't know, I can switch it up. Trev, you know me, I always want to look different."

Trevor laughed. "I wonder what our daughter will think … Are we going to eat? Please say yes, I'm starving. Afterward we can decide what to do with the rest of the day. Franny said we should come back tomorrow morning, but I still feel we should poke our heads in."

"Babe, we all are hungry. Let me give Roxanne a quick call." She called Roxanne's phone, "Miss McNaughton, are you ready to eat? Your father is starving."

Roxanne grunted, "Well, we have been waiting for your call, we're ready. All cleaned up."

"Okay, meet you downstairs."

They reached the lobby, where Rio, Jae, Roxanne, and Zach were waiting.

Trevor couldn't help himself. "I see we are all clean and in our new Target outfits."

Rio looked over at Gina. "What the hell did you do with your hair?"

Gina rolled her eyes and curled her lip. "I like to be different, I'm tired of seeing my haircut on other women, so I bought extensions. I can be whoever I want, I bought assorted styles. You won't know what Gina you're going to get."

Jae was so excited. "Gina, I love this idea, a distinctive look for every mood. I think it will be great for shows."

Rio added, "If we ever get to play shows."

Gina stared down her cousin. "Stop being an asshole, you know that's what we're working toward. You still haven't given us an answer about Boise."

Roxanne stared at all of them. "Are we going to eat or are you all going to bicker about the band?"

Roxanne looked disapproving. "For the record, Mom, there you go again, always trying to be sexy Gina. Long blonde hair, now you fit in perfectly in California. I don't know why you are always changing your appearance, Mom. Are you trying to get attention? Ugh."

Trevor jumped in, "Let's go eat at Fridays and then get to the hospital, we will only stay for a bit. Roxanne, you need to be nicer to your mother, all she does is for our family. Let's go."

The group was appreciative of Fridays' extremely large menu. There was food all over the table. After paying the bill, they called a cab to get to the hospital.

Rio and Trevor figured out they would need to rent a car. Gina agreed that eventually they would need to drive to the Ricci estates. Especially if they were going to stay for a week or so. It was more practical than taking cabs.

They got to the hospital, went straight to Mario's room. He was sitting upright in a chair attached to various tubes and IVs.

Franny was excited. "Doctor Wong wanted your father to sit up after surgery, it helps in the healing process, preventing blood clots and allowing the blood to flow. It's a miracle, truly." Mario looked lovingly at his wife. "I can't fucking take being hooked up to all this shit. They said if I behave, I could go home in about five days. They want to make sure my chest is healing. They opened my whole frickin' chest."

"Daddy, it's called open heart surgery, so yes, they want to make sure your incisions heal correctly. We are going to be here until you go home. Daddy, I looked up how long your recovery looks like. After you leave the hospital, you have six weeks to take it easy at home. Then twelve weeks is your goal for a total recovery. Mom, are you looking for nurses for when he gets home? He won't listen to you."

Franny threw Mario a look. "Gina, you're correct, your father will try to work around me. I'll talk to Doctor Wong about hiring someone. Don't you all look clean. New clothes?"

Roxanne came over and kissed her poppi. "Yes, Nonna, my mother had never been in a Target store. We all did some shopping so we have clothes for a few days while Poppi is in the hospital. Zach and I have a few weeks before we need to go back to school. Football and cheerleading practices start in July. I would like to go home to Montecito for a bit."

Mario spoke, "Roxy, you go to Stanford, really competitive. I'm glad you still do the cheerleading, and Zach, you play football at Stanford? Maybe I should start watching."

She answered, "Yes, Poppi, I am. I'm sure I have been on TV. The entire world knows who my parents are, so they love to catch me on the sideline, it's so annoying. I'm hoping to be a co-captain this year."

Mario looked at Roxanne lovingly. "We would be proud to see you be co-captain. What an accomplishment. Roxy, you have famous parents, that shit is always going to happen, you have to suck that shit up, baby girl."

Franny detected something different about Gina, "Princess, you look different."

Gina sighed, "They are called hair extensions, they are real hair and I want to change my look up."

Franny looked at Trevor, "Trevor, what do you think about the new look?"

Trevor smiled, "Gina looks beautiful. No matter what she does with her hair, I'm good with it." The nurses came in and did their vitals check and asked if Mario was ready to eat something.

He answered, "Are you giving me real food or that Jell-O, broth crap?"

"Mr. Ricci, you are on a heart-healthy, low-sodium diet, so, yes, that is what you are getting. If you are good, maybe we can give you oatmeal."

The nurse left, and Mario made an appeal. "Can one of you get me some real food, maybe a calzone or something?"

They all laughed and told him no way; his diet would be changing once he got home. Mario wanted to lie down. Franny aided him to the bed with all the IVs and monitors. They all sat around telling old stories, and Mario talked about various clients he thought were jerkoffs.

He looked at the "crew" and told them all he was tired and wanted to rest for the evening.

Franny pulled Gina over. "Remind me to talk to Serena about accommodating his new diet. You are correct, his diet has to change, he won't like it … Have you been to the house?"

Gina shrugged, "No, Mom, the limo dropped us off, all our stuff is in Manhasset at your house. Why, you need me to go over to the house?"

Franny whispered, "Gina, I would feel better if you told Serena about changing your father's diet. The nurses have nutrition plans for us to take home."

Gina offered up, "We need to rent a car, it will be easier than taking cabs. I might fly Roxanne and Zach back to Montecito. She wants to spend time at home before she and Zach go back to school. After we drop them off at the airport, I'll stop at the house. By the way, did you do anything to the Carriage House? Or is it the same?"

"Gina, it's honestly the way you and Trevor left it, except no kitchen supplies. I believe someone packed those."

Gina smirked. "It was actually Ant, where is he, Mom?"

Franny looked down, her face drooped, her disappointment obvious. "Ant is an important prosecutor in Dallas. He has a case he can't leave. I know it's killing him not being here."

Gina duly noted that exchange, she would need to dig deeper into that.

Trevor excused himself to get the car. He found an Avis car rental in a shopping area near the hospital. Trevor called ahead to reserve a car to transport everyone.

He whispered to Gina, "I got a van. We need to move folks around. If Roxanne wants to go home, we need to get her to the airport. We can take care of some things for when Mario goes home."

Gina felt overloaded. "Thank you, Trev, for taking care of that. I'll miss Roxanne, but she wants to spend time at home. Marisol will be happy to have her home. It will be so much easier for us. You have to pick it up from Avis, please take Rio to get the car. Take him and try to nail his ass down about Boise. We can get some real music writing done while his mind is relaxed. I know Jae wants to come."

Trevor kissed Gina on the forehead. "Rio is starting to annoy me. He acts like I don't care about the band. Why would he think that? It's ridiculous. We created this together! I'll give him a *talk*. I won't be too long; I'll get Rio to come. Can you check out flights for Roxanne and Zach? I'm glad she wants to spend time back at home. I think tomorrow would be great."

Gina smiled. "Agreed, yes, let's get her and Zach home."

Trevor and Rio went to get the car and Gina called the airline to get tickets. She motioned for Roxanne to come into the hallway. "Delta has two flights that would work for you, one at 11:00 a.m. or one at 3:30 p.m. The other flights are either too early or later in the evening. Which one, sweetie pie, works best for you?" She silently hoped she'd pick the later flight.

Roxanne was fine with the 3:30 p.m. flight. Gina was grateful. Her plan was to let her see her poppi before she headed to the airport. Then Gina and Trevor would go to Manhasset and talk to Serena. Gina thought she could take a minute to spend time with Trevor in their first home together. The home where their love blossomed. The Carriage House.

Franny told her family it was okay to leave for the evening; she loved them all but even she needed rest.

Now with the ability to drive around, Uncle Tony wanted to take the family out to eat. He knew a great Italian restaurant nearby. With the Ricci connection, especially in Long Island, the eight family members were given the best table in the restaurant.

They were all more relaxed knowing that Mario was doing well. And Aunt Deidre absolutely loved Gina's hair.

She told her, "When I was modeling, they would put all types of pieces in my hair for crazy photo shoots. Some were actually quite nice. But Gina, you can rock anything. Good for you, don't listen to Rio, what does he know? He has had the same hairstyle since he was a teenager."

Gina laughed and gave him the finger, reminding him of those teenage years. Bottles of wine were delivered to the table. She was curious how Trevor would react in a social situation, he simply asked for sparkling water. Gina knew Roxanne was watching him. She was still concerned about a slip in his sobriety.

Roxanne announced that she and Zach would be leaving tomorrow. She enjoyed seeing her family, even though it wasn't the best situation. Various family members told her it was good to see her. Uncle Tony ordered a special dessert for the table, zabaglione, with fresh fruit. It was Gina's favorite Italian dessert next to Italian pastries.

After the restaurant they rode back to the hotel and said their goodnights.

Gina reminded Roxanne, "Get all your things together and I'll get you a suitcase tomorrow. I'll send your other luggage to the house. Your father and I are going to Nonna and Poppi's house. You and Zach have some rest, you'll be on a plane for five-plus hours. Your father and I will be going back home to Montecito. We will have some time together at our *real home*. Love you Roxy, don't forget that."

Roxanne sighed. "I know that, sometimes it's simply hard to be the daughter of Gina and Trevor McNaughton. The world thinks you're so cool, it can be a lot. I have to learn to deal with it better, you both aren't going to change."

Gina smiled. "No, sweetheart, it's what we have done our whole lives. We love what we do and we make people happy. That's a special gift to give. You want to be a child psychologist; think about how you will change some young person's life. It will be so rewarding. My dear child, goodnight, see you in the morning for breakfast."

They kissed goodnight. Trevor had parked the van and shouted, "Roxanne, doesn't your father get to say goodnight?"

Roxanne ran up to Trevor and flung her arms around him. "Good night, Dad, I see you are staying away from alcohol. I'm proud of you."

Gina smirked at Trevor. "She is still that little girl who thinks her daddy is the greatest."

Trevor glanced at Gina with his arms folded. "You aren't jealous of that, are you?"

Gina laughed, considering what Trevor just asked. "Absolutely not, are you serious? She was always a daddy's girl, that's all. You are still her number one, over Zach, which should make you happy."

Trevor took that information in, happy he was still Roxanne's number one.

Roxanne and Zach flew home the next day. Marisol would pick them up at the airport. Gina reminded her to call when she got home.

GINA
GOES HOME

TREVOR GLANCED AT GINA. "I'm so happy Roxy chose to spend a few weeks at home. We should be back before she leaves to go back to Stanford."

Gina agreed; however, she was more excited about the prospect of going back home. "Baby, you are correct. I'm accustomed to it being solely us, without our daughter judging us. Trev, she has her opinions, all we can do is love her no matter what she thinks."

Jae was silent in the back seat until the subject of Roxanne came up. "You know, Gina, you would think she would be more sympathetic to you since she kept the truth from you. You are the best mother. I remember when she was born. I don't know kids, I don't understand them. But both of you have given her so much."

Rio was waiting for his chance. "Are we going to talk about the band right now? I mean, seriously, we need to. If Jae and I come to Boise, we can do writing, and maybe we can plan some dates to play venues. I mean, Skip would arrange them, but we could pick the best ones. Promise me that we will do that."

Trevor smiled. "Rio, I'm still working out some of my rehab moments. I feel stronger but need a couple more weeks to relax. When Gina and Jae do this last interview, we have to relive all the crap. The falsehoods about my wife and me. Being uttered by a psychopath, truly he is. Mayfield is a problem we will have to deal with once back in California. After the interview, I promise Perfection will be at the top of the list. You should take advantage of the relaxation in the surroundings you'll be in. You need to get off the merry-go-round, my friend."

Jae agreed, "He does need to relax, he is wound up so tight. Rio is always too focused on Perfection. You know you are, babe. I know I'm going to enjoy Boise."

Trevor passed the gates to the Ricci Estate and drove down the street to Rio's parents' home.

Rio looked at the house. "It's been a while since I've been here, it's still home. Mae probably has something special planned for my return. Okay, you two got what you wanted, we're coming. We have to decide what time we are going to the hospital tomorrow. May I suggest getting there around ten or eleven? Jae and I are going to crash hard."

Gina smiled. "You both have fun crashing. How about ten thirty, we will split it down the middle."

She looked at Trevor. "Are you excited about going to the Carriage House? I totally am. I do have to talk to Serena before we get settled in, though."

Trevor understood. "Do we need to take her shopping?"

Gina laughed. "Are you kidding? She has a Ford Expedition, she's fine. I'll give her a list of suggested meals from the doctor. But honestly, I'm not sure how she is going to feel, not cooking all those special Italian meals. I'm doing my part for whatever Franny needs. I'm actually starving."

Trevor looked at Gina. "Baby, we're on Long Island, we'll order takeout."

Trevor punched the code to the gates and drove past the Carriage House, where Gina and Trevor's brilliant love affair began. They continued up the winding, immaculate driveway to her parents' immense house. They let themselves in.

Serena came out, surprised. "Oh my goodness, Princess, look at you. I have missed you. Long hair again. Trevor, how are you?"

Gina was happy to be home. "Serena, I wanted to give you a suggested meal list for Dad when he comes home. He can't eat pasta every day. He needs to have a special diet, especially for about three months. Are you good with that?"

Serena surveyed the meals. "Princess, if Mario needs to eat special, we cook special. He gave your mother and I a scare."

Gina smiled. "Serena, I knew you would appreciate the situation. Mom has to get a nurse when he comes home. She'll keep him in line. If you need me, we are staying at the Carriage House."

Gina kissed Serena goodbye. "Serena, our luggage was dropped off. Do you know where it is?" Serena walked over to the dining room. "I had them drop it all here. I will see you again, Gina?"

Gina hugged her. "Of course you will. We are off to the Carriage House."

Gina couldn't hold her excitement, she felt it was so special. They parked in their old spot; they carried what they had and ran up the stairs. Gina still had the keys on her key ring. She opened the door and turned on the soft lights, it transported her to their first night.

She went into the bedroom. "Oh, shit, Franny wasn't kidding, it's exactly how we left it. We took the bed for the Hollywood Hills house, there's no mattress."

Trevor was practical. "G, there is another bedroom we can sleep in."

Gina countered, "Maybe by the fireplace. I know it's not freezing but for the mood. The comforters are still here. We can cuddle up by the warm fire and relive some of our best memories."

"I agree, but our best memories are still in front of us. I'm not going to lie, thinking of some really sexy things we did here?"

Gina smiled. "That's my husband. What should we do first? Let's find our luggage and see what we want to eat. Oh, I'm thinking I want to take a shower."

Trevor grinned. "Gina McNaughton, you are a temptress."

They opened their suitcases, pulled out their new clothes, plus what they had packed from Boise. They hung them in their old bedroom. Gina picked out all her special toiletries, found towels, couldn't wait to take off her clothes. Trevor heard the shower; he walked in without hesitation.

"That didn't take long," Gina said coyly. "So, what's your move, Trevor?"

He smiled at her and showed her his move, one that he had used on her many times. It felt like they were in their twenties again.

Gina packed the beautiful satin robe Trevor bought her and slipped it on after her shower. She removed her hair extensions and met Trevor in the bedroom. "You still love me, baby?"

He shook his head. "Crazy woman, what do we want to eat?"

Gina's head was running through all the choices, shouting them aloud, making faces with each choice. It came to her, she punched Trevor's arm. "I want Thai food, we haven't had that in a long while. Pick what you want, I'll order. Do you plan on being naked for the delivery?"

Trevor pulled out those old, raggy, torn sweatpants.

Gina smiled. "After we get our takeout, I know you have many moves left to show me."

Trevor was a bit confused. "G, are we pretending to be who we were here over twenty-five years ago or who we are now? I'm trying to get my libido in the right direction."

Gina pondered that question. "That's an interesting thought, Trev. Do we want to be the twenty-somethings that lived here or us now? The couple we are now is beautiful. We have lived a full, happy life with one hiccup. Something we learned from both of us. I like who we are now, people who are more mature. We have a deeper sense of our love. Can you get your libido in that direction?"

Food was delivered with extra paper plates and chopsticks. Gina opened the bags and set them up in the living room. "Now eating this could get me excited, I'm starving."

Trevor laughed. They sat on the living room floor and turned on the TV. Gina flipped through the stations; she couldn't believe what she landed on. The Entertainment Channel, and there he was, Paul Ryan.

Trevor was angry. "Turn that shit up, I want to hear what that asshole has to say now."

Gina knew Trevor was fuming. "Trevor, don't get upset; whatever he says we'll deal with it. Jae and I will do that interview, I believe it will go over well."

Trevor, enraged, insisted, "Gina, turn it up."

Ryan's interviewer, Susan Fine, one of the minor interviewers from Entertainment Channel, asked Ryan a question.

"So, how do things stand with you and the band Perfection?"

"They fired my firm with no real grounds. I believe Trevor McNaughton was behind the firing. He is afraid of me being near his wife for obvious reasons."

"You believe there were no grounds for your firing. However, you claimed you had a solicitous romantic relationship with Gina McNaughton. All indications are that those accusations aren't true. Don't you feel that is a good reason for being fired?"

"Who is saying that it didn't happen? They wouldn't know the truth."

"Paul, people are asking why you are so focused on Gina McNaughton. She has been a happily married woman for years. What made you think she was interested?"

"Sometimes you meet someone and you can feel their interest. I met Gina at a meet and greet many years ago. She was extraordinarily interested in what I did for a living. I believe by her taking time with me that she was interested. She couldn't act on that attraction because her controlling husband was close by. I built up my public relations firm with many rock bands and other celebrities. I hoped over those many years that I would get to work with Gina. Once I started working for Perfection, I knew Gina would be interested, away from her husband."

"Paul, that is quite a story. You are saying that you waited years to get to a woman who has never once mentioned you. Of course, she is calling you a liar. I admit this seems a bit unbelievable, maybe a dream on your part."

"Susan, sometimes relationships take time to marinate in a person's head. I knew Trevor McNaughton had issues. I was gladly there for her when it all fell apart."

"Paul, Gina and Trevor McNaughton have always been in love, it's hard to believe that she would run away from that relationship. It is known that Trevor has had some issues with his sobriety, he worked hard on getting better. I personally believe that she wouldn't start a heavy romantic relationship with anyone. As it turns out, they are back together and seem extremely happy."

"Of course, they are in a deep codependent relationship, he rules what she does. She's afraid to go against him."

At that point, Trevor threw something at the TV. "What the fuck is this guy doing? If this is a way to get you, this is some fucked-up way. People know some of the insane shit he has done. Legally, this is an issue we will manage. Gina, we need to exploit his delusions and obsessions. I'm sure the public will see him for a deranged lunatic."

The interview continued.

"Paul, I know that Perfection and the McNaughtons are about to sue you for slander, perhaps other issues. Why would you continue discussing this matter until the legal issues are resolved?"

"I have nothing to hide and Gina knows I will always be there for her. I promise to be ready when she needs me."

"You really don't think that would happen. Again, I know the McNaughtons have taken a trip to reconnect. Personally, Paul, I don't see Gina McNaughton doing anything like that. Well, thank you, Paul, for your side of things. It remains to be seen what will happen next."

Gina looked over at Trevor's shaking body. "Babe, I know you are jumping out of your skin. I believe we found our interviewer; she seems sympathetic to us. I would like to approach her for an interview, sooner rather than later. We should fly her to Boise. I want this shit finished by the time we reboot the band. I don't want fans, anyone for that matter, to think Paul Ryan has any place in my life. He just showed his psychotic nature."

Trevor, frightened, wild in his thoughts, "Gina, would you go to him for any reason if we had a fight? Would you run to him?"

Gina looked astonished. "Trevor McNaughton, I swear, what the fuck is in your head? How could you even think that, after all we have been through to push past this insanity? I have told you, showed you how much I love you. The fact that you would say that to me right now is extremely hurtful. I thought we were going to have a sexy night together, but you hurt my feelings on such another level. I can't believe you right now."

Gina ran off into the bathroom, angered and wounded by Trevor's comments.

Trevor's phone rang, it was Rio. "Dude, I hope you weren't watching TV right now? Paul Ryan is a firestorm we need to extinguish immediately. Trevor, you there?"

Trevor was deflated as he answered, "Yes, I saw it with my wife. I asked her if she would run to him if we had a fight. I totally fucked up with Gina, she's crying."

Rio was pissed. "Trevor, why the fuck's sake would you say that to her? Gina fucking loves you more than her own life. Bro, I don't know how you are going to make this better. Fucking fix it."

Trevor sighed. "My insecurities got the better of me, it reminds me that I'm still not fully recovered if I can say that shit to her."

"Trevor, you better do something, women hold onto that shit. Make it better." Rio ended the call.

Trevor hated the idea that any man could cross over into his territory, the love of his wife.

Trevor's phone rang again. He saw it was Roxanne; he wasn't going to take the call.

He walked to the bathroom door. "G, I know what I said was wrong, I own that. My own fear got the best of me. Please open the door. I still want a romantic night with you."

"Are you serious now?" she yelled through her tears. "Why would I want you to touch me after what you said? How hurtful, Trevor. Do you not trust me? I have never given you a reason not to trust me, but you have. I still found it in my heart to forgive you. How dare you say those things to me."

Gina was sobbing as she spoke. Trevor knew how to unlock the door and did so. Gina was sitting on the floor, crying her eyes out.

He tried to touch her, she jerked away. "Don't touch me, you don't trust me."

Trevor begged, "Baby, I am insecure when it comes to that man. You can't even believe how painful it is when a man tries to invade your world, your woman, your life, it's staggeringly personal. I lost control, lashed out, and that was wrong. I learned all about misplaced feelings in that facility. I had been doing it my whole life, until you showed me what love was like. You are the person I always wanted. Please let me see your face, I hate when you cry."

Gina looked up at him, tears streaming down her face. "I want you to see me cry. I want you to see what I did while you were gone. This is the way I looked; do you think it looks attractive? This is the way Paul Ryan got to see me when he came to our home. I honestly thought we'd have a romantic night here together. Here, in the place where our love exploded, and you ruined it."

Trevor got teary himself. "Baby, let's have that romantic night, we can still do that. Your husband couldn't help himself. I'm insanely jealous of this crazed man. That's my problem to work out, it's not you. Gina, please ..."

Gina threw her arms around his neck. "Don't ever, ever question where I want to be. I'm right where I need and want to be." She leaned over and grabbed his face. "I love this face, I loved it for over twenty-three years, with those beautiful blond curls and all that facial hair, look how we grew up. I still think you're the sexiest man." Gina sniffled. "I get you're still working out some feelings and how you deal with them. This is one I will oversee. Me and Jae, the truth. Can you fully trust me?"

"Obviously, I trust you, my entirety. Can we make up?"

Gina laughed through her tears. "Baby, do you mean make up or make out?"

Trevor looked up. "Possibly a bit of both. Can we finish our cold food?"

Gina cracked a smile. "We have a microwave, you know."

They turned off the TV. They both had phone calls from Roxanne, but no need to call back right away. They finished eating, somewhat quietly. Gina sat in Trevor's lap on the floor, touched his face, unshaven and full of love. She went into their old bedroom, brought in the two comforters, laid them down, and piled the pillows on the floor.

She dropped her robe, her naked body in front of him. "Trevor, what's your next move?"

He stood up and ran his hands all over her body, she melted at his touch. He kissed her neck; she drew his body into her and started kissing his neck. Her hands slid off his sweatpants. They stood with nothing on.

She kissed him, and he picked her up and laid her down by the comforters. "Baby, I'm going to love you in every way."

Gina smiled. "I didn't expect anything less. You didn't take one of those pills?"

Trevor was surprised. "No, not at all."

"Too bad!" she teased.

They soon fell asleep, fully spent.

WE GOT OUR INTERVIEWER

IN THE MORNING GINA FOUND coffee and a French press, along with some Styrofoam cups that would work. She brewed a fresh batch and handed one of the freshly poured cups to Trevor.

Gina offered up, "We agree, maybe calling Roxanne right now is not something either of us wants to indulge in."

Trevor was aggravated from the interview. "We not long ago dropped her off. I could use a few days of no Roxanne. She probably called about the Ryan interview. I know it upsets her, I'm not ready to have that conversation with our daughter. What she saw must have been hurtful. We will call when our emotions are in check. In total transparency, your cousin called last night. He was freaking out about the Ryan thing. Rio is tremendously fixated on getting Perfection back to work. Any part of the Paul Ryan story, he wants dealt with before we get fully back to the grind."

Gina sipped from her cup. "Trevor, let's get them to Boise and I'll make arrangements for the interview. Get that distraction done and work on our music. We still have a few more days of dealing with Mario. Getting him home, a nurse to watch him, then we can slide out. Franny will want things her way. She needs to be in control … Can we stop by a bagel shop so I can get a good New York bagel?"

"You can always have what you want. You were demanding last night, I loved it."

Gina smiled slyly. "Trev, that's why it's called make-up sex, I make up what I want you to do. I'm going to take a quick shower. We ought to be at the hospital soon. We have to pick up my noisy cousin. It's amazing that Jae puts up with him. But she loves him."

Trevor winked at her. "G, some people might think that about us."

Forty minutes later they picked up Rio and Jae.

Rio asked politely, "Did you two have a nice evening last night?"

Gina knew where he was going. "Yes, we did, it was a late night. What about you? Did you have fun *crashing*?"

Gina knew she hit a nerve with Rio; he was quiet about his sex life with Jae. He always knew that Gina and Trevor needed their *alone time*. However, Gina knew through Jae that Rio was extraordinarily needy in their relationship. They too needed time alone. She would never reveal what she and Jae spoke about, that was their bond.

Gina broke the silence. "Hopefully Dad is progressing nicely and that incision is healing. Franny won't leave but she does need to go home before Dad does. She will need to interview nurses; they are both massively meticulous in who gets into the Ricci Estate. One of us needs to stay with Dad and try to pry Franny from the hospital. Trev, babe, I think that's you. She loves you and will listen to you. I can manage my father. Rio and Jae, I'll need your help at the hospital. Uncle Tony will be there, you will have to neutralize him, Rio. He will want to be with Dad as much as possible. You and I can manage those Ricci men."

Jae went to a place Gina was hoping no one would mention. "Gina, that interview last night was horrific. I can't figure out how someone could go on TV and blatantly lie. We need to get our interview out there."

Gina sighed. "Well, I was hoping we wouldn't go there, but yes, Jae. I want that interviewer. I want Susan Fine to come to Boise. We do our interview with her as soon as possible. Are you ready for that? It may get messy. I believe she will be open to hearing our side, which is the truth."

Trevor was getting uncomfortable hearing the conversation. "All I want to say about this is, show Ryan to be the villain. An obsessed man, that is who he really is."

Rio looked at Trevor. "Hey, man, don't fuck with your hands. We need them, he's not worth risking your livelihood."

Gina slammed the car door and pointed her finger in the air. "We are here at the hospital, no talk about Ryan. We're here to make sure my father is going to go home soon. We need to get him better. So we can move forward with Perfection."

They arrived at Mario's room; he was back in the chair, with less tubes.

Franny was excited. "Doctor Wong said your father's recovery is moving faster than he would have thought. We are hoping he can go home in two days; that's wonderful news, isn't it?"

Gina was happy that Mario would get to go home soon. "Mom, if that's the case, we need you to go to the house and find a nurse. I'm sure if you ask at the nurses' station, they could give you names. You can't interview here; you want them to see the house. There are a lot of stairs. You may have to turn your office into a room for Dad."

Mario was staring at both his daughter and his wife. "You both are talking like I'm not fucking here. What the hell, don't I get a say? I'm still the head of the household."

"Dad, you need to slow it down for a few more weeks. You can't go into the office yet. We know you, the Italian Stallion, you are not. Please go with the flow. We want that strong ass man we all love. Don't be mad because we want the best for your recovery. Mom, do you want me to talk to the nurses?"

Franny never missed a beat. "Gina, you are correct, they need to see the house. I want someone who appreciates our need for privacy. If I go for a few hours, who will stay with your father?"

Gina explained the plan. "I'll stay with Dad if you're okay with that.

Trevor will take you to the house. Let's set things up for tomorrow. This way there are plans in place for Daddy's return home."

Franny was amenable to this plan. The two couples stayed for a few hours, to make sure plans were made. Mario was moving around a bit. Gina felt that the Ricci family dodged a bullet, her father would rebound. It was lunchtime at the hospital, Mario reluctantly ate the bland hospital food that he was served.

Frankie and MaryAnn came to visit with their four adult children. Gina couldn't figure out what she didn't like about them. Franny had the same misgivings. Franny asked Gina to stay longer since Frankie and crew were there. She felt more at ease with extra people around.

After a short visit, Mario told everyone to go home. It was about four thirty in the afternoon. Mario was working hard on his recovery. He wanted out of the hospital. He felt that he could work on his strength with less people around.

Ant was still wrapped up in a particularly important federal case and couldn't make it out to New York. Gina felt bad, she would have liked to have spent time with him.

Franny told the family it was all right to leave. Tomorrow would be an early day.

The four younger Riccis got into their van, along with Uncle Tony and Aunt Deidre. They were dropped back off at the hotel. It was an exhausting day at the hospital. Gina couldn't wait to get back to the Carriage House and take a shower.

PERFECTION'S RETURN

ON THE RIDE HOME, RIO PRESSED HARD about the band. "Why don't you two go back to the Carriage House, take a shower. Then Jae and I will come over. Let's look at the venues and start plotting out our shows."

Gina kept quiet, she wanted Trevor to speak on this. "Sure, Rio, I know you are anxious about Perfection's return. I'm not making promises yet. Still, let's look at the top ten. Are there more than that? I might be open to a couple more dates."

Rio had a spark. "Yeah, man, we have about twenty-five medium to large venues that would like us to do a stand-alone concert. Skip needs to start planning months before we play. You know the circus, Trevor; we got to get in."

Trevor relented. "Fine, we will look at things. No calls to Skip yet. You have a car at the house, so you bring over some kind of takeout. Jae, I'm sorry, you will be bored as hell."

Gina sat back and let Trevor take control but added, "Don't come over right away, seriously, I need to take a shower. You know hospitals have tons of germs floating around. I have to wash them off of me."

Rio laughed. "Sure, Gina, we know. Therefore, you two fuck your brains out, it's cool."

Gina was pissed. "Let me ask you, my cousin, my brother, why is our sex life so dominant in your head? Have I ever asked you about what you and Jae do in your sex life? I would never. So why is our life so interesting?"

"Because you put it out there onstage every time you perform. It's cool, people love seeing it. I also remember when you two first met. You needed to have your *alone time*. Come on, Gina."

"Rio," Gina scolded. "Please don't bring it up again. It's getting old."

Trevor nicely said, "We'll see you later, around seven-ish? Bring food, we don't care what."

As soon as they stepped out of the car, Gina went on a rant. "I swear, I hope he is different when he and Jae are alone. He is being a dick, a little bitch, because he has to have his way with Perfection. What is it going to be like when they come to Boise?"

Trevor calmed her. "He is being a little bitch. We do have to start moving on things, though, Gina. Clearly our sex life is on Rio's mind, have no clue why. Imagine what other people think."

Gina smiled. "People think we are much in love, that's fine with me. People can imagine whatever they want."

The two arrived at the Carriage House. As they entered, Gina was already pulling off her clothes.

Trevor followed. "So are we having a playdate? Or did Rio ruin it?"

Gina smiled as she pulled off her bra and lacy panties. "Nothing he can say can ruin this." After the shower ritual, Gina put on some cozy sweatpants and a tank top. Trevor did the same and took out the two guitars he had with him.

He looked at Gina. "I would love to put music to 'Almost Done.' We would have to add more lyrics. But I think it's a great song for our fans. Our song about what we went through and how we came out of it. What're your thoughts?"

Gina got close and smelled his clean body. "I love that. Tommy has other ideas, reworking some of our unreleased music. We can do new music and also remaster what we have. I love you, Trevor McNaughton, I know I overreacted last night. We can't let anything or anyone divide us." Trevor put the guitar down. "G, I never should have said what I did. I never doubt your love. Ryan is so irritating me; I took it out on you."

Gina added, "When do we address Brian Mayfield working with Ryan? I still want to see Mayfield deported. I will chase down the band he is working with. I'll talk to their manager and try to get him out of Los Angeles."

The doorbell rang. Rio and Jae were holding two bags of Chinese takeout.

Jae came through the open door. "We didn't know what to get, so we got about the entire menu."

Rio had handwritten notes that he took from Skip. "Can we eat and discuss at the same time?" Trevor looked completely relaxed. "Yeah, why not."

They sat at the table with paper plates and napkins; each piled their plates.

Gina asked, "Don't you think New York Chinese takeout is better than any other place?"

The group laughed, off to a good start. Jae likely had a talk with Rio.

Rio dove in, "Gina was correct, the first show we do is in Los Angeles. We owe them a concert. Red Rocks would like us to come back; we could do a live recording. Vegas would like us to spend three nights at Caesars, but that counts as one venue. Madison Square Garden would like us to have two nights, again, one venue. I would prefer doing a live recording at MSG, it's our home. Miami would like us to come back, requested Gina wear something see-through. We have requests from Canada, Trevor. Vancouver and Toronto would be in the top ten. Milwaukee has an open-air concert. Sturgis Motorcycle Rally and Daytona Bike Week want us. Hardcore rock is what they want. I heard they are nuts, definitely necessary for our comeback. Orlando wants us there badly, with the amusement parks, that's a sellout. Last in the top twelve. Get ready, Gina. An appearance on the kickoff show for the Football Conference Championship. Don't say you don't love that."

Gina looked at Trevor. "That's impressive, it is more than ten shows, technically it's fifteen. Are the other contenders as good as these?"

Rio said, "There happens to be one show we have to do. The Daisy Point Rock Festival at Jones Beach. There are five top bands, no headliner, you get a slot, you could be first, middle, or last. I don't know how they choose."

Gina looked at Trevor. "Anytime I can play back here, I'm in. Now that there are sixteen shows, we will write our latest music. We trinkle it out as we play. Something new, it gets exposure. When we put out an album, some of the music is already out there."

Trevor thought, "These performances aren't one after the other, they are distributed over months. We could put together an album, as Gina said, introduce a few songs. I'm guessing after we put a whole album out, we would tour again."

Gina needed to give a hopeful message. "Baby, we might not tour for a year or so, you'll be strong enough."

Trevor thought for a minute. "I like these stand-alone shows, but G, those motorcycle rallies can get extremely outrageous, half-dressed women all in the audience. You need to contain your jealousy."

Gina laughed. "Who said my outfit won't be outrageous?"

Rio threw a shrimp in his mouth. "We are clear on this; I'll call Skip tomorrow and tell him we have all five members in agreement. This is a major step, I feel better about going to Boise now. Let's celebrate, I have a few joints."

Gina glared at him. "Hold on, all five members, did you talk to Ian and Jeff before us? I don't want Skip confirming any venue until I am on the call with him. You understand, Rio, that's why I am involved in the business end. And yes, I would like to indulge in that joint. Rio, of all people, you know that Trevor can't smoke weed."

Rio apologized. "Geez, shit, I can't believe I forgot. No, I haven't, but they want to play, surely they will be on board."

It was mostly Gina and Rio smoking a joint. Jae indulged a little. That work plus the weed made the group tired. Good nights were said.

Gina shut the door. "That sounds like some impressive plays. How are you feeling about it all?" Trevor grabbed her face. "G, I feel like I want to get back out there. We need some Gina opening covers. The audience loves seeing you do an incredible cover, parading your stuff. Think about it."

Gina smiled. "I will be super sexy. On another note, I have three names from the nurses for Franny to interview. The interviews would start at eleven thirty. Can you get Franny back to Manhasset by eleven?"

Trevor agreed he could. They got ready for bed and agreed they would sleep in the guest bedroom, and sleep was all that was on their minds.

BAGELS
FOR MARIO

THEY GOT UP AROUND SEVEN THIRTY to get ready to go to the hospital. Gina made coffee and called Trevor; he was slow to get up this morning. They got dressed and drove to the hospital.

They stopped at Gina's favorite bagel store in Manhasset along the way. She got a bagel with lox spread, and some extra bagels for the house and hospital.

They went directly to Mario's room. "Hey, people, look at me, I'm walking around."

Franny looked a bit concerned.

Gina asked, "Dad, should you be out of bed or your chair?"

Franny interjected, "The doctors want him to walk around, get his feet underneath him. He's doing remarkably well. We are still hoping he can come home tomorrow. A day earlier than we originally thought. It's God's work."

Trevor encouraged Franny. "Speaking of Mario's departure, we need to get you to Manhasset to interview nurses. There may be traffic on the expressway."

"I don't want some person dictating every move I make," Mario declared. "Especially someone I don't know. Trevor, can you vet these people? I don't want just any person in my house."

Franny touched his arm. "Honey, don't worry, I won't have anyone take care of you that I don't feel comfortable with. Gina talked to them; she knows what would be acceptable."

Trevor was trying to get Franny out the door.

Gina moved things along. "Mom, you need to leave now with Trevor. I'll be here with Dad. If you need to know anything important, I'll pass it on, go."

Trevor grabbed some of Franny's belongings and gently touched her arm. "Let's go, Franny." He finally got her out the door after a bunch of kisses for Mario.

Gina sat down, opened her bagel, and started enjoying it with her latte.

Mario was salivating at the scrumptious treat in her hands. "Princess, you're eating that in front of me, you kidding me right now?"

Gina apologized. "Dad, I'm hungry, sorry. Did they change your diet yet?"

"Slightly, I can eat toast, fruit, and oatmeal still."

Gina pulled a bagel out of the bag. "Here, take one, don't tell anyone I gave it to you. I'll deny it anyway."

Mario smiled. "I taught you well, Princess, deny, deny until you get caught, and if you get caught, still deny … I heard the nurses talking about some interview that prick Paul Ryan gave. I believe your mother caught some of it. You want to talk to me, Princess?"

"The nurses were talking about the interview? What did they say? Mom watched some of it?"

Mario cut her off. "Princess, does it matter? This prick is starting trouble for you and your husband. I heard he had some nasty accusations against Trevor. I know it's not true, Trevor never had a chance to control you. If it were the other way, I could see you holding his balls in your pocket. You need to come back at this jerk off, Princess. How do you plan to attack him?"

"Trevor is extremely hell-bent on going after Ryan. It hurts him very personally. Ryan said I would run to him if I ever had a fight with Trevor, he would be waiting for an eternity. The interviewer rebutted most of what he said. She seemed to believe our truth. I know Rio is afraid to put Jae out there for an interview. She wants to do it, her idea. We will sue the SOB for slander, and our manager has talked to a judge about a restraining order for Trevor and me. Plus Perfection."

Mario lay down. "That's my girl, go after his jugular right away. Fuck me, Gina, the whole family knows how much you love your husband. The whole frickin world, Princess. Take him down, and if you need help, you tell Uncle Tony and me, if I'm able to do anything."

Gina smiled but was teary. "I know I could come to you, that would be easy. There may be a time when I need your help. Trevor and I have to attack him as a unit. With no question anyone ever doubts what we say. We aren't going to talk about that bullshit. Can we drop it for now? What are you most excited about going home?"

Mario yawned. "Sleeping in my own bed, knowing your mother is right there. Having Serena cook some awesome food—"

"Daddy, you know they don't want you walking up and down stairs for a while, things might not be exactly the way you want, but you will be home."

Meanwhile in Manhasset, Franny interviewed the three candidates Gina found. She picked an outstanding, qualified nurse, Renee. She understood discretion and was qualified with cardiac patients. Franny liked something about her, that's all that mattered. She could start the next day, even if Mario didn't come home. She would get things organized and institute any changes.

Trevor sat in the kitchen with Serena as she fed him breakfast and kept feeding him. The two enjoyed talking.

Serena mentioned, "I heard some man on television talking about you and Princess. The Riccis could help."

Trevor laughed. "I'm aware of that, this is personal. Gina and I are content in our life. We bought the house in Boise for winters and family Christmases. Roxanne loves to ski. After things settle down here, we are going there for two weeks with Rio and Jae. Write music, make plans for Perfection, it's time to go back to work."

Franny walked into the kitchen, overhearing some of the conversation.

Franny smiled. "We are lucky that Jae is truly a Ricci, fighting for this family. After I finish this tea, I'm ready to go back to the hospital. If Mario doesn't come home tomorrow, it will be the next day. As soon as that happens, I want you to go to Boise. I'll be fine, it's been a week, I love that you all came. It's time, Trevor. You and Gina need to get back to what you do. If I need either of you, I will reach out. Be the rock stars that you are and take care of the Ryan situation." She kissed Trevor's forehead.

Franny was ready. "Trevor, I would like to get back to my husband, and it's about an hour away, hopefully no traffic." She said goodbye to Serena and walked outside to the car.

Back at the hospital Gina and her father were talking about some fun times they had as a family. Gina understood that even though her parents seemed distant when she was younger, the Ricci family actually had many fun family trips. She looked at the time. Trevor should be heading back to the hospital. She turned on the TV, hoping she wouldn't see anything about her and Trevor. She turned on the Sports Channel, she knew her father loved all things sports. No mention of celebrity news. About an hour and twenty minutes later, Trevor and Franny walked through the door.

Franny went up to Mario and planted a sweet kiss on Mario's lips, then summoned a smile for Gina. "How has the patient been. Behaving?"

Gina winked at her father. "Yes, he is doing well. He is keeping up with sports, which makes him happy. Did you find a nurse that fits Franny Ricci's qualifications?"

Franny was impressed by the amount of detail her daughter put into her request. "The list you gave me was impressive. Renee, a qualified cardiac nurse, will start tomorrow. She wants to prepare the house for when your father comes home. I'm happy I didn't have to ask. Excellent job, Princess, knowing what your father and I would find acceptable. Sweetheart, they are keeping you one more day, they want to make sure your chest is healed."

Mario threw his hands in the air and uttered Italian swear words. "Franny, my love, I sincerely want to go home."

"Dad, one more day isn't going to hurt. It would be reasonable to listen to the doctors."

Mario was ticked off. "Fuck me, one more day, I think I'll go crazy. The food sucks, I got nurses checking everything, I mean everything. I don't like these nurses checking in on the privates. You get me? I feel violated. Damn."

Gina grinned. "I guess we will stay one more day, Daddy, next we are off to Boise. Don't you want to see us one more day?"

Franny looked at Gina and Trevor. "Now that you are together, can you explain this man, Paul Ryan? Why does he continue with lies about you? He seems to live in some type of fantasy world when it comes to you, Gina. Please tell me you have a plan to refute him."

Gina dropped her head and took a deep breath. "Mom, I don't really want to relive this again. I spoke to Dad about it. We are overseeing this personally and legally. Jae and I are giving one more interview with that woman who interviewed Ryan. That's it, no more, please, can we not?"

Franny looked at Trevor. "This is the plan, Trevor, you agree then?"

Trevor scowled. "This is personal. I am not a violent man but I would love to hand this guy his balls on a plate. Fuck him up badly."

Franny winked. "Trevor, we know people who could do that for you."

Gina announced, "We bought the house in Boise to relax. That's what we plan to do."

Mario was firm. "Princess, I love seeing you, we all need to get back to our lives. That includes you. Promise me when I get out, you'll leave for your new house."

Trevor reassured him, "We will look into getting a private jet, how's that?"

Collectively they agreed that it was a great plan and were sure that Rio and Jae would agree. Gina and Trevor said goodnight and took the ride back to the Carriage House.

MAKING PLANS
FOR BOISE

"SHOOT! TREV, REMEMBER, ROXANNE CALLED each of us after Ryan's interview? We need to call her back, or maybe you should call her. Let's tell her we have things under control. Roxanne worries about us. She's already pissed off."

Trevor grabbed her hand and kissed it. "You are correct, we better call that daughter of ours."

Roxanne picked up after the first ring. "Dad, what took you so long to call me back? Did you think I didn't see that interview? Are you and Mom trying to avoid me?"

Trevor actually said, "Yes, we were. We had our own feelings about it. We didn't want to speak to anyone until we determined how we would deal with it. Roxanne, your mother and I are especially capable at dealing with this asshole. As much as we love you, this is our relationship out there. It's all lies, you know that. I know you're worried that something will go wrong, but your mother and I have always been a team. Please know you don't need to worry."

Roxanne took a deep breath. "Fine, you must have some plan. I guess I'll wait for the next bomb to drop."

Gina heard her. "Rox, there are no bombs. We have a plan, please let us do what we need to do. Don't worry. There are no surprises, you can relax." Gina knew she had to accept the blame. "Roxanne, I am sorry. Your father and I had to digest what we watched. We are pursuing all legal avenues."

Roxanne was resigned. "Okay, I get it, you know what you're doing. That's all I needed to hear. When will you and Dad be coming home? Is Poppi going home yet?"

"Yes, he is going home tomorrow. He is doing fantastic, can't wait to get home. He doesn't realize it isn't Mario Ricci's plan. He will be fine."

Roxanne acknowledged what her parents said. "Well, thank you for the update. Take care of what you need to do in Boise. Zach went to see his parents. Marisol and I are having fun cooking and going out to fun stores and even restaurants. We can't wait for you two to come home. Marisol misses you."

In unison Trevor and Gina said, "We miss you too. Promise, we will keep you updated. Love you."

Trevor had a gleam in his eye. "Now we can enjoy one last night at the Carriage House. How about that?"

Gina smiled. "Are you thinking of a playdate? Because I would love that, it's been hectic. We were making some new memories at the Carriage House. We had that awful fight. Rio, relentless in discussing band business. I believe we lost track of the magic that place holds."

"We won't let that happen tonight, baby."

Gina squirmed in her seat. Having a playdate with Trevor always made her have that feeling, like they had their first night together. Gina remembered how sensual that night was. It was the first time a man made her feel overloaded with emotions. All that trapped sexual energy she never felt. This beautiful, long-curly-blond-haired, half-shaven man had ignited primal feelings. She couldn't believe he would be interested in her. She felt terribly average, but Trevor McNaughton from Vancouver made her feel like a beautiful woman. She remembered how slowly he took her clothes off, both enjoying every minute. It was love, right from the beginning. Gina felt that bolt of lightning run through her body.

They pulled into the Ricci Estate, walked up that flight of stairs, turned on the soft lights.

Trevor pulled Gina into him. "I love where this is going."

"Come over here and make out with your wife."

Trevor leaned over her so she was lying down on the couch. They kissed passionately but in a sweet, loving way. Not like teenagers waiting to get to the next level. Gina took off Trevor's shirt, she loved feeling his chest. She kissed his chest and broke away from their kiss. She quickly moved to start unbuckling his pants, grabbed his soft ass, her hands caressing him.

Trevor was impatient. "Are you playing with me, Gina?"

Gina was full of love. "No, I get excited, having a weakness by touching your body. I've known every part of your body for over twenty-three years. Always you, oh shit, that would be a great song title."

Trevor was stimulated. "Right now, I'm interested in something else from you, not song titles."

Gina laughed. "We want the same thing, go and take it. Like that first night, take it."

Trevor couldn't wait to strip her down. They gave each other all the love they had, like they always had done.

Gina remarked, "I would love to have you all night."

Trevor dragged her to bed. "You are a bad woman, Gina McNaughton."

Trevor called private jet companies in the morning. He wanted a small jet that could fly out of Long Island's MacArthur Airport directly to Boise. He was able to make reservations for this afternoon at 2:30 p.m. The flight would be over five hours. Luckily, they'd gain two hours in time zones.

After Trevor made the plans, Gina called Rio.

"Hey Gina, what's up? You got some good news?"

Gina smiled as she answered. "I do, Rio, we have chartered a private jet for Boise leaving today at two thirty. You in, correct? My parents want Trevor and I to start working again, my father should be leaving the hospital later this afternoon. Franny has a private nurse there already, we can leave. You ready to go to work?"

"My sweet Gina, always flying private. I personally prefer it; glad you were able to get a jet."

"Dude, we always fly private. Not sure what you mean. We tour, it's private, we go on trips, private. It's not new. We rushed to New York on commercial, we had no choice. You make me laugh; we are Ricci's, privileged."

"You are once again correct, Gina. Jae is excited about going. I have no idea why, but she can't wait to go. Now I can tell her we're going. Hey, you don't have a car out there, do you?"

Gina thought about it and Rio was correct, only the RV was there. "Rio, can you rent a car? I need to get ready to go to the hospital. I want to talk to Mario's doctor so I know his recovery plan at home. I feel better leaving knowing what direction his recovery at home looks like."

"Gina, I'll get the rental car for today, no worries. Okay, we doing this?"

Gina simply said, "Get ready, we are off to Zen," and hung up.

Trevor asked if Rio was happy with the itinerary.

Gina wrinkled her nose. "I can tell he can't wait for the reboot. I'm going to try to write that song, 'Always You.' You inspired me."

Trevor smiled. "I'm glad you were so inspired by last night. If you want to write the song, do it."

Gina headed to the bathroom while Trevor tuned his guitars.

"G, we have to go to the hospital for final instructions for Mario, right? We should get there soon; they release your father sometime today."

"Babe, I'm heading for the shower now."

The McNaughtons prepared themselves and drove to the hospital.

Rio drove his parents' car to the hotel in Stony Brook and picked up

Tony and Deidre. He told them he was leaving early in the afternoon to go to Boise with Gina and Trevor. Individually Gina and Rio were taking care of their responsibilities in New York before they left.

Gina yawned while they were in the car. "Trev, I'm so looking forward to Boise. I can't remember what the house looks like. We didn't get to spend any time there … Shit is about to get real again. You can take it on; Trevor, you are the best fucking guitarist."

Trevor smiled. "I'm glad I have my wife's approval. You still feel up for writing that song?"

"I have my notepad. I have it in my head. I can write while you drive."

ALWAYS YOU

I look at my life, a movie played up on the screen, I knew it was Always You. From your first kiss, I dreamed of a life that led us to where we are, that was you and me.

My heart knew it was Always You.

Always you to love me, to be the only person who could make love to me. To excite me the way most people dream that they could feel. We have a life that might seem to some a life filled with lights, a life of applause. We never forget that if I didn't have you, it would mean nothing at all because it was Always You.

Chorus

Always You in the morning to begin my day, to make love to you in the bright of day and in the starlit and moon-filled night making love to you every night. I always knew, it was Always You.

Always You to have and hold. Always You to be my love, a love that lasts for an entire lifetime, I'm lucky to say I have that special feeling that was Always You.

Always You to be my love, Always You to go through the times When life seems so hard, Always You when it just ain't right.

Always You fighting to keep the haters far away and protect the love we share. Always You to keep those fans who want us to share more and our most intimate of details. We both know that we will never share what our private love affair is.

Always You in my bed, making love to each other the way only we can. Always You to hold onto, I never thought through all these years that you and I have something more, most only wished that they could have. Always You, it's Always been just you and I and it will be to the end of our days, Always You

Chorus

Gina and Trevor entered Mario's room. He was sitting on the edge of the bed, waiting for Doctor

Wong to discharge him from the hospital.

Franny was pacing, smiling nervously. She had Mario's things packed. "I'm sure your father will be sent home today, likely this afternoon. Doctor Wong wants to check his stitches. It appears to be healing fantastically. Renee, our nurse, has the house prepared for his return home … We want you two to go to your new home and pick up your careers. Trevor, please tell me you are leaving."

Trevor looked directly at Franny and Mario, "We have a private jet leaving at two thirty today, you are sure it's squared away for us to leave?"

Mario looked at both Gina and Trevor. "Please, get back to your work, which would make us happy. You took the time to spend with us and each other, now go back to fucking work. Be those people who the entire world wants to go and see. Damn, Perfection is your baby. Frickin' go out there and kill it."

Gina ran to her parents. "I love you immensely and I'm ecstatic, Daddy, that you have recovered so quickly. We are ready to go back to work, Rio and Jae are joining us. We will be able to get some real work done."

Franny walked over, gave them a kiss, and told them it was time to go. The McNaughtons walked out of the hospital, called Rio and Jae, and told them to be ready to get picked up. It took about an hour to get to them, and Rio and Jae were ready with their suitcases. Uncle Tony and Aunt Deidre were there to say goodbye to the group of four.

"Go be those rock stars that you worked so hard to be," shouted Deidre on their way out. "We love you all, it's time."

BOISE IS CALLING

OFF THEY WENT TO MACARTHUR AIRPORT to their private charter. They returned the rental and found the hangar where their jet was waiting.

Jae was excited. "I can't wait to see this new house, you must have fallen in love, Gina. Montecito is spectacular, this must be equally beautiful."

They stepped onto the plane and there was a flight attendant with food and drink waiting for them.

Gina plopped down into her seat, exhausted. "Between my dad, Franny, Roxanne, and the Paul Ryan situation, I am mentally drained. I did, however, write a song. I believe we can make it something special, it's a bit of a love song. I think we can make the chorus a bit harder."

"Gina I'm glad you got your sense of writing back. We need you to put words to some of the ass-kicking music I'm thinking of. Trev, you are that star guitarist?"

Trevor sat close to Gina and wrapped his arm around her. "I'm ready, I have my talented, beautiful wife to thank for getting me ready to work. Let's do this, I'm ready to put an end to Paul Ryan also. We're still doing the interview, correct? Did either of you reach out to the interviewer?"

"Once we get situated in Boise, I'll make the phone call to set it up," Gina told her husband. "I'm sure that interviewer will be hot to hear our side of things."

Trevor kissed her forehead. The four of them relaxed for the five-hour plane ride. Once they arrived, Rio found a place to rent a car. The group went to the realtor's office to pick up the keys to their house. Dennis Tate was happy to see the McNaughtons and told them he had a friend pick up their RV and park it at their estate. He also assured them that all the furnishings were in place. The sale of their new home was dealt with without any issues. Trevor thanked him and asked for directions. It had been a while since they were in Boise. Trevor had forgotten how to get to the house. Dennis told them he would drive them there.

"Trev, we haven't even driven into downtown Boise to see where stores and shopping are. Jae and I will need to go buy food. We will take the car and figure out our way around to do some shopping."

They entered the house and it was exactly the way Gina remembered it. She fell in love with it once again. A respite from their crazy life. A home to share with their family and friends.

She twirled around the living room. "Look, three separate places in one living area, we all get to spread out."

Trevor dropped their suitcases in the master suite. He looked around and went into the bathroom. It was how he remembered, but better, like a spa retreat. A shower with two shower heads and two jets. Exactly what he loved to have for his playdates with Gina.

She walked into the room and put her arms around his neck. "I love you, thank you for giving me this quiet space away from the madness of California and New York. It's precisely what we need. Any time we feel stressed, we come here, look at the foothills, and get creative."

Trevor flashed a wicked smile and led her into the bathroom. "I definitely can get creative in that shower."

Gina placed her arm on her hip. "You know what, Trev, I always find it fascinating how your mind goes straight to the most sexy thing. I need to show Rio and Jae to their room. I do need to leave if we want to eat. You don't mind spending an hour or so with Mr. Dickweed, Rio Poole? He will hammer you about the music."

Trevor smiled once again, "G, you go take care of stocking up, I'll manage Mr. Dickweed for sure. But Gina, promise me you will call that interviewer today. I want Ryan ripped apart before we get back to Montecito."

Gina touched up her makeup. "Trev, honey, I promised you it's my top priority. First let me get some stuff in this house. Love you, bye."

Gina called out for Jae. "Jae, you ready to go food shopping in Boise, Idaho?"

Jae pranced out of the fabulous room Gina offered to them. "Gina, this house has such a peaceful vibe. I know you feel it. I want to find a beautiful wind chime. Relaxing sounds, bells set the mood. My housewarming gift to you for the Boise vibes."

"Jae, whatever you like. Let's go food shopping, I'll die if I don't have my morning caffeine. I have to get a barista machine." Gina ran into the kitchen and found the previous owner had sold them the whole shebang, small appliances, dishes, the works.

Gina said, "I guess when we said we wanted the furnishings they took that to mean the entire house. Great for us."

She called out to Trevor and Rio and said they were leaving. The ladies were ready to hit the town.

Trevor and Rio brought their guitars out to the deck and made themselves comfortable.

Rio took in their surroundings. "Man, this is some peaceful place. I see why you wanted a home here, it's serene, great for writing. The views are spectacular. Trevor, seriously, talk to me about the interview. Do you think that will make Paul Ryan back off? Or do you feel another attack can follow? I mean, dude, I support my wife wanting to do this. You know a prick like Ryan keeps coming back. He is obsessed with Gina, no doubt. I don't want him to go talking about my wife too."

Trevor sighed. "Listen, Rio, I get you want to protect Jae. But neither of us were there at the house watching my wife torturing herself and that asshole relentlessly going after her. Jae did see those things. We have to try. We're a family together, plus the entire band. We have the truth, that's all we need."

They laughed and started playing some chords and pieces of music they had in their heads.

Meanwhile, in downtown Boise, the ladies found a huge farm-fresh shop including only locally-sourced items. They bought food for two weeks. Gina found heavenly coffee beans, they had a floral scent to them. This trip would be worth it for that alone. Gina and Jae packed up the provisions in the car. The two walked down a main street, surveying some unique, trendy clothing stores. They found a beanery, an ice cream shop, and a New Age store, which Jae wanted to run into to find some feng shui articles for the new house. She found what she was looking for, a beautiful wind chime that made serene music. The house would fill with melodic tunes with a slight breeze.

On the way back, Gina looked over at Jae. "Thank you for all the good juju you bought for my new house … I have been thinking about the interview, are you still good with doing it? Was I oblivious to how obsessed he was?"

Jae brought her hands to each side of her head in amazement. "Gina, it was obvious from the moment he met you that he was infatuated with you. That's why he took on Perfection. You were so worried about Trevor, you never saw how crazy in love he was with you."

Gina knew when she was in Hawaii, and Paul planted a big kiss on her in the hammock. She also had a huge secret, that one night Paul took advantage of Gina being drunk. She would never tell anyone, *ANYONE*. If Paul ever spoke about that night, Gina would totally deny it. Her father always told her, deny, deny, deny.

Gina decided to tell Jae about the kiss. "Jae, I do have one thing I need to tell you. I need to get it out. I was resting in a hammock on the beach and Paul came over and planted a huge kiss on me. It took me a minute, at that point I threw him off of me. I instantly thought about Trevor. He could say that happened, but Jae, I won't admit it."

Jae placed her hand on Gina's shoulders in a protective gesture. "Gina, you never have to talk about that, he took advantage of you. Resting in a hammock with your eyes closed, relaxing, that's on him. You don't have to talk about that, never. I got your back. I could name every sad song you played over and over."

Jae added, "Let's try to call that woman from the Entertainment Channel and get this over with." Gina looked lovingly at Jae. "Thank you for having my back, I know we are family. But I hope Rio truly knows that he married a beautiful, genuine woman. I hope that he isn't a giant dick to you."

Jae laughed. "Gina, he is a pussycat with me. I know how much he loves me. Honestly, he treats me like a queen."

Gina pulled into the driveway and opened the garage to park their rental. She walked into the living room and saw Trevor and Rio jamming on their guitars outside through the full-length window. Gina paused and listened for a moment. She loved the music that was emanating from her backyard. She walked outside and put her arms around Trevor's neck and kissed him. "I hate to break this up but we need help with the bags in the car."

Trevor kissed her cheek. "You got it, babe; we can get back to this."

Rio got up. "I guess there is no Mae, Serena, or Marisol to help with this stuff."

Gina gave him the side-eye. "Rio, you're not that spoiled that you never took shopping bags out of a car. Guess what? Here in Boise, we take food out of the car. Get moving, my brother."

Jae held a handful of shopping bags and kissed Rio as he walked by her.

Trevor took an armful of shopping bags and set them down, then made two more trips. "G, did you buy out the store? It looks like a bounty; you plan to do some significant cooking."

Gina slid her body into him. "Well, there's no help here in Boise. I will be doing the cooking. I promise I will be available for writing and listening to the latest music. As soon as I put this away, I have a phone call to make."

Jae poured some glasses of wine and recognized her mistake. "Trevor, I'm so sorry, I forgot, please forgive me."

Trevor waved it off. "Jae, no worries, I am strong enough to refuse it."

Rio looked around. "Hey, where'd Gina go?"

Trevor simply told him, "She's making the phone call to hopefully arrange the interview."

Gina didn't have a special phone number; she called the Entertainment Channel. She asked for Susan Fine, the Paul Ryan interviewer. She let the receptionist know that Gina McNaughton was on the phone and she wanted to be put through to Susan.

After about three minutes, the receptionist came back on, "Mrs. McNaughton, I'll connect you with Susan."

Gina waited, Susan Fine came on the phone. "Is this Gina McNaughton for real? I was hoping you would contact me. I am guessing you saw the Paul Ryan interview. I thought I was fairly hard on him. I don't believe what he said, Gina. If you are willing, can we sit and talk?"

Gina paused. "Susan, guess what, that is exactly why I am calling. Jae Poole and I would love to give you the truth. Jae was with me every day that Trevor and I were separated. She saw Gina McNaughton raw and vulnerable. She also witnessed the relentless nature of Paul Ryan. Can I fly you up to Boise, Idaho? We recently bought a home here. Do we have an agreement?"

Susan Fine could not contain her excitement. "I would love that, get the real story. I knew, Gina, there was a deeper story here. I can come up the day after tomorrow, is that too soon?"

Gina exhaled. "Susan, the sooner the better, I'll have someone pick you up at the airport. If you wouldn't feel uncomfortable, I have plenty of room at my house. I would love to have you as our guest."

Gina was sure Susan Fine felt like the biggest story had been dropped in her lap. "I would love to be around you and Trevor. That would lend so much credibility to your love story. Do you think Trevor would speak to me?"

Gina laughed. "I think you could get Mr. McNaughton to give his opinion on this whole situation."

"Thank you so much for this opportunity. I have to admit I'm a bit starstruck by this whole idea."

"Susan, you will be seeing us as regular people, not rock stars," Gina reassured her.

"That's even better, Gina. Thank you again."

Gina asked Susan to send her airline information and she'd send a car to pick her up. She walked into the kitchen, where the threesome was sitting around a table covered with cheese and crackers.

She announced, "The interview with Susan Fine will be the day after tomorrow. I told her she could stay here to get a better idea of our relationship, Trev. Plus, having Rio and Jae here is an added bonus. Trev, you and Rio might be asked for your input, I wouldn't think that would be an issue."

Trevor looked at his wife. "I'll do anything in my power to put Ryan in the ground. Expose him for the unraveled human excrement that he is, you know that. Thank you for getting this done. Once we get through this insanity, we can concentrate on the music. I love you, Gina McNaughton."

BOISE
CHILL VIBES

RIO LOOKED UP FROM THE CHEESE and crackers. "You and Jae are doing this, okay. I guess I should be prepared to say my piece in this. Yes, let's do this, no more distractions. We should be back in Montecito in two weeks. Ian, Jeff, and Kevin are itching to get into the studio. Skip is waiting to book those dates we talked about. Tommy can't wait to get us recording. Enjoy the next two weeks. Afterward, it's showtime."

Jae leaned over him. "My love, you need to relax and enjoy. I know the music is important but don't overlook the peacefulness of where you are, chill."

Gina noted that when Jae voiced her point of view, Rio relaxed a bit. She had led him into a different space. Jae was right, Rio loved her so much.

Gina looked at the two guitarists. "Why don't you two go back and play some more. I will prepare dinner. Chicken marsala with sautéed asparagus with hollandaise sauce. Does that agree with the gentlemen in the house?"

Rio laughed. "Gina, you going to show us your culinary skills? I knew you baked Nonna's desserts but I didn't know you could actually cook, other than Italian food. Is that why Trevor loves you so much, you feed him well?"

Gina swatted her cousin on the arm. "No, you asshole! It's all the other amazing things I do for him. Keep a house, sing, write music. Other issues we won't speak about. But it doesn't hurt to know how to cook."

Trevor smiled. "Rio, she is a multitalented woman. Gina does everything well. She is the whole package."

Jae was laughing. "Rio, I think Trevor topped you, my love."

The men continued to jam outside while Gina cooked. Jae kept Gina company.

"Do we know anything about Susan Fine other than she doesn't appear to like Paul Ryan, or doesn't believe him?" Jae asked. "Should we be nervous at all?"

"Jae, she actually seemed starstruck about meeting the four of us. That's a bonus. Honestly, she is a fan girl. That works in our favor. She said she wants to get to the truth. Don't worry, Jae, this should be one of our easier interviews, no stupid questions."

Jae poured herself and Gina another glass of cabernet. Then she asked Gina, "Do you ever feel guilty drinking in front of Trevor? I mean, it must be hard for him to refrain from drinking."

"Trevor has his sobriety under control, I honestly believe that. Which brings us back to what we'll tell Susan Fine. I'm not going to share how horrible it was for Trevor in rehab. I'll focus on telling Susan that Trevor is in control of his sobriety, that my love for my husband has never been stronger."

Jae nodded her head in the affirmative, knowing the whole story. "Trevor has a sad story, Gina, it's like he never had a chance. He did turn to music, focusing on something he excelled at. He's so talented. Didn't he know Ian back at that time?"

Gina sighed. "Yes, Ian went through many of those things that led to them drinking also. Ian never turned back to those demons, though … We should set the table; food is almost ready."

As they set the table, Trevor walked over to his wife, put his arm around her, and kissed her, "Rio, I was so lucky that night at Glen Island to find that woman in the white crochet dress. I have loved her since that magical night."

Gina narrowed her eyes. "Enough of memory lane, food is ready, let's eat."

The cheery group continued with a lively conversation, lots of laughing and reminiscing. After they ate, everyone went outside, and Rio and Trevor entertained the group with their guitars. It was peaceful. Jae was there to top off the wine glasses.

After a bit, the two couples were ready to go to bed. Gina told Jae they would produce some mock questions and answers to prepare for the interview. They hugged, and Jae thanked her for the opportunity to relax and get in tune with nature.

Trevor waited for Gina to clean up in the kitchen, then he sat at the kitchen island and peered through her with a gleam in his eye. "Do you know what I'm thinking, G?"

Gina knew that look. "Are you thinking that this is our first night at our new house and you want to christen our bedroom, yes?"

Without hesitation Trevor answered, "Exactly. G, you need to be a bit quiet. Rio and Jae are here."

Gina gave him a fake stern look. "What makes you think they aren't doing the same thing? Come on, let's go to bed."

Trevor led Gina to their beautiful new bedroom. It had a modern feel to it. Gina's style was more traditional; however, this house represented a respite. She liked the minimal modern feel to relax in. The room was huge with a California king-size bed.

The colors were sedate, soft blues and greens. The moment the door closed and locked, Trevor grabbed her around the waist and kissed her, hard and enthusiastic. Gina didn't protest when Trevor couldn't control his libido.

She pulled away for a moment. "Trevor, I know where I want you to go."

He smiled, knowing what she was thinking and what he was planning, "Come here, let me strip you down, I want to take my time."

Gina added, "After that, I get to strip you down. We will do it together, okay, baby? I need you to come here and kiss me."

He took his time undressing her, caressing every body part he uncovered. Gina pulled off his shirt, she kissed his chest and then his neck. Her desire was taking over her. Gina grabbed his face and kissed him hard. He reached over and freed her breasts from her pink lacy bra. He leaned over and kissed each one tenderly and lovingly. He next reached down in one swipe of his hand and pulled her matching rose lace panties off her body.

Gina backed up against the bed. "Baby, I'm lying down, I want you to take me hard and rough."

She knew that made each of them crazy. He began sweet and slow; at that point he looked into her eyes and gave her what they desired. Hard and rough, biting each other all over their bodies. Trevor loved it when Gina asked for it rough. It allowed him to take her over in any way he chose. He became highly stimulated, which also made him really vocal. Trevor pulled her up to him and she wrapped her legs tightly around him. He played with her, stopping and then continuing hard and rough. Gina was so excited, she shook with pleasure. Trevor rolled her on top of him and let her take control of him hard and rough, teasing him until he begged her to finish him. After they were overcome with ultimate pleasure, they rolled over and looked into each other's eyes.

Gina spoke first. "Are you happy that you got to make love in our new house? We have done the same exact thing in every house we owned. But I love your consistency."

Trevor caught his breath and rolled over onto her. "I truly need you so much. You inspire me in my music and every part of my life. I am happy we bought this house. It's peaceful, I think it's rubbing off on Rio. He won't admit it. He is a jerk sometimes."

They laughed. Gina snuggled up to him, "I want to fall asleep wrapped in your body." Trevor pulled her close. The first night in their new house was beautiful.

The next morning Gina got up early and prepared breakfast. Jae followed the smell of bacon, waffles, and hash browns downstairs. "Gina, can I help with anything?"

"Jae, could you set the table for our lazy men? That would be great. Did you sleep well? Or did you sleep?"

Jae giggled. "Rio was so relaxed that he was particularly horny. It was a long night."

Gina smiled, "I knew he was a freak; I love it. I have to call Susan Fine and get her flight information. I'm also going to ask her for a transcript of her interview with Ryan. I want to debunk everything he said point by point."

Jae grabbed a piece of bacon. "Great idea, I first want to talk about you and how you dealt with being alone, the impact on your psyche. Next, we go in and pull apart Paul's story."

Gina liked it. "Let me make the call, she'll be here tomorrow."

Trevor shuffled out of the bedroom. "It smells like Gina's waffles, where is she?"

Jae sat down with her coffee. "She is calling Susan Fine for flight information and to get the transcript of the Ryan interview."

Rio tumbled in. "Why is Gina asking for the transcript?"

Jae folded her arms and made it clear to her husband. "Babe, so we can talk about what Ryan said. We tell our story."

Rio grunted and grabbed a cup of coffee. "So, Trev, you want to play some more music later? We have some good solid music going on ..."

Gina stepped out of their small office. "I have Susan's info and she already has the transcript of Ryan's interview. Jae, we need to work on how we'll begin our interview, any thoughts?"

Jae spoke firmly. "Yes, what a total mess you were. Nobody could pull you out. Marisol and I watched you fall down."

Gina looked saddened. "I hate to keep telling people I fell apart but it's the truth."

Gina looked at Trevor and Rio. "What are you two going to do as we work? I heard you play; it sounds like you have some good tunes coming out."

Rio was excited. "I love the tunes Trevor and I have going on. Boise is getting our creative juices alive."

The group enjoyed the view of the foothills behind them while they enjoyed mealtime. It was serene. Gina cleaned up and announced she was going to take a shower, then get to work. Trevor excused himself and said he was also going to take a shower.

Trevor walked to their bedroom, disrobed, and met Gina in the bathroom, already in the middle of her shower. He didn't miss a beat. "G, you jumped in without me, I thought we could have a playdate in our new playroom."

Gina grinned. "I was waiting for you to excuse yourself from our guests. Get in here, it's even better than our shower at Montecito."

Trevor walked in and kissed her as the water cascaded over her face, "Gina, I feel so relaxed, buying this house was a great idea."

After a little fun in the shower, Gina came out and put on her silk robe. She looked through her limited clothing options. Comfortable, expensive sweats and a shirt. She got dressed and informed Trevor of her schedule for the day.

Gina said, "Trev, babe, I'm going to sit with Jae and get a plan of action for the interview with Susan Fine. I want to be prepared for anything that may come up. I need Jae to feel comfortable in what she is prepared to say."

They exited their bedroom to find Jae and Rio sitting outside taking in the view. Rio looked more relaxed than Gina had seen him in a while. The band business was consuming him and not in a healthy way.

Gina walked out to meet them. "You two look so relaxed. Who said Boise was a crazy idea?"

Rio was in full swing, drinking early. "Gina, I have to admit, it's nice to be away from all the shit in California. No one here to grab a picture of you coming out of a store, that shit can drive you crazy. It's chill here."

Gina sat next to him and put her arm around him. "Bro, sometimes you need to take a step back and enjoy the beauty of nature and life. I'm glad you're chill. You and Trevor are still working on music. What I'm hearing sounds great, very melodic; I like it. Maybe stick in a harder edge."

Gina and Jae walked arm in arm out to the driveway through the gate and down the street in comfortable silence. Trevor and Rio stayed back at the house to go over music. They spent a whole afternoon playing for several hours.

"Rio, man, I'm calling it for today. I'm exhausted. I am still catching up to playing mode. You good with that?"

Rio got up and stretched his legs. "Trev, are you worried about that interview tomorrow? I don't want to see my wife or Gina put in a tough situation. We sure this Susan chick is cool with our ladies?"

Trevor looked out in the distance. "Rio, as sure as we can be about anything. I think after seeing that interview, she is the best bet we got."

Rio pulled out a joint and lit it. "Oh, shit. Trevor, man, I'm sorry. Does it bother you if I indulge?"

Trevor waved him off. "No, Rio, I'm good, you have a party. Let me ask you, we go on tour, you going to go nuts with the blow, or have you cut that out?"

Rio looked tense and uneasy. "Man, don't say anything, not even to Gina. Jae was going to leave me because I was doing too much partying. Remember my second DUI? Jae had to drive me around. One day she told me, if I didn't get my shit together, she would leave me. I had no choice, just like you. You love someone, and you figure out you can't live without them in your life. I couldn't, and you hated to be away from your wife. Look at you two now. I can't wait to see what Gina pulls out of her ass for opening covers for shows. She will put it all out there."

Trevor laughed. "That's my wife, the sexier the better."

At that moment Gina and Jae walked through the door.

Rio quickly said, "Gina, reservations to somewhere in Boise. Our treat for having us here."

Gina looked confused. "Since when do the Riccis have to treat family members for being family?"

Jae was excited. "I'm going to freshen up and get ready for an evening out."

"I'll be right there, babe. Gina, promise me, protect Jae tomorrow. Not sure she totally is aware of what she is getting into."

Gina said, "Rio, I'm not going to pretend that this won't be hard. Remember, it's Paul Ryan we are after, not to put blame on ourselves. We are family and that prick isn't going to take that away. Got it?"

Rio said that he understood. Trevor and Gina excused themselves to get ready for a night out.

"G, I know you are strong enough to manage this," Trevor said as they walked to the bedroom. "I have faith in us; you have all my love. You were there even when I dreamed you, encouraging me to get better. It's that faith that will get the truth out. Are you ready for an evening out?"

Gina nestled in Trevor's arms. "I'm ready for it all, baby, we are good."

The two couples found a Korean restaurant; Jae knew what to order for the table. At that moment they were recognized by a diner in the restaurant.

A man came up to their table and asked them, "You're all in Perfection, aren't you?"

Trevor answered, "Yes, we are, like you, we are trying to have a nice family meal. Is there something we can do for you?"

Unexpectedly he said, "I own a small bar a few blocks over, maybe you could surprise our patrons and come in and sing one or two songs. It would make the folks in Boise go nuts."

Trevor thought for a second. "When would you want us to show up? We'll be unavailable for a day or two. I suppose we can come Friday, if that would work for you. But no publicity, we walk in and play some acoustic songs."

The bar owner was thrilled; he would take anything. Trevor took his information and promised they would be there.

Gina inched closer to Trevor in bed. "Trev, that was a wonderful thing you did for that guy. Say you love me and let me hold you now."

Trevor kissed her forehead and pulled her in tight. "No worries, G, I got you. Come closer and I'll wrap you up."

Gina surprised Trevor. "I'm thinking I may want to go home to Montecito sooner than planned. We have been away for so long. I love it here but I think it's time to be back with our people. I want to be home before Roxanne goes back to school. The New York trip wasn't a joyful experience. We need to have time with our daughter. I've been thinking about the LA concert and I'm having ideas for opening numbers. That tells me I'm ready to perform. What do you think?"

Trevor sighed. "G, I think you're right. We need to go back to our real home. We'll leave a few days after the interview. Does that sound good?"

"Really? Are you ready to be Trevor McNaughton again?"

Trevor beamed. "Baby, I'm ready to go back to our life."

Gina got teary. "Good to know, I was worried you weren't ready. I'm happy to go home where we have all our memories. I don't have to worry that you won't be there to share the memories we created. Make more memories, hopefully with Roxy."

Trevor pulled her even closer. "I want you to get rest for that interview. You shouldn't hold back any of your feelings. Remember, if you need to cry, do it. This time I will be there to protect you. Let's go to sleep."

SUSAN FINE
COMES TO VISIT

THE NEXT MORNING GINA MADE blueberry biscuits with a lemon glaze. She thought it would be a nice touch for Susan Fine to see Gina as a homemaker, not the well-known rock star. She was coming at twelve forty-five, along with her crew.

The crew was staying at a hotel in Boise. Susan arrived promptly at twelve forty-five. She was petite with a short haircut, she was cute. The Entertainment Channel always had the most put-together interviewers.

Gina greeted her at the door. "Hello, Susan, we have been waiting to do this interview. I hope you are ready to hear the truth. It might get emotional; are you ready for that?"

Susan looked starstruck. "Gina, this is an honor, the public wants the *real story.* I have my personal views on why Paul Ryan would say some of the things he said. I don't want to share them until after the interview. Jae Poole is joining us, correct? She is a huge part of the interview."

Gina motioned her into the living room; one section had four club chairs and a round cocktail table. "I thought this would be a perfect place to hold the interview. Can I get you anything? I have any type of coffee drink and I made some homemade biscuits."

Susan, shocked, "Wow! Gina McNaughton bakes. I would love a cappuccino and would be happy to try some homemade whatever you made."

At that point Trevor and Rio walked into the room, trying to get a read on Susan.

Rio whispered to Trevor. "She doesn't look cutthroat, right?"

Trevor simply said, "It's on now, Rio. It will be what it will be. I think you should know Gina and I plan to go back to Montecito sooner than we expected. We will do that favor for the guy in town and hopefully we can get a jet to leave Saturday. Gina and I want to get back home and to work. I would imagine you're happy with that."

Rio beamed. "Fuck, yes, man. Let's get serious and get Perfection back into the conversation. Man, that's great news. I'll call Skip and have him get the troops together, Monday? You realize that during the time you both were gone, Perfection has hired ten roadies, three pyrotechnic guys, and five lighting crew guys. Perfection has grown."

Trevor knew this would eventually have to happen. He knew Gina always wanted to be involved in the hiring of Perfection's staff. Gina was not able to deal with business for those months. Skip was the manager and had to start ramping up Perfection's staff, even if Gina McNaughton got pissed off. Trevor felt he would put a pin in that discussion. The producer, camera, and lighting people arrived; the interview was getting real.

Gina got up and went over to Trevor and Rio. "Are you two going to be hovering around? It may make it difficult to have the conversation, with all the emotions. Susan may want to talk to the two of you, but not at once. I love you two, but let Jae and I start this, we cool?"

Trevor hugged her. "You go, baby, say your side of things, and bury that asshole. I'll be available if needed. Go slay it." The crew was ready, and Jae came in and took a seat in one of the club chairs. Gina brought out water bottles for everyone and sat down. She looked at Susan. "Let's get this done, okay?"

"Gina, I asked Paul Ryan where he stood with Perfection as your PR guru. He told me that he was fired because Trevor McNaughton, your husband, was afraid of him being around you. Is there any truth in that statement?"

"I guess some truth; he was fired by Perfection. He fixated on me. Paul said terribly inappropriate things to me and many of those inappropriate things were said in front of Trevor. He also kept telling me that Trevor was addicted to substances, which of course I knew. I did not ever give up on Trevor as I watched him spiral out of control, that's not the way my marriage works. He told me he took the job to get closer to me, a happily married woman. Susan, that's fucked up. Who is the villain here? I became focused on addressing Trevor's struggles with addiction."

"Mr. Ryan has said he did have a relationship with you, Gina. Now I know, something had happened at your last concert in LA. You refused to go onstage, are these two things connected? I'm trying to figure out why Mr. Ryan is claiming a relationship with you."

"No, those two incidents are not connected in any way. I did refuse to go onstage after I saw my husband unable to perform, he was a mess. That made me see red. I always protected Trevor from those demons that creeped in. I told him I wouldn't do it again, my mistake. He promised he would get help; I didn't believe him. I should have. I did destroy the backstage, I'm not proud of it. I was a sobbing mess, seeing my husband unable to do much. I asked for a car to go home to Montecito and my cousin and Jae got me out of there. I will say our manager tried to convince me to go onstage. Jae told him there was no way. Paul Ryan informed me that he would address the issue of the concert being canceled. He also told me I deserved a better man, like him, and not a loser like Trevor. Nobody puts my husband down. Simply put, there was no relationship, it was one that Paul concocted in his head. He rented a house extremely close and would come over in the evening with wine and a joint. I needed the joint. I was a mess. I had no idea where my husband was. I thought he ran off with some young groupie, I assumed the worst. I told Paul every night that I was not interested in starting any type of relationship with him. I was mourning a marriage of over twenty-three years. I told him to give me a minute, and he wasn't ending up in my bed. He said he could wait. It's bizarre, so crazy."

"Okay. Jae, you have been silent, but I know you want to tell people about Gina's journey from your perspective. You saw her every day, how bad was she?"

"It was ridiculously hard to see Gina in the state she was in as a family member. Her depression was deep; nobody could pull her out. Watching such a vibrant woman sink so low was upsetting. Let's face it, she thought Trevor threw her away for another woman. There were days when she didn't even shower. I remember putting her in the shower several times. After months of watching this, I knew Paul Ryan was trying to work her. He was the one who bought the tickets to Hawaii. Gina never left the house. Rio would stop by a few days a week. He couldn't face her, and Roxanne didn't see her mother for five months. Roxanne knew Gina would know she was hiding something. Gina thought Roxanne knew where her father was and didn't want to tell her about some young groupie with Trevor. It was truly a shitshow."

"Jae, you said that Rio knew where Trevor was the whole time. Didn't Rio or Roxanne feel that Gina should know where he was to keep her from her pain?"

"Rio didn't even share that information with me, he knew I would tell Gina. It was Trevor who told them he wanted to prove to Gina how much he loved her by getting himself clean. This time it was his love for her that made him commit to a program. The whole time he was in the facility, he knew Paul Ryan was hitting on Gina. That made Trevor work hard to earn his sobriety. He wanted to come home. And Paul knew where Trevor was the entire time. Roxanne was strong-willed and chose to be the one to tell her mother. Gina cried and yelled, I'll never forget it. I thought my husband was wrong in keeping it from her. The next day I asked her if she could find forgiveness in her heart. We all knew she loved Trevor. Their love was electric, that's what Rio told me. I left her to think. A few days later, Trevor showed up. Well, their love was strong enough to overcome a five-month separation. That's the love story.

"Never, let me repeat, never was Gina remotely interested in Paul. He thought he was clever; he's just a delusional lunatic. That's the truth."

"I asked Mr. Ryan about the slander case that you have against him. I realize it is a legal matter and you may not be able to discuss it. However, he said he has nothing to hide and that Gina could come back to him. What do you feel about the response?"

At this point Trevor walked in with Rio. Susan Fine was happily surprised to see him.

"I want to answer this," said Trevor. "We are working with our attorneys to see if we have a hard case for slander. My wife running back to him, this is a man who sounds unhinged. As I can assure you, that will never happen. We also found out that Ryan and a man named Brian Mayfield worked together to get me back on all the substances I had issues with. Mayfield also created a situation that my wife could not tolerate. It was a plan to break us up. Gina and I took an RV trip up the coast from California to Vancouver to give us some time to reconnect. We weren't rock stars, we were two people in love, enjoying nature and each other. When we take our alone time, we find time to write songs. More so, discover how much we rely on each other. We bought this house as a respite for our family to get together for holidays. It's time for us to get back to California, to record and write. We will also be doing some stand-alone concerts. I'm ready to go back to work. Paul Ryan should now keep quiet. He is not affiliated with our band. He should stop spreading nonsense. It's not true, none of it."

"As a fan of Perfection, I am pleased to know that all is well in the McNaughtons' house. I'm not sure how many people actually believe Paul Ryan. I think after

seeing this interview those nonbelievers will see through any other stories that may come out."

The crew stopped the cameras and Susan thanked the McNaughtons and Pooles. "I feel that this interview is a high point in my career."

Gina asked Susan when she planned to leave. When Susan responded she was heading back tomorrow and would be going back to her hotel now, Gina wouldn't hear of it. Instead, she chose to make a real Italian dinner and invited the interviewer to join.

Susan looked on, watching in awe that this rock star was whipping up a special feast for her. Gina moved around the kitchen effortlessly. Susan called her an all-around woman, which Gina loved. While she cooked, Trevor occasionally walked in to check on things and give his wife a kiss. Susan got to see the love.

"You are in for a treat," Susan. "I'm cooking Italian, which I love to do. Plus, you're hanging out with family—four members of Perfection. Maybe you will get some info on the band's next moves. Our table talk goes off track sometimes."

Susan was definitely a fan girl. Gina wanted to use that to her advantage. Jae got a few bottles of wine.

They sat around the table as Gina was serving the food. "Susan, so you know, we are heading back to Montecito shortly. We have a lot of work to do for Perfection. It's our baby, all three of us created Perfection. I'm sorry, plus Ian and Jeff, I can't leave them out. Trevor and I also want to spend time with our daughter before she goes back to Stanford. Roxanne is our joy. Rio, are you happy we are going home?"

Rio sipped his wine. "Hell yes, I'm happy, it's about time the two of you are done with your *alone time*. We need Perfection time. I know Trevor's got great ideas for the music, and didn't you write two songs, Gina? Have you thought of the covers you want to open shows with?"

Gina was serving food. "Yes, dickhead, I have. I want to sing a different cover for each show's opener. I want to try and not repeat a song. That might be difficult for the rest of you to learn. What, something like fifteen different covers. Or should we resurrect some of our old club songs? I'm open to that, it has to be sexy. I'm going to go over the top."

Trevor looked at his wife. "What do you mean over the top? Not Gina McNaughton wearing see-through clothes. I love that you want to *sex* it up. Can I at least see what you plan to wear?"

Gina was shocked. "Trev, you never were concerned before, why now?"

Trevor sat back and said two words, "Paul Ryan."

Gina was puzzled. "What does he have to do with anything? He's nothing in our world."

Rio cut in, "Gina, you can *sex* it up but remember you're not in your twenties anymore. You might want to reel it in."

Gina looked at Rio with daggers. "Are you fucking kidding me? You're a dick for saying that. You've had the same hair since you were ten. You still wear skintight pants, don't you? All of you do, I think you should wear something looser. How do you like that? You're a douche right now."

Jae chimed in, "Rio, she's right, you all haven't changed your look, why should Gina have to?"

Gina grimaced. "Susan, what do you think about our dinner conversation? You can't get more personal than what these guys are saying, what're your thoughts?"

Susan Fine couldn't believe she was part of this conversation, "Gina, you have always been a trendsetter. I think whatever you choose to wear will be exciting to see."

Gina winked at her new friend. "Thank you, Susan, enough about clothing. What time do you leave tomorrow? I want to get you a car to drive you to the airport and will pick up your crew also."

Susan fumbled around in her purse. "I'm leaving at 1:35 p.m. I guess I should leave around eleven-ish."

"No problem, we will take care of that."

Mealtime talk subsided from Perfection and shifted to Susan's best and worst interviews. She told them that Paul Ryan's interview was in the top five. However, she believed their rebuttal would be the pinnacle of her career. The four let a nervous laugh out. Susan told them that the interview would air the following day when she returned to Cali.

Trevor's face lit up; he couldn't wait for that interview to air. After dinner, the group enjoyed some more wine. Gina and Trevor finished cleaning up in the kitchen while everyone retired to their rooms. Gina was astonished by Trevor's remark.

"I can't get over that comment you made about my clothing, Trevor. You have no reason to be insecure or jealous, why say that?"

Trevor helped her load up the dishwasher. "Gina, you always have put yourself out there. Don't get me wrong, it has helped Perfection be who we are. Baby, tone it down a bit, that's all. I love you. Can't I be a bit protective of my wife?"

They walked into their bedroom.

Gina teased, "Damn you, Trevor McNaughton, you know I can never say no to you. It's a deal. We need to start looking at jet charters. Tomorrow is Friday, you promised that guy we would sing a few songs at his bar. We can leave on Saturday to go back to Montecito. My plan was to stay here longer, but we need to get back. Poor Marisol, she has been holding down the fort for a long while. And we need to spend some quality time with Roxanne."

Trevor undressed. "I don't want to get in too late. I need to check the studio. I know it's being used, but that's my baby. All the new equipment we bought, making sure it's tight. You better let Marisol know we are coming home. I'm hoping for some damn good Mexican food."

Gina put on the white nightgown Trevor bought her; she was already on the bed.

Trevor eyed Gina. "That nightgown, I love it but I hate that it reminds me of detoxing. I did buy it for you because I thought it was beautiful."

Gina smirked. "I can take it off, if it bothers you."

Trevor laughed, "That was happening anyway."

MONTECITO IS CALLING

THE NEXT MORNING GINA MADE an early breakfast to send
Susan off. The car came for her and she thanked them for the interview
and the hospitality.

Rio looked at Trevor. "Want to jam and write some music?"

Trevor knew that was utmost in Rio's mind, he wouldn't let it go.

Trevor relented. "Of course, let's go outside."

Gina relaxed in the great room and Jae came down and joined her.
"Jae, I can't wait to go home. It seems like it's been forever. With my father
getting sick, Roxanne, Paul Ryan, I feel like I can breathe a bit. I can't believe
I'm saying this, I can't wait to get back to Cali."

Jae smiled. "It's been a hectic couple of weeks, but things will get normal.
We will see Lisa, steal her away from Ian one afternoon. Lisa and Ian are so
grounded, it's incredible. We can have our lady lunches, be normal."

Gina gazed. "Be as normal as we can be. The paparazzi will be waiting.
I'm glad that the interview will be aired before we get back. People will be
asking questions. I will simply say, 'Did you watch the interview?' … It's
really hot in here, isn't it?"

Jae looked puzzled. "It's on the cool side, Gina. Hope you're not
getting sick."

After a few hours, the guys came in. It was Friday, and Trevor promised the bar owner a few songs tonight. Gina reminded him they needed to make flight arrangements. They chartered a jet for 1:10 p.m. on Saturday. Gina got underway with packing, she didn't want anything to delay their departure.

Trevor came into the bedroom. "G, I don't even know what we are playing tonight, any thoughts?"

"Babe, we have to play acoustic, so that leaves out a lot of our catalog obviously. I know we did 'Found You' acoustically, it is your first song you wrote about our love. How about 'Plush?' Rio may hate it but the audience loved it. That's two songs, we need one more. We should ask Rio; he is playing the guitar. Hold on, we can do 'You and Me,' the song that Roxanne joined us on the stage for, remember?"

Trevor agreed with her choices. "G, I haven't really sung in a long time. We sang to each other on the road, but there was no one to hear us."

Gina raised her eyebrows. "I haven't sung either, it would suck if we sounded bad. We are bailing out of Boise anyway, so what will be will be. I have clothes for tonight, and clothes for the plane, otherwise I'm packing everything."

Trevor, Gina, Jae, and Rio dressed like rock stars. Even though this was a small venue, they knew it would get play in the media. Gina figured it would play well in Boise, then get national attention. Which would be a great backup story after Susan Fine's interview. They drove and found the bar where Trevor agreed to play. The establishment was the typical bar with pub food. They all laughed, remembering they got their start playing in bars like this in the early days. The host was surprised to see four members of Perfection and found a table. The owner, Wes, found them and told them how much he appreciated them doing this. The reluctant four ordered a few drinks while they waited. They were having fun listening to the band on stage. They all understood this was a jumping-off point to be discovered. Approximately one hour later, Wes went onstage and introduced the three members of Perfection.

Trevor told the audience they were happy to perform for them. He went on to tell the crowd they were part-time residents of Boise.

Gina leaned into the microphone. "Hello, everyone, I'm Gina McNaughton, you knew that. We are excited to play a few songs for you; however, we are all rusty and apologize ahead of time."

Rio rolled his eyes when he knew "Plush" was the first song. Gina's voice was perfect, but the rest of the band would be rusty. The next song was "Found You," an iconic Perfection song. The crowd was clapping before they sang the first note. Trevor's and Rio's guitar playing were solid. Gina and Trevor began to sing their love song. Trevor looked at Gina as they sang, making Gina feel a bit emotional and the song even more authentic. The crowd was going crazy seeing how much this song meant to her. The last song they played was "You and Me." Gina thought of that incredibly special moment when five-year-old Roxanne McNaughton came onstage to be with her parents.

The crowd stood up, cheering and clapping and not believing they just had a mini concert from Perfection. The band left the stage, shook hands with a few patrons. Told everyone it was a pleasure to stop by and meet some of their Boise neighbors. Wes thanked them and told them he couldn't wait to share the story with the press.

Once in the car, Gina spoke first. "Now we have a story to follow up with the Susan Fine interview. Oh, no, did we miss the interview? It's airing tonight!"

"Don't worry," Trevor reassured them. "I recorded it just in case it aired while we were out."

Relief washed over Gina, Jae, and Rio, this was a big moment. They needed to watch for so many reasons.

They all walked into the living room. The air stank of nervousness. Trevor found the recording and hit the Play button. The show opened with some B-list actress who was arrested for a DUI.

Gina laughed. "Well, if we are following that, we'll look great."

No one else was laughing. Susan Fine appeared and Trevor turned up the volume. "I recently had the pleasure of sitting down with three of the members of Perfection and the guitarist's wife," Susan announced. "The purpose of the interview was to clarify the preposterous claims that Paul Ryan is putting into the public domain."

Jae said, "That's a good start, getting her opinion out there."

Trevor just wanted to hear that Paul Ryan was eliminated in the thoughts of the public. He was fired up as the interview began. Gina watched carefully. Susan did not cut much, which pleased her. The truth was out there for the public to see and ponder what was real.

Susan went on to tell her listeners how the McNaughtons had a very normal home life and there was no doubt about the love they shared. She went on to say that Paul Ryan's claims were completely unfounded. And that Jae had made it abundantly clear that the two had a moment of separation. That separation only strengthened the love that the McNaughtons shared. Susan also commented on the closeness of all four family members. She went on to express her feelings about Paul Ryan.

Susan said, "I'm not sure why Paul Ryan puts out a false narrative about Perfection, mostly about Gina and Trevor McNaughton. I met with the McNaughtons. They are a happy, extremely in-love couple. Jae Poole, Rio Poole's wife and Gina's close relative, shared how Trevor's rehab affected Gina. A sad moment for sure. It sheds light on the fact that maybe Paul Ryan has a bit of an obsession with Mrs. McNaughton. Mr. Ryan seems to have some mental struggles, or it might be a dislike for the band. He certainly was never a love interest for Gina McNaughton. Paul Ryan's reasoning for his attachment to Gina is convoluted. I believe Mr. Ryan had better find a different story or fade away from the Perfection narrative. I tried to contact Paul Ryan to get his response to the interview, but he is refusing to speak on this subject. Is it because of legal matters connected to the story? Who knows? Perfection is working on their latest music to stay on top of rock's most beloved bands. Sorry, Paul, you need to get the memo. I'm just reporting the facts."

Trevor pressed Stop on the remote and everyone looked at each other.

"Ladies, fantastic," Trevor said while rising out of his chair and clapping. "I don't know how anyone can conclude it was unauthentic. Rio, say something, man. It was gold."

Rio was slightly tempered. "Yes, this was exactly what we wanted. Beautiful. I don't think Ryan is done with us, though. I feel another storm coming. I hate being that guy, just saying. Great interview and I think we will get some good juju from tonight. Some national rag or TV channel will pick up the story. Excellent work lovely wife and my badass cousin."

Gina stood up. "Well, we are leaving tomorrow to go back to our real homes. I am packed. What about you two?" she asked Rio and Jae.

"We are packed and ready to go home," said Rio.

The Pooles and McNaughtons relaxed outside, taking in the beauty of the foothills and the Zen vibe before going to bed. Tomorrow they would all be back home in California.

Gina was restless, she couldn't sleep. She was worried how the press and the public would react to their interview. It appeared to be favorable to them, but would people believe Paul Ryan's story or Gina's?

HOME SWEET HOME

THE PLANE RIDE HOME WAS QUIET, no talking about business. Once back in Cali, things were about to get real. The interview would also be out to the public for viewing. Gina couldn't wait to find comfort in her beautiful home in Montecito. She woke up in the morning after about three hours of sleep. She was nervous, the interview, Paul Ryan. And another chilling thought: *Where is Brian Mayfield?*

They gathered their luggage and waited for a car to take them to a private hangar, where Rio's car awaited them. He drove the McNaughtons home. An ecstatic Marisol and gleeful Roxanne greeted them as they walked through the door. Hugs and kisses, followed by a display of all the food Marisol had prepared for them. They weren't hungry but talked for a while about all they had been through.

Roxanne was thrilled to see her parents. "I thought you were going to spend more time at the Boise house? Is there a reason you came back earlier? I did watch that interview. Is that the reason?"

Gina grabbed her daughter. "Roxanne, it's been a long while since we have been back to *our home,* this is our family home. All the memories and life we built together. We wanted to come home. Your father and I were hoping to spend time with you before you go back to school. We can do whatever you want. As far as the interview, no more talk about that maniacal piece of shit. I won't even say his name. Don't worry, Roxy, all is good."

Trevor put his arm around Roxanne's neck. "Can you stand your parents doting on you until you leave? Honestly, I have lost track of time."

"I'm waiting for the cheerleading practice schedule. Then I'll know. I will also know if I'm co-captain, fingers crossed!"

Gina said, "Roxy, what an accomplishment, I will be so thrilled."

Gina was at her favorite appliance, the espresso machine. Making a lavender latte.

Marisol told them she would leave them so they could get comfortable back home.

Gina, Trevor, and Roxanne sat in their living room and looked at the Pacific Ocean out of their window. They all cuddled up on the sofa.

Gina could barely talk. "Trevor, this looks so beautiful. I'm so happy to be back at our real home. Not the Carriage House, not Boise, our family home. I look around and see the happiness we created here. Roxanne, you are a beautiful young woman; you're intelligent, athletic. Roxanne, you are the full package. Okay, family, I'm so tired. If I fall asleep here, just leave me."

Trevor remarked, "G, I noticed you had a hard time sleeping, what's up?"

"I thought certainly we would be surprised by photographers and all that crap, but no one seemed to know we were coming home, except Susan. She didn't give us away, thank God."

Trevor reached over. "Come over here. Put your head down on me and go to sleep … I want to check the studio, but I'll stay here until you fall asleep."

Gina drifted off in about fifteen minutes. Trevor gently slipped out from under her and walked down and checked out the studio, which looked exactly as he had left it. He walked back up to the house and found someone at the gate delivering a package. He guessed it was the copy of the interview Susan had promised them. He would keep it in their home office for now.

Gina slept for about three hours and woke up out of sorts, not knowing where she was.

Trevor heard her stir from the kitchen and told her, "Baby, we're home, it's okay. Why not come over here and get something to eat? Roxanne and I may eat everything."

Gina was woozy. "Looks good, not sure if I'm ready to eat. Wait, do I see Marisol's homemade guacamole? Maybe I am a little hungry."

Trevor looked into her eyes. "Guess what I got?"

"Trev, simply tell me, I'm not into guessing."

Trevor held out the package. "It's the interview."

Roxanne looked on. "Why do you want that? You already saw the interview."

Gina said. "It documents what was said in case we need it for a legal case. Don't you worry. Let's sit down and eat as a family in our home."

They ate Marisol's array of Mexican wonders. They laughed and talked about nothing. Just being a family. Roxanne helped Gina clean up. Then she told her parents she was meeting some friends later.

Gina was still tired; it was a long way to get back to Montecito, their family home.

Suddenly a thought struck her, "I was thinking, next weekend we should have a Perfection and crew kickoff party. It would be nice to see everyone and let them know we are all in. It would be nice to see Skip and Tommy. We should also meet the new people we have on the payroll. I would also like to invite the Montecito Moms and families. Roxy, you can see your friends. I'll have it catered; I don't want Marisol cooking for that many people. What do you all think?"

Trevor leaned over and kissed his wife. "Gina, I think that would be a wonderful gesture. We need to let our people know we're back and committed to the band. Glad to hear you are thinking of what's good for Perfection."

"Well, Trev, that's next weekend. The rest of this weekend, I want to relax and enjoy our home, being here with you and Roxanne."

Roxanne said, "I'm going to change my clothes and visit some friends." She told her parents she'd maybe see them later. Roxanne was happy to be hanging around with her friends in Montecito. Gina and Trevor told her to have a fun time.

Trevor went over to their music system. As musicians they had a turntable, cassette, CD player, and the best quality reel-to-reel player. It had the best sound quality. Trevor went to put the music on in the living room. Then he sat down next to Gina. "Nothing Compares 2 U" blared through the speakers. He didn't know Gina's sad songs were queued up on the player.

Gina sat up. "Trev, no, this was my playlist for when you were away. Please turn it off, it brings back bad memories." Gina's eyes teared up, it was painful.

"G, please let me hear what you were listening to. It connects the dots for me; how hopeless you felt. It's okay, babe, I want to hear."

Gina sat back and tried not to let her emotions roll over her; nonetheless, when she heard "My Immortal," the words stabbed at her. She couldn't control her tears. "Baby, turn it off."

Trevor pulled her in. "G, it's okay to cry, this is a sad song."

"Comfortably Numb" came on next, Gina remembered how she sat with bottles of wine and a pile of Valium. Luckily Jae came over. All those memories washed over her.

She clutched Trevor's shirt. "Don't you dare ever do that to me again. If you want to listen to the playlist, it's fine. I sat with you visiting the spot where your mom passed. I should let you hear how I was in a dark pit of despair. But now I have you home, so this is just a bad memory."

She rested her head in his lap. He stroked her hair as he listened to song after song, it affected him also to hear Gina's pain.

Trevor listened to Gina's sad songs. He was moved, then said, "I know you're full from eating; hearing that music, G, I want to ask you, I would love to go in our room and make love to my wife."

Gina looked up, staring at her husband. "Mr. McNaughton, I was waiting to see how long it would take you to ask. Making love in our own bed, what a treat. Wait, do we know when Roxy will be home?"

"G, that's why we have a lock on the door."

They walked hand in hand into their bedroom, stripped down, and made love. They heard the gate open and knew Roxanne was home. The lovemaking session was done.

RASPBERRY CHOCOLATE CHIP CRUMBLE

IT WAS A LAZY SUNDAY MORNING. The McNaughtons slept in, then floated around the house without a care. Roxanne baked chocolate chip cookies.

Gina went down to the studio to check things out, especially her office. She knew Skip was taking care of things. She just needed to see all the paperwork. Trevor walked into the studio, sat down, and began playing his guitar. Gina listened to his hard-edge song. A thought came into her head, a song, "Touching You All Over." A sexy song, a dirty song, Gina loved the idea. The lyrics came to her quickly as she scrawled them on a piece of paper.

TOUCHING YOU ALL OVER

I'm sitting down, I look at you, you know I just want you to touch me all over. Take those hands, put them down my pants, just go ahead, I want you to be touching me all over.

Your smile betrays you, you act like I don't know you, but
I know you want to have me touching you all over.

Shit, babe, go ahead between my legs, I will love how you play the
game. You play me like your guitar, I promise you I'll be screaming
for you to do more, take me all over, babe, flip me over and have
your way because I need you to be touching me all over, and when
you're done, I promise you I'll be kissing you with my face between
your legs, and I'll be loving you and touching you all over.

Chorus

You know I need it; you know I want it. You know we both need
to have it, so just let me have a taste of you, and then you take a
taste of me because I'll be touching you all over. Damn you, babe,
I love how we play the game. So, let's be touching all over.

Gina interrupted Trevor, "I wrote a little song I want you to look at. It's not done, but it's a start."

Trevor took the paper, as he was reading it his eyes widened. "G, you wrote this in the past few minutes? The song does go with our harder edge. G, I think the band will definitely want to record this. Were you motivated by something?"

Gina shoved him. "Trev, get the hell out of here, of course I was. This is kind of our life. People think they know it, but let's give it to them. If we are *that couple*, let's happily embrace it. Are you embarrassed to sing this?"

Trevor looked at the words again. "Actually, no, it crosses over, dudes and chicks will be into it. I'm surprised you wrote this. It's okay, I'm into it."

Gina made sure Trevor knew this song needed a lot of guitar and a heavy bass line.

Gina went into her office and saw proposed concerts; she reviewed the dates and venues. She hoped that Los Angeles was the first show.

The band felt they needed to do a makeup for the last show that was canceled.

Perfection always had Gina open with a cover song. A song that was kick-ass. Something where Gina could come out with a big entrance. She had given thought to what she wanted to do.

Trevor came to his wife's office. "You know, Gina, we spent three hours here already. Let's go back to the house, I'm thinking of the Mexican food in the fridge. Where is our daughter? Out and about?"

Gina was proud. "She is baking chocolate chip cookies. I'm hoping my baking skills rubbed off on her."

As they strolled up the slate walk, Trevor picked up Gina. "Come on, bitch, after we eat, I'm going to do to you what you wrote in the song, but dirtier."

Gina reminded him, "Babe, I know we have always been carefree but Roxy is home. Let's wait and see what she is doing after dinner."

Trevor groaned. "You're right. I forgot she is actually spending time with us."

Gina reminded him, "I wonder when Zach will be appearing at the house. I'm sure they plan to go back to school together."

Trevor groaned again. "Why did you remind me of that? I was hoping we'd have more alone time with her before Zach whisks her off."

"Babe, you say these things about Zach. You are always more than accepting when he is here. I remember him calling you Trevor."

They opened the door and were hit in the face with the sweet aroma of freshly baked chocolate chip cookies. Gina yelled out, "Roxy, my goodness, it smells like heaven in here. Is this dessert for tonight?"

Roxanne was confident about her project. "You can have some. I made them for a party tonight at Felicity's house. Her parents are away. Don't say anything to Laura."

Trevor and Gina said, "No, we won't."

Gina pulled out Marisol's leftovers. "Leftovers? Everybody on board?"

Once again, the three McNaughtons sat at their kitchen island enjoying a meal together. It was an early supper, knowing that Roxanne was going to a party. They sat and laughed about some of their Montecito friends.

Gina asked, "Is this a sleepover party? I don't want you to drink and drive. You know better, you can wake us up if needed."

"Probably going to spend the night, it might be a rager. It has been a long time since we all have spent time together. What car can I take? The Porshe?"

Trevor was not amused. "Roxanne, that will never happen. I don't think your mother has ever driven it."

Gina shook her head *no* and told her to take the Mercedes. Within twenty minutes she was out the door.

Gina looked smug. "Let's get some ice cream, I'm dying for the raspberry chocolate chip crumble at Saffron's. We will get it and come home, promise."

Trevor grabbed the keys, they got in and out of the store with a pleasant, "Welcome home, McNaughtons."

Gina brought the ice cream into the bedroom and told Trevor to hang on. She came back with some whipped cream. She was afraid it would be bad, but it tasted fine.

Trevor was already sitting on the bed naked. "G, what's up with the ice cream and, oh, I know where this is going. Let's go … Who's first?"

Monday morning arrived. Marisol was in the kitchen preparing breakfast. Gina woke up first, threw on her sweats, walked in, and wished Marisol good morning.

Marisol smiled. "It's so good to have you and Mr. Trevor home. I missed you tremendously. How is Mr. Mario? Is he doing better?"

Gina sipped her latte. "Yes, he is. Franny is in total control of him and he is expected to make a complete recovery."

Marisol crossed herself. "I'm happy to hear that, and Mr. Trevor, he is doing okay?"

Gina took another sip of her latte. "Marisol, he really worked hard while we traveled all around. He is happier, it reminds me of how he was when Roxanne was first born."

Trevor walked in, wearing those old sweatpants. "Good morning, Marisol, the food smells great."

He leaned over and gave his wife a kiss. "Good morning, baby. It feels good to sleep in our own bed again. Slept like a baby."

Marisol poured him coffee. "You are happy to be home, Mr. Trevor. The house and I missed you for a while."

"Marisol, I can assure you that the house and you will never miss me again. G, I don't know when those guys are going to get here. We should eat quick and get down to the studio."

Trevor grabbed a quick nosh and announced he was going to shower.

"Ugh, okay. I was hoping to enjoy sitting here for a moment and enjoy my latte. I guess I'm taking my shower now. Thanks, Marisol, I'll eat this beautiful homemade donut on my way out."

Walking into the bedroom, Gina heard water running. Trevor was already in the shower. She peeked in. "Want company or are you in a hurry to get to the studio?"

Trevor looked apologetic. "G, I'm excited to see Ian and the other guys, do you mind? We can always make time for a playdate later."

Gina understood his excitement. "Trev, you go play with the guys, this is a big moment for you. You haven't seen them in a bit, I get it, I'll be down there soon."

Trevor got dressed and walked down to the studio.

Gina was excited to see the band, however, she wanted Trevor to be there to welcome them. Trevor had a moment touching all the equipment, looking at his collection of guitars. Trevor was plugging in his favorite guitar when he turned around and saw Ian.

Ian became emotional. "Hey, mate, it's been a good while, how the hell are you? I missed the fuck out of you. Did you let the demons fly?"

Trevor hugged his old friend. "I'm good and missed you too. I did have some emotional moments while in Vancouver. I was lucky Gina got me through them. I can't believe how much I hurt her by not being honest with her. It kills me. Did you see her those months?"

Ian was honest. "Dude, I saw her briefly, she was a mess. Lisa came over a few times. It was difficult for her because she knew there was nothing she could do to make it better. But you two worked it all out and we are here. Hey, mate, I can't wait to see where we are going musically." Jeff sauntered in. "Hey, Trev, what the fuck, how is it going? Good to see you, man. You look great, ready to write some impressive tunes."

Trevor hugged Jeff. "I can't believe I'm saying this to you, but I missed you too. How are things? Are you straightened out?"

Jeff knew what he meant. "I, unbelievably, am dating a *nice girl*. She's a production assistant for a film company. It's much better not to date the rising star, too much work and ego."

Skip, Tommy, and Kevin walked in.

Tommy at once walked over and hugged Trevor. "I am so glad you came out the other side. Many people don't, Trevor. You put in the work on your sobriety, marriage. I knew you and Gina would fix any issues you had … Enough of that. I can't wait to get to the business of making good music."

Skip looked at Trevor. "Good to see you where you belong. How was the RV trip? Get enough of nature? Seeing you is so much better than talking on the phone. I suppose Mrs. McNaughton has specific topics to discuss. It's back to work."

Trevor saw Kevin come in and walked up to him, "Man, it's been a while."

Trevor had a bit of a speech to all assembled. "Look, I'm back at a hundred percent. There still may be fragile edges. I have the tools to work those out. There was a moment I never thought I could get here. I'm sorry you all had to put things on hold. I appreciate your faith in me and Gina.

More importantly, giving Gina and me the space we needed to work out all our issues. I should have been transparent about my struggles. Gina and I are doing outstanding. Together we wanted to get home, get back to work, we're ready. Where the hell is Rio?"

Gina finally waltzed into the studio, "What a sorry-looking group of assholes," she teased. "Team, I'm here to write and I'm here to make sense of these concert dates. Here are the words you want to hear—Gina McNaughton is back, bitches. Wait, someone is missing, Rio is late? The person who was relentless in getting us back to work?"

At that moment, the door opened. Rio Poole the rock star walked in. "Hey, fuck off, I get to be late, I'm related to these two."

Tommy immediately took control. "Look, I would like to redo some of the songs in the vault. If there is new music, we should look at that first. Afterward we can go over the older stuff and rework areas we can remaster. Slowly we can introduce it into a new album. Are we in agreement with the plan?"

They all agreed it was a great plan.

Trevor threw out, "My wife wrote three songs. I think her last one should get you all in some kind of mood."

Gina laughed. "That's correct, I wrote a filthy-hard rock song. We need to get dirty, it's acceptable now. Before sensors would have made us change it. Now anything goes."

Tommy's interest was piqued. "Gina, you're right, all lyrics and songs are acceptable now. There is an audience for every type of music."

Rio chimed in, "I can get into playing songs that have filth."

Gina gave Rio one of her fake smiles. "I will concentrate on totally writing filth for you, Rio." Then she was all business. "Skip, let's look into these stand-alone concerts that are definite. You spoke to selected venues, correct?

We will work on that together. I would like to meet the new employees who have joined us. I trust you all, but I need to know who I have working for us. Did Trevor mention we want to have a Perfection kickoff here at our house? All employees, families, significant others, whatever. It will be a catered event, no need for anyone to bring anything. Trevor and I feel we need to embrace this reboot. We want to thank you all for your patience with us. You think that would be a good vibe?"

Tommy interjected, "Gina, you don't owe anyone an explanation. I think it would be a great bonding time before the demanding work sets in. These concerts would be over a year out. It's going to mean driving cross-country once again. Arduous work for the road crew."

Gina agreed. "I know, but this is the direction we are taking. We are going to work our asses off, come home, and after that go back and do it again."

Gina motioned to Skip. "Let's go into the office and try to sort out this show schedule. I've been waiting to work on this."

Skip followed Gina to their office. "Gina, I want to tell you again how sorry I am for not telling you about Trevor. I promised him."

Gina stopped him. "Skip, I'm not upset any longer. I may not agree with Trevor's logic but I have him back whole. It was a journey, one I never want to have again. I needed to take that road trip with Trevor. We learned things about each other. Over twenty-three years of marriage, feelings locked away that we never knew about each other. That is the treasure."

"Gina, I'm so happy you made it through that terrible patch. Ready to go to work? Let's take a look at the shows."

"Skip, you know the first show we do is Los Angeles. Never will we talk about what happened again. We canceled the concert. I don't want to do anything until we give them an amazing show. I have a great opening number planned. I need a sax player, a keyboard player, and two screens with videos of me singing the chorus of the song. I am envisioning coming out with a light show and pink smoke. I want to sing, 'Would I Lie to You?' Heavy guitars, drums, and of course the sax is key. I want to have an outfit that I pull off as I strut across the stage. No worries, nothing terribly revealing, Mr. McNaughton would be unhappy. We can manage that now with the crew we have, correct?"

Skip agreed. "We can manage it, no problem. Can I bring up a sore subject, Paul Ryan? We know the lies he has been spreading. You, Trevor, and Jae did some damage control. However, I think he's coming after you and Trevor. He's lying low after that interview, but the grapevine is saying otherwise. Gina, some men can't let things go. I'm being honest, aware, and prepared."

Gina's eyes widened, and a lump formed in her throat. "Like what? He has to be unbalanced, maniacal to do something."

Skip mentioned, "As you know, he worked with Mayfield. Mayfield has a big mouth. He is working for some mid-level band in LA. He has been gossiping that Ryan isn't done with you and Trevor. He doesn't say what's in store. He is dumb but not that stupid. If he knows details, he isn't sharing them."

Gina tried to contain her aggravation. "I don't believe we need a public relations firm. We are capable of taking care of any dirt internally. The way the Ricci family deals with problems. We don't need any more mistakes like Ryan. Are we clear? Let's sit down and look at the schedule."

Skip placed the top requests out for Gina. "Some dates are not flexible; we would need to work other dates around those."

After hours of planning and Skip calling the venues for availability, they came out with the following schedule:

Los Angeles	July 15	The Wiltern
Caesars Palace, Vegas	July 28–30	The Colosseum Theater
South Dakota, Buffalo Chip	August 8	Sturgis Motorcycle Rally
Morrison, CO	August 20	Red Rocks Amphitheatre
Orlando, FL	August 29–30	Amway Center
New York City Live	Sept 29–30	Madison Square Garden

Charlotte, NC	October 10	PNC Music Pavilion
Miami, FL	Dec 28	Miami Beach Bandshell
Football Kickoff	Jan 29	TBD
Vancouver, Canada	Feb 24	PNE Amphitheatre
Toronto, Canada	Feb 28	Danforth Music Hall
Daytona, FL Bike Week	March 10	Full Moon Saloon
Washington Park	April 12	Milwaukee Rock Festival
Jones Beach Theater, NY	May 26	Daisy Point Rock Festival

"Skip, this was mind-blowing. I'm exhausted. We've booked all our stand-alone concerts for an entire year. We will also be working on our latest music. I would like to think about making some videos. Do we still do videos now? I see them online. We will need a production company that we can work with. I'm sorry, I remembered one more item. I need you to hire two bodyguards. I need people to watch my back or anyone in the band. I am not very trusting these days. I want two big dudes who can kick ass if needed, got me?"

Skip looked a bit surprised. "Gina, you are serious? You feel that threatened?"

Gina stared with lasers and arms tightly folded. "Yes, I'm fucking serious. Apparently, my edicts of no groupies, no hangers-on, no crazy fans, no drug dealers have not been taken seriously. I'm not having it. As you said, we have no idea what Paul Ryan will do. So, yes, fucking find me some huge-ass dudes. Additionally, where is Brian Mayfield, the supplier of drugs and alcohol? Do you know? Those restraining orders need to be in place, and bodyguards need to be hired before we travel to any shows. I think we have taken care of most of our business for today. I guess I should see what's going on in the studio."

When she got there, the band was taking a break.

Gina looked at Tommy, "You letting these guys off easy, Tommy?"

He simply said, "These guys are soft. I'm breaking them in slowly, later

I'm going to be pummeling them hard. You too, Gina. Have you thought of your openers?"

Gina knew but wasn't ready to share yet. "I spoke to Skip about what I want for the Los Angeles show. I will give you my ideas later. I need fifteen openers, maybe more. I might want to resurrect some of our music from our early band days."

Rio groaned. "Oh, no, Gina, really, haven't we played that shit to death?"

Gina glared. "Well, Rio, I have some ideas. If you have suggestions, let me know about it. Tommy, did you get a chance to see any of my songs?"

He looked a bit uncomfortable. "I did see the latest one you wrote. It's not what I expected from you. We can definitely work with a harder edge. Let's break for today. I heard about the party next weekend, Gina. Anne and I will be there. I think it's good to have a nice get-together before we start shouting obscenities at each other. See you all tomorrow."

The guys started packing up and were happy to be calling it for the night.

Before they left, Gina shared the concert schedule. "Look, I tried to spread things out for the entire year. There are some dates that are not flexible since they're part of an event. Skip and I called venues and worked everything out the best we could, spread out, not overwhelming. We play the concerts and work on our music. We add our latest music a little at a time. We all in agreement?" There were groans, but it was agreed.

Trevor looked around. "Good work, my brothers, see you all tomorrow."

Gina waited for him to put his guitars away, he meticulously wiped each down from fingerprints, sweat, whatever.

Gina asked, "How was it playing, practicing with Tommy?"

"It was great to get back into the groove. I'll tell you what, it is draining. Tommy going over things four or five times, I know we got it. It's one more time. I've been away too long; I need to get back in that groove. I'm really looking forward to having a nice quiet meal with my wife and daughter. Let's go see what Marisol made."

They walked arm in arm to the house. They hoped Roxy would be home to join them. In Gina's mind, there was a countdown to when she would be leaving.

Once they walked through the door, they could smell Marisol's special roast beef.

Gina walked up to her fancy barista machine. "Hold on, Trev, I need a strong cup of coffee after talking with Skip about protection for the band."

Trevor didn't flinch. "G, if you think we need bodyguards to prevent the wrong element from coming backstage, I'm all for it. No PR firms, are you going to be the point person for bad press?"

Gina brought over her mug and snuggled up next to her husband. "Do we need to talk about that now? I'm so exhausted after working with Skip all day long. I have to say, I wonder if Skip is missing a beat. He was telling me that Ryan was waiting to come after us. Part of me thinks he might be friendly with Ryan. I don't know, it's a feeling, Trev, I can't shake it. When the subject of PR firms originally came up, he had Ryan's firm all wrapped up. Why? Did he know him already? Did Ryan work Skip because he thought he was weak? Skip allowed the Mayfield situation to get out of hand after I told him to fire him and deport that asshole. I could be wrong, Skip has been with us since the beginning. I hate to think about firing him now."

Trevor sat up. "G, do you really think that? I personally would feel wounded if that was the truth. He was there when I was in rehab and was exceptionally supportive."

Gina conceded, "Baby, I don't know, maybe because I'm tired. Skip couldn't believe I wanted bodyguards. The band, primarily you and me, needs protection. Skip was shocked. His response should have been 'No problem.' Ugh. I don't want to discuss our first day back into the circus."

Marisol set dinner on the table, it was her zesty Mexican roast beef with new potatoes. It was killer.

Roxanne came floating downstairs. "Good late evening, parental units. How was your first day back at work?"

Trevor eyed his daughter. "It was work. Went over things many times. It can be frustrating. How was your day?"

Roxanne eyed her parents. "I got a facial. I feel very relaxed, and my skin is glowing."

Gina laughed. "Yes, facials are relaxing. I wish I knew. I would have gone with you on another day … I have to plan this party. Can I count on your help?"

Roxanne was happy to help her mother. She knew Gina had great taste, just like her Nonna.

Marisol boasted, "Mr. Trevor, I made one of your favorite Mexican feasts and a special dessert."

"Marisol, you are spoiling him," Gina kidded. "You know you can get to him through his stomach."

Trevor laughed. "I'm ready to eat. Marisol, will you join us?"

"Oh, Mr. Trevor, I will another time. I am going to the movies with my friend. You, Mrs. Gina, and our Roxanne, have a nice dinner together. I made my flan that you love for dessert, it's in the refrigerator. You all enjoy, I'll see you in the morning."

They all said goodnight, took a deep breath, and dove into their tasty meal.

"Babe, do you mind if I have a glass of wine? I need something to take the edge off from today. We knew it would be heavy work and it was."

Trevor grabbed her hand as she got up. "Gina, don't ever feel I'm holding you back from a glass of anything. I'm good with it. Enjoy."

Roxanne paid close attention to how her mother navigated her father's addictions.

Gina went into their wine fridge, grabbed a cabernet, and placed the bottle on the table just in case she wanted another glass.

Gina sipped her wine. "I'm sorry, Roxanne, you are old enough, would you like a glass?"

Roxanne simply said, "I'd love one."

Gina looked at Trevor, excited. "Do you want to hear about my opening number for the LA show?"

Trevor was enjoying his dinner. "Sounds like you have something big planned."

Gina looked into his eyes. "You know I do. I want to sing 'Would I Lie to You?' I'm interested in what you think."

Trevor swallowed. "G, I'm sure you've put a lot of thought into this. Baby, whatever your vision is, we will make it happen. I'm more focused on whether Ryan is waiting for us. G, if I see him, I'll be making sure he doesn't get up. He can even sue me for assault."

Gina looked worried. "Trevor, no way. He's not worth you getting arrested, seriously, baby. We have been through enough, please promise me. That's why I want bodyguards. I'm concerned about Mayfield making a reappearance too. I would like to have a beatdown with him. But I'm not willing to go to jail for a complete asshole drug-pusher."

Roxanne looked shocked. "Dad, Mom is right. Why would you risk getting arrested when it comes to Paul Ryan? Please don't."

"Gina, I can't promise you I won't do anything if I see him. You need to trust me, this is personal. I love you. I won't do something that will hurt us."

Gina implored, "That's why I want the bodyguards, let them do that dirty work. Let's not talk about this. I'm enjoying this dinner and this glass of wine. Besides, we have that dessert to look forward to."

Trevor finished eating. "I am looking forward to that dessert. You are right. I'm exhausted, aren't you?"

Gina looked at Trevor, who was laid back. "I am but the wine is making me mellow. I'm happy to snuggle up in bed, find a good movie. Let me get the flan out."

They enjoyed dessert and went to their bedrooms for a quiet evening.

Trevor reached over and pulled Gina next to him. "G, I love this relaxing in bed, having you close to me."

Gina snuggled under his arm into his chest. "This is my favorite place to be."

Roxanne came downstairs and knocked. "Are you two decent?"

Trevor told her to come in. "What's up, Rox? Are we going to see Zach before you go to school?"

Roxanne got between her parents on the bed. "I got a letter from school letting me know I need to be back right after the Fourth of July. I have a few days. Cheerleading practice is serious. Zach has full football practice. Oh, yes, I am co-captain of the squad. Zach will be here a few days before we leave. I would like to fly back. Is that a problem?"

Gina squinted her eyes. "Congratulations, my love, on the captain thing! It's not a problem. Dad or I will arrange your travels when we get a solid date. We are about to watch a movie. Do you want to join us?"

Roxanne slipped in between her parents just like she did when she was younger. The three McNaughtons snuggled up together. Gina thought how perfect life was right now. Surrounded by the two people she loved the most.

GINA'S SETLIST

THE NEXT MORNING GINA WAS DRINKING her latte and getting ready for the day. She sat on the bed looking at what she had to do. The band, the party. She let Trevor know what her day looked like.

Gina sat for a moment and went through a checklist for her day. "I'll quickly visit and see what Tommy wants from me. I'll let him decide when he wants me. I'll give you my song list for openers. I need to go to the caterer today about the party this weekend. I'm taking Roxanne to get her involved, I think she will enjoy it. I know it's short notice. I hope I can get what I want. You okay with that plan?"

Trevor was sitting in the bedroom listening to Gina's day. "G, we need to plan the party. Meeting up with the ladies is great. Right now, I'm walking into the shower and wondering if my wife is following me."

Gina gave her wide-eyed, sly smile. "Yes, I think you owe me a playdate."

"Mrs. McNaughton, I am here to make your wishes come true."

Shower time was a happy one. Then the two got dressed together. Trevor threw on loose-fitting pants and a T-shirt. Gina chose a more businesslike outfit since she was meeting the caterer.

They said a brief good morning to Marisol and Roxanne. Gina reminded Roxy about going to the caterer. She said she would be ready.

The McNaughtons walked down to their studio. Skip followed closely behind. "I see I'm the first one here. Since it's the three of us, I put out the word about the bodyguards that Gina requested. Trevor, are you on board with this?"

Gina was seething but Trevor said, "Skip, if my wife wants bodyguards or security people, please fucking do it. Why would you push back on this?"

Skip fumbled over his words. "I just needed to know that you were on the same page."

Gina let loose. "Skip, never question what either one of us says to you. Trevor and I will always be on the same side. Why do I feel that there's more going on here? Are you tired of working with Perfection? You have been here since the beginning, you have done a wonderful job, with the exception of Mayfield and Ryan. I'm feeling a lot of pushback from you, something has changed. What is it? You're pissing me off big time."

Skip stuttered, "You know I love this band, I was here from the beginning. Things are different now. Perfection is successful, we have arrived. My work is slightly different, that's all."

Gina didn't accept that answer. "I would think you would be elated. It's a higher level, Skip. That means more responsibility to keep us always moving forward. Like getting us a high-quality production company for videos. We also need to find a sound production company to help record the live performance at Madison Square Garden. Is this too much for you?"

Trevor knew Gina was baiting Skip, he interjected, "Dude, right now we need the band and staff to be working harder. We had over a six-month absence. We need to punch it to a higher level. You're on board, right? I need your knowledge of the band and all the players. You good?"

Gina was the person who would be in your face, Trevor had a softer touch.

Skip tried to defend himself. "Gina, the last thing I want to do is piss you off. Everyone knows not to piss off Gina McNaughton. Of course I'm on board. I remember all that we went through to get here. Yes, I'm in."

Gina sat back. "Well, you are going to be busy. Let's start getting all the equipment for my opener in LA. Get the bodyguards, get a crew in to record MSG. Start searching for a production company to be ready when we do the music videos. Trevor, Rio, and I want to be there for the last two tasks. I'm involved in the business for a reason. Soon I'll be busy rehearsing and recording. So, step it the fuck up."

Skip left to go to his office. Trevor gave Gina a disapproving look. "G, you need to reel it in with Skip. I know you think he didn't take care of the Mayfield and Ryan situations the way he should have. But ease up, baby, we can't have him walking out on us now."

Gina sighed. "Fine, for you I'll do anything. Before I go to the caterer, I want to talk to the band, Skip, and Tommy about the songs I picked as openers. I'm not changing my mind on the Los Angeles show and the festival at Jones Beach. I'm open to suggestions on the rest."

As they were talking, the guys trickled in.

Gina forgot to call Lisa and Jae about getting together. She went to a corner to call the ladies and arrange plans.

Rio's voice barreled through the room. "Gina, let's talk about what the hell you're singing at these shows. I'm a bit concerned about playing our super-old covers. I mean, what the fuck? We are one of the hottest bands, we can't find something better than 1979?"

Gina stood against the wall and glared at her cousin. "First, good morning, also fuck off. I'm going to tell you. I printed out a cover list last night."

Los Angeles
Would I Lie to You? Break Stuff—big screens, light show, pink smoke

Red Rocks
Eminence Front, All My Love, Tuesday Afternoon, Every Breath You Take, Plush

Caesars, Vegas
Fell on Black Days, Love Is Alive, Fame, All of My Love, Tear
Us Apart

Sexy with Trevor, Sturgis
Fame, I Just Want to Make, Love to You, Feel Like, Makin' Love,
Rock and Roll

Charlotte, PNC Music Pavillion
All My Love, Houses of the Holy, Need You Tonight, Trampled
Under Foot

Orlando, Amway Center
Can't Get Enough, Gimme Shelter

MSG
I Just Want to Make Love to You, Shattered, Murder By Numbers,
Never Tear Us Apart

MSG
No Sleep Till Brooklyn, Need You Tonight, Loser

Miami
Mystify, Bell Bottom Blues, Rock 'n Roll Fantasy

Football Kickoff
It's Only Rock 'n Roll, Let's Spend the Night Together, Perfection
Classics

Vancouver
Every Breath You Take, Can't Get Enough, Plush

Toronto
Heaven Beside You, Roadhouse Blues, Wicked Garden, Plush

Daytona Bike Week
Fame, Break Stuff, Let's Spend the Night Together, I Just Want to
Make Love, Tuesday Afternoon

Daytona Bike Week
Rock and Roll, Addicted to Love, Black, Fame

Jones Beach
My Sacrifice, Can't Get Enough, All My Love, Surprises

Gina looked at the band, she couldn't read the room. She made it clear
that Los Angeles was going to be what she wanted, with a sax player and
keyboard player.

Of course, Rio spoke first. "I don't hate them, we need fifteen, maybe
more. I know these songs, not too much practicing."

Ian said, "I can play anything, it's not a big deal, I'm good."

Jeff laughed at Gina. "You know I always wanted to play 'Love is Alive,'
it has a great bass line. You remembered that, didn't you?"

Gina glanced at Jeff. "We finally worked it into our repertoire, Jeff."

Trevor was the last to comment. "G, I'm good with all these openers.
What's up with 'Fame' being sexy? You want to rework the song, don't you?"

Gina grinned, which meant of course she did. She waited for Tommy
to get to the studio. Gina wanted his approval. Although she was going
to sing what she wanted. Once Tommy came and gave his blessings, Gina
would move on to the caterer. Tommy showed up about twenty minutes
later. Gina wanted to be the first to talk to him.

She confidently spoke, "Here is my list of covers for the show dates.
These guys are fine with all the songs. I will tell you I want to rework 'Fame.'

Make it very sexy with my husband, dirty sexy. I think we should release it as a video first. Get buzz, then perform it. Thoughts?"

Tommy took the list and reviewed it. "You guys don't need much practice with these songs. Gina, you are going over the top with 'Fame.' I can picture you all over Trevor. Correct?"

Gina looked happy. "Yes, Tommy. I'm glad no objections. I'll explain my vision later. I'm off to plan the party."

LET'S HAVE
A PARTY

GINA AND ROXANNE MET WITH a local caterer. Rosco was well known by the Montecito elite for excellent food and specialty drinks. He would also arrange for the bars. Gina planned a buffet-style meal, with choices for each person's liking. Roxanne reviewed the dessert menu and convinced her mother to include a few elaborate desserts—Baked Alaska, crème brûlée, chocolate molten lava cake. Gina knew Roxanne's weakness was desserts. She wanted her daughter to be invested in the party. They went to the florist and had arrangements made. White roses, peonies, hydrangeas, snapdragons. Plus beautiful greenery. All the vendors assured her they could accommodate her plans in the short window.

Gina told Roxanne she needed to make a call to her Beverly Hills hair stylist, Tammie. Gina offered Roxanne a cut, color, or whatever she wanted. Roxy agreed to go but didn't know what she wanted yet.

Gina called the only woman who could transform her into a fresh look. "Tammie, hi, it's Gina McNaughton, I was hoping to make an appointment to come down to see you. Can you get me some long blonde hair extensions and sew them in for me?"

"Of course, Gina, what, we not loving the G-Mac anymore?"

Gina sighed. "I'm so tired of seeing women with my hairstyle. While I was in New York, I bought some cheap hair extensions. People loved the look so I'm going with it. Can you do it for me?"

Tammie was more than accommodating. "Gina, of course, when do you want to come down?" Gina pictured her schedule in her head. "Tammie, I would love to come down today, but I'm tied up. Do you have time tomorrow? I know it's short notice. My daughter might want a haircut, I'm sure there is someone who can take care of her."

Tammie put Gina in her appointment book for two tomorrow. "I will make time and get the good stuff. I have a great stylist for Roxanne, no problems there."

Gina took a breath. "Thank you so much, Tammie, see you tomorrow."

Gina and Roxanne made it home after a busy day of party planning. It was fun but also exhausting. She was happy to get home knowing she had managed all the Perfection party details.

Gina dropped her purse down on the dining room table. She was feeling flushed again; she checked the thermostat as usual. "Marisol, does it feel hot in the house?"

Marisol pressed her hand against Gina's forehead. "No, Mrs. Gina, are you getting sick?"

"I guess I've been running around doing too much. Have any of the guys come up here looking for food?"

Marisol giggled. "No, Mrs. Gina, no one except Mr. Trevor to get another flan, he sneaked it." Gina laughed. "I'm going down to the studio to check in. I'll have a cup of java and then go."

Gina drank her brew and still fell asleep on the couch.

Trevor came up from the studio around six and woke Gina up. "Hey, sleepyhead, I thought you were coming down. Did the party planning go well? It's not like you to not show up at the studio and fall asleep in the middle of the day."

Gina yawned. "Baby, I'm feeling run down. And I was feeling hot before. I need to take more vitamins. The party and all the work for the band. I can't afford to be sick …"

Trevor sat next to her. "Baby, rest up."

"Are you hungry? I'm sure Marisol made something to eat."

Marisol came over. "Should I place the food on the table?"

Gina sat up on the couch. "Trevor, you, Roxanne, and Marisol eat. I had a tasting of all of Rosco's cuisine. I'm not hungry."

Roxanne came downstairs looking for something to eat. Gina told her it was time for dinner. "Should we expect Zach here for the party this weekend? Or is he still enjoying being with his family?"

Roxanne thought about it. "I could ask him. How would he get here? His car is at our apartment at Stanford."

Gina sighed heavily. "Roxanne, we can fly Zach here for the party on a private jet. Don't you agree? Is that something he would be agreeable to? Would his parents object to him spending less time with them? Let's be real, sweetheart. If Zach comes to our house, he is staying until you go back to Stanford. I'm just worried that his parents might not like the idea."

Trevor interjected. "Can you find out tonight so we know what we are doing? The party is only days away."

Roxanne looked at Trevor. "Dad, you are sounding more like Mom all the time. Yes, I will call him tonight. I'm sure his parents won't have an issue."

Gina motioned to Trevor. "Trev, Roxy, go eat, I'm fine here. Roxanne, thank you for helping me today. Tomorrow we are driving to Beverly Hills to get our hair done. Babe, I hope I'm not missing anything important in the studio."

Trevor ate and talked about the songs Gina wanted to sing. "G, how are you planning to sex up 'Fame?'"

Gina laughed. "Trev, leave that up to me, I know how to play up to you."

Roxanne rolled her eyes. "Yet again another sexed-up stage show. It's embarrassing."

Gina's look was narrow-eyed. "Roxanne, I know you hate it. But this is our job. We need to stay relevant. In today's music world, dirty is in. Sorry, tell your friends you can't control your parents."

Roxanne finished eating and declared she was going to her room to call Zach.

They laughed, knowing that would be their daughter's response. After their meal, Trevor dragged Gina to bed. "I want you to relax, come on, I'll massage your head."

Gina showed some disappointment. "That's all?"

"Let's see how you are in a bit."

Gina fell asleep on Trevor's chest. He kissed her goodnight and let her remain there for the night.

SHIT GETS REAL

FOR THE REST OF THE WEEK, it was putting their latest music together with lyrics, some of which Gina wrote. Other songs that the rest of the band put together. Gina had her hair appointment with Tammie in Beverly Hills on Wednesday. It was long days for all, arguments, Tommy making revisions. Completely what Perfection expected, it was truly back to work. Gina excused herself on Friday, she was making last-minute preparations for Saturday's party. Rental furniture, tent and a DJ booth, dishes.

She also arranged for Zach to get to the house at around four thirty on Friday. She went upstairs to Roxanne's room and made sure guest towels were all laid out. Gina always felt she and Roxanne were at odds. She couldn't fathom why, but she was thankful that the time they were spending together was pleasant, no sniping at each other.

Gina lost track of all the extra equipment, large urns, serving platters; it was overwhelming. Gina was a pro at parties; she just needed to get her head around it. She couldn't concentrate. Had she thrown herself back into the business too fast? Many thoughts ran through her head. She was hoping Roxanne could help her.

Trevor came into the house. "G, Tommy is asking for you to come down to the studio. He wants to hear your thoughts on the redo of 'Fame.'"

Gina glared. "You got to be kidding me right now. I'm in the middle of this party shit and Zach will be here in an hour. Why didn't I get some kind of notice?"

Trevor walked up to her; he placed his hands on her shoulders. "G, are you okay? It's not like you to come at me like that. Is this party stressing you out?"

Gina became teary. "I'm there to write only. Now I'm wanted in the studio, and poof, magically I'm supposed to come down and explain how I want the song to be done. Trev, I know how I want it all to play out. I simply can't think straight right now. I'll go down and tell him myself. It's not your issue, it's mine."

Trevor backed off, sensing something wasn't right. Gina put down some rental vases. "Let's go, I'll tell Tommy what I'm thinking."

With that they walked down to the studio. Trevor grabbed her hand. "Baby, you sure this whole party thing isn't taking too much out of you?"

Gina was flustered. "Trev, I need a moment to relax and breathe. But I will tell Tommy, if I'm needed, to please let me know ahead of time. I know the way I want things to flow, but it's not a switch that turns on and off. I need to get into the groove of what's going on around me."

Trevor reassured her. "Come on, baby, you go and tell them. I'm right beside you."

Tommy was happy to see Gina. "There she is, our sexy lead singer, what are your thoughts on 'Fame'? I'm interested in how you want to play it."

"Well, Tommy," she said in an atypically cocky voice, "first, I would have liked to have had a little notice. Right now, I'm dealing with the party setup. If I'm coming in for input, I would like a day to gather my thoughts. I do know how I want this played. Trevor and I split singing the lead, with each of us singing the 'Fame' part. I want to be specific in my movements to the song, which will be played a bit harder, and I plan to plaster myself on Trevor's body as we sing, like a lap dance. I mean, that's what people want, me being sexy with my husband onstage. I would like to run through it, but next week. I can't run through it today."

Tommy eyed Gina. "Gina, I apologize for the short notice. You're absolutely right … I believe I get where you're going, I like it. We would definitely need a run-through to see if we are on the same page. I get it, you want to basically dry-hump your husband onstage."

Gina exhaled. "Yes, if I'm being honest, I want to play up to the decadence that Sturgis is, that was my plan. The Sturgis crowd would love us doing 'Feel Like Makin' Love' into 'Can't Get Enough.' That also would be extremely hot and sexy. I'm thinking of the venue and what the crowd wants. If I'm seeing topless chicks screaming out, I most definitely need to put a bit of raunch out there also. That's what I'm thinking. You folks can think I'm nuts."

"I don't think you are," Tommy said thoughtfully. "You have the right idea. Gina, can you spend time in the studio on Monday so we can start creating that and what you want for LA?"

"Thank you, Tommy, yes, I will be at the studio Monday."

Gina was relieved and happy. Now she could put her stamp on the shows, and she wanted her new song introduced in the set. "Well, thank you for letting me get that out. I really need to get back to the house. Zach, Roxanne's boyfriend, should be coming any time. I want to be there when he arrives."

Trevor also wanted to be there for Zach's arrival. They walked back to the house. "G, you feel better now that you explained your vision?"

Gina took his hand. "Most definitely, it's nice being heard. Remember, Trevor is going to be nice to his daughter's boyfriend …"

Trevor made a face, then promised he would behave.

Gina hugged him. They met Zach on his way into the house. "Zach, so good to see you, are you ready for this chaos of a party?"

He shrugged and the college kids ran up the stairs to Roxy's room.

Marisol reminded Gina that dinner was in thirty minutes.

"Trevor, is the band almost done? I would love to have just family while we eat, without the crew at the studio."

Trevor agreed. "G, I'll call Tommy and tell him to wrap it up for today. Tomorrow they all get to party."

Gina kissed him softly on the lips. "Don't ever forget you keep me sane in an absurd, insane world."

Every person left but Rio, he assumed he was invited to dine with his family. He burst through the door. "Family feast sounds great. Jae will be here soon."

Gina tilted her head in a cocky way. "Did I invite you? Now that you are here, no talk about band business with Zach here. Can we solely have family talk?"

Jae arrived and they sat down to Marisol's Mexican wonders of food. There was laughter and happiness around the table. Gina sat back and took it all in, this was her family. Even though they all annoyed her in one way or another, she loved every one of them.

EVERYTHING PERFECTION

THE DAY OF THE PARTY, the house was buzzing with activity. Gina knew to step back and let the people she hired do their jobs. Roxanne and Zach sat by the pool and watched as water lilies and candles were set into the pool.

Gina and Trevor hung out in their room, sitting on the chaise lounge. Gina, exhausted, looked at Trevor. "I'll be glad when this is over. Next time, when I think of one of these ideas, remind me of today."

Trevor laughed. "My baby, you always go over the top. It's one of the many reasons I love you." Gina groaned. "Trev, I guess at some point we need to get ready."

Gina was direct. "I am laser-focused on meeting our unfamiliar staff. I don't want any fuckups this time."

Trevor motioned to her. "Let's take a shower and get ready."

The house looked amazing, the tent with beautiful floral tiebacks, every table with blush and sage-green linen and flowers to match. The food included Korean ribs, beef tenderloin, every type of appetizer. Gina surveyed the outside, it was to her liking, with the backdrop of the Pacific Ocean making it exquisite.

The guests started arriving, she couldn't wait to see the Montecito Moms. She missed them; they were there when she was at her lowest. She observed people she didn't know, they must have been new Perfection employees. Gina grabbed Trevor and walked up to anyone unfamiliar and introduced them as the McNaughtons. They tried to get a feel for these new employees. They seemed competent and were on their best behavior. The band trickled in, Gina knew she could say a quick hello and they wouldn't be offended.

Tommy and Anne walked in. Anne went to Gina immediately. "Gina, I'm so happy that life gave you back all that is important. I love the long hair; it's a great look for you."

Gina was introspective. "Thank you, Anne, it was all a journey but it was worth it."

At that moment Gina saw them, the Montecito Moms. They couldn't contain themselves, giving hugs and kisses, and compliments on her new hairdo. Some of their girls came. Roxanne was excited to see her old friends. The party was going according to plan.

Trevor called for everyone's attention. "This is incredibly special, we wanted to thank you all for coming tonight. You are all important people in Gina's and my life. We wanted you all to know that we have never been happier. Perfection is coming back strong, life is good. The best is still to come. Let me bring my wife up here. Gina?"

Gina stood next to Trevor, slid her arm around him. "This is a special moment for the McNaughtons and to all of you who are here. All of you are significant in our lives. We have so much more to give and show you. We love you all."

Gina gave her husband a sweet, long kiss. The party continued without any incidents. Roxanne and Zach hung out with her friends. The party was perfection. People said their goodbyes, but Rio and Jae stayed.

Rio sat back and lit up a joint. "As usual, you two, another great party. I got to meet the new employees. They seem fine. The test will be the LA show. Gina, you want a hit?"

Gina relented. "Sure, I'll take a hit. I'm exhausted and it's hot, right?"

Trevor looked concerned, "G, babe, it's actually a bit cool out and there's a nice breeze. You're hot? You pushed yourself with the party."

Rio was high. "Gina, you're nuts, it's beautiful out here, breezy. I guess being a host gets you going. After this joint, I guess Jae and I will go home. I promised no talking about band business. I was a good soldier."

Gina took the joint. "I needed this."

Rio got up. "Let's go, babe, I'm tired, we need our *alone time*."

Trevor and Gina sat outside and looked up at the sky. "Trev, it's beautiful looking at the stars. Remember when we looked at the sky on the road? The stars were so bright."

Gina, with so much love in her eyes, grabbed his face. "Trevor, you are so handsome. I want you, can we go inside now?"

Trevor had a naughty look and picked her up. "G, you always read my mind."

Roxanne disappeared somewhere with her friends. Gina and Trevor had the playdate that they missed earlier.

The next morning Marisol made homemade donuts, eggs, pancakes, and bacon. Roxanne and Zach were already downstairs consuming all the goodies when Trevor and Gina sauntered out in their sweatpants and tees.

Gina smirked. "How nice is this, my daughter home having her favorite morning feast?"

Gina made cups of java for her and Trevor.

Trevor looked at his daughter. "Roxanne, I hope you had fun last night. We hardly got to see you. Is it acceptable for your father to sit with you?"

Roxanne groaned. "Of course, Dad, I enjoy being with you."

It was a lazy afternoon; the caterer came to clean up most of the party rentals. Music blasted through the house and the McNaughtons relaxed on their couch listening to music to get inspired. Roxanne and Zach hung out with her parents listening to music, enjoying family conversations. It was one of those family moments they would remember.

Monday came, which meant work, the Los Angeles concert was three weeks away. Gina wanted this to be a concert LA would remember. She walked into the studio. "Let's get to it! I want to sing, 'Would I Lie to You?' I told you the scenario. When do we start recording me singing the chorus, we need videos. I would like to see the ideas for the light show, if possible. Did we get a saxophone player and a keyboardist? I think we should keep them around since some of our covers might need them for several shows."

Tommy was eager to share. "Maxie, you remember him from Brown Fence, my engineer. He is a sax player, he's doing studio work. I'm sure he would love to climb on board. I can find a good studio key person. Let's talk about 'Fame,' and your song 'Touching You All Over.' You are really putting your sexuality out there. Trevor is on board?"

"Tommy, I'm good with it. I want people to see we are truly back as a couple but stronger and sexier."

Tommy wanted more, "Let's run through the number without the sax and keyboards for now. I'll get them in here tomorrow."

The band didn't miss a beat; they ran through the song and Gina's voice was right where she needed it to be. Tommy made them run the song about five times. He was happy with how it came together. For the first time, Gina heard the music for "Touching You All Over." It was hard and edgy. Gina made some additions to the lyrics and she and Trevor made the song a hard-edge love song. They went through it about ten times to ensure that each member was adding their flourishes. Tommy had them practice some of Perfection's older songs. They were getting close to being stage-ready. Practices all week lasted hours. Going over the songs several times until Tommy felt it was the right mix of every instrument. Gina was always afraid that too much practice would make Perfection overworked before the night of the show. She went along with the plan this time, but noted this for future shows. Friday of that week, Maxie and a keyboardist, Mike, came to practice with the band. Getting down their part for playing in the opener.

Gina wanted to get an idea of how the opening light show would look. This was her intro to take the stage. The lighting crew walked her through it, it was on point.

The show needed to have Gina's recordings plus videos. She picked a black leather catsuit and a seductive nightgown, and she'd style her hair with wavy, long blonde curls. The practices continued to be grueling for the next two-plus weeks. Tommy was able to get them access to the venue so they could run through the show with all the pieces in place. Tommy was pleased that the close-to-six-month absence hadn't slowed the band down.

The night before the show, Gina and Trevor stayed at the Hollywood Hills house. Gina's favorite cloud bed was there.

Roxanne said she and Zach would drive from their home in Montecito to downtown LA.

Gina cuddled up to Trevor. "I'm so exhausted from the practicing, I hope I have something left for the show."

Trevor pulled her up on top of him. "G, once you're up there parading your stuff, it will overtake you. It always does. What about this outfit that you're stripping off yourself?"

Gina laughed. "Trevor, it sounds worse than it is. I had it made by some new designer; he's a kid actually. I dramatically pull off sleeves, part of my hem, and part of the top. It's to make the audience think they are getting a Gina who is about to show them something. I'll also have my long blonde hair in. I get to be different again."

Trevor kissed her. "Would it be asking too much if I could have this Gina? The one I get to see." Gina looked at him lovingly. "Baby, you have every Gina there is."

They enjoyed the Hills house for the night. Gina knew the significance that house held for them. She tried to bury those feelings. She let that past go. Gina had what she needed, Trevor.

Perfection would show the universe how their absence made the band hot, edgy, setting the standard for other bands to follow.

Gina wondered what was ahead for her, Trevor, and the band. She was excited for the yearlong tour, but thoughts of Paul Ryan and Brian Mayfield lingered in her mind. Would they sabotage all the McNaughtons had worked for?

Gina McNaughton has no idea her world is about to change.

PLAYLIST FOR PLAYING ROUGH

Comfortably Numb	*Pink Floyd*
Can't Find My Way Home	*Blind Faith*
Can't Get Enough	*Bad Company*
Music Is a Circus	*Perfection**
Almost Done	*Perfection**
Lost Our Way	*Perfection**
Life Flies By	*Perfection**
Break Stuff	*Limp Bizkit*
Punch the Night	*Perfection**
I've Been Waiting for a Girl Like You	*Foreigner*
Trampled Under Foot	*Led Zeppelin*
Always You	*Perfection**
Nothing Compares 2 U	*Toni & Chris Cornell*
My Immortal	*Evanescence*
Touching You all Over	*Perfection**
Would I Lie to You?	*Eurythmics*
Wicked Game	*Theory of a Deadman*
You and Me	*Lifehouse*
Roadhouse Blues	*Doors*
Heaven Beside You	*Alice in Chains*
Bell Bottom Blues	*Eric Clapton*
Wicken Garden, Plush	*Stone Temple Pilots*
Touching You All Over	*Perfection**

ACKNOWLEDGMENTS

THE THIRD BOOK OF THE *Perfection Saga, Playing Rough,* shows us that forgiveness is something we all need to learn. As with the rest of the series, I have interwoven snippets of my own life, so the story is very personal.

With every new book I have learned so much in how to improve my writing style, edit my own work, and try my hand at marketing. I have said before how I truly have the "A Team" supporting me, holding me up with so much care. I have *brought the band back together.*

First, I want to thank my "team leader," Polly Letofsky of My Word Publishing. She calms me down when I'm feeling stressed. She is a very groovy lady whom I trust with my work.

My editor, Cheryl Jaclin Isaac of CherylJI Editing, is the most thorough and intelligent person when it comes to manuscripts. She sets me straight on so many levels. I have learned so much from her. How lucky I am to have her working on my manuscripts with a different set of eyes, always understanding my vision. She is treasured.

The beautiful visionary Victoria Wolf of Wolf Design and Marketing creates my book covers, websites (which she also updates almost instantly), and much more. She always comes through with the *Perfection Saga*'s unique look. I have received many compliments on my books' artwork. Thank you, Victoria.

Andrea Vanryken joined the *Perfection* team on this third book as my proofreader. Thank you, Andrea, for jumping in and doing a great job. I appreciate you understanding my story and vision.

I work with a brilliant marketing guru, Mary Walewski, who tackles the challenging job of marketing a book, consistently finding creative ways to put my books in front of you. Mary promotes my books in various ways, including at conventions, book festivals, and book clubs. It is an all-year job, even when there isn't a new book out. Thank you for helping me learn new ways of bettering myself.

There are many people I need to thank on a personal level. My bestie Holly, who has shown me how to have fun again, and what true friendship really looks like. My other besties who know who they are: my Bama ladies, Bev, and Lynda, who goes all the way back to high school. I apologize if I forgot any other besties. I love all you ladies. The support you give me means so much.

There are also people in my life that I see every other week or month who ensure my hair and nails always look perfect, making me feel my best and keeping me sane. Thank you to Jamie, Amanda, Dale, and Ximena. My friend Tammie, who appears in my books, gracefully deals with my frequent requests to change hair styles with her simple comment, "What are we doing today?" She's the best. I also want to let the following people know how much I appreciate them for seeing me every other week for seven years, taking care of my nails and other beauty needs: Annie, Kim, Nelson, and Abby. You are always sunshine, especially when I'm stressed out. I appreciate you all so much.

Thank you to my three daughters, who I can't even quantify the amount of love I have.

And to the little love bug Miss Truffle, my not-so-miniature dachshund, thanks for keeping me company as I spend long hours writing. Dog Mom Love.

Last, to all you indie authors our there like me, don't get defeated, don't let others make you feel you aren't good enough. Write, write, and write. You have a story to share. Do it!

ABOUT THE AUTHOR

BETH PELLINO-DUDZIC was born in the Bronx, New York City. Beth grew up in Westchester County for most of her life. She received a BA in Business Administration. She then moved to Honolulu, Hawaii, where her three daughters were born. She came back to Westchester to raise her girls and worked at IBM upon her return.

Although the story is fictional, it was part of the author's early history. The story developed over decades in her head; it was waiting to be written. The *Perfection Saga* series has become Beth's passion. The characters and events in the story are close and personal to her. When not writing, Beth's favorite pastimes are cooking and baking; she claims to make the best New York Cheesecake. She also hosts a monthly book club with her friends. Beth is an avid football fan of both college and the NFL. Beth has another other passion: her miniature dachshund, Truffle.